GATE OF
THE TIGERS

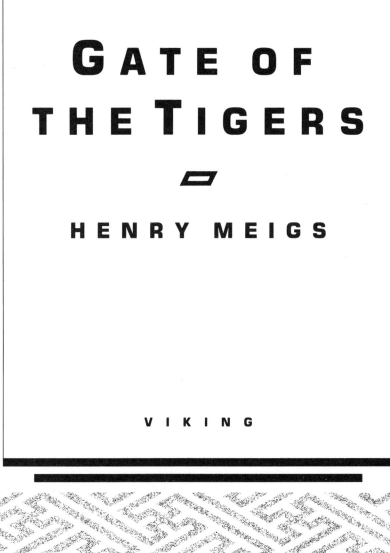

GATE OF THE TIGERS

HENRY MEIGS

VIKING

VIKING
Published by the Penguin Group
Viking Penguin, a division of Penguin Books USA Inc.,
375 Hudson Street, New York, New York 10014, U.S.A.
Penguin Books Ltd, 27 Wrights Lane,
London W8 5TZ, England
Penguin Books Australia Ltd, Ringwood,
Victoria, Australia
Penguin Books Canada Ltd, 10 Alcorn Avenue, Suite 300,
Toronto, Ontario, Canada, M4V 3B2
Penguin Books (N.Z.) Ltd, 182–190 Wairau Road,
Auckland 10, New Zealand

Penguin Books Ltd, Registered Offices:
Harmondsworth, Middlesex, England

First published in 1992 by Viking Penguin,
a division of Penguin Books USA Inc.

1 3 5 7 9 10 8 6 4 2

Excerpt from *Bushido, The Soul of Japan* by Inazo Nitobe is reprinted
by permission of Charles Tuttle Co.

Excerpts from *The Hagakure* by Tsunetomo Yamamoto are from the
translation by Takao Mukoh, published by Hokuseido Press.

LIBRARY OF CONGRESS CATALOGING IN PUBLICATION DATA
Meigs, Henry.
Gate of the tigers / Henry Meigs.
p. cm.
ISBN 0-670-83620-6
I. Title.
PR9515.9.M45G37   1991
823—dc20   91-50149

Printed in the United States of America
Set in Trump Medieval
Designed by Ann Gold

FOR MY MOTHER AND FATHER

AND

IN MEMORIAM TO PADDY,

WHO GAVE HIS LIFE IN ORDER

TO SAVE A FRIEND

Our sense of revenge is as exact as our mathematical faculty, and until both terms of the equation are satisfied we cannot get over the sense of something left undone. —Inazo Nitobe

Bushido, The Soul of Japan

GATE OF
THE TIGERS

PROLOGUE

On the black firebombed rubble in front of the palace, rows of white-clad, sun-darkened men knelt with military precision. Near them the inner moat, which normally protected the palace with placid algae-green water and centuries-old stone, was scarred black from incendiaries. Bloated bodies floated in water but the skies today were clear. U.S. bombers would not return; the war was over.

At noon in a high, nervous voice the emperor had broadcast the surrender: the first time his words had ever been heard by the Japanese public. An American airborne unit would land at Atsugi Airbase that afternoon, the first day of peace for the Japanese empire. The men, all descendants of the major samurai families, knelt together on the blackened debris, oblivious to everything around them: the strangely quiet skies, the watchful sentries on the palace walls, the weeping groups of relatives gathered nearby.

Many of the men held high commands, yet there were soldiers of all ranks. One principle bound them together: that surrender was unthinkable. And so their request for extreme unction. That honor had been reluctantly granted by the imperial household.

One group of watchers stood apart, privileged above the others. Attended by a group of staff officers and a Shinto priest was a small boy with his mother. Although the boy's nostrils filled with the suffocating odor of burnt and rotted flesh and his eyes stung with the acrid fumes of the hated incendiary bombs, his face showed no emotion. The deadly preparations on the scorched field were already accepted as part of his existence; his past and his future. He took in everything with stoic composure, a serenity that belied his youth. As the son of a general, a warrior of the Satsuma clan—the clan to which the empress had been born—he, too, was expected to carry on the tradition of his class: patriotism and loyalty. Filial piety. Reverence for ancestral memory. Disdain of life and companionship with death.

The priest detached himself from the group. He moved forward to the general, bearing the kiriwood stand on which a *wakizashi*, the ceremonial dagger of chosen death, was wrapped in parchment and rice paper. As if greeting an old companion, the general took the *wakizashi* in both hands, raised it to the level of his head, bowed, then placed it precisely in front of him. For a moment he looked up into the broad sky. When his eyes returned to the *wakizashi* they were relaxed, almost smiling. Carefully he unwrapped the dagger. The blade shone like ice in the early afternoon sun. The handle was of worked metal in a chrysanthemum design that indicated linkage to the royal family. The general allowed his upper garment to slip down to his waist, exposing a thickly muscled torso.

The boy shut his eyes and prayed.

Of Amaterasu Omikami, sun goddess of his eternal race family, he asked for acceptance of his honored father into the world of darkness from the world of light. He promised to perform *misogi*, ablutions, each memorial day until he was granted the opportunity for atonement. To ensure her aid, he called her name three times before opening his eyes: *Amaterasu Omikami, born from the left eye of the Great Sky Father, sister of the moon and storm, ancestress of the royal line. Protector of my fate.*

His mother took his hand. She was as proud of her son as she was anguished for her husband, who would make the ultimate sacrifice of obligation to his country. Akiko Mori wore a formal kimono of black silk, with the mark of their famous house in white silk, the color of purity, on the back. The house of Mori. A samurai family that made its name during the thirteenth century fighting brilliantly in the service of a major lord of Kyūshū, the southernmost island of Japan. In 1868, the Mori joined the leadership of a band of revolutionary samurai who carried out the political coup that brought about the breathless change of the Meiji Restoration—they helped to lead a series of extraordinary reforms that brought public education, did away with warrior privilege, opened public office to all, and abolished estate distinctions. The Mori name quickly became revered throughout Japan. Akiko sighed and shook her head. Now the grand history of the house of Mori had been irrevocably tarnished.

In this sadly concluded war, the general's soldiers on the islands of Iwo Jima, Tobruk, and New Guinea had fought well and bravely; but they had failed. To honor that bravery, the general must allow those that survived the foreign onslaught to live in the spiritual peace of defeat. His life would be presented as atonement to the emperor and to Nippon, the eternal abode of the gods and the spirits of their ancestors.

The priest, youthful in face, approached Akiko to speak. "The dictate of bushido is quite clear," the priest intoned, glancing to where a staff officer had brought a final cup of sake to the general. The boy would always remember the priest's voice. Reedy and high it was. Nervous. But of what? "Your husband is satisfying the station of his rank. No responsibility falls to his offspring."

The priest turned to smile at the child and was met with a hostile stare. Flustered, the priest turned back to the mother again. She bowed low, weeping silently that she could not join her husband in his glory. But she must fulfill the obligation to their only child. Strength grew in her heart because she understood that their son was strong in spirit and would grow

3

to a man of the warrior clan who would fulfill his obligation to his family. A strange peace suddenly began to flow through her body.

The priest returned and presented her husband's death haiku:

All kinds of love,
The dying threads
Were white at first.

Over five thousand bodies were counted later. Within months, traveling by word of mouth, news of the deed had become known in all of Nippon.

Tora-san was the way Japanese referred to the general when they mentioned their most famous warrior in public. It was a code name for him and for his loyal retainers, who had followed him in death on the blackened earth before the emperor's palace. Tora-san, the Tigers.

The name came to mean much more than that, finally, when the humiliation of the peace agreement was known. It came to symbolize for every Japanese who had lived through the first military defeat in the nation's history that their country had gone down disastrously but with honor, with humiliation but, in the end, with pride.

Several years later, General MacArthur's command was asked permission by a local council to change the name of the intersection nearest to where the ceremony had taken place. The Americans could see no reason to deny the request, although the new name puzzled them.

The crossing was renamed Toranomon, "the Gate of the Tigers." To the Japanese it would ever after mark the place where the magnificent ones had passed to their ancestors.

PART ONE

KIN-YOBI
GOLD-DAY

FRIDAY, OCTOBER 9, 1987

I know not how to defeat others; I know
only how to win over myself.
—Yaju Munenori,
  Sword Instructor
  to the Tokugawa Shogunate

CHAPTER 1

GOLD-DAY, 5:00 P.M.

It is not easy to prepare oneself for total patience. It is acquired through abstinence and discipline. Through avoiding spontaneity and pleasure. Above all else, patience is what the Public Security Bureau of the Tokyo Metropolitan Police requires of its officers. Tetsuo Mori seemed to be born to it.

His childhood had been difficult, but Mori never thought so, except for the sight of his mother's tired face as she worked from dawn to late at night to keep them alive after the war. He felt no different from others of his age. He was a small, scrawny lad, but so were all children of this war. During his primary-school years, he walked the streets of Tokyo earning money for schoolbooks by selling kindling scavenged in the foothills, or grass for tatami mats, or, failing that, he would carry lanterns in the frequent funeral processions. But although he was like the others, he was also different: in the calm, expressionless eyes that commanded respect; in the way he spoke, without ever smiling.

Mori and his mother had lived in a tiny two-room apartment—one room of six mats, the other of three. When he complained of their crowded condition, his mother chided him. Space was more important for the mind than for the body, she told him. Grow your mind. Learn to think!

7

At the time Mori entered middle school, his mother proudly gave him two books of his father's, which became the cornerstones of his life: the *Hagakure* of Yamamoto Tsunetomo—the foundation of Bushido philosophy—and the *Analects* of Confucius. He took up Zazen at a temple and worked out regularly in a local judo training center. Sometimes, in his early teens, he would wander off into the Tokyo foothills and fall asleep on a cushion of pine needles alone. When his mother found out about these excursions she never scolded him. She had been raised in the Satsuma clan tradition, where men's and women's clothes must be washed separately. As much as she could, she protected him from that moment when he would take his place in society and fulfill his obligation to their house.

———

Inspector Mori held the Japanese teacup like a day laborer, his thumb on the lip and forefinger on the bottom to prevent burn. Periodically he drank from the cup, but his calm eyes remained fixed on the Japan Electronics Tower entrance a half block away.

Downstairs in the police box someone had turned on the play-by-play of the Japan World Series. Mori immediately regretted the ten thousand yen he'd placed on the Seibu Lions. The Yomiuri Giants were ahead by one.

Beside him, the ancient Defense Intelligence Agency colonel growled an obscenity about the frivolity of baseball, got up, and closed the door.

Too wise, Mori decided, staring at the officer's back: one who never allows himself good humor. The colonel was completely bald and scarred from all the wars since Manchuria. They had met only that morning at the agency. "American bitch should be any minute now." The colonel had looked out the window, then at his watch. With a quick jerk, his bullet head indicated the entrance to the skyscraper. Mori nodded. The Japan Electronics Tower was an elegant symbol of Japanese postwar resilience; a hushed and carpeted showplace of sixty-five stories. Thirty billion yen invested in the structure,

8

the richest by far of the nine "earthquake-proof" skyscrapers in the Shinjuku district.

In his stockinged feet the colonel paced the tiny second-floor room of the police box. The tatami floor was shiny from wear. The colonel stopped to open the window a crack and allow chill October air to flood the room. Mori studied him briefly as he stood there staring out at the Japan Electronics Tower as if that were the real enemy.

The wise find pleasure in water; the virtuous find pleasure in hills. Mori smiled that the passage from Confucius came to him readily. The wise are active and joyful; the virtuous are tranquil and long-lived. Mori's ancestors would not approve of this colonel, who was wise yet unjoyful; unvirtuous yet long-lived.

Mori looked down at the complicated glass maze which served as entrance to the tower. Two floors where the foreign girl worked were advanced research laboratories. The briefing this morning had been vague about the girl's research responsibilities. Japan Electronics Corporation, the colonel had said, was working on a dramatically new computer. It involved high-speed microcircuitry research, ceramic compounds which when supercooled allowed electrons to travel without producing heat. Mori hadn't been particularly interested in listening to electronic theory. His role in this business was relatively simple, and he had been well trained for it. He was to follow the girl; to find out everything about her. To determine whether she was a spy.

Total patience was to assume nothing, to be nothing. Mori forced himself to relax, to save himself for the moment when pursuit would begin and all energies would be consumed in stalking the prey. While one part of his mind watched the JEC entrance, fragments of the past continued to swirl through his brain.

———

"*Shinyo*," his mother would explain softly in the moments they shared during those early years. It meant "trust." Reliability. It was the goal of a man of honor, she would say and smile sadly. Young Mori would nod his head knowingly and repeat, "It is one who fulfills his commitments at whatever cost." Then she would kiss him, sometimes brushing a tear from her eye, saying it was the hibachi smoke. And she would tuck the padded quilt around him, reading from *The Heike Story* or from *Momotaro the Peach Boy* until he fell asleep.

He'd studied the *Analects* each night his mother was out working. It never occurred to him to complain. It was his *unmei*, his fate. Thus without his realizing it, the course of his life was determined at a very early age.

When he passed the exam for First Higher School, his mother, wearing her finest kimono and clogs, took Mori on the old wooden train down the coast to Atami. It was spring, the sea sparkled with joy, the *mikan* trees were bursting with fruit; the air was alive with the wonderful scents of azalea, young bamboo, and camphor wood. Yet his mother remained solemn all the way to the outskirts of the hot-springs resort town.

The temple was on a steep hillside overlooking Atami Bay, and the five hundred steps one had to climb to reach it ensured seclusion from all but the most determined visitors. A shrine to Kannon, goddess of mercy. The shrine was dedicated to the memory of Japanese officers and men killed in the Pacific Island fighting. During Occupation it had been deserted, an ideal location in which to conceal her treasure.

His mother had pulled a scented handkerchief from her obi and fanned her flushed face. Mori had felt very proud of her; she looked so remarkably beautiful that day. It was the first time she'd brought him to the shrine. And the last.

They moved together to the darkened interior, where the plain metal box rested, painted against salt winds that blew from the Pacific.

"Your father is here," she said simply, and bowed low. Then she lit a candle to the goddess of mercy and took silver *hashi*, which were chopsticks, and a small porcelain bottle of sake from her handbag. She dipped the *hashi* into the urn that they found inside the metal box, and she withdrew the sticks and held them over the flaming candle. Then she opened the bottle

10

and poured sake over the *hashi* and released the purified ashes of the general, the boy's father, into two tiny cups.

"It is a Satsuma sake of your warrior ancestors," she said, and handed him one cup. "The time has come."

The fourteen-year-old bowed as he took the cup from her and made the most solemn commitment a Japanese could make. "I will avenge my father's death on those countries and people that caused it." Then he drank the Satsuma sake mingled with the ashes of his father.

———

The early morning briefing had been held in the basement of the small but very exclusive Yotsuya Self-Defense Forces compound. Part one was slides. Under the terms of treaties with the United States, Japanese advanced computers, used in avionics or missile targeting, could not be sold to COMECON and Muslim countries. One slide listed the code name of each restricted Japanese computer. The next slide showed maps of the Soviet Union and the Middle East covered with red dots like a skin disease. All the dots were numbered. The final slide listed advanced Japanese computers alongside the locations where they had turned up inside Iran, Iraq, and the USSR.

The lights went out and a film came on, also without introduction. Even in poor lighting, one could see that the foreign girl was attractive, an open, guileless face and a marvelous bustline. The surveillance camera appeared enamored of her profile.

When the lights came on, Mori saw that an officer had slipped into one of the empty rear seats. He introduced himself to Mori. "Yuki's my name." The colonel had stood up and bowed. "Covert operations of the Defense Intelligence Agency." His manners were cursory. "The police are considered a sister service; that is why we help one another occasionally." The word *help* was emphasized. Mori understood that the agency didn't want to appear to be soliciting assistance from the police.

The colonel smiled suddenly. "I was with the TOKKO before the war."

Mori bowed. Acceptance into the prewar TOKKO, the Thought Control Police, was an honor accorded only to the highest-ranking graduates of the major universities. Communists, during TOKKO's tenure, had been virtually eliminated from Japan. In 1946, by the wisdom of American G-2, the TOKKO had been dismantled. Under MacArthur's benevolence, Communism had been reborn: riots, strikes, and street marches. Mori's own division, the Public Security Bureau, which kept tabs on terrorists, radicals, and foreigners, had been ordained in secret, and too late. Banned from the organization charts, and thus without legal status and public funds, the PSB had never been able to live up to the TOKKO. Mori was trying to think of a compliment to pay the colonel when Yuki began his formal and thorough debriefing.

His first question dealt with how long it took the girl to reach the station. Each day she made the same journey. A stopwatch had been cleverly superimposed on the lower right-hand corner of the picture frame showing elapsed time.

"Seven to eight minutes in the three series," Mori said. He was accomplished at these sessions, as he was at tailing suspects. He knew how to keep out of target sightlines, how to maximize surveillance distance, and he had an uncanny feel for what a suspect was going to do next. For this was his job: He followed foreigners such as the girl, found out their secrets. Under certain conditions, he destroyed them.

"Excellent," said the colonel. "We'd heard you were quite good."

It was the kind of debriefing that case officers like to make after a particularly important sighting. Apparently they considered the girl of good potential for their operation. Finally Yuki's barrage of questions stopped. He stood and touched the back of his hand to his upper lip as if to stifle a cough. Then he withdrew a pen from his left breast pocket. Using it as a pointer, he indicated the first location on a slide map. "El-Tuwaitha," he said, enunciating the word carefully. "I don't suppose you ever heard of it." Mori shook his head.

"A few miles from Baghdad," Yuki said. "An Iraqi rocket and missile research center. Stolen computers there numbered ten and every one on the restricted list. The KGB was supplying them. To prevent the Soviets from acquiring military-application computers from Japan, a monitoring system had been set up two years ago. Called Exodus Sixty, it placed monitors in local high-tech firms to check sales and exports to Communist countries. In addition to her research chores, the American girl was also one of the monitors. She was, however, apparently doing much more than that for the U.S. government."

Yuki's pointer marched to Oakland, California, to Nord Aviation, where the sophisticated components for the space shuttle were made. Six months ago, Yuki said, a copy of a stolen Japanese Fifth Generation computer showed up there. It was now believed that the Americans were attempting to insert a huge intelligence network into Japan's most sensitive industry—computers and microchips—where the United States and Japan were fiercely competitive. The girl was believed to be the U.S. resident, in charge of running and expanding the network locally. But they didn't know for sure.

As he listened, Mori felt his interest grow. A U.S. spy then! The first time in postwar history they had come even close to one.

———

Today Kathy Johnson was dressed in a tight-fitting tailored suit, for the cool October weather. From her thirty-third-floor office, she could see the eight other uniquely sculptured towers of Shinjuku shimmering against a white sky. Each of the earthquake-proof shafts was set apart to be admired from nearby viewing areas and parks like a collection of rare pagodas.

Kathy's specialty, until four years ago, had been the Josephson junction, a microscopic switch that, when cooled by liquid helium, operated faster and used less power than semiconductors. When developments in superconductor materials had made the Josephson less attractive, she'd switched allegiance. More recently, supercooled ceramics had become her love. She wasn't one for long runs in her field; not with developments moving so swiftly.

Kathy was blond and attractive, a gift of her Scandinavian ancestry, and wore her hair a trifle longer than one might have expected of a researcher. Like many California girls, she kept a tan and preferred lipsticks in more violent shades of red. The firmness of her fine legs and the tightness of her waist suggested surfing and other water sports in her youth. One reason the Japan Electronics Corporation had asked her to work in Japan, she knew, was because Japanese males admired her figure.

Her clothes were fashionable without being flashy. She had a no-nonsense approach to life; for everything there had to be a solid reason.

Although the R&D offices had recently initiated random body searches, Kathy wasn't particularly concerned. Kobayashi, head of afternoon security, had received several liters of Rémy Martin from her Hong Kong trips; gold in Japan thanks to protectionist tariffs. He usually just waved her through.

Kathy checked her watch and gave herself another five minutes. She took out a comb and cuffed her blond hair until it was full and shiny. Then she checked her lipstick and straightened her jacket so that it showed her figure to full advantage. She looked out the window. Pollution from nearby Kawasaki mingled with condensation mist from Tokyo Bay. A round China red sun hung in the white afternoon sky like the Japanese flag. A final check of her watch. The heavier the rush-hour crush, the greater the protection, was the theory. She didn't look forward to Tokyo subways. For a moment, she thought of California and sun. Real sun. God, how she missed it!

———

The World Series game was in the top of the eighth, the Giants ahead. The colonel reached for a pair of low-power binoculars and handed them silently to Mori. A blonde glittered briefly in the JEC lobby. It was her. Automatically, Mori searched the street for backups; no cars were parked in the vicinity and the sidewalk was clear.

The girl spun blithely through revolving doors in a thin-ankled two-step. Carefully, Mori checked off recognition points one by one: shiny helmet of golden hair; stain of mascara and sea-green eyes; confidence of long-legged stride.

Mori slipped into his shoes at the door as Yuki continued to watch the girl. "Not too casual with her," he admonished. "Remember, even the devil at nineteen was irresistible."

Mori grinned perfunctorily and disappeared down the stairs. The foreign girl had turned east, headed for Shinjuku Station.

Mori stayed a good sixty feet behind even though she did not once check her back. She ignored several obvious opportunities, including shop windows in Nishiguchi, and a storefront crowd which was watching the World Series on TV through the glass. Mori felt disappointment; the girl was obviously an amateur.

Her final chance was the newsstand opposite the station entrance. She appeared to hesitate over the English-language newspapers but did not turn. Mori followed her into the caldron of Shinjuku Station.

She was taller than the Japanese girls; 165 centimeters, her dossier stated. Mori preferred the grace of Japanese form to foreign height and color. A Japanese girl's skin, like rice paper, absorbed the light; foreign skin, like foreign paper, only reflected. Translucence versus glitter. He suddenly thought of his wife, Mitsuko. Her skin was like the very finest shōji.

In the streaming pandemonium of Shinjuku Station, where five million commuters passed daily, Mori shut off all other sight and sound. If she was going to lose him, this would be where she'd try. It was only the girl and himself now. Only her heels sounding on the spotless tiles and her breath hollow in the cloud-white throat.

Hurrying, she had turned away from the main ticket gates to follow signs down tiled stairs for the Marunouchi Line. She selected a 140-yen machine, which meant no more than seven stops. He watched as she impatiently waited in line for her ticket to be punched.

Kathy Johnson tossed her golden hair, checked her makeup in a compact mirror, and remembered her instructions to take evasive action on the train platform. She didn't think she was being followed but she decided to follow her instructions anyway.

Once on the platform she let several trains go by. It was nearing peak commuter hour. A Marunouchi uptown pulled in at the same time as the downtown. Exiting crowds boiled together. With perfect timing, she turned and bolted for the downtown train just as the doors were closing.

She fell against the wall of Japanese men with a sense of relief. The doors hissed shut. That would take care of any followers. She turned her mind to what lay ahead. Sukiyabashi crossing, the middle of Ginza at the height of rush hour. Excellent cover. Eyespot would be the red lapel pin as always, if they didn't miss each other in the crush.

The train lurched as it started and several Japanese male bodies collided with hers. A hand grabbed her for support. High on the thigh. It was starting already. She concentrated on *katakana* posters over the windows. One advertised a mansion in Tokorozawa: dining room, kitchen, and one bedroom of 480 square feet. The price was one-half million dollars' yen equivalent. Typical living quarters for upper-middle-class Japanese. She thought of her spacious condo in Newport Beach, then stopped herself. Better not, she thought. It would only increase her loneliness. She tried another poster.

Here, a bride looked at her, smiling with a slight overbite, wearing a frothy gown of infinite bad taste. The marriage package included either a Japanese ceremony or a nice Catholic church you could rent. Loan of the gown. Reception replete with semifamous master of ceremonies. A forty-centimeter cake and a three-day Hawaiian honeymoon. Group rates available. Jesus! Unbelievable.

At each stop, the press of Ginza-bound men clamped more tightly around her: Shinjuku Gyoen, Yotsuya San-chome, finally Akasaka, where gloved pushers packed the passengers in from behind. Evening rush hour boiled toward its peak. She wondered how Japanese women took it so stoically. The close-ness of Japanese males with their after-shave and cologne mixed in dizzying variety. Their strange absence of body smell. Breath an astringent odor of rice and seaweed. Harsh thighs against hers. Hands. In New York or Paris or London the girls would scream epithets and fight back. Here the pretense was all that mattered. "Face," the Japanese called it. Jesus, what an uptight place!

Fingers on her hips as the train suddenly lurched to the left. An accident. Only she knew better. "The Touch"—*Chikan*, the Japanese girls giggled in the washrooms. Another brush of her hips as the train gathered speed in its dash for the Ginza. The Road of Silver. I could kill him, she thought, remembering what was in her purse. Another touch. This time her bra. Nibbles of animals attracted to succulent food. She felt the anger in her throat and fought against it. Her instructions were clear on this point as on everything else. She knew the crowds were her best defense and made surveillance virtually impos-sible. To gain something one must inevitably give up some-thing. Control's words. Finally she relaxed.

———

Inspector Mori had missed by the narrowest of margins getting into the last subway car. With a reflexive lunge he managed to jam his left hand into the rubber door separators of a car three from hers. With all the desperate strength he could mus-ter he prevented the doors from closing completely and lock-ing. A uniformed pusher started angrily for him but he had just enough strength left to force the door and squeeze through into the packed interior. He heard the platform all-clear whis-tles and felt sweat on his back underneath his shirt.

Chikisho bitch! She'd sucked him in with that benign act and he'd nearly let it work. A hated American. Three cars away was the symbol of all that had gone wrong for his family. And he had been ready to give her the benefit of the doubt. The colonel had been right when, toward the end of the briefing, he'd explained his theory.

The Americans, he had said, were so far behind the Japanese

that they had only one option left: theft. The Soviets were even farther behind. Here it was, 1987, and both superpowers' advanced computer programs were in shambles. Foreigners had never learned to work in teams. "We're not talking supercomputers here," Yuki said. They were mere number crunchers. Cray Company, with their Cray 3, still had Japan whipped. But supers were old ideas. The future was AI—artificial intelligence, machines that actually thought and spoke. New-generation machines. Orders of magnitude faster than anything in the West. Here, the Americans, like the Soviets, lagged far behind. JEC had been working on AI. And Kathy Johnson was somehow involved in a possible attempt to steal the latest prototype.

Carbon monoxide, sulfuric dust, the smells of cheap tobacco and soy sauce greeted Mori when he emerged from the subway at Ginza-Sukiyabashi. The girl was ahead of him in the crowd. A tiara of enflamed neon atop the Sony Building flashed on, challenging the darkening sky. Her skin and hair gleamed incredibly white, then changed colors in the moving artificial light blazing around the broad intersection. For the moment he was quite close to her. He could sense, almost feel her confidence, the confidence of a woman used to male eyes. There was even more: an animal sexuality, the vibrancy of one who luxuriated in excitement and risk.

Mori tore his eyes away from her momentarily and scanned the intersection. The logic was that she wouldn't try an open contact. One of the buildings, perhaps. An unbroken wall of Japanese waited patiently on all sides for the next light change—the "scramble," as the Japanese called it, a light-change system where pedestrians crossed from all sides at once. Behind Mori was the Ginza-Sukiyabashi police box, done up in that awful red and brown siding that the vast Japanese middle class considered upscale. It was built like a house. A steep gabled roof sprouted loudspeakers and searchlights. From the speakers, baseball play-by-play could be heard: another service of the Police Community Relations Division. Nobody out. Yoshimura up. Tokyo Giants at bat. The first pitch was a ball.

A music tone for the blind chimed as the pedestrian signal turned green. A mass of Japanese swept from all sides of the crossing. Mori joined the flood, keeping the girl in the corner of his eye. A wave of oncoming pedestrians carried him away. He was not concerned. Her head bobbed like a golden cork in a black sea.

Yoshimura grounded to first, and the loudspeakers came alive with the near hysteria Japanese display at baseball parks. It was one of the few public places where emotion was forgivable. One out. The stadium crowd was chanting Shinozuka's name as the leading hitter came up to bat. "Shin-ozu-ka. Shin-ozu-ka!"

It was at that moment that Mori saw the foreigner making his way across the intersection through the crowd. The Caucasian's face was hidden from view, but Mori noted heavyset shoulders, a hatless shock of brown hair going to gray. He did not ride the wave of the crowd like a Japanese but fought the tide, shoving bodies roughly aside. A dark raincoat was held over one arm. Incredible! A U.S. contact was meeting her here?

The man angled through the crowd toward the blond girl, like a powerful swimmer fighting a strong current. Instinctively, Mori threw his weight against the crowd and edged closer to the two. The foreigner was near his goal, but the girl did not see him until he stepped into her path and said a word Mori could not overhear. Something was wrong. The girl searched the man's face with puzzlement. Then Mori saw her express another emotion. Fear!

Japanese pedestrians skirted the two foreigners as they faced each other in their own tiny arena. Shinozuka took a curve ball for a strike. It was the top of the ninth, the Giants ahead. Mori watched the foreigners, wondering what he should do. There was obviously not going to be an exchange. The man had taken the girl's arm and she had shrugged him off. A faint ironic smile touched her lips. As she stared directly at the man, she reached calmly into her handbag. Metal flashed briefly in her hand. Her face suddenly contorted.

Someone shoved Mori—he couldn't see. Desperately he dove through the crowds, crashing into the wave. Then he saw.

The first bullet had hit her in the stomach; the second, a head shot, exploded her blond hair in a final swirl of gold. Her lower face was replaced by a jagged tear through which blood poured. She lifted her hand to touch it in astonishment. Mori kept lunging at them, screaming at the crowd. Shinozuka had doubled into the right-field corner; loudspeakers were roaring like an animal gone berserk. A third and final eruption; her chest.

Her body started a slow, agonizing spin toward the concrete, eyes surprised, mouth agape. The foreigner had turned away flailing into the crowd. Mori noted a red scar from his ear to his collar. Then he was gone.

Cries of terror mingled weirdly with shouts of joy. Police whistles shrilled. The girl was lying still in a spreading slick of blood. People were backing away. Slowly at first, then with ululating frenzy, the hysteria took hold. Men bellowing. Woman screaming. Crowd energy pushed and shoved Mori until he could no longer tell in which direction the killer had escaped. He cursed the crowd's insanity but his voice was hopelessly lost in the blind madness that had overtaken it.

G O L D - D A Y ,   6 : 3 0   P . M .

A mobile investigative unit radio car picked Mori up after the ambulance had gone. They found him staring at the intersection from a small park next to the crossing. Aoyama was waiting in back.

"The chief is a bit upset," Aoyama said. He looked at Mori's face. "What happened?"

"She was shot. A foreigner was waiting for her."

"She's dead?"

"Hai. She drew first. One of his bullets exploded her face. Dumdums perhaps. I had almost reached them."

"Poor foreign bitch."

Mori didn't care very much for Aoyama. He spoke five languages, wore French ties and British suits, and exuded an expensive American after-shave most mornings. He was early forties, younger than Mori, and, as the resident computer expert, had become the superintendent general's personal assistant. Mori had once accused him of being *batakusai*, a sycophant for anything foreign, and Aoyama had promptly retaliated, spreading rumors that Mori suffered from pre-Meiji neurosis. A *bushi*. A man of violence who lived in the past.

"Chief wants to see you. He was on his way home when it came in over the 101 desk."

"You know what he wants?"

Aoyama smiled and shook his head.

"*Chikisho*," Mori spat. "Can't you talk?"

"It's a shame you haven't read American literature, Mori. There's a very fine book by Melville about a man in search of a white whale. When he finally finds the whale, it kills him."

They drove the rest of the way in silence.

At the main VIP entrance of Metropolitan Police Head-quarters, they got out and walked into the shiny new granite foyer. The security guard looked at Mori questioningly, since he was still in civilian clothes and didn't have a lapel pass. Aoyama nodded that it was okay, then led the way to the elevators. The chief's office was on the top floor in what was known as the "penthouse." Mori said nothing on the way up. The secretary had already gone, and Aoyama knocked on the chief's door, opened it for Mori to enter, then closed it, leaving Mori alone.

The superintendent general bowed stiffly, not taking his eyes off Mori's face, as if searching for symptoms of fatal disease.

"*Gokurosama*. You have done very well." The chief spoke without enthusiasm. Mori noticed that there were lines under his eyes and that his voice was hoarse. He motioned Mori to sit.

Mori settled in a chair with a view of a flower arrangement. God, Earth, and Man. He wished it were that simple, and thought of the chief's wife, an insipid woman who bowed too much and dyed her hair. He guessed the flower arrangement was hers. Foreigners, he recalled, offered flowers to their dead. Japanese gave money instead. Flowers were for the enjoyment of the living. He wondered if the American girl had liked flowers.

"Well, the Giants won today, didn't they?" The chief managed a smile that was too bright, too happy. Mori understood that he was angry. "Puts them ahead in the series, doesn't it? One nil?" The chief had one of those executive chairs you could lean way back in without falling over, and he did so, amazing Mori by his balance. Then he clasped his hands behind his neck to complete the performance. Mori wondered briefly if he should applaud.

"Lions couldn't hit Nishimoto's sinker, that was the real problem. I believe it was on the speaker at Sukiyabashi intersection. Did you hear any of it?"

A warning buzzed in Mori's head. The chief had already checked with Traffic at Ginza. "Only a part," Mori said, quickly deciding against elaboration. He'd also noted that the chief was a Yomiuri Giants fan. They were the establishment team, after all; the favorite of all elected officials like the chief who were at the top of the state hierarchy. It was natural, Mori felt, that he would root for the Giants.

The chief continued to study Mori's face as if trying to decide something. He suddenly righted himself and pressed a button. "Maybe tea would do," he said. "My girl has gone but Naomi is out there, I'm sure. New girl."

The rumors had it that the chief was the justice minister's boy, a National Public Safety Committee appointee. A politician first, therefore; you had to remember that. It wasn't his fault, really, Mori reminded himself. It was the nature of his job as head of the largest police force in Japan. Mori recalled the chief's extraordinary indirectness from previous encounters. The more elaborate his manners, the more serious the offense.

The chief opened a lacquered seashell box and offered Mori a cigarette, longer than the Mild Sevens Mori normally smoked.

"They're foreign. I hope you don't mind."

There was that strange searching scrutiny again. Mori accepted one, then lit the chief's cigarette and his own.

"And your young wife." The chief took his first puff. "Mitsuko, isn't it? Still with the government job? Quite a girl, I hear."

He'd been checking the files, too, Mori understood. Probably had Naomi, the "new girl," do it to get the name straight. But the key word was *girl* instead of woman. Mori knew what the talk was in the bureau. Japanese didn't approve of older men marrying younger. A mistress, fine, but not marriage. It went against the grain. Mori's first wife had died ten years ago. They'd had no children.

Mori nodded. "She's fine, sir. Selected for ICOT recently." ICOT was a government-backed research group attempting to develop a revolutionary new computer.

No surprise in the chief's voice when he agreed that was quite an honor. Apparently, they'd kept up on his personal side as well.

Does flower arranging interest her? If so, the chief said, she'd have to meet his wife, Mayumi. He prattled on as if they were at the Nippon Club for drinks. Mori brushed aside the formalities. Mitsuko was quite busy, really. No time just now. Then he explained what had happened: that the girl had died before the ambulance arrived; and that it was his fault.

The chief reluctantly nodded as if confirming a difficult point of *go* technique. He sucked air between square white teeth with a long hissing noise and offered an oblique reply. This was between foreigners, after all. Fortunately, no Japanese were involved. And, by the way, had Mori gotten a good look at him?

A dance, Mori thought. Music provided by the state. The steps already learned. "The KGB and CIA," Mori agreed. Very clean, in fact; only an American dead. And the other foreigner with a nice scar behind the ear for identification. But Mori hadn't gotten a good look, really. Perhaps it had been the baseball game after all. He gave an approximate height, size. The nondescript clothes that didn't look Russian. The raincoat.

"Not a Russian?" The chief's eyes narrowed with the suggestion, as if to warn Mori that this part of the dance was more difficult—the steps quite intricate. Then the chief waved an arm: "Of course, he wouldn't dress to look like one of his own then, would he?"

His good humor thus restored, the chief was suddenly out of his chair poking around the room as if searching for precious treasure. There were piles of paper on side tables and chairs. Finally he found an envelope and handed it to Mori. "Best we could do on short notice."

The inspector went quickly through fifteen photos of varying quality, most of the faces grainy with the porous effect of a telephoto lens. He shook his head finally and returned the pictures to the envelope.

By this time the chief had found a second envelope amid the disorder. Again none of the faces fit—and anyway, Mori doubted that he could positively identify anyone if he were sworn. The chief did not appear displeased. "We didn't think so either. But the minister called. I had to assure him we were making a thorough investigation. I really don't agree that this concerns us though, do you?" The chief didn't wait for Mori's reply. "After you leave me I'm afraid Colonel Yuki wishes to use some more of your valuable time. Our Defense Intelligence chief. Didn't tell you that, I suppose, did he? Very modest personality. Would you like to phone your wife you'll be late?"

Mori knew his wife wouldn't be home yet. "She's used to it, sir," he said.

The chief nodded sympathetically, leaned back, and squinted at a point on the ceiling. "Your mother still live with you, does she?"

Mori didn't reply at once. He recalled that there was a dinner tonight with his wife's sister at some eel restaurant in Akasaka. He hadn't been looking forward to going anyway.

"It's working out then," the chief concluded, supplying his own answer. "I mean, you know how it can be with a young wife, a mother, and all."

Mori agreed he knew how it could be. He also understood, or was meant to understand, the brass were on to the problems of his marriage. But why were they so interested?

The chief had turned to watch him thoughtfully, nodding as if very pleased. It was the signal that he had finished the niceties and that hereafter no mercy could be expected. He asked about the exact moment the girl was shot. Mori explained that the girl drew first, which somehow startled the chief. In all that crowd? He shook his head. And then they moved on to what Mori had done to stop it.

The crowd. The noise. The suddenness of the shooting. When Mori had related the facts it was clear he'd done virtually nothing. But the chief acted impressed and shook his head

25

admiringly as if Mori had been the hero. For a time the chief didn't speak; a pleasant smile remained on his lips. Finally he asked in a very soft voice:

"And how did you feel about the girl? Her being shot in front of you and all?" The chief might have been asking Mori about how he'd enjoyed his dinner. The control he displayed was quite remarkable.

"I was upset," Mori said. "I cursed the crowd. I felt anger."

The chief nodded carefully as if not to disrupt the logic. "Nothing will go on your record, you understand. I am simply trying to ascertain the state of your mind at the time. You say you felt anger. Where was your anger directed, Mori-san?"

Mori fought the sudden confusion storming through his brain. "I don't understand, sir."

The chief's face glowed with warmth as he apologized if he'd gotten his facts wrong. But at times hadn't Mori shown a certain xenophobia? A hatred of all things foreign and all foreigners? "Not that I can blame you, understand," the chief concluded.

"That has nothing to do with—"

"You don't blame foreigners for your father's death?" The chief raised his eyebrows and waited to see if Mori wished to interrupt again. Then he continued. "Not uncommon among children of our war dead, I might add. After all, you witnessed his chosen death as a child. You hate them because you fear them. In particular, Americans and Soviets. Nothing to be ashamed of; but it might have traumatized you under certain conditions of stress. Caused an inability to act in spite of your brilliant record with foreigners. Frankly, there'll be some who'll say you could have stopped it. That you let an assailant escape. Or did you want the girl to die? Was it an indirect act of revenge? I would only like to know what you think. I can protect you. I am one of many who respected your father."

After a brief silence, the chief smiled paternalistically, a father with a difficult son. He explained that the Public Security Bureau, as a confidential branch, had to bend the rules sometimes. Then he asked how Mori supposed it would go down in the Diet if the Socialists and the Communists found out what they'd been doing today in Sukiyabashi? "The media would savage us, am I not right?"

Mori rose slowly. "I will resign my position. There will be a letter on your desk in the morning; I will assume full responsibility."

The chief's laughter was sudden but without harshness. As one laughs at a backward child. Resignation wouldn't be necessary, he explained, becoming thoughtful again. Actually they had something rather more complex in mind for Mori. A way for Mori to put things right with his father once and for all; and also to help his country. Although the latter apparently hadn't been at the top of Mori's list, now, had it?

Mori flushed, but the chief simply lifted his palms upward: "You have thumbed your nose at our system of advancement and sequestered yourself in the PSB backwater to wage your private war against the *gaijin.* You believe it has gone unnoticed? Do not be naïve."

Mori squeezed his eyes shut as if to close out the words. Again he saw the long rows of white-clad figures kneeling in black powder. His father lifting the *wakizashi* and the field of toy figures following. As the knife flashed in the sun, Mori felt bile rise in his throat. The chief's voice brought him back to the room:

"Bursting with talent and nearly to your prime, yet you choose to be left behind by the likes of Aoyama, your good friend Watanabe, and others of your age group. There's only one answer, isn't there? That's why I've called you here tonight, Inspector. I don't like to see a good man go to waste. I can offer you one final cleansing victory that will purge your soul and satisfy your house."

The new girl arrived with tea, carrying the black lacquer tray carefully. The two handleless cups smelled of good tea, not the kind served in operations. When the girl had gone, the chief tested his, making a sucking noise as was common among the Japanese, drawing in air with the tea to cool it.

"Oolong," the chief said. "From China. Supposed to keep you thin." He took another exploratory sip. "She's boiled the leaves too much and almost ruined it. Really a problem the way these younger girls treat tea leaves." He put the cup down and belched. Then he proceeded to explain.

Mori was to investigate the dead American girl. Had she been spying for the United States? Who was her control? Which U.S. agency, if it was that, and they certainly hoped it was. What was she after? Now that the girl couldn't tell them— and that had been the original plan all along, for which Mori was at least partially responsible—it was his *giri*. Obligation.

Meanwhile, Homicide Division would find her killers. Colonel Yuki's team would help. That shouldn't be difficult since it was obviously Soviets. Mori would be assigned as liaison to the American investigation team. That should make his work easier. His approach would be a data swap. When Mori had uncovered the U.S. espionage activities, and Yuki with Homicide had found the killers, they would put the two pieces together.

The chief paused to look carefully at Mori. "The spy scandal of the century, Mori-kun. A huge media event. This is what we are hoping, anyway."

"Why not just terminate the bastards?" Mori said. "On both sides."

"Because, Inspector, public outrage will allow us to take the first step to change the course of Japanese history. To move from the child dependent on a foreign protector to an adult that decides alone. The first step to protect our strategic high-tech. Diet approval for a huge new security agency to rival what we had prewar."

The phone rang. The chief lifted it impatiently and listened. Then he grunted and hung up.

"Well, you are in luck. That was Colonel Yuki's office. Something about a meeting with the Americans tonight, so he's canceled your meeting I'm afraid." The chief folded his hands on the desk in front of him. His fingers were short and blunt. They still looked strong. "An operation of which your father would approve, I am sure. You are free to refuse of course. We can find someone else. For example, Aoyama has specifically requested he be put in charge."

Mori stood up suddenly and bowed. "That will not be necessary, sir."

When Mori had gone, the superintendent general switched off his recording equipment and dialed a special telephone number. Then he pushed a scramble button on his console. A voice on the other end replied:

"Yes?"

"The decision has been taken, Minister. Inspector Mori will be Tamon."

"That is satisfactory." The voice was calm, unmoved.

"Everything in his background indicates he is the ideal candidate."

"I have several questions before I can give final approval. We should meet if possible in one hour. I leave for Kyushu later tonight."

"Agreed, sir."

The superintendent general of police carefully replaced the receiver and took a deep breath. The minister would agree. There was no alternative. Tamon had been an appropriate name. It was one of the four Japanese gods responsible for protecting Japan from its enemies.

CHAPTER 3

GOLD-DAY, 7:30 P.M.

The telephone purred calmly twice, an electronic buzz that characterized the latest-model Tokyo phones. Ludlow, struggling to the surface of consciousness from sound sleep, brought the receiver to his ear.

"This is Graves. I have orders from the DCM."

The voice was tense, clipped, with an East Coast accent. He was using identification code.

Ludlow fought to concentrate through the haze.

"I just said . . ."

"I damn well know what you just said."

Ludlow was wide awake now. The code registered. The Tokyo station chief had properly identified himself. DCM meant deputy chief of mission, the specified code. He looked quickly around the cramped embassy flat they had assigned him. His not-yet-unpacked bag lay where he had flung it two days earlier when he'd arrived from Hong Kong.

"I want a tack in thirty minutes exactly." The station chief's tone had hardened perceptibly. "Roppongi *kōsaten*, the all-night bookstore side. The opposition is hopping tonight so watch your back, my friend. We have an Echo Echo. The car is a white Nissan Sports."

The phone went dead in his ear and Ludlow slammed the

receiver down. God, what time is it? Why can't they say what they mean. A young one fresh from Washington. It never changed. Full of importance and the ridiculous jargon. An "Echo Echo," for Christ's sake. Years ago they had all been his juniors; one by one he'd seen them move past him up the ladder. London, Brussels, and the real plum, Frankfurt. He'd never learned.

Ludlow checked his watch, noticing not for the first time that his hand was not entirely steady. Instinctively, he went to the window. There was a wall and a guarded gate. Cars were parked along the narrow street beyond. Harmless and empty except for one. One would be a watcher. Perhaps curled on the back floor using mirrors. Ludlow didn't know it. He assumed it. The front door was out. It was just 8:10 p.m.

Roppongi, Tokyo's own Broadway and Piccadilly rolled into one, was the second problem. His control had picked it for the crowds, he guessed. They liked the security of familiar surroundings, the Roppongi crowd did. Shelter for the foreign bar girls, the models, the out-and-out hookers. The hunters and the hunted. A strange foreigner would stand out like a copper penny in a goat's ass. He hoped the new man was punctual and wondered again what was at stake. Hong Kong had been rife with rumors.

From his nondescript luggage, Ludlow rescued a crew sweater, then dark pants and a stained suede jacket. His finest evening wear. Outside, as he made for the garden behind the apartment complex, the chill night air shocked his lungs. Peshawar and Hong Kong had thinned his blood. He prayed that the new man would not screw it up. Nervous voices did not belong in the Asian theater. And Echo Echo meant emergency. However, it was about time. He'd been sitting on his fanny in Hong Kong for over ten days recovering from the "accident" in Peshawar. Then two days in Tokyo cooling his heels, waiting for Graves to call.

At the end of the garden, Ludlow reached a brick wall. Favoring his right leg, he tumbled over it carefully. He dropped into a deserted lane that funneled to a wider street and then a stoplight where it joined the broad pavement of the road to Roppongi. He had fifteen minutes left. Plenty of time: he could walk it.

He went swiftly up the hill, pulling the suede collar more tightly around his throat. Ludlow walked like an American, without straightening his back or exaggerating any part of his stride, as if he really didn't give a damn what others thought of him. Unless you watched Ludlow closely or had seen his medical report after Peshawar, it was almost impossible to detect his slight limp.

In point of fact, Ludlow had been treated at a hospital in Peshawar, though the accident had occurred on the wrong side of the Khyber Pass. He had been instructing a Pathan team on the use of the Stinger hand-launch missile. The Afghans had picked up the hang of it quickly. Their third sortie in the Pandashar Valley tested them against an armored Soviet patrol. The guerrillas had taken out a Hind chopper and Ludlow was grinning broadly when a Kalashnikov heavy machine-gun round blew a small piece of his calf away.

He'd made it out on his own, with a triplet of Soviet ears presented to him as a parting gesture by the Pathan mujahedeen chieftain, the highest accolade available in those parts. The exchange did not end there. Ludlow also came out with what he had gone in for, or so he thought: Pathan word they would turn over wreckage of the brand-new titanium-plated Soviet Hind helicopter they had trashed. The United States was desperate for a sample of the new product. He wondered now if the promises had been kept. Once in a goddamned great while they were. Of course he'd never know. Only some invisible hand back in Washington that chalked up the tally on his scorecard and decided his future knew for sure.

Ambiguous victories and vague defeats: that summed up what it had been like since coming over. In military intelligence they jumped all over the smallest mistake. You eventually found that out if they sent you to some godforsaken place lower down the pecking order, or pulled your plug with a very polite letter inviting you back to the United States for refresher courses. If you'd won, nothing was ever said. Silence was the reward. And a certain enhanced courtesy when the senior people came in on their annual trips.

Not that he really cared. It was the nature of the game, and they'd told him at the outset not to expect an ego trip; if you want that, join the fire department. The glamour of the service had been badly punctured since the Alan Dulles, Beetle Smith days. Still, he'd taken a bad spill, careerwise, in Colombo, and the memory rankled. It would be nice to chalk up a big one and know about it for a change. He'd hoped Tokyo might be the place to get back on track. Now he didn't think so. Not with a control like this one. Graves sounded like a hundred others he'd met.

The road to Roppongi was a confusion of lights; the overhead Shuto Expressway gave it the appearance of a vast erotic cave. Schools of taxis floated curb to curb, their Empty signs lit, waiting for long-distance riders or for those who held up two fingers, meaning "will pay double." Cutting through the jam of taxis like elegant fish were the latest toys: shiny Mercedes, Nissan Zeds, a Rolls or two, and Italian racers. All the equipment, including the cabs, was as shiny as the Mirror at Ise.

That explained everything about the Japanese, Ludlow decided as he walked. A diseased man takes many baths, as they themselves pointed out. Their society was sick, run by a powerful elite that controlled the individual so cleverly, so cleanly, that it got by as democracy. A Marxist's mouth watered when he understood the full implication of what the Japanese leadership had accomplished.

Japan now had the most highly structured society in the world, an especially remarkable feat since it did not require the enforcement of a KGB-style organization to assure conformity. The Japanese had done it mentally. The seed was planted at birth and flowered with adulthood. The sickness was called *giri ninjo,* a web of obligation which every responsible Japanese assumed as duty—but only to one of his own race. A duty carried with him to the grave. It explained why Japanese had so little violent crime in their own cities, yet during war could massacre thousands of Chinese civilians; why they never crossed streets against the light and rarely

33

broke the most common local laws, yet used every trick to invade overseas markets. Why they remained corporate legends, ignoring personal reward for the profit of their corporations—the glory of balance of payments. For Nippon. Shinto mind control and Zen discipline. With it they had nearly won the Second World War and were now winning the economic one. Their closed system made the Marxist revolution look like the dance of the sugar-plum fairies.

Knots of Japanese stood or walked, gestured, talked, laughed; decided where to go, then went. Neon shouted in various hues, from the moving *kanji* of the Miami Coffee Shop, where the foreign pros congregated, to the sophisticated tones of Coco's, a host cabaret where high-bred Japanese women went to be entertained by men.

One heard that it was changing; that youth was resisting the harness imposed on their elders. But one had heard that for every generation. If it ever did turn, Japan would require a huge security agency to contain its masses. All hell would certainly break loose.

Ludlow watched a flushed crowd of youngsters swirl by. Japanese males and females of all classes and age categories drank, but particularly the young. It was considered social, it was considered a necessity. To ease the pressure of the web. To permit one to say what one really thought and then excuse it later as drunken insanity. Thirty thousand Japanese committed suicide a year, Ludlow had been told. Published stats refuted this embarrassment. Accidental death was the rug most of the numbers were swept under. Accidental turning on of gas jets; accidental walking into the sea. Ludlow didn't wonder why.

They swirled around him, perfumed and well dressed; but he saw the permanent cost in their eyes. No wonder Tokyo was one of the more active fleshpots of the world. But it was mainly kept by the Japanese to themselves.

From the more dimly lit entrances doormen clapped their hands as if calling the gods at Meiji Shrine and beckoned passersby to rediscover their youth. Heavy makeup and the latest European fashions were in, being led toward fates that bore the names: Rosemarie's, the Rising Sun, Hama's, Pub Cardinal.

Ludlow had five minutes to go when he reached the core of the district, Roppongi Intersection. Hawkers littered the sidewalk with cheap jewelry and blinking sweatbands, or grabbed passing arms with offers of more temporal consummations. Ludlow waited at the curb for the light change.

He was a solidly built man for his age—which was thirty-eight, although his passport stated he was forty. He looked older. His skin was burned dark by too many Asian suns and his curly black hair was going to gray like an aging karakul. His Washington dossier classified him as a field operative, a low rank for his age, mainly because he'd been offered a long-term contract by the covert Directorate of Operations and had turned it down. That was his reasoning, anyway, since Colombo. It held water best after several drinks.

Since he offended most of the Operations career men he worked with—he seemed to make a point of it—his only job security lay in the fact that he was technically very good at what he did. In the jargon of the intelligence trade, he was a locksmith. To the inner circle at Operations in Langley, despite all his shortcomings, Ludlow was rated the best of his peculiar breed in Asia. There wasn't a weapon that he could not fire and take apart blindfolded, Eastern or Western, nor a computerized security system yet devised that he couldn't sort out, given time. He was the kind an intelligence service likes to keep in its stable for those extraordinarily infrequent occasions when the stakes are out of all proportion to slights incurred or remuneration paid.

Graves did not show, and the bookstore was exposed, Japanese style, no doors, just stalls of books and magazines. Ludlow's anxieties grew as the minutes ticked off; he couldn't hold here forever. A steady crowd that read without buying was heavy in the adult-comic and porno section. Bunko, the Japanese called it. Printed junk food. The only cars slowing were cabs looking for riders.

Ludlow pulled a magazine from a rack and pretended to read. Adult porno cartoons. The cutting edge of the most incredible magazine sales boom of the century, the Japanese admitted.

Figures were cleverly drawn so they looked neither Caucasian nor Asian. All the girls were of heroic proportions, full-busted and long-legged. One page showed just a conch shell. Japanese censors still did not allow explicit art. The shell symbolized all that was feminine; yet on commercial TV they were allowing rear nudity in golden-time spots, and frontals on the erotica panels after eleven p.m. It had been explained to him quite late one night at the Okura Camellia Bar by a self-proclaimed expert from Protocol Section.

The frenzied emphasis on sex among Japanese males was simply one way of letting off steam since they were trapped by their highly structured environment—the dull conformity of their lives and the predictability of their futures. Most Japanese husbands were unfaithful. It was expected.

Sex was risk. A symbol of escape.

A gleaming white Nissan Sports pulled to the curb, the front door swinging open. Ludlow was inside and the car moving just as the lights changed. This all took less than ten seconds. The driver turned right, down the hill toward Kasumicho, shifted gears expertly, and carefully checked the rearview mirror. For a while neither man spoke.

"Perhaps if you acquired a less conspicuous car."

The driver's eyes flicked to the fender mirrors as if Ludlow had reminded him.

"Yes. Sorry about the delay. The opposition has been beefing up their Japanese team. They've a lot more on the streets now than in your day."

Instead of telling the new man to stick it in his ear, Ludlow lit a cigarette. Graves had one of those accents that made everything he said an insult.

"I'm not a street man," Ludlow said. "Never claimed to be."

Graves drove stolidly on, preoccupied. Superior. Graves of Washington. He had a thin hawklike face with a genuine wariness about him as honest men do who are forced to consort with thieves. Ludlow quickly inventoried the dark suit, rep tie, suspenders, and preppie watchband. A Soviet-Asian network was at stake, so the rumors went in Hong Kong. God help us if this was the talent level at the helm. Ludlow coughed and dragged on his cigarette for solace.

They turned at Kasumicho so they were on the road through Aoyama Bochi, the tombstones hidden among the shadowy cherry trees. There was no traffic now. No one following. Graves was driving carefully, well within the fifty-kilometer-per-hour speed limit, coming to full stops at all the deserted crossroads. Ludlow began to feel ill-at-ease. At Aoyama-dori the car turned right down the broad separated avenue and picked up speed.

"You speak Japanese?" Graves fell into the occupational gambit of probing for something the dossier might have missed. "Your file says you spent two years here with State Department cover a while back."

Ludlow's smile was ingenuous. "Why in hell would I want to speak Japanese?" He had found that language ability was a weapon it was best to conceal.

Graves shook his head as if he'd hoped for a better start. A look of doubt crossed his sharp features. "Look," he hissed suddenly, "I didn't ask for you. This was Washington's idea. And to be honest, the last thing I need right now is a reprobate castoff from military intelligence with a spotty success record in the Central Asian Section, stability question marks in his file, plus a recent wound to muddy my waters. Understand?"

Ludlow's chuckle rumbled from deep within his chest to the surface of his face. Laugh wrinkles feathered the corners of his ferocious eyes. The taut mouth relaxed into a grin. The ridge of his crooked gladiator's nose twitched. He took out an old plaid handkerchief and blew his nose loudly, which brought his features back into control. He sniffed and said, "Damn, Graves, you're a real charmer, you are."

Graves's grip on the steering wheel tightened. His knuckles whitened. "Just telling you what your file says. It's nothing personal."

Ludlow shifted his bulk in the seat as if to get a better look at the station chief. "I don't really care what my file says," Ludlow said softly. His fierce black eyes glowed with sudden

37

volcanic energy. "To be honest, I don't like you either, Mr. Graves. Now, are we gonna do this? Otherwise let's turn this faggoty car around . . ."

A vein appeared suddenly on Graves's forehead and danced in rhythm to his heartbeat. He took a deep breath. "Did you know Kathy Johnson?"

"No." Ludlow's massive shoulders relaxed.

"Green eyes," Graves said. "Not a real beauty but a great figure. Worked for Sixty."

Ludlow nodded curtly.

"Shot three times this afternoon. Middle of a downtown Tokyo street. Some fucking Japanese cop saw the whole thing and let the bastard get away."

Ludlow grunted and said nothing. Team Sixty worked with Exodus, a Science and Technology op run out of Washington. Mainly protection of Free World high-tech. From what he knew it wasn't that successful in Asia. Certainly not enough to justify extreme prejudice from the KGB executive section. It didn't add. Sixty agents were mainly greenies and women. Unless Graves was lying about the dead girl's assignment, which was probable. Either that or it wasn't the Soviets.

Graves's nasal voice interrupted Ludlow's thoughts: "The girl worked at a Japanese company by the name of Japan Electronics Corporation. High-tech of course. Hot new computers."

Ludlow continued to study the road. "So you believe she was running a pre-op validation when she was taken out?"

Graves looked remarkably surprised, and Ludlow wondered briefly if he hadn't underestimated his control.

"How did you figure that?" Graves's tone was neutral.

Ludlow smiled. "Why else would I be sent in if not to collect some prize from a Japanese laboratory?"

They reached Yasukuni-dori near the Outer Moat and passed Ichigaya Station. The car stopped in front of a large barred gate. A Kevlar-helmeted sentry surged from the darkness looking like a World War II German paratrooper. Except that he was Japanese. Ludlow could see another Japanese soldier carrying a new American M-16A2 at port with bayonet fixed.

Nice single-shot weapon, Ludlow recalled. He'd tested it for some Chapa tribesmen at the Darrah gun bazaar. They'd bought a crate although he'd explained you couldn't piss around the automatic grouping. Too much kick.

Graves showed a pass and said a name, "Snow." The soldier took the pass to a sandbagged guardpost and went inside. A light came on and Ludlow could hear the jangle of a telephone. The heavy-barred gate started to open automatically even before the guard emerged. As the soldier handed Graves back his pass, Ludlow glimpsed a flash of red and blue shoulder patch. Japan Self-Defense Forces Headquarters Regiment.

They drove up a winding road between rows of spiny cedars dominated by a huge floodlit red and black antenna that towered eerily into the night sky. A control room one hundred feet up was lit like a late-night restaurant. Without asking, Ludlow knew that they were inside the highly secret Self-Defense Forces headquarters compound, operation nerve center for the security of the Japanese islands. Formerly it had been the U.N. Forces Far East headquarters, and, during World War II, the command center for the Japanese Imperial Army.

They stopped in a nearly deserted visitor's parking area and Graves turned to him: "You will be in a holding pattern for a while, so your orders have been changed. DDO now wants you in charge of investigating the girl's death." He yanked the hand brake tight for punctuation and perhaps something more. "It's really the Science and Technology boys' problem, though, the way I figure it." He got out of the car and, without waiting for Ludlow, strode ahead down a path toward a two-story building where lights burned.

Ludlow cursed under his breath and slowly opened the car door. He wasn't a detective, for God's sake. He traced Graves's steps down the path. As he walked he wondered what was really going on. He'd heard of a bitter power fight between Operations and Science and Technology. Could his assignment to investigate the girl's death be connected? If, as Graves had said, Kathy Johnson was working for Science and Technology, it was really their affair.

Operations was the covert directorate, and none of the other sections were allowed to poach on its operational preserve. Operations handled all actions where "risk," as defined by the agency, was involved. One such definition was "collections category." "Collections" was the polite term in vogue for acquisition of high-tech data and prototypes of friendly and unfriendly competition. Roger Harrington, director of Science and Technology, placed his orders and Operations made the collections. But Ludlow had heard the rumbles that Harrington wanted his own collection team. Harrington was trying to usurp the role of Operations in the ongoing CIA power struggle. And Kathy Johnson could have been one of the pawns in Harrington's game plan.

Many old-timers were jealous of Harrington's spectacular rise in the CIA. The Directorate of Science and Technology was the new darling of those who understood the importance of high-tech superiority as the key to future economic growth and power. Science and Technology was now challenging Operations, the traditional kingmakers, in the CIA power hierarchy. Such rivalry was good, Ludlow believed. It reenergized the lower echelon, forced leadership to change. It also scared the hell out of those agency conservatives who could not accept the idea that scientists might one day run the CIA. Ludlow wondered again if his assignment to investigate the girl's death was somehow connected, if it was part of an Operations attempt to thwart the DS&T's surge toward power?

He reached the building where Graves waited impatiently. The station chief jerked his head toward the entrance:

"Japanese intelligence lives here." He laughed harshly in the silence. "Eunuchs they are. MacArthur took away their balls. The hard vicious boys of the Kempeitai were mostly shot after the war. That left the Japs without an answer to enemy covert organizations: Soviet, Chinese, North Korean. You see, in his great wisdom MacArthur banned Japan from establishing its own security agency. It would take an act of the Diet to change the laws of the land, and the Communists have shot down every attempt so far. Not enough public support. We suggested they and a bunch of hotshots over in the police organize this with the understanding we provide operation backup and protection from foreign agents. Over the past several years it hasn't worked too well. Technically they're free to do as they please."

Ludlow nodded. What Graves was saying was well known. Japan had traditionally lacked an effective counterintelligence service. "So, Japanese intelligence still has the same problems?"

"Yep." Graves nodded sagely. "The Soviets have one hundred agents here going wild. They steal everything the Japanese make, smuggle it out before it's available in the stores. Local KGB resident has received every medal they give." Graves opened the door. "On top of that there aren't any decent espionage laws in this screwed-up country."

Graves went inside and Ludlow followed. "Snow is pissed, so let me do the talking, right?" A sentry saluted and silently preceded them down a polished hall. He had apparently been waiting for them. The same army as anywhere, Ludlow decided, as he viewed the long sterile hallway pockmarked with mysterious doors. Attached to each was a precise military label on white cardboard. They stopped in front of a door that bore a neatly printed name and rank in Japanese and English: COLONEL N. YUKI, DIRECTOR, DEFENSE INTELLIGENCE RESEARCH GROUP.

Their guide knocked, opened the door, and stepped aside. Yuki's office was like any other military cubbyhole Ludlow had ever visited, except that in Japan, it seemed, the higher the rank the greater the disorder. Filing cabinets were ajar along one wall. An old gray walrus of a safe guarded another. Windows were shielded by olive-drab blinds. A black lacquer tea table stood strangely out of place surrounded by battered, disorganized chairs. On the table a chipped white Japanese teapot with bamboo handle and butterfly design presided over a covey of teacups already used. Yuki apparently kept a late schedule. A metal ashtray on the table was full and the room reeked of cheap tobacco and green tea.

The Japanese intelligence officer was sitting cross-legged in the only armchair, barefoot but otherwise in uniform. A pair of *geta* sandals waited nearby on the floor for boarding. He made no move to get up.

"Evening, gentlemen." Colonel Yuki's mouth twitched in what might have been a smile. He nodded at Ludlow, the older of the two, since in Japan age meant rank. Graves rushed to cover the error.

"Good to see you again, Colonel. This is Brown, my assistant."

Yuki snapped shut a file he had been reading and dropped it carefully on the floor beside him. The colonel's black eyes pierced the room. He motioned them toward chairs. There was a brief moment of silence as each side appraised the other. The colonel had the quicker draw.

"You people could have at least told me." The colonel's voice was soft but intense, a low hiss that was punctuated by a sudden thrust of his shaved head toward Graves. A cobra testing its opponent's nerve. Ludlow began to savor the moment. Graves pursed his lips as he sorted options. Yuki didn't give him the chance to regroup.

"Is he the one?" The colonel's fierce eyes swung to Ludlow.

"Yes, sir. Mr. Brown has the assignment now."

Ludlow didn't know whether to laugh or protest. He decided to keep silent.

"You have caused me to lose face to my superiors. Please understand my position."

"Jesus, Colonel. We're not exactly overjoyed she got blown away either. No one expected what happened. As you know she was only an Exodus Sixty. Working for the Science and Technology crowd. I don't have anything to do with them."

"What was her role precisely, Mr. Graves?"

"She was monitoring shipments of high-tech strategic equipment from Japanese companies to certain Middle East and Hong Kong buyers. There is a very active KGB network specializing in Japanese equipment, as we both know."

The men allowed a silence to develop for the moment, each for different reasons. Graves made the first mistake.

"There are no strictly applied laws against industrial espionage in Japan, and this remains of concern to my superiors in Washington. The Soviet KGB resident . . ."

The colonel's eyes had squeezed shut as if he were experiencing pain. His face flushed. His voice was ominous as he interrupted Graves without opening his eyes.

"The girl is dead. All of us regret that. But it does not excuse the fact you deliberately planted this person inside the research group of a highly sensitive Japanese electronics firm, for what reasons I'm sure you'll not reveal."

This was not a question from the Japanese. More a challenge. Graves decided wisely not to touch it.

The colonel opened his eyes slowly, daring Graves to reply. Then he continued, fixing his attention on Ludlow as the lesser offender: "I have advised Japanese police to cooperate with you in every way."

Ludlow smiled for cosmetic effect.

The colonel's gaze returned to Graves as if to settle the point. "Mr. Brown has responsibility for the investigation then?"

Graves ducked his head as if dodging a blow.

"In return," Yuki continued, "there will be no . . . adverse publicity, shall we say. The event will be kept out of the media to the extent possible. But we will share every piece of information that Mr. Brown develops, yes? The courts here are ours as you know."

"Everything will be shared," Graves agreed, ignoring the irony, relieved to be rounding the last bend and heading for home.

"Who will my contact be?" Ludlow asked after deciding it was an inappropriate time to remind Yuki that trial by jury was still unknown in Japan. They held a unique record among the advanced countries of the world for convicting innocent citizens. They also led the world in solved crimes.

The colonel hesitated for a moment. Ludlow thought he saw, for the briefest second, a loss of control reflected in the colonel's eyes. If he didn't know better, he would have said what he saw was hate.

"That will be Inspector Mori. I'll get his phone number if you wait a moment. Meanwhile you may want to read the forensic report."

Yuki eased himself out of the chair onto the *geta* with surprising agility and handed Graves two smudged yellow carbons, barely legible. Graves, content for the moment the chain of command was at least working properly, passed one to Ludlow.

Female. Caucasian. Hair blond. Natural brown. Height 165 cm. Age 24. Time of death: 6:03 p.m. Cause of death: gunshot wounds, total three. Round X fired from distance of fifty centimeters horizontal, into lower abdomen severing appendix, large intestine and lodging in pelvic cavity. Round Y fired upward at 76 degrees through the jaw into the brain causing extensive damage, primary cause of death. Round Z fired upward into her chest hitting number three rib left side and penetrating lung. Preliminary ballistics analysis indicated .45-caliber hollow points were used. Source NA. Manufacturer NA.

The report was signed and dated, "Y. Komatsu, Oct. 9, 1987."

Yuki returned from a filing cabinet and handed Graves a dog-eared card with the police officer's name and phone number.

"Monday afternoon, Inspector Mori will be waiting to show Mr. Brown our forensic work to date on the case." Yuki paused. "There was one other reason I asked you to stop over tonight." He returned to his chair and, after sitting down again, retrieved the file from the floor and flipped through it reflectively.

"In here is a Defense Agency review recommending reconsideration of all U.S. intelligence installations on Japanese soil." The colonel tapped the file with one finger as if it were a live animal he wanted to taunt. "That means, Mr. Graves, every shred of CIA electronics, the analytical teams and field staff at your embassy, Yokota, Tokorozawa . . . and that covert dish in Misawa monitoring the Russians. All the NSA crap."

Graves started to protest.

"Come, Mr. Graves. It is our business to know what is going on in our own country. You underestimate us."

"This is connected to the girl's death?"

"Of course not, Mr. Graves. This is simply an issue that

44

surfaces periodically. The timing is unfortunate, however, wouldn't you agree?"

Graves's hawkish features appeared to tighten in the glare of lighting. "Colonel, our security team is here to help protect your government and your high-tech from our mutual enemies. What is proposed would remove a vital shield."

"Indeed it would." Yuki clucked his tongue, commiserating. "I couldn't agree with you more."

"For example," Graves continued seriously, "we have just sourced a proprietary in Hakodate. Possibly a Soviet conduit using the Northern fishing fleet."

"The brilliance of the CIA effort never ceases to astound us." Colonel Yuki shook his head admiringly. "Without your assistance the Soviets would no doubt pick our high-tech plants clean." Yuki's voice was without the slightest hint of malevolence. "We must get together and work something out." Yuki paused to glance at his watch. "Not tonight however, I'm afraid. It's much too late and I believe it would be more productive if just the two of us could meet." The colonel beamed at Ludlow to confirm this meant no offense. Yuki had risen to his feet.

"Certainly." Graves stood and urged Ludlow up. "Thank you for seeing us at this late hour."

"The pleasure was all mine," Yuki said sincerely.

As they walked to the car, Graves enthused over what a truly good meeting it had been, very frank exchange of views. Didn't Ludlow agree? When they reached the car, Graves unlocked the trunk. He lifted a tool kit from the interior and slammed the trunk shut.

"You're going to vet the girl's place tonight if you don't mind, Bob. I'll drop you since it's on the way." Graves walked around to the driver's side and got in behind the wheel. Ludlow shook his head. His weathered features tensed as he hefted the tool kit. His battle-hardened eyes narrowed to slits as he pondered this new problem. He opened the car door and slid into the other seat.

"You want to tell me what the hell is going on?"

Graves started the engine, and listened to it with his head cocked to one side. "She was a Sixty, so she has a code book stashed in her room. Also, you heard the man. I want you to check her pad thoroughly. See if she has anything else incriminating. Espionage tools. Pages of books with carbon indentations. You know what to look for. If Harrington over at Science and Technology has been up to any tricks I'm going to have him for lunch." He swung the sports car out onto the gravel drive. "One more thing, Ludlow. This isn't Central Asia. Why don't you buy some clothes? Charge it to expense if that's the problem. I'll see it's covered. You know how fussy the Japanese are about appearance. You look like you're about to rob the jewelry department of a convenience store."

Ludlow said little all the way to Azabu Juban. He was considering why it was he always ended up working for people he didn't like on assignments he didn't understand.

CHAPTER 4

GOLD-DAY, 8:00 P.M.

The justice minister's office was in an older building that also housed the National Police Agency. It was conveniently near MPD Headquarters, the Diet, and the Foreign Office.

The superintendent general of police was shown into the minister's visiting room, which instantly clarified its master's heady status in the power elite of Japan. The furniture was period French and almost comfortable. Statues of two samurai from the Heian Period were beautifully carved in wood, aged to a magnificent patina of dun and mahogany. On one wall was a priceless piece of calligraphy by General Hideyoshi himself from the years he ruled both Japan and Korea. The justice minister believed in history, and considered the present posture of Japan a temporary aberration.

The minister burst into the room at flank speed.

"Perhaps you'd like a drink?" His voice was robust, almost a shout. He headed toward a polished cabinet which the superintendent knew contained a brilliant collection of sakes and whiskies.

The SG shook his head. He wanted to shorten the meeting, not lengthen it. Less exposure, less risk, he reasoned.

The justice minister accepted his refusal in midflight, altered course, and dive-bombed a fragile chair. He was large-

47

stomached for a Japanese, with a cheery directness about him that was completely deceptive.

"Then let's get on with it."

The minister settled himself in the chair as a bear settles on the bank of a river to await fish. His watchful gaze fixed on the police chief, a habit he had acquired while serving in the Diet, and which lent credibility to the misapprehension that he was an entirely honest man.

"The girl under surveillance died at three minutes past six, sir. The U.S. embassy has been notified."

The minister clucked his tongue. "Shot in the middle of Ginza? What is our city coming to?"

"The MPD takes full responsibility." The chief said this a little too loudly.

"Nonsense! I'm not faulting the MPD. Point is it wasn't a job for the police force in the first place."

"Maybe not, sir."

"Let's be honest . . ." The minister fidgeted until he found a cigar, lit up, and exhaled a luxurious cloud of smoke. He pointed the cigar at the superintendent general of police. "Yuki over at Defense runs a mediocre intelligence operation. That's an optimistic evaluation, you understand. Not his fault really. He's just not too bright and he's understaffed. Always looking in your pockets; ever since that awful MicroDec disaster."

"Yuki's role in the investigation will be limited."

"That's what I wanted to hear."

"He's agreed to the minor assignment of contacting the Soviet embassy and screening all staff there."

"Very good. It's the Americans we want, Chief. Let's not forget that. The death of the girl doesn't change a thing. You must find out the truth about her."

"An investigation has begun, headed by Inspector Mori. The one I mentioned on the phone. He will liaise with the Americans."

"Any relation to the general?"

"His son, sir. He's our primitive. Rumor has it that as a boy he drank his father's ashes in one of those savage clan rites." The chief paused to confirm this had not unduly disturbed the minister. "So there are two Moris. One that lives in the past and obeys the ancient cult of his samurai ancestors—the pledge of vengeance to his father's memory. The second Mori lives in the present as if the other half did not exist. Not so unusual for those whose formative years were split by the war; what came before and what came after were like night and day."

"Good. Sounds like just the man for the Americans. He's not to be told all of it, is he, Superintendent?"

"Just need-to-know, sir."

"And the evidence against the girl. What do you have so far?" The minister settled more comfortably in his chair.

"An escape route to North America. A gun."

"Excellent. You realize what this means to us."

"Yes, sir." The chief vigorously nodded his head.

"Global power is no longer measured in military terms."

"I didn't believe it was, sir."

"Economic power. There's the key. Even the Soviets understand the change. There is only one way to grow economic power of course."

"Technical know-how, sir. But we have to be able to protect it. This is the problem."

"Right you are. A legalized and strong security agency is vital. Stronger than the prewar TOKKO. The public does not understand. So they must be shocked out of their apathy. We must rally their support."

"Scandal involving the Americans would do it, sir. A fallen blossom never returns to the branch."

The minister of justice waved his cigar. "We need a monstrous scandal. No doubt of it. One that will make the public demand that the Diet give them a decent security agency. The Communists notwithstanding. Then and only then," the minister smiled, "will Japan awaken from its long and peaceful sleep."

"Rearmament?"

"Why on earth rearm unless the Americans insist? An armaments industry? Yes. An industrial-military complex? Yes. But to my point. Economic power. Export. Imagine it! Strategic high-tech export! Aerospace export. Far bigger than electronics,

cars, textiles, by a large multiple. A huge industry, Chief. One
our country has been prevented from entering by the terms of
the San Francisco Peace Treaty and certain U.N. statutes written at the end of the war. Archaic. Ridiculous. Imposed on no
one else, not even the Germans. Awaiting only the proper
catalyst to put them in the shredder of history. Scrap paper.
Forgotten."

"If she was a proper American spy, then?"

"That should do." The minister grinned. "If we sell it to the
press correctly. Now how about that drink?" The minister rose
with some difficulty and headed toward the liquor cabinet.
When he'd selected a good brandy from his collection, he
poured two shots neat and handed one to the superintendent
general.

"There is one more issue I should tell you about, Chief."
The justice minister squinted at his subordinate as if reassuring
himself of the need to confess. "A certain element in our government believes the Japanese–U.S. Security Treaty should be
scrapped. They also question the wisdom of Japan's continuing
to define itself as a member of the Western bloc—drastic
thoughts, I will admit. However, the world is changing. A
recent best-seller by a Tokyo University professor proposes
just such concepts."

"Third World issue?"

"Right. Democracy versus fundamentalism. Is this not
where the world is heading? A period of turbulence, who is
to say?"

"Oil, of course."

"The U.S.'s highly ideological views are hostile to the Third
World."

"To the Muslim fundamentalists, I agree. Seventy percent
of our oil supply and growing yearly."

"So while no one expects any immediate shifts, a little spy
drama would not go unnoticed in Baghdad or Teheran. It would
show that our heart is in the right place. Plus the Soviets are
hinting at the return of our northern islands, which could open
up a broad-scale economic relationship. Not only Siberia."

"And the U.S. is a stumbling block?"

"Let us just say that a falling-out between Tokyo and Washington would not dismay Moscow in the least."

"Then an American spy scandal would have wide-ranging impact."

The minister of justice smiled pleasantly at the chief of police. "Yes, I suppose it would." He lifted his shot glass. "Shall we drink to a victory for the home team?"

CHAPTER 5

GOLD-DAY, 8:45 P.M.

Mori surprised himself and arrived at the Minagawa eel restaurant in Akasaka Mitsuke before nine p.m. The restaurant was a gathering place for the expense-account rich, done with Meiji-era motifs; woven rice straw ceilings and prints by woodblock master Hokusai.

There were nine people at the table. Mori's wife was sitting next to an attractive woman he did not know. When he arrived, both their heads came up like deer startled at a lake by hunters.

Mori bowed. "There was an emergency. Sorry I'm late."

Mitsuko rolled her eyes and managed a smile. "I don't think you've met my friend, Erika, from ICOT."

"No. Delighted."

The stranger dipped her head and said her name. "Erika Hosaka." She kept her eyes averted. It was bad manners to look a member of the opposite sex full in the face on first meeting. Mori's brother-in-law, Kazuo, stood to introduce Mori to others at the table. He wore an expensive double-breasted suit and a diamond ring on his little finger that looked nearly a carat. Tonight, besides Kazuo's wife, Miko, and Mitsuko and Erika, he'd invited an advertising executive from one of the larger agencies with his model girlfriend, the owner of a growing convenience-store chain, who was there to escape his wife and to visit a nearby cabaret later, the president of the second-largest instant noodle company in Kanto, who wanted to discuss pricing, and the oldest son of the owner of the largest supermarket chain in Northern Japan. His father couldn't come. Kazuo's company was the largest food broker in Kanda.

When Mori was seated like the others on a *zabuton* cushion on the floor before the Chinese black pine table, their count came to ten. The floor was of tatami mat, in an alcove raised off the main floor of the restaurant. Kazuo's connection to the Minagawa's owner had secured them this exclusive location. Shoes were removed and left in a row as one stepped up into the tiny room. The walls were of textured sand, with occasional insets where valuable blue and white Imari dishes were placed. The room had sliding shōji doors, which remained open so that they could see other diners as well as be seen themselves. The effect was one of intimacy without isolation.

Seated next to his brother-in-law at one end of the table, Mori listened as the conversation ebbed and flowed. At times a current topic, such as the latest scandal in the Diet, would catch up the entire table in a chaotic exchange of opinions. At other times, male guests would pair off to discuss more intimate topics: prices, discounts, the launch of a new product. Golf scores. The soaring cost of TV ads. The women kept themselves occupied with flattery of one another's clothing, deprecation of their own homemaking abilities, namedropping of chic restaurants visited, and the recent women's rights movement, which Erika insisted on bringing up.

Mori drained his glass of beer and Kazuo refilled it. Kazuo was younger than Mori by several years, but had been extremely successful in the marketing wars.

"Busy?" Kazuo filled his own glass.

Mori shrugged. "It's been quiet as Aoyama Bochi cemetery."

"Then why don't you take a week off? I'm going to Taiwan Tuesday. I could expense you as international staff." He poked Mori in the ribs and glanced over to where his wife was deeply engaged in conversation with Mitsuko and Erika.

"Love to," Mori said without commitment and studied his wife. Mitsuko's face was oval with high cheekbones that cast shadows when she smiled. Her eyes were jet black and full of humor that offset the severity of her elegance. She wore her long hair straight back and tied tonight. It fell below her small pear-shaped breasts when she combed it out in front before she slept.

Her sister Miko was a slightly less brilliant rendering by the same artist. She was packaged in the latest Hanae Mori fashion and her hair shone from the recent attentions of a Roppongi beauty parlor. Erika, the third of the trio, had the best figure, and male eyes around the table kept sliding to her.

Mori had heard his wife mention Erika's name several times. The two women were members of a team that was competing fiercely with the United States and the rest of the world to develop a new kind of computer, one that his wife claimed would revolutionize the world, although Mori never could quite understand what all the fuss was about. Computers didn't hold any interest for him. Erika was a relative newcomer to ICOT, as he recalled, and worked on the public relations side. The number of foreigners curious about Japanese accomplishments had recently surged.

A waiter took orders. More wine for the women, with eel salads. Lambrusca was fashionable among Miko's mah-jongg crowd and she insisted that all the girls try it tonight. Blue eel on rice, more sake and beer for the men. The eel came with a sweet shoyu sauce that soaked through the rice and was considered a delicacy.

Kazuo had launched into an expert discussion of eels; varieties from Taiwan were larger and tastier than the local types—a distinction which, he pointed out, was often applied by Japanese men to Chinese women. It was said that when Chiang Kai-shek fled the mainland he took the most beautiful Chinese females with him. Mori listened patiently to the age-old arguments about Chinese skin being smoother, Chinese legs longer, Chinese breasts more shapely, and Chinese love-making more passionate.

"I have a lady in Taipei who beats your wife's friend, Erika, by ten kilometers." Kazuo had lowered his voice only a little.

"Not at all like a Japanese woman either. You know exactly where you stand."

"Sounds expensive."

"Who said romance was cheap?" Unabashed, Kazuo put the Kirin bottle down. "Particularly in the developing countries. I look on it as an Oriental. I'm helping to sustain the GNP growth rate in a sister Asian market. The yellow races must stick together."

Actually Mori didn't dislike his younger brother-in-law—if he'd just keep quiet. Few escape their past in Japan. Kazuo Takeda's parents had been traveling *botefuri*, chicken merchants, who settled in Tokyo.

"What I can't figure is you, Inspector." Kazuo shook his head. It troubled him that Mori was only an inspector. A graduate of Gakushuin, the peer's school—one who had gained admittance by ancestry rather than wealth or acquaintance— and a member of Tokyo's elite, Mori should have done better. Kazuo pointed an unsteady finger at Mori. "One who exults in self-sufficiency and therefore does not contribute to society. A true samurai, I suppose you will tell me? Embodying the spirit of Yamato Damashi, of warrior Japan? Insistence on spiritual and physical perfection? Piss on the GNP?"

"Materialism doesn't interest me," Mori smiled. "You on the other hand are a product of the postwar system. The emperor is no longer god, so business replaces him. Now every company president becomes a local god."

"Possibly," Kazuo said.

"Possibly, my ass. This is how the system works. The Japanese organization has become the house, the feudal lord. People like myself become the servant, the clerk working for a master. Education promotes social group consciousness, assures the traditional system will survive in spite of great social change. Each group infects individual actions, alters ways of thinking, eliminates spontaneity. So you wonder why I do not allow myself to be infected? Why I stand apart?"

"Have another beer," Kazuo suggested. "It sounds like you had a bad day."

Over dessert fruits, Kazuo inquired innocently about Mori's mother. Mori replied perfunctorily and sensed unpleasantness ahead. He checked his watch and calculated that she must be into the question period at the Rojin Club by now. Wisely she had opted to attend a lecture at the seniors' club on Nobunaga, one of Japan's great warlords, rather than have dinner with relatives.

Kazuo looked up cheerfully from his beer. "You should take Mitsuko out more. Loosen up. From what I hear you're always at the Ginza bars. Get her away from the *shutome* mother-in-law. Her spirit is the same as yours."

"I take her out several times a month. She likes my mother, as a matter of fact."

"What does a dinner cost?" Kazuo continued as if he hadn't heard. "She seldom goes anywhere, Miko tells me. Buries herself in her job. Not good; you could lose her, you know. We invite you to parties at the new house, you never come. Bad. You should make some contacts, develop options to get out of that police yoke and earn some real money." Kazuo glanced appraisingly at Mori's suit.

Mori lit up a cigarette. His head suddenly ached. Perhaps it was fatigue. He saw the blond hair, backlit by a spray of blood, the disintegrating face. The chief's words echoed hollowly inside his head: *If my facts are right at times you have shown a certain xenophobia. A hatred of foreigners . . . Frankly, there'll be some who'll say you could have stopped it. That you let an assailant escape.*

"Food is a very profitable business," his brother-in-law was explaining.

"I don't know anything about business," Mori protested, and wondered what the truth was. Could he have stopped it?

"It doesn't matter," Kazuo argued. "Business is a game like police work is a game. You should consider getting out of the police."

Mori shook his head and tried to smile. Miko was looking across at them now. They've set this up between them, Mori thought.

"Consider Mitsuko's position, for a change, if you won't think of your own, then." Kazuo was leaning a little too heavily on his elbows. "You could have a much better job with your family background. Travel. Mitsuko would love to see the world. Hell, you never even take a vacation, I'll bet."

Mori glanced at his watch. "Something usually comes up. Last summer we went to Kamakura several times. And to the mountains during rainy season for bamboo."

Loud laughter from the other side of the table interrupted them. Mitsuko's face and Erika's were flushed with wine. They were looking down the table away from Mori and Kazuo, their mouths locked in formal smiles.

The instant-noodle president was nearly hysterical with mirth.

"Well, it's true," Erika said and kept the smile in place. When well-bred Japanese disagree they invariably smile or laugh.

"I hire women, lots of them." The president regained control.

"On a temporary basis I would guess. And when they get pregnant you let them go; no leave, right?" Erika had an angelic face and spoke with a soft, melodic voice but her words struck bone.

"It's what everybody does," the advertising executive broke in.

"Men are the aristocracy in Japan," Erika said, with stoic simplicity in her pure voice—a beautiful child telling strangers her doll is broken. "Lifetime employment with all the benefits is only for men. Japanese women are underprivileged."

Kazuo looked desperately to Mori for help. Mori simply smiled back at him. He happened to admire women who spoke their minds. This was Japan's new breed of female; he sensed the competitive spirit behind the childlike simplicity of her words. He listened as Erika explained how women were a growing part of the work force, and how feminization of the work force could cause regeneration of a decent labor movement and reaction against the stifling cocoon of a paternalistic society.

"Tell me something," the president ordered suddenly. "What kind of a radical are you, anyway? A Communist?"

Erika laughed. A pure musical sound. Innocent as a school-yard full of children. Animated laughter was bubbling on all sides now. The women had their hands in front of their mouths and Miko was wiping tears from her eyes. Kazuo fled toward the toilets. Attention at the table had clamped firmly on this beautiful new girl.

"Young lady, would you like to tell me what kind of a job you have?" A smile continued to split the president's face.

"I work at ICOT."

"The Fifth Generation computer project," the president mused. "I thought they only hired people who weren't trouble-makers, Erika."

"At ICOT we're all troublemakers," Mitsuko interrupted with uncanny timing. It was one thing to be tough on an unattached girl who had no close relations in the group. But to take on the sister-in-law of the president of the wholesale company with which you wanted to negotiate a new price was a different situation. Mori had to admire his wife. She smoothly diverted the table from the confrontation by describing what ICOT was doing to develop computers with artificial intelligence. How all the researchers were under thirty-five and brilliant. There was no doubt that they would develop a new computer generation before the Americans. She showed a shade too much loyalty there for Mori's taste, but the dinner did end on a peaceful note.

As happened at the end of most Japanese gatherings, everyone rose as a group. While they were waiting for coats, Mori found himself next to Erika, his wife, and Miko. Erika smiled at him incautiously.

"I hope we meet again. Your wife and I are good friends."

"You are welcome to our house any time," said Mori, since to say anything else would have been rude. Then he added, "Where did you work before ICOT?" It was an innocent question, since all members of ICOT were drawn from one of the large electronics companies or, like his wife, from government.

"I was with Japan Electronics Corporation," Erika said, and

smiled. "Mitsuko tells me you work as an officer with the police."

Mori nodded. "Yes. A dull administrative job, I'm afraid. Traffic."

"Only whenever he has a date with me," Mitsuko said with a hint of malice in her voice, "he seems to come up with an emergency."

"Promise it won't happen again," Mori bowed.

Mitsuko gave him her broken-promises smile. It was reserved for missed appointments, forgotten anniversaries, lost flower bouquets, inadequate commemorations. Mori knew he was a terrible husband. He was a solitary who enjoyed the games of chance he played with his nation's enemies. He had little time for anything else.

Erika's cheeks had flushed, perhaps with the wine. Up close, Mori noted that her figure was even more startling than he'd imagined.

"Maybe you knew an American girl who worked at the JEC Shinjuku Research Laboratory," Mori blurted out suddenly, with hideous timing.

Erika's eyes clouded momentarily, then cleared.

"You must mean Kathy Johnson. Everyone knows her. Why?"

Mitsuko was suddenly very interested in where her husband's eyes were. "Do I know her?" she inquired innocently.

"Oh no," Erika said. "I meant the people at JEC. She's awfully sweet for an American. We'll have to get together sometime."

Then she turned back to Mori. "How do you know her?"

Mori took a deep breath. He hated to mix business with pleasure, but in this case he had no choice. The beautiful Japanese woman might know something about the American girl that could be vital to the case, no matter what the others thought.

"She died earlier today," Mori said. "No one is sure what happened. Some say it was a traffic accident. Others, that she was mixed up in a smuggling operation. No doubt all her friends will be questioned."

59

That night Mori couldn't get to sleep. Perhaps it was too much booze and eel. Or the nightmare of the American girl's death scene, which kept replaying in his mind. When they'd arrived home his mother had still been out. They had taken baths hurriedly and made love, thankful for the privacy. Mitsuko always worried that his mother could hear. A full moon lit the shōji of their bedroom window, filling the ceiling with black and white squares. Mori turned on his side, away from Mitsuko, who was breathing evenly with sleep. Something was seriously wrong with their marriage but he could not easily define it. Perhaps, he thought, he should begin as the Christian savants had done in trying to define their god: by defining what it was not.

It was not as simple as Kazuo implied. His brother-in-law's heavy-handed advice tonight had attacked the symptoms and not the disease itself. He didn't see her enough, that was true. But his work came first. In Japan all wives understood that. Even if he came home early every night and took her out faithfully to dinners and shows on weekends, he doubted that their relationship would improve. Trust, he decided: there was the nub. It wasn't that he'd hadn't tried to explain numerous times that he'd taken a vow. He was committed, like a priest. His work came first. Even before they were married he had admitted he was a dead end, without hope. The hours were horrid. He spent all his money in bars with sources, contacts, possible leads, and other lowlife. This was line-of-duty, but police expense accounts were ridiculous if the job was to be taken seriously. And he had debts. *Kamisama!* God! Money was a scourge. He reminded himself of the feudal lords who, during the Tokugawa Era, had been forced to spend half their time in Tokyo with their samurai retainers. Life in the capital had been expensive even then. They had become heavily indebted to merchants and brokers. Many were ruined, ending up as slaves. No doubt Mitsuko worried about his future. There he could not blame her. They could ill afford to buy a house; prices had skyrocketed. Well, he had been honest to her before the marriage about his money affairs as well as his job. And about the fact that his mother must live with them. No doubt she'd thought she could change him. This was why she did not trust him, then. Her failure to change him, his mother's domination of the household, the feeble attempts of relatives like Kazuo's tonight, these things had embittered her.

He considered the promise by the chief again. If he could find out the truth behind the death of Kathy Johnson, then could he purge his revenge commitment? Solve the problems of his marriage? He didn't think so. Life was not as simple as flying a kite.

He got up quietly so as not to disturb Mitsuko's sleep, and went into the bathroom. There he opened the tiny window and took a deep breath of chill air to clear his lungs, his troubled thoughts. Inadvertently, he looked out. The moon bathed the street with an eerie luminescence. It glanced off the glazed tile roof across the street, and off the windshield of the black car parked several houses down. He looked again. The car, he was quite sure, didn't belong to anyone in the neighborhood. While he was watching, a leg in the front seat shifted and settled into more comfortable stillness, blending again with the interior. He closed the window silently and turned on the water to wash his face. He felt a prickle of excitement. They were watching him. The ones who were running Kathy Johnson, no doubt. A big white whale, Aoyama had intimated. Only this one he would kill.

CHAPTER 6

GOLD-DAY, 11:00 P.M.

Ludlow took his time before entering Kathy Johnson's apartment. Even before the simplest incursions, which was what he considered picking up her code book to be, he liked to achieve devout concentration. He came to that pitch after a half-hour stroll through the Moto Azabu section, which was where she lived. It was one of the most expensive residential sections in Tokyo; a hilly area of wide streets lined with basswood, maple, and Japanese pine. Some homes even had large lawns, an incredible luxury in Tokyo. There was an air of sustained wealth, of huge bets that had been placed and won. Ludlow walked all the way to the Azabu Lawn Tennis Club, which the crown prince frequented, then back. Finally he arrived at her apartment. It was a luxury condo in blond concrete with tinted windows for the lobby door. Ludlow pushed the door open and went in. He wondered what bet Kathy had placed. And why she had not won. Perhaps her apartment would reveal some clues.

Directly ahead of him was a security guard's window. When a face appeared in it he waved and cut left for the elevators. From the guard's room he could hear the TV tuned to the eleven-o'clock Fuju Network sports roundup. A gleaming elevator door opened quickly for him and he hit the ninth-floor button. Number 903, Graves had said.

When he reached her door, he paused and extracted the scarred old lighter from his pocket. After Colombo, the habit had stuck. After Colombo, it had become clear to Ludlow that an element of chance accompanied the most commonplace operation. His planning in Colombo had been first rate, and look what had happened. He rubbed the smooth surface of the lighter for luck.

The anticipated spring lock on her door disappointed him with its simplicity. Two tiny rooms with a kitchen alcove. She'd favored pinks and pastels, stuffed animals on the couch. He started with the bath—an absolute barrage of feminine objects, from the latest in glossy lipstick shades to funny plastic bottles with embossed hearts that turned out to be douche. He moved on to her bedroom.

A picture on her night table was striking and he paused to take it in; she was much better-looking than Graves had said. Ludlow experienced even less confidence in Graves's judgment. But it was the man in the picture who attracted Ludlow's deeper concentration. They were in bathing suits on a broad veranda overlooking a tropical beach. A white comber in the background was about to break. The Caribbean, probably. They were a striking couple, one that would turn heads. The man was tall, casual, angular, young. Ludlow knew right away who he was: Roger Harrington, the one who directed Science and Technology, the current bane of Graves's existence. Ludlow removed the picture from its frame. On the back, written in one of those old-fashioned pens that took real ink, was *With affection and love. R.*

Her closet revealed a broad range of high-quality, fashionable clothing, with labels from London, Paris, and Malibu, carefully hangered as if they didn't belong to her. On the floor behind the clothes was a large Samsonite. Ludlow opened it quickly and dumped the contents onto the floor. Besides an assortment of sports clothing and an inventory of pantyhose, he found a packet of letters from an address in Wyoming and statements from American Express advising her that her account was overdue. He opened the letters and quickly read.

They were all signed Carl, in a looping hand, and dealt with the limited range of subjects available to one in confinement. Return address was the United States Correctional Institution in Laramie, Wyoming.

Ludlow's fetish for thoroughness took him to the walls next and an unexpected prize. In the dining room a kimono of inferior silk was hung on a lacquered bamboo pole. The garishly colored kimono itself merited only brief curiosity. It was the bamboo pole that piqued his interest, for in it, as he checked the hollow interior, he noted the artificial stops.

Dutifully he admired the workmanship, as one artist admires another's craft. They'd run a threadlike antenna the length of the bamboo and out behind the kimono. One side of the pickup box slid open to reveal a 1.35-volt mercury battery. The thing looked Japanese. He set out with renewed interest in search of her code book. The high-grade microphone tap he pocketed.

The remainder of Ludlow's search went slowly. No amphetamines, Dexedrine, ludes, or dupah, the Malaysian's choice. She wasn't doing cocaine. None of the mournful aberrations that offset stress, and signal impending tragedy. Kathy Johnson, whatever her other faults, hadn't been doping. He soon discovered that she had, in fact, been an astute professional.

After forty minutes of fruitless search he found the book; it was in a ventilation duct over her bed. With it was a large manila envelope. He quickly checked the contents. The findings sent him sniffing to other parts of her apartment a second and third time. The report itself was in Japanese, with a complicated grid of numbers—apparently the results of a product test. A computer, no doubt. Also in the duct, bound by a rubber band, were half a dozen onetime code pads.

He found the Minox ingeniously secured in the back of a wall clock. The miniature camera was loaded and ready to go. Her radio was more difficult. He didn't locate this until he discovered a false bottom in the toilet septic tank. It was a beautiful made-in-U.S.A. device, with five crystal options. With it was a tightly folded sheet on which were transmission frequencies and times. All wrapped carefully in waterproof material.

Ludlow left the building as confidently as he had arrived, with a nod to the old security guard as if he'd lived there for years. It had already occurred to Ludlow that whoever owned the hidden microphone would be around eventually to pick it up.

On the way back he became ravenously hungry. He found a sushi restaurant open late, and gorged himself on *uni* and *chu-toro.*

———

It was after midnight when the totally bald gentleman in a neat pinstripe suit rapped on the security guard's window. He flashed his ID, Defense Intelligence Agency. There'd been an accident in Ginza. The foreign girl in nine-zero-three. The guard's mouth gaped at the news. A policeman would be arriving shortly for her door. Meanwhile no one was to be allowed in the room. The gentleman, showing an expensive piece of *washi* paper with a large red seal which confirmed authorization to search the room, borrowed her key. When he returned, his face was red. He asked if, by the way, there'd been any guests this evening?

The old guard pulled a face and sucked air through his large gold-capped teeth to demonstrate concentration. After too much thought he said three. No four. And one of them a foreigner.

The bald gentleman nodded carefully. Was the *gaijin* wearing an old suede jacket and wrinkled brown pants? A bit hard-looking? Yes, the guard said, his eyes widening in amazement. The bald-headed gentleman said there would be several more of his men along in a half hour or so, who would like to get a statement from him. If there were any problems, be sure and let him know. He left a name card which read Defense Intelligence Agency with a number in Yotsuya.

PART TWO
TACHIAI
(THE CONFRONTATION)

Bushido I have found out lies in dying. When confronted with two alternatives, life and death, one is to choose death without hesitation. —Yamamoto Tsunetomo, *Hagakure*

CHAPTER 7

THE BEGINNING

Ludlow arrived at the embassy early Monday morning in order to get organized. Never having conducted this kind of investigation before, he had little notion what to do now.

First, there was the problem of how to handle his discoveries from Johnson's apartment. He certainly didn't want to show anything to Graves yet. Graves would go right for the DS&T's throat, and then Ludlow would get nothing done. So this was his first decision. Until he could get a perspective on the radio, the camera, and the rest of it, he would avoid bringing them to Graves's attention. He needed more facts about the girl's death.

His first action was to send a memo to his old State section, Political 2. Anything historical on Inspector Mori? He was to meet Mori this afternoon at police forensics. Then he phoned Graves. He told him he'd found the code book but not about any other finds. Last, he inquired discreetly about their good mutual friend, Colonel Yuki.

Graves, for his part, had been most careful. He had trouble, for example, recalling that he'd sent Ludlow to the girl's apartment in the first place, until he'd confirmed that Ludlow was calling from a secure extension. Then came the delicate part.

"I'm checking into several discrepancies," Ludlow said. "Like to see her file if I could."

"Nothing fancy, Ludlow. Keep it straight and simple. The names of the Russian heavies that were involved and whether they were local boys or Moscow Center."

As to Ludlow's polite questions about Colonel Yuki, Graves's answers were equally circumspect. Yuki was the U.S. contact with Japanese intelligence, such as it was. Ludlow would please stay the hell away from him.

As for the man himself, Graves did say that Yuki had been TOKKO under Kishi in Manchuria. Then back to Tokyo for the Great War. He had surfaced again in one of those postwar G-2 cells that General Willoughby, MacArthur's main man, had belatedly scraped up to head off the Japanese Left. The Americans had recruited General Arisue, the former chief of military intelligence, and seconded him to a fictitious historical section. Yuki was part of that until the Public Security Bureau came into its own in '48. He changed his name after the war, but Graves couldn't remember what it had been before. When Kishi was made prime minister and Nakasone was moving up in Defense, the colonel had taken the Defense Intelligence job. Graves gave this information reluctantly, then told Ludlow he couldn't see him today. "Meeting," he whispered urgently. "Sorry, old man." He'd collect the code book later in the week.

A reply to Ludlow's State memo came by phone soon after his conversation with Graves. A Japanese girl named Hiroko remembered him and asked how everything was.

"I'm fine, Hiroko," Ludlow said, trying unsuccessfully to remember a face. "Just perfect." All he could recall was a big girl. Wide shoulders.

She'd called him right back, she said, because his inquiry concerned the son of a very famous general, General Mori, an outstanding general during the war. Mori's grandfather had led the Satsuma Rebellion. The family was quite famous. The current Mori was a member of the Tokyo police special branch. The Public Security Bureau. Surveillance section, specializing in radicals, terrorists, and espionage counteraction.

"You're quite sure?" Ludlow had asked. "He's not in Homicide?"

"Not Homicide," Hiroko had replied sweetly.

"How about the father? What kind of background? Still living?"

"An opponent of the Tojo war cabinet who was expected to become one of the leaders of postwar Japan. The day the emperor announced surrender, he committed suicide. He became a national hero. A martyr."

Ludlow expressed his thanks and suggested they have lunch soon. He did not ask why an opponent of the war cabinet would commit suicide when the surrender was announced.

Since Ludlow had been assigned as cover to the Public Affairs Section, he was required to sign in and out of the embassy. For the time being, he had a tiny cubbyhole office and desk. Before heading out of the office that morning he registered a checkout time with reception and Mori's contact number at the MPD for anyone who wished to reach him that afternoon. Then he went out the embassy gates and down the hill. He walked past the NCR Building until he reached the Ginza Line entrance at Toranomon. Sukiyabashi was only two stops.

It had rained earlier that morning and the pavement was puddled and shiny. As he slogged along he recalled the phone conversation with Graves. It had confirmed his intuition. Ludlow was being used as a stopgap, a warm body to fill in until Washington made a proper decision and sent in an expert with credentials. They'd want a man with boundaries predefined by the National Security Council, the Congressional Committee on Oversight and possibly the White House itself, especially if the dead woman's family had connections.

At Toranomon he boarded the downtown train. The Ginza Line was the noisiest and the cheapest line in Tokyo.

He thought about Yuki. What shore had he washed up on? he wondered, as the train rattled toward Ginza. Yuki was surely one of the Old Boys. Yuki and Prime Minister Kishi must have met in Manchuria. TOKKO members were an elite, selected from only the brightest law-school graduates. There would have been only a handful of them in China. Yuki must have been useful to someone like Kishi, who had been a high-ranking administrator of the colony, a man committed to Japan's greatness. Somehow, Yuki had proven his value, and sealed his future. Otherwise, when Kishi became prime minister, there would have been no appointment to head the Defense Intelligence Agency. A debt had been paid.

One should not underestimate the elderly colonel. Yuki had known Kishi when he was alive, which meant he'd known the younger brother, Eisaku Sato, who also had been prime minister. Then had come Tanaka, and finally Nakasone. They were all cut from the same cloth. And behind these front men, the real power: Bamboku Ohno, Kodama, Osano. The Kuromaku. The Black Mist. Men who had earned their fortunes during the war or before and had influenced Japan's postwar political destiny. Scattered to the winds these names were now, but new blood had replaced them.

Ludlow turned his mind back to Kishi to remember what he could.

Sallow-faced Nobusuke Kishi. Grandmaster at the game of Japanese politics. A follower of the fascist Ikki Kita in the thirties who became second-highest-ranking civilian in Manchuria during the turmoil there. Then minister of trade and industry and vice munitions minister in the Tojo war cabinet. Kishi had been arrested at the war's end by U.S. MPs and designated a Class A war criminal. At Sugamo Prison he befriended Kodama, who with others financed the postwar conservative government. Kodama was later indicted in the Lockheed scandal. It was said he had built his fortune on the prewar pillaging of the Chinese economy through a Shanghai front company.

After three years at Sugamo, Kishi was inexplicably released. Nine years after he walked free from Sugamo, Kishi became prime minister. It was one of the most remarkable political comebacks in history, but went unadvertised in the West. Certain historical aspects were embarrassing.

The subway squealed to a halt at Ginza. As Ludlow emerged, the sky was bruised and overcast. A bullet train roared nearby on its way south to Hiroshima. Autos stalled in the morning rush hour that would last until noon. He intended to visit the Sukiyabashi *kōban* and chat with the police, then survey the murder scene. Afterward, he would wander over past Kabuki-za to Tsukiji fish market, where you could still get sushi for under two thousand yen on the luncheon specials. Who cared if they were cutting it thinner now? It was the only thing Ludlow really liked about Japan.

The police box at Sukiyabashi was a few minutes from the Ginza subway exit. Outside the open door a sign with the number of accident fatalities and injuries so far today indicated a zero and a three. Ludlow went inside to find a youthful police officer seated behind a desk filling out a report. Behind him on the wall was a detailed blowup map of Tokyo. The rookie's English was surprisingly good. "Can I help you?"

Ludlow pulled a name card with the frowning eagle of the United States in its upper right-hand corner. "Robert Brown," it read. "PAO." Public affairs officer. "I'm here to discuss the incident yesterday evening."

The rookie stared at the name card briefly, then handed it back to Ludlow. "Sor-ry, Mr. Brown. Not authorized to speak about."

Ludlow took a deep breath. He'd been taught what to expect. In this nonconfrontational society the Japanese react poorly and unpredictably to frontal attacks. The last embassy briefing Ludlow'd been to a year ago explained how there were over two hundred times more robberies annually in New York City than in Tokyo and how Japan's lawyer population was only three percent of that of the U.S. He didn't care. He also knew that there were those wonderfully infrequent occasions when acting like an American could get results.

He thrust the name card back in the youthful policeman's hands. "Let's cut out the bullshit. Who's in charge here?"

A superior magically appeared. Ludlow turned to him and pointed at his card. "American trashcan," he said and waited impatiently.

"American *taishikan*," the rookie translated to his ranking officer. "American embassy."

"I'll handle it," the officer said in Japanese, then turned to

Ludlow and spoke in English. "Wouldn't you like to step upstairs? There's a room we can talk. I hope you don't mind taking off your shoes."

Ludlow allowed himself to be led up the narrow stairs.

"You haven't been in Japan very long, Mr. Brown, I assume."

"Only a short while," Ludlow said, following the officer into the room. He handed Ludlow his name card. Inspector Takihashi had thick wrists, a slim martial-arts build, and a face full of confidence in what the body could do if necessary. "Do you have some sort of identification besides this name card? A passport will do."

Ludlow handed over the bogus passport he had used to enter through Narita immigration, then sat cross-legged on the tatami. Takihashi retrieved a phone from the floor and dialed a number. "Confirm to U.S. embassy please," he said in Japanese. He slowly read the passport number and carefully spelled the name. Then he turned back to Ludlow. His uniform was newly pressed, Ludlow noted, his hair cut militarily short. Flecks of gray confirmed a lack of vanity; many Japanese men over forty dyed their hair. "We should have confirmation within several minutes. Meanwhile, please tell me what you'd like to know and why you cannot follow proper channels to find it out."

Ludlow grinned convincingly as if it were obvious.

"Let me answer your second question first." He placed the officer's name card on the tatami in front of him like a businessman after an order for U.S. goods. "As a matter of fact I am to meet an MPD officer at your headquarters this afternoon."

"And who is that please?"

"Inspector Mori. He will take me through forensics, review what happened, answer questions. The reason I'm here is to prepare myself firsthand for the afternoon session. I want to familiarize myself with the intersection. I don't mean to disrupt the normal procedure of your police box." Ludlow had heard that their police were a lot like the Russians: if an issue wasn't covered in the written manual, there was little chance for a creative discussion. Still, it was worth the try.

"You are responsible for the investigation then? From the U.S. side?"

"For now. Yes."

Officer Takihashi stared thoughtfully at the phone, which refused to ring. "Your MPD contact this afternoon," Takihashi said, speaking in fluent English, "will provide answers to all your questions. They know more than we do. The officers on duty last night are not here today. I am very sorry."

Ludlow took a deep breath. He'd forgotten how frustrating the Japanese could be, how they were always willing to outwait you. The phone call was part of it, no doubt. The final excuse, if necessary. "Okay," Ludlow barked. "I'm here because we both know this is one hell of a dicey situation, Officer Takihashi."

"Dicey?" Takihashi repeated the English slowly. A dictionary suddenly appeared in the officer's hands. Sanseido's English to Japanese. Pocket Edition.

"Forget the dictionary, it's not there." Ludlow struggled to keep the anger from his voice. "Difficult is what I mean. Dicey. Difficult."

Takihashi nodded with extreme politeness.

Ludlow pulled his voice back together. "An American citizen has been killed by another foreigner under your very eyes." He pointed out the second-floor window to the intersection only yards away. Takihashi's eyes followed his gesture, then returned to Ludlow's face. Attentive. Wanting to please. A charade carefully choreographed. "In the English-language newspapers this morning," Ludlow continued, "I note a very small article which stated the girl died in an accident. Fine. Tokyo doesn't need more bad publicity besides its smog and traffic. This isn't what really concerns me. Your country is known as one where formal systems of justice are not embraced as they are in mine. Unlike the United States, you do not eagerly assign right and wrong. You prefer extrajudicial resolution of disputes . . ."

"Pardon me?" Takihashi fumbled for his dictionary again.

"Negotiated settlements," Ludlow said irritably. "Compromise, which does not assign moral fault so no one loses face."

Takihashi's face lit up. "Ah yes. Sometime it is so. But only when both parties are at fault." The officer smiled helpfully.

"What concerns me," Ludlow said, his voice beginning to show frost, "is getting clear-cut answers from your headquarters people. I thought it best to find out what I could on my own."

Takihashi nodded with great empathy. "In this particular case, Brown-san, I do not believe it will be problem." The phone rang. Takihashi lifted the receiver. *"Moshi, moshi."* He listened, watched Ludlow, then spoke hurriedly in Japanese. "No. The man's a recent arrival; he doesn't understand Japanese. So it's not a TFA listing on the State Department registry? Only TF . . . yes, I understand that would indicate he's not a routine placement. I will be careful. Yes. Everything else is under control. We've checked the park the assailant fled through. Nothing. The *gaijin* will give us no problems. Sayonara. So be it."

Takihashi hung up and smiled at Ludlow with renewed goodwill. "Your ID has been confirmed. If the American's killers are caught they will certainly be prosecuted under our law. Please trust us, Mr. Brown."

"The chances of her killers being caught aren't very good, I'm afraid." Ludlow offered a glacial smile.

"Perhaps you are making it more complicated than it is; why not wait and see what forensics provides this afternoon. You might be pleasantly surprised."

"You still haven't found the murder weapon?"

"No murder weapon." Takihashi stood and gestured amicably toward the stair. "I'm very sorry we can't be of more help today. *Domo sumimasen.* Stop by again if you don't get what you need from forensics. Stop by any time."

———

Ludlow stood in the small park ignoring his hunger pangs. Barely the size of a tennis court, it huddled between the Hankyu department store and the international arcade. If his understanding of the officer's phone conversation was correct, the police had already searched the park. But for what? Since the killer had not dropped his weapon in the street, he would have discarded it as soon as possible. This park would have provided the first real opportunity.

Azalea, camphor trees, and ginkgo grew beside a fountain which climbed two meters. The earth around them had been raked by a zealot. A morning crowd on concrete benches—too low and narrow for Western hips—smoked, stared dully at the pigeons, or read the morning papers. Two tramps with plastic bundles of clothing at their feet slept, heads tucked into collars like shabby birds. Unemployment was gaining popularity.

At the rear of the park was a building of properly aromatic public toilets, and a room for garden tools. Squatting farmer-style next to it, attempting to repair a plastic scoop, was an elderly lady wearing a green lapel tag which read, HIROMI YAMAZAKI, GROUNDSKEEPER. The tool room was open and Ludlow, as he approached, could see rakes and straw brooms all neatly stacked inside.

"Hello," Ludlow said cheerfully in English and squatted beside her.

Hiromi Yamazaki turned to eye the intruder, then returned to her repair job.

"Do you work here every day?" Ludlow switched to Japanese.

The old lady stopped fixing the scoop and looked at him suspiciously.

Ludlow smiled as pleasantly as he knew how. "The park is nicely kept. You must spend lots of time here. Do you work by yourself?"

The lady looked at her watch. "I'm busy," she said. "Today is my busy day." Her voice was streaked with downtown Edokko origins. "Why don't you come back tomorrow if you want to talk. *Sumimasen.*"

"I'd like your help," Ludlow persisted.

"Help?" Hiromi stared at Ludlow narrowly as if he'd made an obscene proposal. "What kind of help?"

Before Ludlow could answer, one of the men on the benches called her name.

She got to her feet carefully. "It's my busy day," she said, and shuffled off. She couldn't have been over five feet tall. The client whispered into her ear for several seconds. Her seamed face remained expressionless. Then she shuffled back to Ludlow.

"I hope you don't think I'm selling spring," she said, and settled on her haunches once again, her face a wrinkled mask. She picked up the scoop and turned it slowly in her hands as if she were examining a work of art.

"I don't believe you're selling spring," Ludlow replied earnestly. It was a term the Japanese used for the oldest profession in the world.

A phone rang. Ludlow looked around. He spotted three public phones on the edge of the park. Nice modern stands in green and white with Plexiglas shields to keep off the weather.

Hiromi muttered as she got to her feet again. As she walked over to the phones her hand flew through her pockets until a slip of paper was found. She referred to this as she talked on the phone, speaking with an air of importance for several minutes. When she was done she moved among the benches, talking unhurriedly with at least ten of the loungers. Ludlow waited until she had once more settled near him.

"So they're running at Oji today?"

"They're surely running at Oji," she replied majestically.

"Used to run only once a week. Saturdays."

"Economy's better. Now it's three times a week." Hiromi spat on the ground with authority. "There's the series on, too, and winter sumo in another three weeks."

"Business must be good."

"For an old lady it's better than selling spring." She tilted her face sideways at him and Ludlow let her have her joke. "However, normally I don't deal with foreigners. Too many problems. How much was it you wanted to place?"

"Ten," Ludlow replied without thinking. He'd put in for nonvouchered expense. "You have any hot ones?"

Ludlow's legs had cramped and now they nearly buckled as he stood up. He walked over to the toolshed and had a good look around before he put the ten thousand yen on the floor and came back to stand near her. He was certain if he tried to squat farmer-style any longer he wouldn't be able to get up.

"Rising Sun in the fifth," Hiromi said confidently, and went through the motions of recording the contract. A crumpled paper appeared and was returned to her pocket with a trace of smile.

"Were you here during the commotion Friday?"

"You with the police or just her friend?"

"A friend." Ludlow chose the lesser lie, although if she was that quick she'd probably already made up her own mind. "I'm trying to locate someone who was with her. A foreigner. He might have come through your park after it happened."

Hiromi Yamazaki shrugged her tiny shoulders. "Didn't see a thing."

"Maybe you found something he left here."

"Like what?"

"Possibly a weapon."

"Oh, *kamisama!* God! Here we go again. The police have been all over that. Picked my garden apart next morning too. Didn't find a thing. I told them the same thing I'm telling you."

"How about anything unusual that happened right after the commotion. You saw nothing at all?"

"No. Nothing except for a drunk."

Ludlow put his hands in his pockets and turned to go. Then he stopped. "A drunk?"

"Yes. He came into the park and was sick right after it happened. In the fountain. I had to drain and clean the damned pond first thing next morning. Afterward he went over to the curb and stood there staring at the intersection and all the nonsense going on. Sort of in a daze. Finally a car pulled up and the drunk was helped in. Not a regular police car, mind you. Special."

Ludlow nodded and asked what the man had looked like.

She gave him a pretty good description—wide-set eyes, thin build, fortyish, the age when men start to frequent the Ginza bars.

Later Ludlow searched everywhere in the park where a weapon could have been hidden. He found nothing. On his way out he picked up a discarded racing sheet. He checked the fifth race of the afternoon. Rising Sun was a 60-to-1 shot.

CHAPTER 8

THE COINCIDENCE

Mori took the *wakizashi* from the god shelf, felt the coldness and beauty of its ancient tempered steel. Downstairs he could hear his wife preparing breakfast, and the far-off chant of his mother at morning prayer. The familiar sounds were reassuring, the throb of the prayer drum hypnotic. In the bath the heater had been lit and water was running so it would be hot when he shaved.

At the age of seven, although it was no longer legal under the imposed democracy, he had been given this short sword and instructed in the rite of *gempuku*, how to draw the razor-sharp edge of the sword across the abdomen and then up to cut the carotid. Chosen death. There was no word in Japanese for suicide. His father and his grandfather had chosen to retire from the world in similar fashion. Reverently, he returned the weapon to its place of honor, clapped three times to attract the gods, and bowed to the two pictures placed squarely above the Shinto ancestor tablets.

Carefully, he studied the pictures. His grandfather, Saigo Mori, had a bull-like face with the direct eyes of a Satsuma clan warrior. His hair was cropped short and he wore a shirt with the collar of a military tunic. He had been a leader in overthrowing the Tokugawa shogunate, a three-hundred-year era that had brought peace but had stifled Japan's economic development. Saigo Mori was known as a general passionately loyal to the emperor—a loyalty born of tradition—and scornful of Western dress. In 1890 he had retired and opened a military academy. His school attracted thousands of young men, from all prefectures of Japan, who would be samurai idealists. When in 1895 students agitated against the Meiji government, then attacked and seized the local arsenal, Saigo Mori reluctantly agreed to lead them. He knew the cause was hopeless. They went into battle against the emperor's army on the harsh volcanic ridges near his home, using two-handed swords. Outnumbered, General Saigo Mori's troops were driven off the mountains and destroyed. The general committed hara-kiri at sunset that evening.

Strangely, after his death his reputation became larger than life, his name revered throughout Japan as one of the country's greatest heroes. In schools and households his picture became fashionable. For he had been the last of the classic samurai— a man spartan in his own tastes yet generous and sacrificing to others. Historians did not consider him disloyal for directing his young soldiers against the emperor. For they had fought not the emperor but the clique that surrounded the imperial highness. In recognition of Saigo Mori's vast reputation, the emperor awarded his son, Mori's father, the title of baron. It was held until MacArthur, as part of Japan's democratization, revoked all inherited titles. Mori bowed to his ancestors' spirits. He hoped he would never be forced to choose between his country and his honor.

He knew this was an aspect of Japan that *gaijins* would never understand. When the enemy appeared, one must fight him even though it was insanity. Never calculate. Freedom of spirit comes only when you are constantly prepared to wager your life.

He doused his face with cold water and prepared the razor. He was one of the few Japanese who had to shave every day and had hair on his chest, something Japanese women greatly admired as a symbol of virility. He had failed to produce offspring, however, and this had been a constant source of humiliation. The doctors had told him that he and Mitsuko were both normal, but perhaps the tension of his occupation reflected in his wife and caused failure to conceive. A good Japanese answer; no one was to blame.

Mitsuko had prayed at Hiroo Temple for a time and purchased special amulets for fertility. For a while she cried late at night when she thought he was asleep, and on several occasions offered to annul their marriage. Once she even suggested he take a mistress who could conceive his children. He forbade her to speak of it again. After that the issue was never raised.

She had taken a job against his mother's wishes, but he had sided with Mitsuko. And now there was the Mercedes. Every morning for the past month the same car had picked her up after he left. Someone from the office who lived nearby, she'd told his mother. It was Mori's place, as husband, to wait until Mitsuko chose to explain.

The phone interrupted his thoughts. Mitsuko called from downstairs.

His office told Mori that the meeting was confirmed. The foreigner would be at the MPD on the dot of three. A car would pick Mori up this morning. Hurriedly, he finished his bath and went downstairs to eat.

It was normal that little conversation took place at breakfast. Morning *kiyai*, harmony, was more important than at other times of the day. The spirit was most vulnerable in waking hours. His mother greeted him first, as was proper, then retired to her room.

Mitsuko smiled as she came into the tiny dining alcove with miso and rice and grilled *tai* fish. Mori sat on cushions at a low *kotatsu* table that had an electric heater underneath and in winter could be covered with a quilt to keep them warm. Few homes had central heating. She knelt as she served him, tucking away an errant strand of hair. Her skin was of a whiteness that was quite remarkable for an Asian; the true sign of royal blood, some said.

Mori wiped his mouth and put the lacquered *hashi* down.

"You enjoyed the dinner with Kazuo and Miko Friday night?"

Mitsuko had been kneeling formally on her shapely legs.

She nodded like a schoolgirl with a single dip of her head, eyes averted. Her hands smoothed the *yukata* against the back of her thighs to keep it from wrinkling.

"We should go out more," Mori said. "Take foreign vacations. When this is all over we'll make an overseas trip." He reached over and touched her hair, her cheek.

"It is not necessary. I am happy." Then she smiled her broken-promise smile. "It is better not to talk about such things. One day if it is real, we will just do it."

"I really mean it this time," Mori said. For some reason Mitsuko blushed. Mori could feel her skin hot beneath his hand. He worried that she had a fever or that she was angry. Or that he was just the cold-hearted bastard Kazuo implied he was.

"You are set in your ways. Enjoyment for you is in your spirit, not in your eyes. You do not take trips."

"No. I do not take trips. But one day I will change. You will see."

"I am proud of you. I like you the way you are."

"Really?"

Mitsuko's eyes briefly met his. There were flecks of yellow in her deep brown irises. Fortunately, she knew a good case of male insecurity when it confronted her. "Of course I'm proud of you." She looked away. "Now I must wash up and get ready. Was the call another emergency?"

"No." Mori looked at his watch and briefly wondered if he'd heard a delicate irony in the question. "My office called. I am to meet a foreigner this afternoon. It is very important."

"Why on earth are you meeting a foreigner?"

"About the American girl who died. The one your friend knew."

"Then it wasn't an accident?"

"No. And the foreigner may be able to tell me what she was doing in Japan."

"You will be late again tonight?"

"It is hard to say."

"Yes," Mitsuko said quietly. She started to rise. Mori raised his hand, holding her where she was.

"Do you mind if I phone Erika, ask her to lunch? She knew the American girl and might be able to help us."

"Was that the only reason you were so interested in her the other night?"

Mori smiled. "Good. You are jealous."

"You are horrible. When is jealousy ever good?"

"When it means I am not losing you."

Outside a horn sounded. Mitsuko went to the front window and looked out with sudden panic, but it was not Suzuki-san's Mercedes. It was a black Japanese car for her husband.

———

Most Tokyoites believe their city will last forever. For it has withstood the ravages of earthquake and firebomb, siege under the Tokugawa, and pestilence with the Kamakura—all this while Byzantium and Cordoba were fading into dust. If Tokyo has a symbol of its permanence, it is the Matsumoto Building on Ginza-dori. Erika had agreed to meet Mori there for lunch.

As Mori waited for an elevator he studied pictures of the landmark on the wall, chronicling its history. There was also a brief commemorative plaque. The elder Matsumoto had designed the original building himself from British brick in 1905; it was the first reinforced steel structure in the city. The steel had been supplied from scavenged trolley tracks, British imports torn up that year for replacement by product of local mills. Japanese nationalism had gained value with the defeat of the Russian bear.

There were also pictures of the famous structure standing alone amid the rubble of Ginza in 1923 following the Great Kanto Earthquake. The elder Matsumoto, wearing a straw hat, peered proudly from an upper floor. Another picture, dated September 1945, showed a higher quality of rubble. This time the building was gutted but the stubborn shell stood to mark the war's end.

In the top-floor restaurant, Mori ordered Suntory and water and pondered the Christian significance of a Jeffrey Reusch poster of an angel with good legs holding cocktails for two celebrants. He'd let Erika choose the venue; this was one of those franchised foreign-style pub restaurants the younger Japanese frequented. Art deco prints. Burgundy leather everywhere. Polished brass. And lacquered wood ceiling fans that turned lazily on leather belts which ran round the room in zigzag pattern. It was enough to make anyone dizzy.

He hoped Erika could give some background on the dead American girl, background not available in files. He'd spent the morning going over interviews with the JEC lab staff. Nothing. If Erika knew her personally, then she could help.

Meeting Erika, he knew, was dangerous. Mori understood he was moving inexorably closer to the edge of a very risky cliff. Stoicism was a stone's throw from hedonism, one could argue. His marriage was already in trouble; he'd have to watch himself very carefully with this attractive friend of his wife.

Erika wound confidently toward him among the tables, a pert smile on her well-shaped lips, her hips swinging with just the right amount of understated sauciness. She walked a little on her heels, her breasts jiggling deliciously under a silk blouse. Mori couldn't decide if she was wearing a bra.

She bowed with acquired shyness and they exchanged pleasantries. Then she ordered a glass of red Mercian wine and looked at him expectantly. "If you like we can get right down to business. On the phone you said it was urgent."

Her voice was cool yet promised friendship if demands made were not unreasonable. She wore a black tailored skirt and wide-heeled shoes with a strap across the back like the girls wore who took part in dance competitions.

Mori placed his black notebook carefully on the table. "I wanted to ask you a couple of questions, that's all."

Erika's large tilted eyes and small face fastened on the book. "Are you going to write everything down in that and report me?"

Mori pretended to smile and coughed into his hand. "Actually, I'm not on the traffic side of police work."

"I know," Erika said quickly as if it didn't matter. She had the manner—like many Japanese girls with superb figures—of sitting up very straight when she talked. "Something to do with terrorists, right?"

"Mitsuko told you?"

Erika's eyes studied Mori's drink. "Mitsuko isn't very good at secrets."

"I see the antiterrorist squad intrigues you," he said.

"I had a course on criminal justice at college. The Sondheim Affair. Student riots of the sixties. The burning of Shinjuku Station." Erika ran her hand through her hair like a model.

"Your professor was no doubt a liberal."

"But broad-minded. He pointed out that Aristotle and Lao-tzu extolled the virtues of political torture and assassination several thousand years ago. Repression is not unique to the Japanese culture although we have certainly mastered it." She crossed her silky legs and smoothed the tailored skirt so nearby tables could not see much thigh.

"All those students received fair trials, Erika." Mori lifted his glass patiently. "I just wanted to ask a few simple questions; not solve the future of society."

"You haven't passed my character test yet, have you?"

A waitress hovered for a landing. Mori waved her off, pleading another five minutes. She left two menus. "Over half the convictions were suspended sentences, Erika. Be fair. What would you like to order for lunch?"

A grin of victory lit up her face. "Which brings us to the subject of Kathy Johnson. That's why you wanted to see me, right?"

"Let's order," Mori suggested. "I'd recommend the *ebi* fried prawn or steak."

"I read an article in the *Asahi* this morning that said she died accidentally. The article was about the size of a postage stamp. So which is it, Mr. Policeman, a terrorist act or an accident?"

"The case isn't closed yet, Erika. I've been asked to take your voluntary statement."

"Like hell."

"How long have you been working for ICOT?"

"Just a few months."

"How long at JEC?"

"Apostasy," Erika sighed. "That's how we all live. Enforced

conformity. But nothing's written down. The freedom of security. What did Kathy do? Threaten to expose the System?"

"I supposed you might know more about that than we do." Mori called the waitress over with an intractable smile. Erika succumbed to the Matsuzaka steak and Mori ordered the fried prawns. Then Mori explained that Kathy Johnson might have been working on something that could help clarify her death. And, no, it hadn't been an accident.

He suggested that, since Erika used to work with Kathy Johnson, she might know what the American was really working on. Possibly Erika had some insight the company couldn't supply, a clue to the motive. Erika guided him with little nods, a pull at her perfect earlobe, the joining of rosebud lips and red wine with an erotic tip of chin.

"Well, she was working on JEC's miniature Fifth Generation machine." Erika looked at him expectantly. "You know what that is?" A nice little flush had crept into her cheeks.

Mori shook his head and plunged into his prawns.

Erika neatly cut her steak into small pieces. Then she explained. Fifths were very special computers because they had huge brains and could think. Just like humans. The problem was size and heat. A 5G required millions of conventional microchips, all power-hungry. Over a gigabyte—a billion bytes of memory. Just for a 5G standard model. No chrome or extras. "You understand so far?"

Mori assured her he did, and she continued in a scholarly voice. When you crowded too many chips together, the heat produced could melt the computer. Unless the distance between chips was inefficient—IBM had a 5G thirty-five feet long—or unless you produced a new microchip that allowed miniaturization.

"So this was what Kathy Johnson was working on?" It was all beginning to make sense to Mori. Kathy had had access to technology that either superpower might kill for.

Erika nodded. She said that Kathy Johnson had been working with a team of Japanese on a microchip with processing speeds orders of magnitude greater than conventional integrated chips. It was one key to the miniaturization of the 5G computer: chips made of supercooled conductors with near zero resistance, which therefore produced very little heat. Several million of these chips jammed together produced only a few watts of heat. Fiber optics in place of wires could further reduce the computer's size. The potential was to make a 5G computer the size of a box for straw sandals.

"A *zori-bako*." Mori kept the awe from his voice.

"Amazing, isn't it?" She leaned forward, finished her wine, and put the glass gently down. She seemed to be deciding something. Finally, she said, "I don't know whether JEC has succeeded or not. It's all been done through the tie-up with ICOT but the project is highly secret. If you want to find out more there's a party at Suzuki's home end of next week. He's head of ICOT. I'm sure Mitsuko will be invited. And husbands are always welcome. I'll be there, too."

Mori thought he detected a hint of promise in her voice. He made a mental note to attend the party. He picked up the black notebook that had been lying on the table unnoticed all this time, turned off the recording switch, then slipped it into his pocket. Standard procedure when statements could not be witnessed.

As they waited for the elevator, Mori could see heavy clouds over the Takashimaya department store across the street, an advance squadron of impending storm. Erika was staring at him thoughtfully. "Perhaps I shouldn't tell you this," she said, "but your wife is very angry you've been out every night recently." The elevator mercifully arrived, saving Mori from any reply.

When they reached the street the cast of the sky had darkened and first drops of rain were falling. Instinctively, Erika took his arm. Mori could feel the swell of her breast. Rain came harder and they ran to the shelter of a taxi stand. There was a growing line but they managed a place under the metal canopy. She continued to hold his arm and lean against him, sheltering herself from the storm. Away from the formality of the restaurant, Mori felt a new phase beginning with this mysteriously beautiful girl.

The rain increased in tempo, raising a mist where it splashed from the metal canopy to the gutter. A relaxed gaiety had overtaken the queue, the banter of those forced to share minor disaster. Mori found Erika suddenly smiling at him, studying his face.

Quite inexplicably Mori smiled back at her and said: "You know, I believe my wife is having an affair."

Erika's reaction was totally unexpected. She threw her head back and laughed. "Listen," she said, now not laughing, "I like you both very much. Please don't ask me to take sides, okay?"

She pulled out a compact to study her face briefly. No cabs were stopping; it was obvious she was going to be late. A frown creased her forehead.

"God, I'm a mess. The rain destroyed my hair. And I didn't bring anything. Let me call the office." She hurried over to a pay phone while Mori held their place. He watched her insert the call card and turn away from him to speak urgently for several seconds. When she came back to him she was all smiles.

"They said it would be okay if I was a little late."

Their turn came. As the automatic door opened for them he watched her get in with open admiration. He was about to give the driver the ICOT address when she interrupted him. "Do you mind if we stop by my place for just a second? I want to fix my hair and it's only a little out of the way."

Her apartment was tiny but fastidious, which meant, Mori quickly decided, that time in the evenings hung heavy on her hands. It smelled of brushed tatami and the scent of French perfume. There was just one room and a kitchen. The bedding had been put away and on the tatami there were two legless chairs that served as back and arm rests, and a small inexpensive table. She preceded him into the room and flung out her arms:

"Well here it is, how do you like it?"

"Very efficient," was all Mori could offer as she waved him to sit. Most Japanese lived like this, he thought, in tiny confined spaces with few belongings that could be picked up at a moment's notice and carried away. *Ippiki unagi*, they called them. An eel's sleeping place. Their history of disasters had conditioned everyone to impermanence. Typhoons regularly lashed across the islands; a devastating earthquake was predicted for Kanto any year now; fire broke out with monotonous regularity since most buildings were flimsy and overcrowded. Japanese in one way or another were inured to having their homes destroyed. So they lived like this.

"Take off your coat," Erika urged. "Relax. I'll be just a minute." Before she went into the bathroom she took his jacket, remarked over the monogrammed initials inside the lapel, brushed it, and placed it in the tiny closet. When she came out a few minutes later she'd taken a towel to dry her hair and sat in the chair next to him. Her thighs briefly brushed against his.

"I don't think you could live in such a place, could you?"

"It would depend on the company," Mori replied.

"If Mitsuko ever kicks you out, you're always welcome here." She laughed with a crystalline sound.

Mori understood what it was that had attracted him to this exotic girl. She didn't play the usual coy Japanese female games of catch-me-if-you-can. She openly shared her innermost thoughts, without any pretense.

Erika stopped toweling her hair as if guessing his mood. "We can be friends?" she asked softly.

"Yes," Mori said. "We can be friends."

"I don't want to break up your marriage or anything like that. But I like you."

Mori stared at her for a moment, uncertain what was being offered.

She looked at her watch. "How about a glass of wine. You have time?"

He nodded, aware the music had been turned on and that things had somehow gone out of control. She brought a Mercian white, rough with the inexperience of the local industry in its blend, but, under the circumstances, delicious.

She curled up in a comfortable ball, leaned against him, and told him about her childhood in Osaka. "Broke all the rules, I did." She suddenly lifted her head to smile at him impishly, like a child will for someone she trusts. Her father drank too much—that was the reason. And sometimes he beat her for being a girl. Now she only liked men who drank a little too much, she concluded, and looked at Mori thoughtfully.

The rain was drumming against the window, but inside the room was warm, appealing. Suddenly, Mori looked at his watch and jumped up. "Sorry," he blushed. "I have to meet a foreigner in about forty minutes. Forgot about it completely."

Downstairs, as they waited in front of her apartment, it was still pouring. There were no cabs. Mori was about to suggest the subway several blocks away when a gray Nissan Gloria pulled up. The front door swung open.

"Thought that was you." A male voice remarkably unsurprised. "Can I give you and your friend a lift, Erika?"

Erika gave a little squeal of delight. "We are really stranded. Thanks, Tomu. I'd like you to meet Inspector Mori. Tokyo police. We've just finished lunch."

The driver—how convenient—worked at ICOT and lived in the next apartment complex. He'd been home to pick up some papers he'd left. Mori said little all the way to the Shiba entrance of the Asakusa Line, where they dropped him. If he had learned anything during his years of police work it was never, ever to believe in coincidence.

CHAPTER 9

UNLUCKY NUMBER

It turned colder that afternoon and a fog rolled in from Tokyo Bay to blanket the downtown area. Tokyo Metropolitan Police headquarters loomed in the gloom like a battleship at war as Ludlow approached in his cab.

Guards stopped Ludlow politely at the door to ask his business. He gave them Inspector Mori's name. Inside the lobby voices resounded off cold granite floors. There was no wasted space; like a battleship, this place was designed for action. The security check was brisk. Everyone evoked an air of concentrated effort and subtle superiority.

To the left of the entrance was a bulletproof glass window from which all comings and goings were observed by two senior officers. When Ludlow was cleared through to a reception area, one of the guards lifted a phone. Mori appeared a few minutes later.

Against the backdrop of disciplined efficiency, the inspector turned out to be an anomaly. He looked barely official. His handsome face and wide-set eyes were circumspect, his suit in murderous disrepair. A jaunty necktie was out of tune with the somber setting. He couldn't have been more than five foot three. His hands, however, gave him away. They were much too large for his size, permanent discoloring marred the swollen knuckles, and when Ludlow shook his hand the skin was hard as iron. Chemical soaks and repeated martial-arts exercise, Ludlow guessed. He'd had drinks once with Carter Wong, the world tae kwon do champ. The police had required him to register his hands as lethal weapons. They hadn't come close to Mori's.

To goad him Ludlow feigned a lack of name cards. He knew that Japanese regarded meeting a person without receiving a name card like sitting down in a restaurant where there was no menu. Name cards established rank, title, the importance of the opponent. Japanese were famous for altering their personalities depending upon whom they were talking to. A country of masks.

But Mori wouldn't react. He kept his head bowed as he showed Ludlow to a bank of steel-doored elevators. Once they reached the fourth floor, Mori straightened slightly. Four was written *shi* in Japanese, he explained in passable English. The floor of death. Four was the unluckiest number in Japan, and some buildings left the floor out. Police forensics, however, had earned the right to it. Mori smiled as if this had no special meaning and opened the door so Ludlow could precede him.

The Tokyo Metropolitan Police forensic laboratory was the newest and finest Ludlow had ever seen. It had a starched whiteness about it which the Japanese love, and which can be found in their highest-image packaging. The floor attendants wore crisp white uniforms, the halls were white, walls and ceiling sparkled like ice caves.

Mori opened another door and ushered the American inside. The autopsy room itself was long, with stainless steel tables lined against one wall. White cabinets were packed with bottled chemicals that peeked through glass doors in a rainbow of color. The floor was spotless tile in white and black, alternating like a chess board.

On a table at the far end the girl's body lay brilliantly lit. A sheet, secured to the table by a Sanyo portable tuned to a Japan World Series pre-game show, modestly covered her legs to the waist. Opposing pitchers were being discussed.

Komatsu, the autopsy part-timer, awkwardly shook the foreigner's hand. His handshake was tentative since most Japanese privately consider direct skin contact—like Western toilets—unsanitary.

By way of greeting to Mori, Komatsu said, "Egawa's starting today. If he gets through six I'll kiss your mother's ass." Komatsu held out a forensic update, which Mori accepted.

Ludlow had trouble hiding his amusement at Komatsu's Japanese. He spoke with an accent of the western mountains, Iwate prefecture, Ludlow guessed. The forensic expert was also stunted from poor harvests and splay-toothed from inadequate dental attention.

Mori sorted through the document, which was handwritten with several *kanji* letters gone astray. During this time the radio commentators argued the game would be decided by Egawa's control versus Kaku's speed. Mori finally declared himself pleased by the report, except for one small matter. Komatsu looked undisturbed.

"Only two bullets were described," Mori continued in Japanese. "Three were fired."

Komatsu sighed. They spoke together hurriedly in their own language. Mori had been advised the American spoke no Japanese; however, he'd noted the twitch of a smile in the foreigner's face when Komatsu opened his mouth. Now Mori wasn't sure about the American's language ability. Japanese language was a mountain few foreigners could climb but perhaps this foreigner was an exception.

Komatsu was explaining that the third bullet had not been entirely retrieved; the current update dealt with what they had confirmed. Mori nodded agreeably. There was a shortage of forensic pathologists in Tokyo—since death is not fashionable among Japanese—and the rule was you humored whom you got. Most of the good ones like Komatsu were hospital-affiliated and only worked part-time for the police. It gave them a certain peer prestige and they had access to supplies from the well-stocked police lab at well below cost. Dr. Hayama, who was in charge of forensics, was also flexible on work output during the time of the World Series.

The Sanyo was going down the starting lineups.

"Was this report sent over to the Americans?" Mori tapped the pages in rhythm to his question.

"Translations were sent over this morning to the U.S. embassy. We were trying to ship her out before the first pitch but if there is no rush . . ."

Mori turned to Ludlow, speaking slowly in English: "We will view the body. Please do not touch anything. Please do not smoke. Two of the three bullets that struck her have been identified. Thank you."

"The two bullets," Ludlow said. "What type were they?"

Mori referred to the notes. "Hollow-points . . ."

The door opened and a short, stocky, golf-bronzed figure in immaculate white charged at them. Dr. Hayama was in charge of both ballistics and the autopsy room. He viewed the part-timers as his sheep.

"Yes. Hollow-points. Hello. Nice to meet you." The doctor had raced up to the American and Mori introduced them with some relief. Hayama's English was as immaculate as his coat. "That's their technical name." Hayama would not be interrupted; this was his domain. "The British called them dumdums after the suburb of Calcutta where they were first produced for rifles. Terribly inventive, the British."

Hayama was balding and broad-faced, with gold-rimmed glasses that glittered in the overhead incandescent light.

"When they're used in handguns we call them hollow-points, not dumdums. Same thing really. Matter of muzzle velocity." Hayama smiled professorially. "In crowd situations they are particularly useful, we understand. The bullet slows after several inches of flesh penetration. Avoids ricochets, innocent people being hurt. Very popular with the U.S. police. Of course they're illegal here in Japan."

"What about the third round?" Ludlow inquired pleasantly.

"It exploded." Hayama grinned without missing a beat. "I'm afraid there's not much to analyze. Shall we have a look at the body?"

Hayama led the way and they moved down the room to the table.

The girl's body was ghostly white, counterpointed by purple

puncture wounds in her abdomen and chest. A satellite system of incisions surrounded the wounds, where Komatsu had gone after the bullets.

Mori could not look at her head. Her jaw was black, as was most of her lower face. The blond hair was caked with black strands of dried blood. Black and blond hair. He felt convulsions at the pit of his stomach. The big American, however, was leaning over the face, somehow immune to the effects of the terrible destruction that had taken place. The Sanyo had completed the starting lineups. Mori switched the radio off.

"This the way she came in?" Ludlow straightened up. "Her face I mean?" The dormant ferocity of his eyes had become more legible.

Hayama and Komatsu both nodded.

"At what angle did these bullets enter her body?"

Komatsu obediently reviewed each angle. Ludlow scowled at the facts; they exactly matched the report.

"Only fragments were retrieved from the head shot," Hayama said. "We'll let you see those under a ballistic microscope if you like. In a day or two."

"Yes," the American said with sudden decisiveness. "I'd like that very much."

As they were leaving the autopsy room, Komatsu apologized that he couldn't see them downstairs today. He had too much work to do. Mori nodded patiently. As the door to the autopsy room was closing they heard the radio come alive. Egawa threw the first pitch of the ball game. It was a strike.

———

The incident that brought Mori and Ludlow into their first conflict occurred after they left forensics and Dr. Hayama. They had, at Mori's suggestion, stopped briefly for coffee in one of the bland conference rooms at the front of the Metropolitan Police building. The fog had dissipated. They settled into identical cushioned chairs and Ludlow briefly admired the view, which was of a moat, a grassy slope to the outer wall of the Imperial Palace, and Kitano, the Northern Keep. Ludlow continued to stare at the view.

"I surely wish I knew what you people were up to," he said suddenly.

The foreigner did not look angry. Mori was sure anger was something he'd recognize. On the American's face instead was only a curious smile.

Without replying, Mori scavenged a package of Mild Sevens and offered the American one. Surprisingly, the olive branch was accepted. Ludlow pulled out a scarred nickel-plated antique and lit them both. Mori stared. It was one of those cheap lighters they sell in the brothel districts of Southeast Asia, and said something perhaps of Ludlow's past. Mori's friend Watanabe had brought one back from Bangkok. The American left it on the table between them.

"Police at the intersection saw the girl killed, I was told." Ludlow exhaled bitter smoke through his nose. "So this morning I went down to the Sukiyabashi *kōban* to ask some questions. The people on duty were very uncooperative."

Mori dabbed his cigarette in the ashtray between them. "That's too bad," he said.

"I also spoke with a groundskeeper at the park off the intersection. She said that just after the killing a Japanese male stumbled into the park and was sick in the fountain. He was taken off in one of the special radio cars only the higher-ups get to use. The description fits you remarkably well, Inspector."

Mori stared out the window. On the slope that led to the palace wall sparrows were searching for food in the grass. A larger bird, a jay, flew into their midst and frightened the smaller birds away. An omen? Mori wondered. The foreigner suddenly spoke, the anger now clear.

"Listen, Ninja, this isn't the goddamned trade imbalance we're discussing here. An American girl was gunned down under your nose. If you want to treat it the same way you people treat everything else, with denials and outright deception, then I'm wasting my time." Ludlow made to get up.

Mori held up his hand, a puzzled expression on his face. "What was that name you called me?"

"Ninja. It's what we call you special branch people. Besides,

I can never remember Japanese names. And it doesn't look to me like you got those hands washing dishes."

Mori looked at his hands and smiled. "Then it was not an insult. Good."

"No. And I know what the Asians say: Do not despise the enemy who is small. I know you could spit on me and kill me, Ninja, but that's not the point. I've got a murder to solve and you're not being very helpful."

"Sit down then." Mori waved him back into his chair. He shook his head. "You are quick-tempered, you know. You may have other faults but I would work on that one first. However, before you get angry again let me tell you why we were not sure how much to tell you. Yes, I was following her. You see, she was suspected of being a major American spy."

Ludlow nodded, then said, "Okay, Ninja, now I begin to understand. Just to keep the playing field level from here on, let me tell you my real name isn't Brown, it's Ludlow, and I work for the CIA."

The rest of the meeting with Ludlow went well, and Mori was more than generous. He explained how the shooting had taken place. How she'd been approached by a large foreigner. How his nationality was being checked. How the MPD had every reason to believe he was a Soviet. How the foreigner had a raincoat over his arm he'd no doubt fired through. How it had been extremely crowded. A miracle no one else was hurt. And finally how he had learned the girl was working on a Fifth Generation miniaturized computer that had military applications.

"What the hell is a Fifth Generation computer?" Ludlow looked dubious.

"A computer that has logic and can think like a human," Mori replied.

"Sweet Jesus." Ludlow shook his head.

"Exactly. The motive for the murder is quite clear. We would like you to admit that she was an American spy. That she was attempting to steal highly important data for the American military. This is the reason the Soviets terminated her."

"Just ridiculous," Ludlow laughed.

Later, when Mori, the chief, and Aoyama were reviewing the tapes, Mori pointed out in a satisfied voice that it was from this point that he knew he could handle the giant foreigner. Emotion was weakness. This foreigner laughed when there was nothing to laugh at and became angry at mysterious slights. The American was unstable, Mori concluded. The chief and Aoyama complimented Mori on what a good start they thought he'd made. "One good deed is better than three days of fasting at a shrine," Mori smiled. He told them he wanted the foreigner's cooperation, his confidence and trust. It would no doubt end up as a trade—he would help the emotional foreigner, the foreigner would tell him all about the girl. At the conclusion of their meeting, Mori told the two, he had asked Ludlow to share all data developed about the girl. The American agreed. As a final test of the American's honesty, Mori asked Ludlow if he spoke Japanese. Mori was now quite certain the American had a passing knowledge of the language.

In a rare display of generosity, Ludlow had said that he did, although he must apologize for the quality, and it would be better if others didn't know. Mori said he understood.

"Learned it in the bars mainly," Ludlow said. "You know what that does to syntax."

"Then you enjoy a drink occasionally."

"Hardly have the time, but yes. Next time you'll have to be my guest."

"Yes," Mori said. "You probably didn't know, but most of our business gets done after hours." He smiled and lifted his coffee cup in a toast.

CHAPTER 10

THE *KANZASHI*

The call from Graves's office did
not produce Graves himself. His secretary had a husky Bacall
voice which asked Ludlow to be at an inside room in fifteen
minutes. Then she hung up without saying good-bye. Secre-
taries mirrored their bosses' attitudes. Ludlow tempered his
anger with the fact that the assignment had begun to intrigue
him. Today he only had to deliver Johnson's code book to the
station chief. Better to keep Graves out of it for as long as
possible. Graves was an Operations politician; he would do
his best to hang the DS&T if he could.

Inside rooms were so named because no windows for acous-
tic pickups were available. To further promote austerity this
one was allowed only a modest table, the cyclops eye of a clock,
a picture of the President. No phones. White static in the walls
ensured internal security; shouts were inaudible in the halls,
which afforded opportunity for extremely frank discussion.
Graves was already waiting for him.

"Contact with Washington this morning." Graves's voice
was brisk, official. A voice that had more important matters
on its mind. "They wanted to know what progress we'd made.
Only that's not the way they put it."

Ludlow set the envelope containing her code book on the
table. "So what's your problem?"

"Roger Harrington." Graves squinted at Ludlow, studying him. "He somehow got approval to come in with his own team to sort out Kathy's killing. Not that you give a damn, right?"

Ludlow took his time answering. He had hoped to avoid being caught in the crossfire of an open war between the DS&T and the Operations Directorate. Now that seemed impossible. In the days of McCone and Alan Dulles, the DS&T had had their own collection team taken away and given to Operations. Ever since, they'd been trying to get it back. Exodus Sixty operations were their foot in the door. They were controlled direct from Washington using stringers like Kathy Johnson or low-level full-timers. Insiders claimed the DS&T was on the verge of being allowed to run their own collections again; reauthorization of a DS&T full-time collection team would signal an unmistakable shift in power. The lion's share of CIA project budgets were already moving to the Technical Directorate. If the DS&T also controlled their own collections, there would be no other group inside the agency with as much power. The top jobs would go to the DS&T. This was the fear of Graves and others; that the CIA would turn into a team of technocrats. As far as Ludlow was concerned, the technocrats might run a tighter ship.

"Hell, Graves, I don't see it matters whether Harrington comes in or not."

"Figure it out then," Graves rebutted. "Harrington has top-level approval to come in and cover his ass!" The inertia of his words carried Graves's hands into motion. They chopped the air as he insisted that Harrington had set up an unauthorized operation in Japan. One that threatened the Soviet Union. One that cost the girl her life. Graves stood and paced the tiny room. It would mean the end of the agency as they knew it— any directorate that wanted to could set up its own private collection team to plunder allies and enemies alike.

Graves stopped to stare at Ludlow. "You don't give a shit, do you? But let me tell you something. The cardinal rule of any intelligence agency is that collection and analysis be kept totally separate." The station chief pointed an accusing finger at Ludlow. "Look what is happening to the Russians!" he demanded. "They're shoveling raw data into their praesidium under the flimsiest pretexts. It's dangerous and crazy."

"Okay," Ludlow said. "Okay. All I want is a shot at finding the girl's killers."

"Why the sudden enthusiasm?" Graves sneered. "You weren't very interested at Colonel Yuki's office."

"I had a look at her over in police forensics." Ludlow placed his hands on the table and folded them. "She was deliberately and cruelly murdered."

"Not after a little extra glory for that Colombo caper, are we?" Graves explored Ludlow's face coldly, like an artillery officer checking a first round placement for correction.

Ludlow took the hit without a grimace or melodramatic smile. For all he knew Graves was right. "Can't win 'em all," he said. "So how much time do I have?"

"Ten days," Graves replied evenly. "Harrington is coming in himself. The great man can't arrive before then. Maybe your police friends will get lucky. There's no big mystery who's behind it, is there? Or the motive? Which reminds me. What did you find at her apartment?"

Ludlow nodded to the envelope containing her code book. He knew Graves was part of a clique that competed for control of the CIA. A clique that was conservative, patriotic, that believed the enemy should be kept in the crosshairs at all times, that interpreted flexibility as weakness and sensitivity as impotence. In Ludlow's opinion, they served a time that had passed them by, a tradition that had outlived current events.

Graves cleared the code book, confirmed a standard Exodus Sixty procedure manual, then fixed Ludlow with his most pedantic stare. "So what else did you find?"

"A few bits and pieces."

"Don't try to cover for them, Ludlow! This is a Science and Technology bungle if I ever saw one. Had the poor girl on an unauthorized operation way over her head." Graves paused as if searching for a proper expletive. "Someone has to stop that bastard Harrington, and it might as well be me. I want everything you found at her apartment on my desk tomorrow."

From the station, Mori could walk to his house in ten minutes. Part of the sidewalk had been cut into steps descending the steep hill for the last part. He went down past the schoolyard and the building next to it that housed the Rojin Club where the seniors met.

He was about to turn into his gate when he noticed the black car parked up the street. Normally this would not have attracted his attention. Attached to the rear fender was a long whip antenna, however. Mori cursed under his breath, slammed open his gate, and went up the front walk. His mother opened the door.

"*Okairinasai.* Welcome home. You should've called, you know. Mitsuko will be late."

His mother was a handsome woman who almost always wore kimonos, dark ones that offset her white hair. Her fingers were long and graceful and her movements flowing and precise. She once had been renowned for her Japanese dance; now she kept her fingernails cut short for the koto, which she played extremely well. A woman of the old way, the neighbors said. A woman whose family even before she married was famous. Pity they'd lost everything in the war.

"How long has that car been parked outside?" asked Mori.

"Never mind about parked cars. Come in and I'll fix some tea." She turned and opened the shōji doors to the tiny dining-living room.

"So whose is it?" Mori persisted as she caught him by the sleeve and led him inside.

Like most strong-willed Japanese women, she was tiny. Her skin was still clear and the color of Shimoda sand.

"It's been there since noon," she said, and steered him to a *zabuton,* expertly stripping his suitcoat as she pressed him down onto it. He was still her child. "I went out to shop, a man was sleeping in it. I came back, the man is gone, the car is still there." She went into the kitchen and came back with tea. "You have a wife who never eats at home and you worry about a car parked in our street." She poured tea for him as she studied his face. "A bit on edge, aren't we? You never could hide the truth."

Mori fished a small box from his jacket pocket and handed it to her with a grin.

"Now look what you have brought me!" She shook her head as if to say, I can't. The koto pick was of the finest ivory, made by the shop of Noguchi in Asakusa with its name on the box. She was as delighted with the box as she was with the gift itself, since Noguchi was the most famous name in kotos, had been at it over three hundred years. She turned the pick over in her hands. "Erika was here earlier. Now there's a nice girl. She left something for Mitsuko. Do you know her?"

"I met her at Kazuo's dinner," Mori said and looked away.

His mother put the pick back in its box. "Well, I wish that Mitsuko could be more like Erika." She smiled at Mori and held up the box. "I will try this after dinner."

Mori sensed something was on her mind. "I'm staying home tonight. Maybe do a little work later."

"That's what you always say, isn't it? Then you're up and off to wherever you go without dessert. Well not tonight! I don't care if the future of Japan depends on it. There, I've said enough. I'm off to fix some dinner."

Mori switched on the TV. For the next ten minutes he watched a litany of the day's tragedies in the Kanto area. Another gas explosion in a Tokyo suburb. An *ijimeru* incident, bullying by students that caused the suicide of a fifteen-year-old. It is our national character, he told himself. We make the best cars in the world, yet blow ourselves up with faults in basic devices; we are the politest race in the world face-to-face, yet the cruelest in mental bullying. Our children learn from us.

Having exhausted local disasters, they moved to international news. Today there were rumors that the United States and Japan had begun talks regarding Japanese interest in designing and building its own fighter-bomber. The U.S.A. was insisting that Japan should buy U.S. technology for the F-16. A formal announcement of the talks would be made at the end of the month.

Sports was last, all of it about the World Series. The Lions had lost again and were behind in the series 2–1.

For dinner they had northern sardines prepared with a delicious sauce, *tofu, horenso* (Japanese spinach), and a side dish of *ebi* fried rice. Though his mother seemed to be in a good mood, her comments were perfunctory during the meal. Actually, she did not approve of chattering over food. With the dessert of Aomori sliced apples she finally came to what was on her mind.

"It is unlike a Japanese wife to be away from home so much."

"She works, Okasan. I married a modern Japanese woman."

"She is not interested in housework. Or cooking. It is an absolute shame the food she serves you. All she thinks of these days is that silly government program and her computers."

"They are doing important work. One day she will grow tired of it. For her to be selected from MITI was an honor."

"But she is late many nights. She leaves me to do all the housework. She spends money like a man." His mother shook her head sadly.

"Okasan, she is just young and too busy with her work to act in the traditional ways." Mori felt a pang of guilt. Could it be that his own late habits had triggered Mitsuko's reaction?

"Every morning she is picked up by that huge Mercedes. What must the neighbors think?"

Mori tried not to react. "It is just someone from her office who lives nearby. She told you so, didn't she? Now how was the Rojin Club today?"

His mother brightened and said they had asked her to sing Enka at a recital in two weeks. Mrs. Watanabe had taken seriously ill. "I don't know if I should," she said and looked at her son.

Mori knew she could sing classical Japanese songs and accompany herself expertly on the koto. "Why don't you do it? All your friends will be there."

"Then I will accept," she said, looking pleased. But Mori knew Mitsuko was still on her mind.

"And a new kimono. You will need a new kimono for the

recital, won't you? We can't have you performing for your friends in something old."

"Well that would be nice, but I really don't need one."

"Nonsense," said Mori. "You'd think we had no money."

———

His mother had bathed and come down to wish him good night. She looked at the clock and shook her head. It was the first time Mitsuko had been away so late, she complained. Naturally she hadn't selected Mitsuko for her son like a good mother should. The blame was partially hers. "I would hate to have to send her away, of course." She nodded sadly and retired to her room off the kitchen.

Mori felt the shock of her words sink in. His mother was suggesting he might have to choose between her and his wife? Traditionally a son's repayment of parental *on*—obligation— would never allow him to go against a parent's wishes. Under Confucian tradition, a son owed his parents for his creation, his well-being, his strength of mind, his talents. More practically, in his case, Mori owed his mother for the house they lived in. It was small by Western standards, only one upstairs room besides the bath, and three downstairs including the kitchen. He'd looked for some time before finding it through a broker. Asking price was sixty million yen. Mori said they'd rent for a while to see how they liked it, then decide about buying. His mother loaned him the key money. And of course prices had doubled last year. He picked up the evening newspaper and wondered if his mother was serious. He hoped not; right now he had enough on his mind.

He had barely opened the newspaper and begun to read when he heard the scream. He dashed to his mother's room. She was lying on her side, holding her neck. Blood spotted the pillow.

The wound turned out to be superficial, a puncture in the nape of her neck. He washed it with alcohol, swabbed it in mentholatum, and bandaged it. Then he looked for the cause. There was a sharp object in the pillow. He pulled it out.

A *kanzashi*.

Long and vicious, the antique hairpin was made from silver

sharpened to a deadly point. *Kanzashi* were used by geisha in earlier centuries to protect themselves and test their masters' food: silver oxidized black when it came into contact with traditional Japanese poisons. His mother had been lucky to escape with only a scratch.

He gave his mother a sedative herb and talked with her until she'd calmed. He told her it was an accident, yet he knew it wasn't. He wondered who on earth would do this and why? He made his mother talk with him until her eyes became heavy from the herbs. Eventually she slept.

He then took the object into the sitting room, where he knelt on the floor and examined it for some time with disbelief. Finally, he went outside into the street and looked up and down the narrow road. The car was gone. The street was empty.

CHAPTER 11

THE GLASER

In a shining forensics annex,
the victim's clothes were arranged neatly on tables in ascending order of intimacy. Only the brassiere and blouse were
brown with dried blood. An assistant brought gauze masks and
white caps for the trio. Ludlow's were too small.

"Japanese are very good at rituals in which results are secondary," Hayama observed dryly. He gestured toward the first
table like a merchant in Asakusa. "Good quality," he said and
lifted the blouse. "French." The skirt and tailored top bore an
Italian label. "The girl had taste." Hayama winked at the
American. "Nothing Japanese." As they turned from the first
table Hayama added:

"The genius, Aoyama, has today completed a fiber check
on his computer, fibers found embedded in the wounds. They
were not of her clothing."

"What did the genius learn?" Mori asked.

"Cotton of quite good quality. A type only produced in the
Soviet Union. Uzbekistan to be precise. Cloth commonly used
in their raincoats."

Hayama chuckled and waved them to the next table, where
he picked up a leather handbag that had been emptied. He held
it aloft triumphantly: "Italian with one improvement."

Hayama deftly turned the bag inside out. A neat cut showed

where they had removed the expensive lining. "Fit right into the contour; impossible to detect from the outside."

Hayama held up a West German passport, a driver's license, and a credit card issued by the Westdeutsche Landesbank. The name on all documents was Katina Josefson.

"Visas?" Ludlow suggested. Hayama had put on special gloves to deal with the articles.

"American and Canadian stamps." Hayama found the pages. "And an ES permission for Hong Kong."

Ludlow turned to the next table with the look of someone who has just heard an obscene joke. An aluminum Beretta gleamed guiltily from the polished tabletop. "Wasn't fired." Hayama had moved quickly ahead of them. "We found it forty centimeters from the body. Diagrams will be in the final report. Only her prints on the weapon. The bore is little used. Apparently she didn't practice much." He moved to another bin.

"Shoes," Hayama announced and lifted the pair. "Not much to say there, I'm afraid." They were low heels.

"She must have been a walker," Ludlow suggested.

"Wouldn't know, sir." Hayama put his hands in his pockets and rocked on his heels. "The bullets are last if you'll come this way." He removed a handkerchief and cleaned his glasses as he led them to the microscopes. He waved the handkerchief at one technician.

"Our serologist is doing a radioimmunoassay to pick up traces of drugs, thorazine to see if she was a psychotic. Or a habitual. Normal procedure. Here we are."

He stopped before a row of comparison microscopes and looked at the technician in charge questioningly.

"Katherine Johnson's rounds?"

The technician nervously peered into one of the microscopes and adjusted a knob. Then he stepped back with military precision. Hayama nodded.

"Round X," Hayama announced. "A hollow-point."

Ludlow leaned over the eyepiece and stared at the small, ugly, mushroom-shaped metal object. It had achieved nearly a 1.35-centimeter expansion, he calculated. When Ludlow was done, Hayama ordered the pieces from the head shot. This time

Ludlow studied the deadly pellets for several minutes. He turned from the eyepiece.

"How many of these did you retrieve?"

"Two," Hayama replied. "Number 12 chilled lead shot. A number were too deeply embedded in her brain to attempt removal. They were the ones that caused death. The point fragmented after penetrating approximately six centimeters, sending shrapnel into her brain with tremendous force. Very cruel."

"You found other traces in the wound?" Ludlow was squinting at the doctor, watching him carefully as a larger animal watches a smaller one it does not want to escape.

"Nylon-plastic, which is what we really don't understand." The doctor removed his glasses and scratched his head as though he'd chosen the wrong iron for an approach shot and now had a difficult lie. It was a rare moment when he admitted defeat on his home course.

"What do you think?" Mori asked the question since he knew advice was not a commodity Hayama dealt in gracefully.

Ludlow was standing close to the two Japanese and he towered over them, deliberating. An expression flickered in his eyes which reflected neither hostility nor friendliness. He reminded Mori of a broad-beamed seaman with the experience of many storms who senses another one ahead.

"All the rounds were manufactured in the United States," Ludlow said finally. "The hollows are Winchester Silver Tips or Federal Lead products. They both look very similar under a microscope. The fragmentation point is a California product that advertises a 98-percent kill ratio. A Glaser Safety Slug. The nylon-plastic trace is its signature."

"We've never seen one before in Japan," Hayama apologized.

Ludlow nodded. "It's a rare species. Does anyone know what the sequence was? Did the Glaser hit her as the first, second, or third round?"

"Second round," Mori replied.

"Congratulations then, Inspector. You've just proven a point."

"What?"

"It was an assassination."

———

Mori and Ludlow had adjourned to the Press Club bar. As they ordered the third round of drinks, a growing frankness marked their discussion. On his side Mori admitted he believed the United States was running a major espionage operation against Japan. The girl was the key. The Soviets had found out about her and taken action. After all, she had a fake passport hidden in her pocketbook with visas to North America—obviously an emergency escape route. She had a gun, and, as he'd told Ludlow in their first meeting, she was in a lab that was researching a dramatic new Fifth Generation computer. All this pointed to the same conclusion: American spy. Soviet assassination. Therefore a foreigner did it.

Ludlow ordered round four before offering his rebuttal. The passport, escape route, the gun. All could be part of her kit for the Exodus Sixty monitoring program. Therefore it was explainable. He said he'd invite Mori to a meeting with DS&T and they could ask the question point-blank.

On the other hand a Minox camera for microfilming, one-time code pads, a short-wave transmitter were found in her apartment. They'd want to ask the DS&T about that, too.

"Until then, Ninja, let's not pull any triggers." Ludlow stared for a moment out the wraparound windows. The violet fires of Ginza neon were turning on. "And it wasn't necessarily the Soviets."

Mori looked up, startled. "You can't mean that."

Ludlow put his drink down. "This is about the time she was shot," he said and stood up. "How tall are you, Ninja?"

"One hundred sixty centimeters," Mori said proudly.

"That'll do. She wasn't wearing heels." Ludlow pointed to a spot two feet away. "Stand there," he ordered. "Show you something."

Mori reluctantly obeyed.

"I bend my arm. I fire the gun. Bang." He aimed his finger

at Mori's jaw. The Japanese instinctively flinched. "So what's the angle of the bullet, Ninja? Best guess?"

"Thirty-five, maybe forty degrees."

"You win another round. What did the forensic report tell us?" Ludlow dug a wrinkled water-stained copy of the report from an inside pocket and dropped it on the bar.

"Seventy-six degrees for the head shot," Mori said without glancing at the report.

"Which means the weapon must have been fired from a lower angle directly upward. And you didn't see this large foreigner fire, did you, Ninja?"

"No. I was pushed just as she was shot."

Ludlow sat slowly down on the bar stool. It was 6:30. Outside in the Ginza, the night had already begun. The early flickering neon had become a full forest fire. It would burn till dawn. Down in the streets the cheaper "polos" would be heading for their coffee shop liaisons. *Dohan*, it was politely called. You paid the girl to have dinner with you. You dropped her at her club. Maybe later you got something more. In the 1960s, with the departure of vast numbers of U.S. military, the polos were no longer considered a necessary service industry. Shortly thereafter, prostitution had been legislated out of existence. No one had really expected legal convention to end human frailty, however. Ludlow stared at the fiery spectacle and thought of the victim.

"Please tell me, Ninja," Ludlow said quietly, "how you take a nearly six-foot foreigner, stand him a foot and a half away from a five-foot three-inch woman with his arm raised, a gun in it, and get the angles in the forensic report?"

Mori sighed. "I think you're overcomplicating things. The foreigner lunged as he fired. You narrow the distance, up goes the angle. Simple geometry."

"Fine," Ludlow agreed amicably. "Except there were three shots. First the abdomen shot. Horizontal. Impossible for a man that height. Then the head shot. She's already falling so the angle should go down, not up. Third, the chest shot, forty-two degrees. Again impossible for a six-footer. A tall man sim-

ply couldn't have shot her at those angles in that sequence."
Ludlow pulled out a drawing he'd made with the angles carefully calculated and laid it on top of the forensic report. "It
couldn't have been a tall man, Ninja. It was a man about five
feet five, I figure. Average height of a Japanese male. He was
holding a device that was fired without lifting his arm."

Mori shook his head and fell silent. Ludlow studied the
lights of Ginza, which had now achieved a halo effect from
either inbound fog, pollution, or a combination of both. He
recalled someone once telling him that depraved acts for hard
currency added more to a national GNP than the absence of
air pollution.

Mori finally asked, "Who could have done it if not this
foreigner?" He was willing to consider Ludlow's angle theory
for now. His guess, however, was that Komatsu of forensics
had simply bungled the angle work.

Ludlow hunched behind his drink as if lining up a weapon.
He knew the Japanese were poor at linear logic on the best of
days. That wasn't a knock. They had logic but it was that of
the go player, who placed his pieces in a seemingly erratic
pattern until the final moves revealed the master plan. Perhaps
that was how this killer worked, he thought, and gave Mori
the alternatives:

"Someone next to the foreigner, an accomplice who saw her
pull the gun; or a stranger who had been hired to kill her. A
shorter person. An Asian. Possibly a Japanese. My vote is for
a stranger. Someone the foreigner did not know."

Mori screwed up his face. "But the fibers found in her
wounds were of a Soviet raincoat. What Asian would carry a
Soviet raincoat?"

"One who wanted to make it look like a Soviet execution."

Mori shook his head. "What country would try such
madness?"

"I don't know, Ninja. Any ideas?"

"None whatsoever." Mori took half his drink in a swallow.

Ludlow spread his hands. "What about if someone thought
she was involved in a plot to steal their very valuable high-

tech? They had her under surveillance. And they decided to set an example because intelligence services around the world had been stealing them blind. Ring any bells?"

Mori set his drink down carefully and stared at the American. "My countrymen would not be so stupid."

————

Mitsuko had come home early. She opened the sliding shōji door to their living room as Mori was taking off his shoes in the *genkan*. His watch read nine o'clock.

"*Okairinasai*." She bowed, trying to hide her Kyoto lisp. A simple blue kimono tied by a dark obi offset her white skin. Her thick black hair was swept up, held by a simple elegant tortoise-shell comb. Silently she took his jacket and touched her hair as if to check for errant strands. Light caught the elegant curve of her neck.

"Is there sake?" Mori asked, knowing there was and that she had made it hot for him and wanted to please him with it. He felt discouraged about his session with the foreigner. If what the American said was true, then Mori's own government was deceiving him. Which made them no better than his wife. He was a cuckold twice over.

She put the sake cup on the low cedar table that had been a present from his uncle, the admiral.

Mori drank the sake she poured for him from the fluted heating bottle. Then he handed the cup to her and poured for her to drink. She smiled with pleasure because it was not every husband that would do this.

"Your mother is sleeping already. She was not feeling well today."

Mori nodded solemnly as Mitsuko poured another sake for him. She was looking at his face intently as if trying to read his mind. Then she tipped her body forward and the momentum allowed her to rise without using her arms. Since the kimono is constraining, Japanese women have perfected this movement, and Mitsuko rose like some beautiful bird, noiselessly and effortlessly. She glided into the kitchen.

She arranged the Imari dishes precisely. Squid in a deep soy sauce flanked by *wasabi* dip and tofu with grated onion and rice. She made a second trip to the kitchen and returned with *surumi* made from fish and crabmeat. For a while Mori ate silently with the black lacquered chopsticks.

"Has she said anything to you?" Mori asked finally.

Mitsuko looked surprised for a moment as if she did not understand the question. Then she remembered. "She showed me the cut. It is healing nicely."

Mori was watching her face. "It was an accident," he said.

Mitsuko nodded her head slowly, her eyes riveted on the table as if she feared to let them move. "Yes," she said. "It was an accident." She started to gather the dishes together and put them on the tray. "It was an heirloom of your mother's that she kept in her *tansu* bureau." Mitsuko's voice was soft and melodic, like a sigh. "She is forgetful. Sometimes I wonder . . ."

"Enough," Mori said sharply. "The matter is closed." He knew she was not lying. That left one last issue to resolve.

Mitsuko rose and took the dishes into the tiny kitchen. Mori could hear the noise of the water heater as she filled the dishpan. Normally she would leave the dishes for his mother to do in the morning. Mori wondered if he should hold his tongue, let her explain the Mercedes in her own good time. Perhaps there was nothing to it.

Mitsuko returned with a white Aomori apple peeled and cut on a pristine plate. It was one of Mori's favorites but tonight he had no appetite for it. Mitsuko returned to the kitchen and began to wash the evening dishes.

"How has the work gone lately?" Mori called to her in a voice not loud enough to disturb his mother.

Mitsuko stuck her head around the corner of the kitchen door to peer quizzically at Mori for a moment. "It is growing in vigor," she said as if referring to a child they never had. Then she returned to the sink.

"Erika was here earlier," Mitsuko added from the kitchen. A short pause. "She said to say hello."

"We had lunch yesterday and she agreed to help out on the case."

"She said you acted horribly. Just like a policeman."

Mori smiled. "I wasn't that bad. How well do you know her?" He wondered why he was avoiding the real issue.

"Erika is my good friend. What a strange question."

"She appears very dedicated."

"Erika is a careerist," said Mitsuko flatly as if she herself were thinking about it. "What kind of questions were you asking her?"

"The firm she used to work for is reported to have produced a Fifth Generation microcomputer—using ICOT assistance. Have you heard anything about that?"

"No." Mitsuko came out of the kitchen to stand in the doorway. She shook her head in bewilderment. "What could that possibly have to do with the police?"

"Aren't you glad your husband is finally taking an interest in your work?"

"There is just soft rice between your ears. Don't bother your head with it."

Mori looked at her soberly. "Would you have told me about it if you really knew?"

Mitsuko's hand flew to her hair and she began to remove hairpins and let the shining black river cascade around her neck. "Go take your bath and stop asking silly questions," she said, and finished removing the pins. "I made the *ofuro* ready before you came home."

As Mori soaped himself on the tiny wooden stool, he considered the incident of the *kanzashi* again. If Mitsuko didn't do it—and he was sure she hadn't—then who? Could it be tied into his investigation of Kathy Johnson's background and death? Could someone be sending him a warning? He shook his head. He must be imagining things; seeking meaning in the meaningless. He stepped into the hot *ofuro*, folded a cold wet towel on his head, and sank gradually into a state where the mind was empty. Where the soul was finally relaxed. Without time there is no eternity, he repeated. He felt the water drain the tiredness and tension from him until he became drowsy. Reluctantly, he rose from the bath. He toweled himself on the tile floor and opened the sliding bathroom door to find the clean *yukata* neatly folded in the perfumed clothes box on the hall floor. He slipped into the crisp nightwear, feeling the tingle from the cold air battling the heat stored beneath his skin.

There are many storms brewing now, he reminded himself as he went into the bedroom. But branches of a willow tree are never broken by snow. One has to live as best one can and, when the time comes, to die well. All else is nonsense.

On the immaculate straw tatami of their bedroom Mitsuko had arranged the bed. She had taken the bedding from the closet, fragrant with herbs, where it was stored during the day. The lower, thicker quilts of heavy cotton served as mattress in the milder weather. In winter she would add a foam-rubber mat to insulate them from the cold tatami floor. No homes were heated during sleeping hours; at least not in their neighborhood.

He climbed between the mattress quilt and upper quilts covered by white cotton that served as sheets. His pillow was laid precisely beside hers; one face of the pillow stuffed with dried rice hulls for summer, the other with goose down for winter.

Sounds of his wife coming upstairs reached him; he turned off the lights and listened to her bathe, and visualized her lithe body in the water, diamonds of perspiration on her forehead. Finally, the water surged as she moved out of the bath to dry herself.

When she slid the bedroom door open, only the gentle glow from the city far beyond reached through their sole window to highlight her shining skin and cascade of hair. The scent of lotus and jasmine was delicate, escaping from her body as she undid the sash of her sleeping kimono before she slid in beside him. It meant she wanted him.

He touched the skin of her shoulder and brushed her small perfect breasts and hips. She quivered and put her arms around him and kissed his neck.

"Please hold me," she whispered, and pulled him against her warm, smooth young body.

CHAPTER 12

THE MICRODEC CONNECTION

In the south wing of the Metropolitan Police Department headquarters, where the Public Security Bureau resides, bomb-proof windows overlook grassy embankments that rise to the hill where the Diet Building imperiously stands. At the foot of the hill a sliver of the Inner Moat feeds into the sacred water surrounding the emperor's palace. Occasionally two swans visit these reaches. Such infrequent visits are considered good omens. The swans hadn't been seen for some time.

Mori set up lunch with Watanabe, who was director of the Second Division of the MPD. This department vetted sensitive high-tech positions. He would know Kathy Johnson's background. Then he called the U.S. embassy to remind Ludlow of the time. He also called Komatsu about the bullet angles, but the forensic lab was offended that their work had been questioned, and acted in the best Japanese tradition by regretting that there wasn't more trust between departments. Komatsu went into unnecessary detail to show that the angles in their report were the correct ones. Mori sighed and hung up. He'd wanted to be sure. Forensics had confirmed that Ludlow was correct. The American's angle theory meant that the killer could have been anyone.

Mori muttered softly as he saw Aoyama enter the room and

head for his desk. No Japanese policeman had an office of his own. Desks were grouped in islands of nine, a number of good fortune. Power, insofar as it existed, was symbolized by less obvious trappings: position of a desk, deference by the tea girls, the quality of evening invitations. Aoyama came over and sat on the edge of his desk.

"Seibu lost again; that's another ten thousand yen you owe me." Aoyama grinned self-consciously and adjusted a new Brioni silk tie. The assistant to the chief had not come by his position lightly. His father was a member of the Commission, as it was called, a five-member board appointed by the governor of Tokyo to decide general rules and policies for the Metropolitan Police Department. It also appointed the chief.

Mori reached into his pocket and handed the money across. "Do not paint the final eye on the *daruma* until the series is over."

"Of course. Same bet for the remainder of the games then?"

Mori nodded. He knew this was not the reason the chief's assistant was paying him a call. Courtesy visits were not Aoyama's style. A message most probably to be delivered.

"How much more time, the chief wants to know. He is not nervous but I would say itchy."

Mori shrugged. "I am doing everything I can. I have been out with the foreigner every night."

"Yes. I've heard accounting is apoplectic about some bill they received this morning from a bar in Shimbashi. Perhaps you are getting too close to this American."

"He took me to the Press Club. I was obligated."

"So what have you learned?"

"That he does not really know what the American girl was up to. He mentioned he found some articles in her room. Promised he would show them to me in a day or so."

"Articles? What sort of articles?"

"Tools of espionage, Aoyama-san. Onetime pads, a radio."

"Good. To add to that fake passport and her gun. The evidence is mounting. Stay with him. Buy him all the booze you like."

"I am only after the truth, Aoyama-san."

"Truth? This is a negotiation you are involved in, Inspector. There is no room for truth. Like our negotiations with the Americans over the trade imbalance. They want something. We want something. Each thinks they are right. We think they bully us. They think we deceive them. What is the truth?"

"Watanabe vetted her when she joined JEC. He has her file. He thinks she is innocent of any spy charges."

"Of course. It would make him look bad."

"The American believes it was a Japanese that killed her. He has an angle theory—essentially correct—that a tall foreigner could not have done it. Watanabe has a confidential file on the dead girl. Enough evidence to confirm a Japanese was not involved. We are going to have a confrontation over lunch today."

"It sounds like the American has put you on the defensive, Inspector. Make no mistake, his sole objective is to throw you off the scent."

"Don't worry, Aoyama-san, I am keeping an open mind."

———

In most Japanese buildings, luncheon facilities were located in the basement. A higher floor, fresh air, a pleasant environment was never allowed; it was as if eating debased the workday. Mori took Ludlow aside before meeting his friend. Ignore coldness and erratic behavior, he advised; then he explained Watanabe's history.

Watanabe had closely cropped thick hair, going to gray, that started low on his forehead. He also had a permanent skin problem that could be mistaken for deep smallpox scars, if you didn't know about his Hiroshima childhood. His face had a set look about it now, the skin neither young nor old after the plastic surgeons had finished with it. The morning of the bomb he'd been out collecting firewood for the noon meal his mother and sister would never eat. Charcoal hadn't been available for months. The charcoal shortage saved his life. He never used a piece of it again.

After they'd taken trays through the line, Mori selected a table. When they were seated he turned to Ludlow. "We have

information about Kathy Johnson you might be interested in."
Mori looked expectantly at his friend, Watanabe. As part of
his job, Watanabe placed police personnel in cover assignments
with business and government agencies to check for penetra-
tions by radicals or foreign governments. It was a thankless
job, since all feared what he might find: a job for one of meticulous temperament and emotional neutrality, which Watanabe had learned walking amid the eerie fire and melted
bodies of the Hiroshima aftermath looking for his mother and
sister.

Watanabe pulled a folder from his jacket pocket. Then, without looking at it, and between bites of curry rice, he gave a
brief rundown on the dead girl.

Kathy had graduated from Berkeley in computer science
with high honors. Her father had died when she was young,
and her mother had raised her. Following graduation she'd been
hired by MicroDec—one of those electronics firms specializing
in microchips that grew like weeds during the sixties in northern California. Perhaps Ludlow had heard of it?

Ludlow nodded. "Read all about the trial in the newspapers
too."

Watanabe, who had neither smiled nor spoken much during
the luncheon preliminaries, held up his hand rather harshly.
He was getting to that and the foreigner would please listen.
As if he privately held a differing opinion, Watanabe described
the MicroDec charges, made one and a half years ago, that
Japanese had tried to steal confidential microchip data from
the company's files. A consultant to the firm was involved.
Watanabe quickly glanced at his folder to check the name.
Carl Lawson. His sale of the data to a representative of three
Japanese firms was taped.

Agents of the U.S. government arrested the consultant and
the representative, who quickly broke down and agreed to cooperate. Five executive engineers of three Japanese firms were
arrested in San Francisco hotels. It was an open-and-shut case.

Carl Lawson's contact inside MicroDec was Kathy Johnson.
However, American evidence against her was insubstantial
and she was not charged. Lawson, who was sentenced to three

years, steadfastly refused throughout the trial to implicate her. The reason, she later admitted during vetting procedures for the Japan Electronics Corporation job, was that they had been lovers.

Throughout most of Watanabe's presentation, Ludlow had appeared uninterested, even bored. When he'd finished shoveling in his spaghetti Neapolitan like a longshoreman, he pulled an old plaid handkerchief to wipe his chin and stare around the room. However, his mind had been turning everything over, examining it for flaws. The Carl Lawson part finally decided him. The letters he'd found at Kathy Johnson's apartment that night had been signed, in a looping hand, "Carl." His address was a penitentiary in Wyoming. It added up, then. The Japanese bomb victim was telling the truth. And apparently the Japanese police were being entirely honest with him. Refreshing.

When Watanabe completed the dossier, he retired again into his wall of silence. Mori cleared his throat to say that it was obvious there was no reason Japanese authorities would do Kathy Johnson any harm. In fact, JEC had hired her to show their goodwill. Also, Mori had just learned they'd scheduled a memorial service for her at a church in Omotesando. Hardly the action of a company that thought badly of her.

Ludlow put his hands behind his head and rocked back in his chair. "Really chokes me up, Ninja. So what are you selling then? Whoever killed her—Russian, Japanese, or polyglot— was working for the Soviet Union?"

Mori nodded. "Someone other than Japan."

"Tell you what I'm going to do, Ninja. We'll meet with the DS&T tomorrow. Find out what they know about her activities. Then let's come back to this issue of whether or not the Soviet KGB was involved."

THE KGB PRIZE

The inside of the Toyota van reeked with stale cigarette smoke; cheap *papirosi*. In front, alongside the driver, Yuri Konstantin chain-smoked and tried to comprehend what exactly was happening. For the head of the Tokyo Referentura, the most powerful Russian in Asia, to have arrived suddenly, unexpectedly, and to be sitting hunkered down in the back of Konstantin's surveillance van near the U.S. embassy compound, meant that he must have stumbled onto something huge.

It had started three days ago when Konstantin radioed in the departure of one Caucasian male over the rear wall of the U.S. embassy compound in Roppongi. At 8:21 p.m. exactly. This did not seem like such a big deal at the time. There had been four such exits since the back-wall watch had been installed five weeks earlier by Konstantin's boss, the Watch Team unit leader Gregorov. Nothing had come of them.

Konstantin's features were Central Asian and his skin still smooth and unmarked. With his Asian face, Konstantin would fit in in Tokyo. He had recently completed his training in Tashkent. The KGB was expanding too rapidly in its Asia-wide operations, this after Moscow Center belatedly recognized the future importance of the Asia circuit. Thus, for recent recruits, the two-year training courses with their careful indoctrination and endless classes had been abandoned in favor of a shorter but more intensive one-year course. As soon as his cram course had finished, Konstantin had been shipped immediately to Tokyo. His visa read: "Clerical Staff, Soviet Embassy." He had been in Tokyo only six weeks when the hell broke loose.

"Go through it one more time, Comrade Konstantin," said the Tokyo KGB chief from the backseat, his voice low but powerful. He wanted to hear it all again.

"As instructed," Konstantin said, "I came on duty at eight o'clock sharp. The van was parked uphill opposite the wall so we had a clear view but could not be seen."

"Yes. Yes. A nice job of positioning. Now, when he came over the wall how did he do it? Like an expert?"

"No. Very carefully. He hung on the top of the wall with his legs dangling and then let go. He had a limp as he walked down toward the main road."

"Good. Describe what happened next, after he came over the wall."

"He walked up the street to Roppongi intersection. It took approximately ten minutes. He was in no hurry."

"And where did you lose him?"

"The intersection is extremely crowded at that time of night, Comrade Director. There are many taxis."

"Hearing a thousand times is not so good as seeing once, Comrade Konstantin. Just tell me what happened."

"I ordered my driver to circle the block while I took up a post at the intersection. This is standard procedure, I believe. The American was reading an obscene magazine in the Sanseido bookstore and apparently quite absorbed. A white Nissan sports car pulled up very suddenly. He raced into it—the car had barely stopped—then it accelerated away. At that moment the lights changed. They turned down the hill toward Kasumi-cho. It was over in a matter of seconds. My van was caught in traffic several blocks away; almost like they had known."

"Yes. May I remind you both again"—Pachinkov's hard eyes took in the driver as well this time—"that this is not a training course in Tashkent. These are highly trained and dangerous

Americans. You, Konstantin, thought it was nothing. Another false alarm. Is it not so?"

The young Soviet Central Asian meekly agreed.

"Details, comrade. Always concentrate on details. Did you get a number?"

Konstantin fumbled for his notes, glad that he had kept them. He hesitated as he glanced at his rough scrawl, then shrugged, tore off the sheet, and handed it to his superior. The KGB chief glanced at it, then pocketed the scrap of paper. "Age. Could you give me anything more on what he looked like?" In the jargon of the KGB the chief was *Kappelmeister*, the choirmaster. It was his job, among many others, to locate the most talented individuals in the Tokyo operation. There had been far too few during his tenure. This boy, who seemed to have the patience of his Pathan ancestors, showed some promise at least.

"Over forty years old and heavyset. Black hair, gray at the temples. Big shoulders and strong-looking but not the usual American embassy type. Not a jogger or a ladies' man."

Oleg Pachinkov, head of Region Seven and Chief Resident of the Soviet embassy, ignored the boy's attempt at humor. He said brusquely, "Describe the limp."

"Like he'd had an accident perhaps, and it was healing." The Soviet Central Asian's answer had come almost too quickly. Pachinkov started to say something when the radio hummed and the Central Asian grabbed the handset to perform a routine check-in. The KGB chief leaned back against the seat cushions and narrowed his eyes, concentrating against his growing fatigue. He was not young anymore and the day had been a long one. He wanted to close his eyes, to sleep, but he knew there was no time; there never was these days.

It figured that the Americans would send in their best man. Why, then, was he surprised? Because he'd hoped against hope that they hadn't discovered the incredible new computer the Japanese had developed. Because he'd assumed the KGB operation to steal the Starfire prototype could be completed without American interference. The KGB plan to acquire the

Starfire was on schedule. However, the boy had described Ludlow perfectly. He was the American black-bag expert in Asia. Ludlow's presence meant the KGB Starfire operation might be running out of time. The Americans might also be after Starfire.

"Comrade, call my car now." Pachinkov kept his voice steady. Never show tension or fatigue. The golden rule. Preparations for entry to the Japan Electronics Corporation laboratory that had built the Starfire were nearly complete. Access was the major problem. Someone with access to the JEC laboratory must be blackmailed or become an unwitting accomplice to the KGB operation. Ten candidates had been selected. Half were those with an interest in the Soviet Union. There were trips recorded to the *rodina* or frequent visits to the gleaming new cultural center near the embassy. Books borrowed with name and address, or balalaika tapes listened to, or Russian-language lessons taken free. Staff chosen for their good looks, their charm; several love affairs already to choose from.

The other half were JEC employees and one married lady with ICOT. Each had weaknesses that could be used to advantage. Surveillance teams were watching the homes of all prospects. A final choice would be made within one week. The ICOT lady in particular was interesting. She and her husband looked about ready for a separation. The lady would be vulnerable.

"The car is waiting, sir."

Pachinkov clambered into the pickup car as unobtrusively as possible. "Back to the embassy," he ordered. He needed time to think before communicating with Center about the American, Ludlow, and what should be done. Once at the embassy he took the heavily guarded elevator to his top-floor office and left orders he was not to be disturbed. For a time, Pachinkov paced his spacious office and looked at the richly ornamented porcelain clock as it ticked off the minutes. It had been a gift from the grizzled old Soviet general who now ran the KGB. The clock had once been owned by a member of the tsar's cabinet. The last one.

Inside the Soviet embassy, the late shift had moved into positions to man the control ops room, the high-frequency radios, and cipher equipment. More than two hours had passed since the chief's return. He had not yet reported in to the general in Moscow. It was eight o'clock in the evening there. Dzerzhinsky Square would be alive with the changeover to its second shift. The old general was Pachinkov's mentor, and they communicated daily. The general would understand that he had not yet heard from one of his favorite subordinates because there was an emergency in Tokyo.

Oleg Pachinkov looked down at nearly a dozen sheets of paper lying crumpled on the floor. The chief was sure that the American was a security systems specialist—the CIA's best in Asia. So how to play the bad news to Center. This discovery had come too soon on the heels of the American girl's death. His people had had nothing to do with this killing. His most trusted subordinate, Sergei, had been set up like an amateur. It smelled of someone inside, who knew precisely how the KGB thought. And now Center was screaming, but what could he tell them? This particular message could be the most important of his career. It would outline how precisely, under his direction, they would steal the hottest piece of high-tech to come out of Japan in this century. The Starfire! The message would also tell how the American, Ludlow, would be dealt with.

When he'd finished the draft he sent it to Ciphers and at the same time asked that Sergei be sent for. While he waited, he reviewed his terse communiqué: The CIA had sent in their best man to collect the same high-tech prize the KGB was after, the Starfire. His own operation was on schedule but now threatened. He proposed to cut the remaining time in half. Unfortunately, this would drastically increase costs and increase risks. They could of course overrule him if they liked. Pachinkov's high-tech collection network competed directly with Colonel Malik's operation. He was head of the T Directorate. Let T Directorate take it out of his hands if they wished. Let it be their burden.

In the message he was succinct about Ludlow. The American would be put under close surveillance. When it appeared that he might be ready to attempt a collection of Starfire, he would be "detained." No more harm than necessary would be done him. He would be released after the KGB operation was completed. For this Pachinkov asked Center approval, with the greatest urgency. Privately, he knew it wouldn't come that fast, that several days would elapse before final reply and approvals would be received. How he hated the Center red tape.

When the door opened, the KGB chief resident did not look up. No one entered his room unexpectedly. Sergei Ivanovich Vasilyev stood at attention near Pachinkov's huge desk.

"Thank you for coming, Sergei. Sit down."

He was a decade younger than Pachinkov, but they shared the same raw-boned physique and the same peasant shrewdness around the eyes. They had been raised in neighboring villages of the Urals. Sergei's official designation was as Pachinkov's GRU chief. But he was also his confidant, the only one inside these embassy walls. Each of them had recently received distracting advice about the other.

He's not long for it, people whispered to Sergei. Why else would this man of deception, secrecy, and darkness be shunted here from London? Get out, they told Sergei, whenever you can. But Sergei understood the reason Pachinkov had been assigned Tokyo.

To Pachinkov they said of Sergei Vasilyev that he once was very good, better than most, in the old hard days of counter-intelligence. East Berlin and Rome. But he was running downhill now. Let him go, they told Pachinkov, and get a younger man to watch after you.

Neither man had taken the advice. Pachinkov settled behind his desk as if they were going to discuss wines. "We have an American. The children found him coming over the U.S. embassy living-quarter wall earlier in the week. He could be here for other reasons but it would be foolish to assume so. He is the CIA black-bag expert in Asia. Have a decent watch put on him and when the time comes I will ask you to pick him up. Use the Yotsuya safe house. Will you have time, Sergei Ivanovich, or should I ask another?"

Sergei smiled. The chief resident never ordered him if there was danger. "I would march into hell to compensate for my stupidity earlier this week, Comrade Resident. When the girl was shot, I panicked. I ran."

"Onlookers see eight moves ahead of the players, is it not so in chess, Sergei? Do not be discouraged. My career and yours are not damaged if we get the next moves right. Fortunately to Japanese, all foreigners look alike. You will not be identified. We are cooperating with them. In the worst case we could send you south; to the ferry for Pusan. The immigration checks on the crossing to Korea are notoriously the most lax in Japan."

"Still, had I known . . ."

"What we still don't know is why. When we find that out, as well as who was behind this, you will have another job to do, whether or not Center approves!" the chief added decisively.

Sergei saluted casually when he left, but closed the door carefully. For a time Pachinkov paced his office, hands clasped behind him. The resident's heavy Slavic features, carved from the blunt serf past of his parents, folded in a frown. During Pachinkov's last visit to Moscow, the general, in the privacy of his own quarters and, encouraged by a good Armenian brandy, had broadly hinted to him of a prize Center position. Director of the First Directorate, no less! If there were no slips. It was the most powerful position inside the KGB next to the chairmanship. Responsible for all Soviet clandestine activities abroad. Illegals, scientific and technical, planning, counterintelligence, executive action, disinformation. Whoever held the First invariably moved next to the top KGB post, the chairmanship. Andropov had gone from the First to the presidency of the Republic.

Could it be that other forces in Center were at work? Had others learned of his candidacy? Could that explain the sudden rash of bad luck? Dubious as it seemed, he'd known cases in the past. Violent ones at that. Tomorrow he would put lines out to friends he had in Moscow. The general couldn't help him there. The KGB chairman was isolated from the reality of day-to-day infighting. For this the Asian chief would be on his own.

THE STARFIRE EVALUATION

A redhead in a white sweater arrived first with coffee.

"I'm Cheryl," she said and smiled at both Inspector Mori and Ludlow. It was definitely the Bacall voice, Ludlow thought, and there seemed to be a thaw in their relations. Or perhaps it was Mori's presence.

Ludlow waved a hand toward Mori. "This is Inspector Mori of the Japanese police. Is it going to be a long wait?" As promised, Ludlow had invited the inspector to the meeting today with the Directorate of Science and Technology.

Mori stared appreciatively as Cheryl smiled at him. Then she turned to Ludlow. "Edgar asked the DS&T gentleman to come over right away. He'll be just a minute."

Ludlow wasn't pleased that Cheryl was on a first-name basis with Graves. He'd been hoping she might become an ally. Ludlow covered his disappointment by leaning down to the flight bag that lay like an obedient dog at his feet. From it he extracted the microphone tap he had found in Kathy Johnson's room. With the smile of a rejected suitor he held it aloft so that Mori would have a good look. Then he asked Cheryl to get it to lab analysis for country of origin and who might have put it together.

She made a breathless acquiescent squeak, took the tiny

probe as she might have a child, and headed for the door. Meanwhile Ludlow watched the inspector's eyes. The Japanese registered no surprise or shock at seeing the probe. No eye blinks or quivers. No dilation of the pupils. Mori obviously didn't know anything about a hidden microphone in the girl's apartment. His reaction, while it did not remove the local police entirely from suspicion, certainly distanced them from it. For some reason Ludlow was relieved.

The Tokyo director of the CIA's Science and Technology Directorate came in just as Cheryl was leaving. His face was gaunt, and his body long and cadaverous. He didn't look like much. The DS&T team was the fastest rising star in the CIA universe, however. He probably had ten doctorates in space technology.

"I'm Jim Cooper," he said, and looked uncertain which hand to shake first.

Mori was introduced in the offhand manner typical among Americans. Formal as Japanese are when first meetings take place, Mori stood, expecting to execute a ramrod bow. He found himself ducking a right cross from the nearsighted DS&T director, who was simply trying to shake hands. Ludlow explained that Mori was helping him with the investigation into Kathy Johnson's death.

"A Japanese cop? Does he speak English?" Cooper looked at Mori suspiciously.

"Only a little," Ludlow said and winked at Mori. For the first time Ludlow detected humor in the Japanese eyes.

"Hate the bastards," Cooper muttered under his breath, and smiled at Mori. "Caught me in one of their road checks driving a friend home; her car. Stop everything except the cabs, they do. Little gadget with a digital readout they put near your mouth and ask you very politely to breathe. I'd only had a couple of drinks."

"Ambassador couldn't help you?" Ludlow feigned anguish.

"No. His office said there was nothing they could do. Bastards took my license away for two years."

Ludlow just smiled and shook his head. But it was one area in which he admired these people. They'd read the U.S. drunk-driver stats. The hammer came down even if you'd had only one drink. Two offenses meant a lifetime driving ban. "Understand they don't have a drunk-driving problem here," Ludlow said innocently.

"I didn't come over for a philosophy course," Cooper snapped. "What's on your mind?"

Ludlow bent to his flight bag with the alacrity of the practiced host who knows his guests are hungry. From it, in order of appearance, he extracted the Minox, the onetime pads, the five-crystal radio, and the transmission frequency notes. These he placed expectantly on the table between them. He lifted the Minox first.

"Where'd you get all this stuff?" Cooper grumped.

"I'm opening a store." Ludlow stared at the DS&T man. "You happen to know where this came from?" He shook the camera in his giant paw.

"No." Cooper looked at the camera. "That's for microfilming, for Christ's sake."

"Ninja?" Ludlow winked at Mori and the inspector calmly shook his head. He understood he was there as a juror, not as a suspect.

Ludlow repeated the same procedure for each of the items. For each there was no reaction, either from Mori or Cooper. The DS&T had apparently not issued Kathy Johnson the weapons of espionage. Which laid open to doubt the issue of Soviet KGB guilt.

There were two items remaining in Ludlow's bag of tricks: the picture of Kathy Johnson and Roger Harrington, and the envelope containing the computer test data he'd found with her code book. The photo he was not going to pass around, since he had already received a satisfactory evaluation. But the computer test data was now the only way he might salvage something of value from this meeting.

As Ludlow placed the computer data in front of Cooper on the table, Graves popped through the door. The station chief grinned exuberantly at Cooper, the smile of old friends, and fell all over Mori, telling him all the wonderful things he'd heard about Japanese cooperation. He could only stay a few minutes, he said, much to Ludlow's relief. Then he noticed the document in front of Cooper.

"What have we here?" he asked enthusiastically as he reached across, picked up the envelope, and removed the sheets of data.

"I don't know what it is," Ludlow sniffed. "That's why I asked for the meeting with Cooper."

"Looks like some kind of test result, doesn't it now?" Graves handed the sheets formally to Cooper. "We'd like to know what you make of this, Coop. Honest injun, we need your help."

Cooper obediently began to read. Meanwhile, Graves was staring at the camera, radio, and onetime pad Ludlow had tried to move out of sight when Graves entered the room. They were now piled next to his chair on top of the flight bag.

Ludlow reached into his pocket and pulled out a packet of Japanese cigarettes. He'd found their stronger taste a pleasant change from the watered-down American brands available in Hong Kong. And he'd felt the sudden urge to smoke.

Graves's eyes swung to the local cigarettes with the superiority of a nonsmoker. "Really gone native on us, haven't you, Ludlow? Could I see what you've got on top of your flight bag?"

Reluctantly Ludlow handed up the camera, onetime pads, and radio. Graves's eyes acquired the gleam of an art collector reviewing a rare and valuable find. "Her apartment, right?"

Ludlow nodded slowly.

Cooper cleared his throat. "Based on a quick and dirty, I'd conclude the data here is about an avionics computer." He removed his reading glasses and pinched the bridge of his nose. "Data is a test-flight result." Cooper's eyes moved to Inspector Mori and he beamed warmly at the Japanese. "That about right, Inspector?"

Mori had been sitting with his eyes closed as if deep in thought. He opened them and shifted in his chair.

"The inspector wouldn't know a thing about it," Ludlow interjected.

Graves was looking dubiously at Cooper. "Fine, you have

an avionics computer. But is it worth our time?" He wanted a no.

"It tests a damn sight better than any avionics computer we fly."

"How much is a damn sight better?" Graves's voice had exchanged hope for skepticism.

"It's a product the DOD and Roger Harrington would love to find under their Christmas tree."

"Wonderful," Graves replied with a thin edge of sarcasm. "Could you be a little more specific here, Mr. Cooper?"

"Sure. Ever hear of Pave Pillar or Stolnaya?" Taking a no for granted, he continued without a pause. Department of Defense, he explained, used the code name Pave Pillar for their advanced tactical fighter program with Grumman. The Soviet's equivalent program was called Stolnaya. The ATF was the next generation of fighter-bombers—boost-glide vehicles that flew to the verge of space. This program desperately needed a total avionics computer, something neither the U.S.A. nor the USSR yet possessed. "The Japanese Starfire computer"—Cooper tapped the pages in his hand—"is just what the DOD has been begging for, one that integrates navigation, guidance, target acquisition, tracking, weapons management, and delivery—"

"Wait. Just wait." Graves was waving his hands as if to shut off the music. "You're telling me one computer can do all that? Since when?"

"Since the Fifth Generation arrived, Graves." Cooper flipped through the pages again. "The Japanese have miniaturized a 5G computer, according to this." He tossed the document on the table. "Besides being a lot faster on the draw than any of our setups, it does away with cockpit clutter. Kill ratios ought to be phenomenal."

"But the prototype is a preliminary stage, right?" Graves protested. "Still tinkering, aren't they?" Graves looked around the room appealing for support.

" 'Fraid not, Mr. Graves. This here is a NO-SPEC."

"Bloody hell." Graves took out a pad and made a note.

Inspector Mori raised his hand.

Cooper looked at the Japanese and then at Ludlow. "For Christ's sake, I thought you said he didn't understand English."

"Only a little," Ludlow replied. "Probably he wants to know what the term NO-SPEC means." He looked at Mori, who smiled and nodded.

Cooper glanced at Graves, who nodded imperceptibly.

"A final test of a military product, Inspector, where it's subjected to the most hostile environment. No specifications."

"So how many years ahead is it?" Graves scowled.

"Tests show a few snarls. But it's about five years ahead of the best we've got on the drawing boards. Maybe more. And they could have it in cockpits next year. I'd have to see the product to be sure, of course." Cooper glanced at Ludlow and fiddled with his glasses.

Ludlow suddenly smiled at the DS&T man with the benevolent grin of a friend who only wanted to share a minor secret. "Let's stop screwing around . . . you already knew about this, didn't you?"

"We only had some very preliminary information. Indications." Cooper pulled a pack of gum. "His crowd," Cooper waved at Mori, "has been very quiet about developments."

Ludlow looked over at Mori. The inspector had shut his eyes as if asleep. Ludlow inhaled an enormous amount of smoke and did not let it out. "Your girl got killed trying to bring out the final test data, didn't she? You had a meet arranged the day she had her accident?"

" 'Course not," Cooper snorted. "Good Lord, you're saying we stole it? This data is a complete surprise!"

Graves stood up. "Love to stay through the rest of the excitement but I have a meeting with the ambassador. The data will be channeled back to Operations Washington."

Cooper was staring at both Operations agents with a growing dismay on his ascetic face. "Listen up a minute, will you?" He peeled a stick of chewing gum and offered it around, Lotte green tea flavor. There were no takers. "This data shouldn't be released yet if you want my honest opinion."

"I'm listening." Graves's voice was expectant.

"It would save everybody a lot of embarrassment if the product turns out to be a bogey. A faked report."

"How could that be?" Graves asked politely.

"Where did you get the test data?" Cooper countered.

"The girl's apartment," Graves said, glancing at Mori.

"Maybe the apartment wasn't secure." Cooper was giving the gum a good working-over. He obviously knew he was on thin ice. Why would Japan fake a miniaturized 5G?

Graves folded his arms and sighed wearily. "It was pulled within four hours of the girl's death. You really think it wasn't secure, Coop? I mean, Jesus Christ, give me a break."

Cooper shrugged and chewed his gum steadily as if waiting for the earth to shift. "I think we better give these people credit for being bright. If they can get this close to a working mini Fifth Generation or fake test results this well, they can also set up a room in four hours. I don't want to make any waves, you understand. I'm really a team player."

Ludlow reached down and picked up the flight bag. He opened it and pulled out the photograph of Kathy Johnson and Roger Harrington. "Maybe Coop has a point after all," Ludlow said and put the picture face up on the table so everyone could see. The picture had already been appraised by a lab expert. Blue Willow was his name. Ludlow could never remember the Japanese. He had examined the picture of the handsome gentleman and beautiful lady for some time. First at arm's length for the balance, then at reading distance for the technique, and finally under a magnifying glass for where the pasting was done. Then he leaned back with a grunt of satisfaction and said, "Yes. It is a collage. But very nicely done. Would the girl like to make some extra money, by the way?"

"So what about it?" Graves's question brought Ludlow back to the present.

"I found the photo in her bedroom," Ludlow said. "If the picture is faked this would place doubt on all the other items found at her apartment, right? It would support Coop's theory that the data was planted along with the articles of espionage to frame her."

"And lay blame for the assassination on the Soviets," Cooper added.

"The picture looks genuine to me," Graves said petulantly.

"On the back is a signed lab report," Ludlow replied quietly.

Graves picked up the photo, turned it over, and read for a moment. Then he shoved it into Ludlow's flight bag with the other spy paraphernalia and zipped up the bag. "Okay." Graves shook his head. "Coop gets ten days to validate. No more." He picked up the flight bag, smiled to the room as if things had gone entirely as he expected, and left for his appointment with the ambassador.

"Mr. Cooper!" Mori's sudden English startled the DS&T man. "Does your Exodus Sixty monitoring program require agents to carry any special items with them at all times?"

Cooper smiled viciously at Ludlow before replying, "A gun, Inspector Mori. An alternate passport under an assumed name and a visa routing to the U.S.A. Why?"

CHAPTER 15

THE KGB PROXY

The Soviet embassy lay sheathed in the silence of late night. Two apartment towers that housed embassy workers showed no lights. Only on the top floor of the embassy offices themselves was there any sign of life. Pachinkov had just phoned the kitchen.

"Katinina, is it? How much more shall we wait? I really can't hold out longer; my friend is developing gas from hunger pains." Sergei's laughter in the background sounded like a bad cough.

"They're in the oven, comrade! You wanted them fresh, didn't you? Hold your pants, it won't be long now." She was one of a select few who could get away with talking back to the chief resident.

"I'm sorry to trouble you," Pachinkov said.

Katinina was not about to accept an apology graciously. "It's past two o'clock," she said grumpily, and hung up.

Pachinkov sighed, spread his hands, and turned back to complete the story he was telling. First, however, he refilled their glasses of wine.

"So they were at the Bolshoi for the Moscow opening of the Kirov Ballet. Brezhnev's wife was there and the general found himself next to her in the lobby. She was nothing but since her husband was then Party chairman he wanted to compliment her. In his usual spluttering voice he said, 'You really are looking magnificent tonight!'

"To this she waved her hand. 'I'm sorry the same term can't be applied to you.' She had the KGB chairman's face in mind, of course; he is not a pleasant man to look at. The general merely smiled politely and said, 'Then why didn't you do what I did? Lie.' "

Sergei pulled at his ear, then smiled blandly.

Pachinkov sighed. "No one ever claimed you were brilliant, Sergei Ivanovich. But I would rather have someone who is loyal and can follow orders with the determination of a bull than one who laughs at my jokes." He finished his wine and refilled their glasses. Sergei managed to look modestly pleased.

"The most difficult thing"—Pachinkov pointed a finger—"is to tell the truth without being rude. It takes years of experience. The danger is you become like a Japanese. You start expressing yourself obliquely. Then you begin to lie."

Sergei energetically nodded his head. "It is better we do not stay in this city too long," Sergei proposed. "One becomes like them."

"I do not believe it will be a problem." Pachinkov looked through Sergei, beyond him.

Sergei nodded his head happily. This was the answer he'd hoped to hear. "Is there any news?"

Pachinkov's shoulders made an exaggerated shrug. "One never knows, old friend. One never knows."

They turned to the business of the nightly debriefing; the progress of the operation to take the Starfire. Even though there had been no word from Center following his urgent cipher indicating that Ludlow had surfaced in Tokyo, Pachinkov kept to schedule. He doubted that Center would take Starfire out of his hands. Whom would they send? How would they get it out of the country? T Directorate was jealous of his success; Colonel Malik would think very carefully before he challenged him.

"What about Ludlow?" the chief asked abruptly, changing the subject.

"He is acting very strangely," Sergei said. "Our checks indicate he arrived two days before the American girl was killed. When that happened everything seemed to stop. He was put in charge of the investigation into her death. He is wandering around Tokyo nights with a tiny Japanese from the police. Days he huddles in meetings at the U.S. embassy or the MPD. It makes no sense."

"A ruse. A cover. Are there any signs that he knows he is being followed?"

Sergei coughed. "I have been using multiple teams and cars. However, you know the caliber of talent sent to Tokyo."

Pachinkov nodded, missing Sergei's evasiveness. His thoughts were focused on another possibility. "Ludlow is an old Asia hand, my friend. There is the danger he may be able to put a name to your face. Even though you are in none of their mug books. This is not only a concern to you but to the Starfire operation. If in their mistaken patriotism the Americans believe you killed the girl it'll get very nasty. Bloodshed. Time wasted. I want you to see that does not happen, Sergei."

"I am taking every precaution, using disguises when necessary. What of the Tokyo police? They have approached the embassy?"

"Yes. But do not worry. We have told them it will take some time to obtain pictures of everyone. Over three thousand staff. A monumental task. Please wait, we tell them. A little of their own medicine."

"And no leads on who might have set me up? Killed the American girl?"

"We are checking out the Japanese terrorists that Center keeps on a leash in North Korea—the Red Army, they call themselves. It could have been one of them. But my contacts think differently. Apparently, Comrade Malik is furious he is not the sole candidate for the head of First Directorate. So there is politicking going on which unfortunately I cannot control. It is not beyond imagination that Malik masterminded the American girl's death to embarrass me. He is too clever to directly involve himself, of course. But he is a genius at exploiting the emotions of others, using proxies for his deadlier games."

"So you think whoever killed her was not of the KGB?"

"No. To be entirely frank I do not. No doubt a Japanese who somehow fell under Malik's spell, a Japanese with an emotional blind spot. Perhaps it was someone who knew the girl. Malik provides information that he knows will trigger a violent reaction. As a favor. He gets something in return. That is what really concerns me if the scenario is accurate."

There was a timid knock on the door. The old lady had arrived with a tray of piroshki. The smell of fresh dough and herbs pervaded their quarters as Sergei opened the door. Meanwhile Pachinkov had put an Orlando di Lasso record on the stereo turntable.

The old lady arranged the fragrant dishes on a side table with silver and napkins. Then she stepped back to survey her handiwork and said, "Why can't you play something less ancient?"

Pachinkov snorted without ill humor and turned the volume up a notch. "So you are another who believes all music began with Mozart, Katinina?" He shut the lid of the player and came back across the room, his eyes on the delicious food. "And that Haydn was dubious and Bach boring? So you are one of the new liberals, Katinina? I wouldn't have suspected it."

The old lady put her hands on her hips. "Why must you go abroad when in Russia there are enough patriotic composers for all. And played on a Gestapo stereo, too."

"Out," Pachinkov ordered. "Fortunately you are too old to be hung. I however must still watch my mouth. On your way." But before she went he poured a glass of white Romanian wine for her, which she drank. Then she curtsied and wiped her mouth and left them to return to more private discussion.

PART THREE

KIBARASHI

(THE DIVERSION)

A calculating man is a coward. To die is a
loss, to live a gain, so one decides not to die.
A man of education camouflages with his
intellect and eloquence the cowardice or
greed that is his true nature. Many people do
not realize this.   —Yamamoto Tsunetomo,
Hagakure

CHAPTER 16

THE CROSSROADS

Friday morning Mori was busy, so Ludlow called the embassy switchboard for a line to Political 2. Hiroko, who had helped him obtain Mori's background, said she'd be delighted to join him for lunch.

They met in the Okura lobby, a quick walk from the embassy compound. She had gained a little weight but still had those wide shoulders, a dead giveaway for a woman who enjoyed nothing better than a day or two in bed with a strong male.

He chose the Okura sushi bar; he was feeling expansive and decided it was a legitimate expense. They had *chu-toro*, and *odori* with the prawn still wriggling, and *uni*, sea urchin, the liquid poured into a seaweed shell. Hiroko admired the view. Ludlow noted she had nice eyes. She was in her mid-thirties, with the good connections that come from time in grade. She wasn't a ranker and probably never would be; however, she had detailed information on the latest Thursday Club meeting and the consular-level tea parties. And she knew the CIA station chief was only a first secretary, which possibly explained his inability to control the boys of the Science and Technology Directorate.

She liked sake and they ended up polishing off three bottles of a good Niigata origin.

"I have a favor to ask," Ludlow said toward the end of the meal. He was now convinced that his angle theory was correct, that the shooter was a Japanese or other Asian. And if Graves declared war on the DS&T there'd be little hope of learning the truth of the CIA relationship to Kathy Johnson. The data he had about her was contradictory. If what Watanabe of the Tokyo police told him was true—that she had been involved in stealing secrets from MicroDec for Japanese firms—then why would the CIA give her a gun and fake passport and ask her to work for them on the Exodus Sixty operation? Or more? There had to be a Japanese connection, probably tied into the MicroDec scandal which had hurt Japanese prestige worldwide and no doubt ruined some local reputations. Could Japanese intelligence have been involved? "I need background on a Japanese intelligence officer who had links to Nobusuke Kishi," he told Hiroko. He hadn't wanted to bring in the former prime minister who once was a class A war criminal. But he needed information; the classified records might give him some clues.

"The intelligence officer is a Colonel Yuki."

Hiroko checked the enamel on her fingernails. Yes, she said, the war crimes interrogations and trial transcripts were microfilmed and kept in Archives. It would be no trouble to pull the documentation on Kishi. Thereafter, the air went out of their conversation. Ludlow wondered if she'd misunderstood. She thought he'd only invited her to lunch for a favor. But he had more on his mind.

Over a melon dessert Ludlow asked about her hobbies, what she did weekends. "I read and climb mountains," she replied. "The Japanese Alps or Niigata. When I read it's mostly history and biographies. The odd novel. I like Kawabata when I am sad and García Márquez when I am happy."

"Then you are an impossible romantic."

"No. I believe we should not divide man from nature nor nature from man. This is the secret of life."

"Good. You will have to teach it to me."

Hiroko smiled and fell silent.

Ludlow noted there was no marriage ring. When the green tea came in the beautiful ceramic to signal the end of the meal,

Ludlow fiddled with his cup. Finally he asked what she would say to a weekend in Hakone? The mountains there were said to be beautiful this time of year. And he'd been looking for the chance to get away. Perhaps they could find a place where man and nature could be one. Just friends, okay?

She laughed delightedly, said he was probably a liar, and added she was busy this weekend but how about the next one?

———

Friday afternoon. Ludlow and Mori walked in front of the palace, a wide plaza of graveled drives, well-kept grass, and dwarf pine with outstretched limbs like Noh players. Before Ludlow had left the embassy after lunch, Graves's office had called to inform him that the experts would arrive a week from Monday. He'd wanted some time; now Graves was giving it to him. The complexity of the case, however, made it doubtful that he would have enough time.

They walked as far as the Palace Hotel, turned, and now were heading back. The eternal groups of joggers puffed by them, many in colorful uniform. The two had worked together for a week now. Ludlow was trying to decide what the next step should be with so little time left. They talked over the case. American bullets, a Soviet raincoat, impossible angles for a tall man to fire from. They agreed that someone other than the foreigner had most probably shot her, that the foreigner might have been set up by a shorter man holding a device held fully extended in his hand. A device that didn't look like a gun.

Japanese Homicide had inconclusive evidence that the foreigner was a Soviet; a high-ranking member of the GRU. The Russians were being uncooperative, Mori said. The question was, who would set up the Soviets? And why?

Ludlow shook his head. He agreed that there were many unanswered questions, that they had a theory but no hard evidence. It was time to begin an action phase, didn't Mori agree? Get out of the labs and offices?

Mori smiled to himself. He hated Americans. Yet here he was worrying about an American. We do not know each other, he paraphrased a famous haiku in his mind. We are united through the mountains we both have climbed. However, his assumption that they had faced similar dangers in their lives, had fought similar demons, was not the only reason Mori had come for the first time to trust an American.

Ludlow had done what no Japanese would do with a foreigner: take him into his confidence. The fact that Ludlow had allowed him to sit in on an internal CIA conference between Operations and DS&T amazed him. And the openness and honesty with which Ludlow had conducted the meeting had put aside all doubts. Ludlow had integrity.

Furthermore, their evening drinking bouts had allowed him other insights into the American's character. Ludlow had an Asian mind. He could quote Lao-tzu and the *Book of Changes*. On numerous occasions, after countless bottles of *shōchū*, he soberly confirmed that he had rejected the pseudo-ideal world toward which humans aspire in moments of weakness . . . "Darkness is better than light, but it is nothing in itself." He agreed on the vanity of all human wishes, the intractability of matter, the unforeseeability of life. He could argue the teachings of Mencius, the Chinese philosopher, or of Japanese Zen, with equal aplomb. He could write Chinese poetry in horrific *kanji* on stained napkins for amazed bar girls. He understood the magnificence of simplicity. Unfortunately, however, the growing closeness of their comradeship and the broad vista of their thinking had not resulted in any decisive breakthrough on the case. It was time to make a change.

"Yes, it is best to get into the field," Mori said. "So where do we begin? What are we after?"

"Every crime has its signature," Ludlow replied as the light changed at the crossing in front of MPD headquarters. "So that's where we start. With the exotic American bullets. Let's find out who supplied the killers."

———

While Mori watched, the chief was writing. For two minutes he didn't look up. Finally he put the pen down.

"Yes, Inspector?" The chief's rich voice filled the room with his friendship. "We have been anxiously awaiting your results. Is this why you are here?"

Mori knew the proper ways to show respect. Aoyama made a point of always holding papers and letting his hand violently tremble during presentations. Others perspired. Some stuttered. It was acquired technique. Self-effacement. The more one showed inferiority, the higher his worth was rated by superiors. Mori had no patience for such trivia. However he did begin with a *"Domo sumimasen,"* an apology for inferior achievement with which all educated Japanese began presentations to superiors. No matter what the achievement had been.

Owing to the good graces of his ancestors, Mori began, there had been a number of successful developments in the case. However, he was reluctant to divulge these until every bit of evidence was in. He would then be able to present a complete and factual report.

The chief selected a paper knife from the clutter on his desk. One of those expensive items from Mitsukoshi replicating the sword of a famous samurai; in this case, Oishi, leader of the forty-seven *rōnin* of Ako. He pointed the sword at Inspector Mori. "When? When do I get your results?"

In order to complete the investigation, Mori continued, several final pieces of data were necessary. The girl obviously was a spy. Of that there was no doubt. The matter of her control, identifying him, still presented difficulty. This could only be obtained by showing further kindness to the American who now wanted to begin a field phase. A search for the source of the American bullets.

"There is a rumor you and the American have become rather friendly." The chief shrugged to show he did not believe gossip.

"Nothing to it at all, sir."

The chief leaned way back in his executive chair and turned the sword of the samurai Oishi in his hands. Finally he said, "What do you consider the most significant piece of information regarding her you have uncovered so far?"

Mori nodded as if he'd expected this question and was only too eager to give a satisfactory answer. "A microphone tap, sir.

149

Found in her apartment by the Americans." He explained how the device Ludlow pulled out before the DS&T meeting was very familiar. Just like Tokyo police use. Or military intelligence for that matter. No doubt a coincidence. His checks had confirmed no authorization to wire her apartment came from the police. Baffling, wouldn't the chief agree? Mori shook his head. Whatever party had inserted the device might have known, for example, precisely when and where she was having a meeting in Ginza the day she was killed. The owner no doubt could provide a wealth of information about the American girl. Could it be a Defense Intelligence operation?

The chief pretended not to be surprised.

Failing that, Mori persisted, he would recommend continuing cooperation with the American. Distasteful as it was. They could not expect any more data about the American girl unless they were cooperative. Homicide had drawn a blank, he'd heard: circumstantial evidence that it was a Soviet. Nothing hard. They were no closer to finding her killers than the foreigner. Not a complaint, Mori insisted. However, that was how most secrets were obtained, was it not? A trade?

The chief replied that chasing the bullets would be time-consuming. With little result. Japanese investigators were approaching it from an entirely different angle. Then he picked up the phone and peevishly called Colonel Yuki.

The colonel arrived less than thirty minutes later. Mori was asked to wait. For another half hour Yuki and the chief thundered behind closed doors like a storm over the horizon. The chief's ill humor, Mori later found, was caused less by the bullet-search request than by his discovery that a microphone tap had been found in the American girl's room.

The colonel made a stiff bow to Mori when he was recalled to the chief's office. The chief began by confirming that the microphone tap had been placed in her room by Colonel Yuki's branch. The Defense Intelligence Agency in future would be more careful in keeping the MPD advised of its actions. Unfortunately the equipment had malfunctioned and the DIA had not been able to gather any meaningful data. That was why the request had come for MPD aid in surveillance and Mori's assignment.

The other issue they had apparently been discussing in privacy was Inspector Mori's role. It was at this point that the chief turned the floor over to Colonel Yuki. The colonel coughed into his hand and said in very polite Japanese that some concern had arisen over the way Mori had handled his assignment thus far. To make his point firmly, the colonel began with the tale of Admiral Perry and the Meiji.

It was a story often told to underscore the treachery of foreigners. A story drummed into the heads of most Japanese students from the time of middle school. Perry, an American admiral, had humiliated their country. Forced unfair treaties on Japan, stationed foreign troops there not bound by Japanese law, insisted on extraterritoriality and preferential low import duties for American goods. It was not a defeat at war, but amounted to the same thing: the Treaties of Commerce and Navigation, forced on Japan because shore batteries knew they were no match for the steam-powered high tech of the good commodore and a quarter of the U.S. Navy. It was the first humiliation by foreigners in Japanese history, and triggered the overthrow of the Tokugawa government and the Meiji Restoration.

The colonel turned a brilliant smile on Inspector Mori. Foreigners were never, ever to be trusted, he concluded. That was a first and inviolate rule. They were ingrates, they rarely lived up to their word. Most significant, they gathered friendships as a prostitute gathered clients, holding them close for one moment and letting go the next. He had half a mind to request Mori be taken off the investigation.

"What is the problem?" Mori asked finally.

"You have been out drinking with the American every night."

Mori, who had been standing at attention, suddenly shrugged and smiled disarmingly. "Where there is light there is also shadow."

The chief had been listening nervously but now he leaned

way back in his armchair and said, "There, you see, Colonel? Just as I told you."

The colonel stared at Mori keenly for a moment. "I would still take him off the case. We are running out of time."

The chief nodded and turned to Mori. "You are getting close to the American in order to determine the American girl's guilt as a spy. This I understand. However, we are running out of time. A new security agency is essential; everyone is counting on you, Inspector."

Mori did a half-bow. "I will do my part." Obligation, he thought. Genesis of Japanese success. We try harder because we fear failure more.

The chief beamed. "Confirmation the girl was a major spy then, Inspector? And soon. Trips have been planned. Just like in Meiji we are already sending out people to study the finest security agencies the world has to offer. Right, Colonel? You have been to Moscow?"

The colonel scowled. "I thought that was to be confidential."

Mori decided that what he was hearing must be true. It was like the Japanese leadership to borrow from history. And every Japanese knew the Meiji history by heart. The public, if they ever found out, would be appreciative. In the Meiji era the decision was made to become a world power. Emissaries were sent abroad for the first time. To Germany to study their army, and to England to study their navy. Japanese forces were trained, supplied, then test-marketed. First against the Koreans. Then against the Russians. With the conquest of the Korean peninsula and the defeat of the tsar, Japan had earned the world's respect for the first time. By force of arms. In later years that respect would deepen.

The chief was smiling benevolently. "We must learn now how to protect our strategic high tech; the new basis for world power. To do so we send emissaries to study the finest examples the world has to offer us in counterespionage—as under Meiji we studied the best armies and navies. Your visit with the KGB was most profitable, was it not, Colonel?"

"Most profitable." The colonel smiled briefly.

The chief nodded proudly to Mori. "There, you see? Others will visit British MI-5, Shin Bet, the CIA, when your work is completed, Inspector. I suppose we should take your *gaijin* seriously then? At least go through the motions, eh? An impossible hunt for a source of bullets, right, Colonel?"

"If you insist, sir."

And so an improbable bullet search was reluctantly approved. The chief appointed Colonel Yuki to provide lists of contacts Mori should visit with his American friend. The bullets were illegal, of course. Thus, they could not have come into Japan through normal channels. Embassy pouches were also no longer an option, ever since a Colombian diplomat had been caught smuggling cocaine in one. The *yakuza* were the most logical source, then. The gangster element. Although, as Yuki pointed out, any Soviet who wanted to could deplane an Aeroflot flight with a pocketful and never be caught. Mori agreed. Then he explained that the American didn't think it had been a Soviet.

The chief was quite solicitous. He offered advice on how to talk with the *yakuza*. They weren't really that bad, he whispered, and told how they had helped put down the Railroad Strike riots and other troubles after the war's end when the Americans came in with their ideas of equality and freedom of speech. "Wasn't for them, we might all be Communists now." He laughed and wished Mori luck in his wild goose chase. Finally, as Mori was almost out the door, he said it would be best if there were some firm results within the next week. He gave that embarrassed little laugh he used to indicate that his decision was final.

CHAPTER 17

A BOTTLE OF
KOSHIN KAMAI

On Saturday and Sunday Ludlow and Mori hunted for the source of the American bullets. Their contact work came up empty. They continued to disappear into the notorious Sanya and other sections of Tokyo for liaisons with the *yakuza;* somber-faced, reticent, and well-tailored gentlemen. Each time they returned with taut smiles, indicating another defeat.

It wasn't until Monday evening, after another futile day of meetings, that they decided to abandon the *yakuza* list that Colonel Yuki had provided. The pattern had become too pronounced, the answers similar, as if rehearsed—as if each had been told what to expect and how to reply. Mori began to use his own contacts. These also failed to produce results but at least the answers provided refreshing variety.

Ludlow capped his frustration nightly by consuming increasing quantities of *shōchū,* a rough alcoholic drink of the Japanese working man. Mori stayed with his beloved Scotch. Tuesday night they again reassured each other that they were on the right track. It was only a matter of time. But time was running out.

Ludlow gave the final benediction Tuesday evening in a Shibuya bar the size of a Western toilet: Find who supplied the killer with those exotic American bullets, and we'll have him by the short and curlies.

Wednesday morning Ludlow stopped by the embassy for the first time that week. An envelope was on his desk from Political 2. He opened it, remembering he had asked Hiroko to scan the war-crimes trial records and see what she could find on Colonel Yuki's connections. He hurriedly glanced through the pages. Mori had scheduled a meeting in Yokohama this morning and Ludlow didn't want to be late, even though they were scraping the bottom of the barrel.

There was a nice feminine note from Hiroko saying that she was looking forward to the weekend in Hakone (which Ludlow had nearly forgotten in the crush of events) and hoping he would find the enclosed interesting. There wasn't much about Colonel Yuki and former Prime Minister Kishi. However, she hoped what she'd uncovered involving General Mori might be useful. This turned out to be something of an understatement. Ludlow read through the underlined portions first. Then, not really believing his eyes, he read the entire document. Shaking his head, he pocketed the sheets and left the office. It was not at all what he'd expected. Perhaps better left alone. He checked his watch; he was already late. He hoped to God circumstances did not force him to reveal the document to Inspector Mori.

———

The waterfront of Yokohama is one of Bushido's most resilient preserves. Shinto loyalty to leadership is as sure in the Ishigami crime family, which runs the wharfs, Motomachi, and China-town, as under the Tokugawa shogunate four centuries before. Shinto theology, then as now, has no place for the dogma of original sin. Extramarital commitment and certain venal affliction are de rigeur today, just as polygamy was practiced openly in earlier centuries. Shintaro Shigeyama, who reigned over the Ishigami crime family, maintained, in addition to his wife, what would have been described in previous eras as one consort and three ladies-in-waiting. The number was more a symbol of prestige than of personal vitality. Mr. Shigeyama was a very busy man. He generously provided each a monthly stipend, however, which paid essentials and was deducted from his business expense. His favorite, Asako the Morning Child, received a slightly heavier bonus envelope at the times of Chunenkai and Bonenkai twice yearly. Evenings she worked at Isamu's Bar in Ginza, and it was she who had arranged this meeting in Yokohama with Inspector Mori plus the very large North American. Shigeyama understood an opportunity when he saw one.

"Hollow-points?" Shigeyama repeated and flicked an imaginary speck from his immaculate pinstripe. He was built like a longshoreman; his apprenticeship had taken place on the docks, learning the family trade. Power was inherited in this industry as in others of Japan, so long as the inheritor demonstrated acceptable characteristics: cunning, avarice, physical strength, fairness to followers, and luck. Shigeyama would have been successful in most any Japanese enterprise had his beginnings been different.

"Forty-five parabellum; I need U.S. product," Mori added.

The introduction of Ludlow had gone more smoothly than anticipated. The Ishigami crime family did a certain amount of business with New York and the West Coast these days. Most recent was a high-stakes mah-jongg joint venture for expatriate Japanese in Fort Lee, New Jersey. As Shigeyama put it, foreign visitors often came to discuss business, take the sulfur baths, visit Hakone, and fall in love with our women. There was no flutter of hesitation about letting the foreigner sit in. Particularly when it was mentioned that he spoke no Japanese. Ludlow was explained as a weapons expert and it was left at that. Inspector Mori, after all, was known to be a man of honor.

For its more decorous transactions the Ishigami maintained a room at the solidly respectable Grand Hotel on the Yokohama waterfront. It was a hotel that had survived admirably in spite of its decidedly British origins—wooden Gothic cupolas on the slate roof and highly polished floors in all rooms that creaked like the deck of a man-of-war when you stood.

"We're not into hollow-points. Very dangerous." Shigeyama stared at Mori. Two of his lieutenants sat across the coffee table watching Ludlow. Mori had taken a velveteen armchair and Ludlow a low-status chair nearest the door.

Ludlow admired the way Mori had handled the meeting so far. Through all the polite preliminaries and informal banter that had led to this point where the serious questions began to be asked, Mori had let the chieftain monopolize the talk, hanging on his every word. Ludlow understood it was important to do this to attain the proper image of respect, without which no questions asked received straight answers in Japan. The preparatory phase was now complete. Ludlow signaled to ask a question. Mori nodded. A foreigner can often ask questions a Japanese would avoid, fearing they are too direct—too blunt.

"Do they get calls," Ludlow asked in English for Mori to translate, "people who make sales offers out of the blue?"

After Mori put it into Japanese, Shigeyama replied, "We turn all inquiries down."

"What is being offered?" Mori was quick to charge the opening.

Shigeyama's heavy eyebrows raised with a shrug of his shoulders, communicating innocence. "Winchester Silvertips and round-noses, homemade single automatics from Manila, Heckler & Koch HK91s from Europe, CS canisters over their shelf life from Korea. They make the shittiest tear gas in the world, by the way."

"Certainly," Mori smiled agreeably. It was a well-known fact that Japan's largest cache of arms, outside that of the Self-Defense Forces, was warehoused by the Ishigami and sister crime families throughout Japan. It was smuggled into the country through ports such as Yokohama, Kobe, Nagasaki, and Fukuoka. None of the weapons were registered; the law did not allow sale of handguns to civilians. Rifles were obtainable with a license, but bullets were strictly rationed and required separate licenses for each purchase and each prefecture where they were to be used.

"How about the other *kumiai?*" Mori pursued his prey carefully. "I'd be interested in a handful of Glasers too."

Shigeyama shifted uneasily in his chair. He had strong

wolflike features, thick hair lightly dusted with white, and a well-kept beard. Weapons were always a delicate subject, the lifeblood of power in the gangs.

"Very few in the country. Very, very few." Shigeyama surveyed his associates. One wore a short crew cut, the other a punch perm. Shigeyama turned to his crew-cut lieutenant, a buyer with *irezumi* over his upper body. They spilled from under his white shirt onto his neck and hands. "What do you think, Kuni?" Tattoos were popular among Japanese gangsters as a symbol of strength. *Sumi*, the colored ink, was inserted painfully by hand as had been done centuries before, confirming ability to withstand pain, and loyalty to the clan no matter what torture might befall the warrior. The lieutenant's *irezumi* were of coiled bamboo snakes, the heads emerging from his cuffs poised hideously on the backs of his hands.

"What you've just mentioned are very high performance rounds. Glasers. There is rumor that a Kobe *Gumi* has acquired several of the armament. Also the hollow-points. We know since our Oehler Chronograph was borrowed. Expansion they got on their hollow-points by using a twenty-five-kilo block of ductseal. Only a rumor, you understand."

"Ask him what results they got." Ludlow spoke up suddenly in English.

There was a brief conference before the answer to that question was provided. For the Winchesters they achieved a 863 feet-per-second velocity on the Oehler. It only registered in feet. And a 1.3 expansion. The Glasers gave them a thirty-centimeter explosion.

"The bastards are lying," Ludlow whispered to Mori. "They've tested the rounds themselves. No rival gangs I ever heard of share that kind of data."

Mori turned to the *yakuza*. "My friend is concerned since he does not understand how business is done in Japan. How when we have something to trade we use the third person so that a direct refusal is not offensive. Now. One of your men is being held by our customs bureau. Most unfairly."

Shigeyama scratched his beard and thought a moment. Then he turned to his lieutenant with the snakes. "Kuni, go get some sake cups. The best bottle." Shigeyama's voice had attained ceremonial quality. For him it would be a very fair trade.

After a heart-rending account of the unjust arrest was recorded—the customs bureau alleged they'd underpriced Hong Kong whiskey imports and were therefore skimming tax—the specific details were attended to. Immunity? Mori turned to catch the nod from the large American. Yes, immunity.

"Nor can we testify. After all, we had no idea how the bullets were to be used. The buyers mentioned a hunting trip in Nagano."

Ludlow leaned forward. "We'll take it. We're not after a trial."

Throughout the exchange Mori monitored the heating of a bottle of Koshin Kamai, an exclusive sake of which only a few bottles were produced each year. They were not sold at a premium; money could not buy them. It was a symbol of exclusiveness rather than wealth. This more than anything else assured Mori that the day would be successful.

Shigeyama then acknowledged that both Winchesters and Glasers had been supplied, half a dozen each. Kuni of the bamboo snakes made the transaction. It was not considered significant at the time. The man who bought them was in his twenties. Japanese. "The transaction was done in this very same room. We'd never seen him before."

"He was alone?" Ludlow asked in English. Mori translated.

"During the transaction," Shigeyama replied. "We had a guard at the front door who made sure the boy cleared the hotel. He got into a black Toyota with Tama plates. That's all he could say about it. Inside were two passengers, one the driver and the other an old fellow, all Japanese."

"Any distinguishing features on any of them?" Ludlow persisted.

"Just the older man," Shigeyama replied. "He was totally bald."

CHAPTER 18

A RELIABLY ASSESSED DEFECTOR

The Kehin Tohoku Express which rattled across the Tamagawa River bridge on the return to Tokyo was full of memories. Everyone has their nostalgic train rides, and this was Mori's. His mother had taken him to live in Senzoku near the Tamagawa when the war ended. She had lost her parents in the March 10 bombing of Tokyo in the last year of the war. One hundred thirty B-29s had dropped incendiaries in beautiful parallel lines across the city. Fresh twenty-kilometer winds had carried the flames. Over eighty percent of buildings in the city had been consumed. Ever since that day she'd insisted they live near rivers.

Beside him Ludlow alternately jeered at the sky, which looked to be fixing for rain, or pestered Mori with requests. "I'd like a picture of the good colonel if you don't mind. Mug shot, and we'll see what their doorman has to say."

"There are millions of bald Japanese," Mori complained, "particularly in Yokohama with those chemical plants in Kawasaki blowing pollution whenever there's a north wind."

"And just on the odd chance," Ludlow continued brightly, "does he have a chauffeured car by any means? Yes, I suppose he does. So what color is it, and the plates if you could be so kind."

Mori was staring reflectively out the window. A large threatening cloud had detached itself from the overcast and was making an ethereal bombing run on their train. Why would Colonel Yuki be involved in the girl's killing? he wondered. He recalled his last meeting with the colonel at the chief's office, then turned to Ludlow. "You remember that microphone tap you found at her apartment. Did it work?"

Ludlow stared at him. "Of course it worked. Why?"

Mori shrugged. "Just this. If Yuki is somehow involved I can prove to you that he is not working for the Japanese government." Before they parted at Shinagawa Station, they agreed to meet that evening. Isamu's in Ginza. Eight sharp.

Back at the embassy, Ludlow headed for Graves's office. As he came out of the elevators he saw Colonel Yuki hurry from the station chief's office and disappear down the stairs.

"He's busy," Cheryl smiled at him.

"Have I told you I'm madly in love with you?"

"I'll ring and see what he says." Cheryl busied her free hand with the top button of her blouse. While she was waiting for an answer she said, "Hear you're going away this weekend."

Before Ludlow could reply, Graves opened his office door and waved the Operations agent inside. "Just in time. I've a bone to pick with you." He closed the door behind them.

There was gray carpet on the floor, a large gray embassy-issue desk with an incredible number of pullouts. One held an on-line computer. Graves eased himself into an imitation leather armchair behind his desk and pointed in the direction of a no-frills gray couch. Ludlow helped himself.

Behind the desk, a large window with those narrow venetian blinds that cost double looked out on a building from which the KGB was rumored to film all embassy comings and goings. Graves surveyed the Wednesday-afternoon disorder of his desk. The pile of paper backup had reached heroic proportions. He selected a file and opened it.

"Now what in hell have you been doing evenings, buying Ginza real estate? You really expect me to approve these expenses?"

"Thought I'd give it a try."

"Ever hear of Gramm-Rudman, Ludlow? Ever hear the

screams from Washington every time I send in the monthly financials? Christ!" He dropped the file on top of the paper mountain.

"You know the Japanese system. Nothing serious gets done at the office. Those thirty thousand bars in Tokyo aren't supported by take-home pay. I have to hold up my end, don't I?"

"Save it," Graves sighed. "Any progress?"

"A great deal." Ludlow knew the rules. Presentation was everything. Succinctness. Crispness. Poise. Mastery of the current jargon. If you could speak and present a beautifully phrased report, little else mattered. First he outlined all the reasons he thought there was a Japanese connection. This had led him to spend the last few days looking for the source of the bullets. And today they had apparently found it. In Yokohama!

"So who was the buyer, Ludlow, spit it out. A Soviet?"

"A Japanese."

"So maybe it was a proxy killing. Or he was just the errand boy."

"There was a party of three. One made the buy. Two waited in a car. I may be able to identify one of them."

"You want to tell me who it is?"

"Not yet. I want it to be a surprise."

"This isn't a birthday party."

"I'm missing several pieces to be one-hundred-percent sure. You remember that MicroDec trial two years ago?"

"Of course. Several Japanese firms were socked for trying to steal MicroDec know-how. Served them right."

"Kathy Johnson was somehow involved in it. The Japanese think she was on their side. Now I'm not so sure. I need to see her file to prove if my hunch is right. If there was widespread organized theft of know-how from U.S. firms and MicroDec was a setup by the American government to put a stop to it, then I believe the motive for her death could be revenge."

"Not the Japanese government, Ludlow, for God's sake. I told you before we have enough problems without taking on the locals."

"Not the government," Ludlow agreed, remembering that

Mori had said he could guarantee their innocence. "A personal vendetta. To settle a score. Revenge."

"I still think it was the Soviets, Ludlow. You're letting an emotional dislike for these people color your reasoning. The Soviets were behind Kathy Johnson's death."

"We could both be right. Espionage is mostly trades, isn't it? Like trading baseball cards. I'll give you Willie Mays for Ernie Banks. Only lives are involved, not bubblegum and cardboard. Maybe Kathy Johnson was traded somehow. To a Japanese."

"You think the KGB found out about this alleged role she played for us in the MicroDec case? Then traded her to a local who'd been hurt by all the publicity?"

"Dunno, Graves. But you know how meticulous the Japanese are about evening scores."

"As you know, my vote doesn't count anymore. If it did, I'd have to say you'd have one hell of a job selling this in Washington. As it is the expert team arrives Monday. Give it all to them. Monday three o'clock at the American Club. They want to keep it informal. Invite your chum along. The Japanese fellow. Never can remember their names."

"Harrington still coming too?"

Graves smiled bitterly. "Yes, our old friend, Harrington too. Isn't that a laugh? I send in a blast recommending his investigation and he ends up coming in to review the entire mess. Can you believe it?"

"Message being delivered," said Ludlow.

"Things are far worse in Washington than I thought." Graves glared out the window.

"One favor, then, if I only have a couple more days. Cooper has been stonewalling on the Kathy Johnson file. I need a peek to tie some loose ends together."

"We can certainly put an end to that." Graves made a note on his pad. "Is that all?"

"I saw Colonel Yuki leaving the office just now. Anything to do with what I'm working on?"

Graves looked at the door to see that it was shut. "No," he said. "Something entirely different." He allowed a pause to

163

intervene. "He's helping me on an operation. We're developing a reliably assessed defector."

Ludlow coughed into his hand. "What the hell is that?"

"We're expecting a high-level Soviet to defect here in Tokyo. Can't tell you any more about it." Graves stood up to see Ludlow out. A mischievous grin transformed his face. For the moment Ludlow felt he was in the presence of a teenager who had received a dangerous weapon as a Christmas present.

———

Ludlow was ready to leave and about to call Hiroko when a thin middle-aged woman in a tweed suit and noiseless low-heeled shoes appeared, file in hand.

"I'm Devon," she said and nearly broke down and smiled. She put the black-bordered file carefully on Ludlow's desk, made him sign three forms, and disappeared toward the elevators leaving a ripple of Yardley toilet water in her backwash. The file title was simply *Kathy Johnson*.

The black border signified top secret, minimum circulation, which was supreme in the pecking order of priority. Ludlow opened the file cautiously as if stalking an enemy that hid somewhere in the words.

Kathy Johnson had been recruited three years ago. Her sensitive position at a leading microchip company no doubt weighed heavily in the decision. How the contact with Carl Lawson began was not clear. That he was also a member of the CIA was confirmed, however, when Ludlow noticed the files were cross-referenced. Carl Lawson had his own file. In the counterespionage division of DS&T.

There is always a little bit of luck in a good scam, and this one had it. Whether the duo had sought out the Japanese or been approached was not stated. After Kathy "stole" the documents from MicroDec, Lawson passed them to a representative of the Japanese companies, and the sale was videotaped. In the trial that followed, the CIA "consultant" was sentenced for public consumption; to escape further litigation, the Japanese companies signed an agreement. Each of the three firms, including Japan Electronics Corporation, was required to pay two million dollars to the U.S. Treasury. The case was closed.

Ludlow stopped reading at this point and squeezed his eyes shut. The data he'd been given at lunch by Mori's friend Watanabe-san showed that the Japanese still didn't suspect a thing. They thought Lawson had been working for them; the same went for Kathy Johnson. This had been one gem of an operation.

After the trial, Kathy Johnson had simply disappeared. There was a brief reference to a trip to the Antibes and addresses at both Mustique and St. Martin, where the highest levels liked to play. There would have been a month's debrief at least for something of this size, Ludlow guessed. After an operation scourging the Japanese, waving the flag, and proving once again the might and right of the U.S., the euphoria would have reached the highest-status Washington offices and opened up the special nontraceable funds.

Ludlow acknowledged that the entire operation was the work of a master. The Japanese must have been stealing U.S. high tech from Silicon Valley, and the U.S.A. set out to slap their hands. But good.

Her masters had set up the next phase with MicroDec. Word was put out of her harassment and subsequent departure. So there she was. Nobody to hire her because of her past tainted by the Japanese. An address was circulated where messages could be left, totally cold. Kathy was despondent.

As in any sucker operation, the mark—the Japanese—appeared to have very little to lose. She was eventually introduced through high-level channels to several Japanese firms. The Japanese were impressed, as well they should have been. A computer-chip expert with microresearch experience in the swift technical currents of Silicon Valley. A girl who had been on their side at the trial. Ludlow wondered briefly if any of her physical attributes had deflected their attention as well. Blond hair. Green eyes. A figure that a Ginza bar hostess would envy. A loyal follower.

In the end the Japanese did the only decent thing. Like other highly structured societies and organizations depending upon paternalism for loyalty, they always took care of their own.

JEC offered Kathy a job in Tokyo. And within the first year, when as a condition of their penitence they were required to join the new Exodus Sixty monitoring system, the U.S. reluctantly allowed them to appoint Kathy Johnson to run it.

The final page of the file was a three-week-old control report stating that Kathy Johnson was progressing favorably and recommending her arrangement be continued. The report originated in Washington and was signed by the code name, Robin.

Ludlow immediately phoned Hiroko. After he'd thanked her for the Kishi data, he asked if she could access the Carl Lawson file over in DS&T. She put him on hold and was back on the line within several minutes. Meanwhile Ludlow had lit up a cigarette. The Lawson file was unavailable, she said. Closed. He'd died several months ago in an auto accident. West Germany. Ludlow thanked her and they exchanged light conversation for a few minutes before he hung up. She was really looking forward to Hakone, she said.

He sat for a few minutes letting it all work through his mind. Revenge. Motive for the Japanese side of the equation. Two of the players that had been involved dead. Coincidence? He wondered who Robin was. Where he was. If he was still alive. Revenge. The classic Japanese kind. Yes. It was possible. Who then? Which Japanese? One of the three Japanese companies indicted? He thought of what he had learned today. The bullets had been sourced by Japanese, one of them older and totally bald. He knew where he must look first.

For the first time since he had arrived in Japan, Ludlow initiated standard avoidance procedure on his way down to the Ginza that evening. Tomorrow he would move out of the embassy compound and follow rules that would make it difficult for him to be followed or taken by surprise. It was best, he now understood, not to take anything for granted.

CHAPTER 19

THE ARGUMENT

Isamu's Bar is located in Ginza
four-*chome* in the heart of the downtown entertainment district of Tokyo. Isamu himself was a rarity in Japan, where
similarity is most often rewarded. His father had perished
flying a stripped Zero loaded with explosives into a U.S. cruiser
later reported to be the U.S.S. *Houston*. Isamu kept a picture
of the cruiser over the bar. There were also battle flags of
various Japanese units, which bar patrons had contributed, and
in the place of honor was the sake cup his father had drunk
from before his final flight—his last toast to the emperor.

Normally foreigners were not allowed at Isamu's. Pricing
was sufficiently vague, Isamu believed, to upset the finely
tuned and overrational Western mind, for one thing. For another, most patrons were on expense account and exorbitant
prices were of little concern. Should that not have been enough,
the Ginza view of *gaijin* drinkers was that they tended to
loudness and ill temper, traits the Japanese disdained until of
course they went on their own overseas trips.

Two places were cleared at the bar for Mori and the American. The inspector had called ahead and promised the *gaijin*
would behave.

The American ordered Suntory and water, which confirmed
he had manners. Mori requested Hiroshima *shōchū* with Sap-

poro beer as chaser to achieve geographical balance. Isamu leaned over the counter to assure Mori he would only charge the normal. The accounts of a Ginza bar are as complicated as those of a holding company in the Marianas.

When the drinks came Ludlow cupped both giant hands around his as if to prevent it from escaping. "I need a last favor," he said. "And then . . . I'll kiss the ass of the next Buddhist I meet."

"You're looking at one."

"Present company excluded."

Mori called Isamu over and inquired if he was a Buddhist.

"Only when somebody dies," said Isamu. "When somebody marries I am Shinto. Otherwise, I am available. Why?"

"Bring us another round," Mori said and looked at Ludlow. "What is it you want?"

"A look at the National Police files on Colonel Yuki."

Mori laughed, shook his head, and drained half his glass.

"Great," said Ludlow and dug in his pockets for a crumpled pack of Peace cigarettes. Mori accepted one and Isamu lit them both before retiring to another conversation. He understood it was private.

"I need this last piece before I make my final report," said Ludlow, understanding they had reached the critical point of the negotiation.

"You mean you've solved it?" Mori took a deep drag on his Peace.

"The Japanese side of the equation, right. The other side has to do with a Soviet defection. I haven't figured that out yet. It was a trade, you see. A swap is what we are talking right here. A Soviet side and a Japanese side. They made some kind of deal. The data in the National Police Agency files on Colonel Yuki would help to tell me what was traded. At least by a Japanese. Not your government, Ninja. I don't think they had any idea of that was really going on."

"Why don't you just ask Yuki?"

"Because maybe he doesn't know or maybe he's involved. Eventually somebody will. I'm just trying to put the facts together."

They ordered another round of drinks and one of the girls from the back tables came over and took Mori's arm. She had a nice face, the kind fortune tellers will tell you brings a man good luck: oval with a slightly uptilted nose and tiny nostrils. A good clean sweep of forehead. Mori introduced her to his American friend. Her name was Asako the Morning Child. She insisted Mori be the first one to sing.

Isamu set the drinks in front of the American as Mori allowed himself to be led to the tiny stage, protesting as he went. *"Kara-oke,"* Isamu said and then tried to explain that Mori was the best there was at the war songs. MacArthur had banned them during Occupation, which perhaps explained their enhanced popularity now. He grinned as if this were a joke.

Mori settled in front of a microphone like it was home. Asako inserted a tape. The stereo sound system filled the back of the small stage with more lights than a space ship. In front of the microphone was a display on which the words to the song appeared as the music began. "Empty orchestra" singing had hit the Japanese executive level with the force of a tsunami. A color video camera in front of the stage had come alive. There were also three TV monitors around the bar for those who did not want to watch Mori live.

The American scowled at all the electronic madness and pitched into his drink. Mori had begun "Under the Cherry Trees of Kudan," which anyone could have told him was to the Japanese Imperial Army what Edith Piaf's "I Regret Nothing" was to the French Algerians. But Robert Ludlow wasn't listening.

The audience was appreciative and the applause enthusiastic. Normally, Japanese don't like to clap their hands unless calling a waiter. Mori turned the stage over to another and headed back toward the bar. Ludlow watched him come, a smile replacing the American's earlier distant stare.

When Mori had regained his stool, Ludlow told him what a really fine voice he had, in such a way that Ludlow almost believed it himself.

Mori took a swig of *shōchū* to rinse his throat. "I have several questions," he said.

"Good. You're even more talented than I thought. You can think while you sing."

"First. After someone is named as the killer, either by yourself or by someone else, what will be done?"

"It's hard to say." Ludlow explained that it would be reviewed in Washington. They would make the action decision there. Based on a tribunal guilty verdict, there could be a formal request to the government involved. Say it was the Soviets. U.S. officials talk to theirs. Often this does not have a satisfactory conclusion. In that case, the United States might take matters into its own hands.

"You execute suspects, then?"

"Rarely. We make a clear decision whether the individual is guilty or not. Then we try to work out some civilized retribution. Terrorists, for example, may be kidnapped and brought back into our country for a formal trial before a jury."

"What if it was a Russian with the KGB? He shot the girl."

"More complicated. If our tribunal finds someone guilty who is working for a foreign intelligence service and the government channel fails, then there is a chance a hunter team will be sent out to terminate him. The KGB does the same. I should emphasize this is a highly unusual case."

"I'm a little hungry," Mori said suddenly. "You interested in some sushi?"

Mori called Isamu over and they ordered *maguro, tako,* and vegetable wrapped in seaweed and heavy on the *wasabi.* Mori sat back and looked at Ludlow. "I can't get you into police records under any conditions."

"Patriot," Ludlow scoffed and watched the Japanese take a cigarette from the pack on the counter. He noticed that Mori did not use Ludlow's lighter although it was available. Instead, to avoid fingerprints or DNA spores, he used his own matches. It was an acquired response, the sign of one who has been in the field many years. A professional. He knew that Mori understood that he was not interested in a Soviet in this case. He was interested in a Japanese.

There was a sudden commotion. A guest entered carrying

a long beautifully lacquered wooden box tied with a silken cord. Isamu rushed out from behind the bar and cleared a way to the tables. A Yokohama firm was in town, Mori explained, adding that it was a liquor supplier; an importer and wholesaler. Mori watched Shintaro Shigeyama, chieftan of the Ishigami *yakuza,* as he was escorted to the best of the empty tables, one that had been reserved and kept open for their most honored guest. There were two men with him, both well dressed. One with a crew cut and tattoos, the other with a punch perm.

"Those are our three gangster friends from Yokohama!" Ludlow started to rise out of his seat, but Mori waved him down. This had nothing to do with them, he said.

The three stayed long enough to present the gift, which turned out to be a valuable sword. It was presented with a brief speech by Shintaro, then handed ceremoniously to Isamu-san, who used the microphone to thank his guests because it was in truth a bonus for their very large business during the previous quarter. Mori smiled at the clever touch.

When the American asked what the gift was for, Mori explained that Isamu had done the president a very important favor. The gift was the symbol of repayment, the recognition of debt incurred. There would be other less obvious repayment as well.

"A large favor." The American had eyed the expensive sword appreciatively.

"Yes. He has told everyone it is for business, but in fact I believe an introduction was made by Isamu recently that was very successful for Shigeyama's firm."

Mori noted that when the sword came out of its box and Isamu displayed its vicious edge, a light jumped into Ludlow's eyes similar to when he had first looked at Asako the Morning Child. As the sword was passed from table to table, Mori explained how such ancient Japanese *katana* were made, the folding and refolding of metal under intense heat to establish a bond so strong it could cut stone. Amazingly, the American already knew this. Although they were common knowledge among Japanese, the American's embellishments—including his knowledge of specific heating temperatures for each stage of the process and of the clays used in the final polishing—reflected no less than a massive intelligence.

When Mori casually steered the discussion to other weapons, the American was equally impressive. He could list all the handguns and rifles the Japanese employed in the Great War and since, what was wrong with them, and how they'd been improved.

"Hobby," Ludlow explained.

The sword had by then reached the heaviest drinkers at the back tables. Each completed several hacks at the air. Finally, to great applause, a former naval officer and kendo fifth dan marched to the stage, where he dueled the microphone with exceptional skill. Urged on by a rising crescendo of banzais, he finally beheaded it, stand and cord. Everyone agreed it was a really superior sword.

At that point the Yokohama group rose and bowed competitively with Isamu all the way to the door. There they allowed him to squeeze in the lowest dip before they departed the club.

Their sushi came in a round, heavy lacquer dish. Isamu set the fish in front of them, peeled two sets of wood chopsticks, and retreated to a neutral corner. Mori had a look about him.

Mori popped an octopus first and chased it with *shōchū*. Ludlow tore after the *maguro*. The American finished chewing first. Reluctantly, he reached into his pocket and felt the envelope from Political 2, heavy with its knowledge.

Ludlow appraised Mori, weighing him. What did Mori want? What was he afraid of? Why should he protect his countryman? If anger would unlock the man, then he would soon find out.

"You have an obsession," Ludlow said. "That obsession is to hit back at the United States in any way you can. Admit it, Inspector. I've been researching you and your father."

"That's not true at all."

"It isn't? You believe Americans were responsible for the death of your father. Not true?"

"He chose death," Mori replied evenly. There was sweat on

his upper lip, however, Ludlow almost felt sorry for him. Mori had two powerful masters. One was his past; the other his future. He feared to betray either. Ludlow had seen it before. In Afghanistan, Laos, and Vietnam. In war zones it was rampant, men who had to abandon their pasts to survive. Men who had tried to live in two worlds but in the end had to choose between them. Mori, Ludlow was sure, hesitated between what he owed the past and what he wanted of the future. Between obligation and reality. Ludlow must destroy one or the other to set this man free. The end was selfish, of course. For without his freedom the diminutive Japanese was useless to him. Ludlow reached into his pocket and produced a folded document.

"What is this all about?" Mori hissed.

"The testimony of a priest. The statement of a former prime minister."

"I have no interest. Ripe fruit on a dead tree."

"It has to do with you, Inspector. Your past."

Mori shook his head with disbelief. "That is impossible. I know no priests or prime ministers."

"No, your father did."

Ludlow unfolded the document and began to read. It was several pages of microfilm copy, the questions and answers of dated interrogations. A number of responses were underlined with red. Hiroko must have read everything pertinent to come up with the appropriate pieces. Carefully, she had pieced it all together.

"The state sent a priest to witness your father's death." Ludlow suddenly stopped talking. Would his revelations break the man who sat next to him? He didn't want that on his conscience. Yet he knew he must go on.

"The priest represented the religion of imperial Japan at the time. Therefore it was the emperor, the state, above all the ultranationalists, who feared your father most."

"What are you trying to tell me, *gaijin?*" Mori's voice, hoarse with rage, had finally broken the boundaries of anger.

"A person of great moral courage was required. One who

would take orders unquestionably and accept blame publicly in a dignified and honorable way. A general would be best, everyone agreed. A military man."

"What are you talking about?" Mori stood up, looking with hatred at Ludlow.

"Nineteen forty-five. The end of the war. The first day of peace."

"I don't want to hear any more. You are treading on ground that is sacred."

"The Japanese high command arrested your father at the war's end, Mori. He was accused of betraying everyone. In fact, there was a huge cover-up at that time. All papers were burned implicating the emperor; the decision to go to war, its conduct, the attack on Pearl Harbor. Your father refused to go along with it. He was tried and convicted of treason in secret. Not even your family knew. He chose to commit seppuku instead of facing a firing squad. The public was told that his seppuku was to accept blame for defeat in the war. Your leaders used your father; first as a martyr to the public to take the heat off themselves; and then as a peace offering to the Americans. A scapegoat. It is all here." Ludlow tapped the pages.

Mori was staring at the American with two fierce ovens of hate. His mouth was working, but no words came. Sweat stood glistening on his forehead.

"Yuki was involved in it. So, inadvertently, was Kishi," Ludlow continued. "You've no call to protect the colonel. He was part of the old crowd. They used your father."

"No!" Mori shook his head vehemently.

Ludlow tried to spell it out carefully. The war criminals, he said, were all trying to escape what they had preached to others throughout the war—the samurai code. Their inner truth was cowardice in the end. It worked for some. For Nobusuke Kishi, however, there was even greater irony. He did not care to escape America's wrath. He did not negotiate with other prisoners to protect against what they might tell U.S. interrogators. He and Hirota and Tojo were the only really brave ones. But others were watching from the sidelines. Others who saw the huge potential of a postwar Japan. Men of wealth and power.

The Kuromaku. The Black Mist. They knew Tojo was finished and Hosaka too old, although both were admired. In Kishi they felt they had their man. A man of character. A man who could lead. It was these people who arranged everything.

"You lie!" Mori was staring at the pages in Ludlow's hands, ready to tear them away. But the American went on in his quiet voice, cutting through Mori's agony.

Suggestions were floated to the U.S. interrogators that Kishi had tried his best to eliminate the worst elements toward the end of the war. They brought up your father as a prime example. A Communist of the worst kind, they claimed. A flaming liberal. "It's all in here." Ludlow waved the pages in Mori's face. "They also hinted that your father was responsible for the worst atrocities. Nanking. Singapore. Bataan. 'It was the Tiger's men,' everyone said."

"Why?" Mori hissed. "Why would they do such a thing?"

"To get Kishi and the others off scot-free," Ludlow explained. "Only two were hung in the end. Tojo and Hirota. Kishi protested, of course, since he was honorable. But even that worked in his favor. It looked to the U.S. prosecutors like he was only trying to be loyal to his countrymen. It bought him three years in prison instead of a hanging. Time for Russia to become a serious threat. For Mao to win in China. Time for the U.S. occupation forces to realize they needed some staunch anti-Communists back in Japanese politics. Yoshida during Occupation. Then Kishi. A gradual escalation in quality. Sato. Tanaka. Nakasone. Colonel Yuki knew all of them. They are still in power, don't you see? Descendants of the same crowd that used your father. You owe them nothing, Mori. You owe Yuki and his crowd nothing. Why protect him?"

Mori's face was bathed in sweat. "You," he roared suddenly at Ludlow. "*Baka yaroo!* Get up. I'll kill you, *gaijin.*"

Ludlow didn't move. Isamu and several assistants rushed over to hold Mori.

"The priest who attended your father's suicide wasn't actually a member of the Shinto faith, Mori-san. He was a member of the TOKKO. The Thought Control Police."

Mori stopped straining against those who were holding him.

He was remembering the young priest, nervous, with that high, reedy voice. Remembering the priest's guileful smile and he— the boy—reacting with instinctive hatred. What was there about this priest?

"His name was Komatsu," Ludlow said slowly. "He was one of several who gave evidence supporting Kishi's innocence to the Americans, statements that finally won Kishi's freedom. Statements against your father. The TOKKO agent had attended your father's suicide masquerading as a priest to make sure his death was carried out. Under oath to U.S. investigators he swore that beneath his robes he concealed a gun that day. His orders were to shoot your father if he faltered." Ludlow selected the last tuna sushi on the plate and carefully popped it in his mouth. Then he rose heavily, placed the document on the bar, and walked to the door.

There he stopped and turned. Mori's eyes were full. He looked at his tormentor, thought of his hand slicing through the American's neck. In one stroke he could destroy this man who had just made his life meaningless.

"The TOKKO agent changed his name after the war, as did many Japanese of questionable war experience. The name he has used since is Yuki. In English that means 'snow,' which is our symbol for purity. A little irony there by the good colonel, I suppose."

Ludlow opened the door and walked out of the bar. On the street it had begun to rain.

CHAPTER 20

THE NATIONAL
POLICE AGENCY

Mori left Isamu's when it was nearly light. His friends had held him back, tried to console him with drink. But he knew he would never be the same. The rain had ceased and the pavement was new and shiny. There were few cabs. He started to walk toward the Sony Building, where there was a stand. From the Boromon Tailor's entrance-way, a voice startled him.

"To the Japanese people."

"Go away, *gaijin*. I hate all Americans. Most of all you."

"Looks like you could use a little help."

"I have decided to kill you."

"You're in no shape right now, Ninja. Why don't you wait on that one?"

"You are not afraid of me?"

"I've had too many drunk Japaners tell me they either love me or are going to kill me. Rolls off after a while, know what I mean?" Ludlow got up and followed the Japanese, who was weaving from side to side.

They crossed the street, to the scramble where it had all started, where Kathy Johnson had been killed, past Hankyu department store. There were no cabs at the stand. Another stand next to the Imperial Hotel was several blocks away. Mori headed for that, his pace somewhat slower.

"I think I'm going to be sick."

They were near the small park Ludlow had searched that first day, and the American gently guided him into it.

"See you don't get any on the pavement," Ludlow warned. "She was damned angry the last time you came through. Not a fan of yours at all, Inspector."

Mori sat down on one of the concrete benches. "Who's that?"

"Lady that runs this here park, that's who."

"I feel better now. Why don't you just leave me alone?"

"Because when I left the bar I was followed. Two men and a lady in shifts. KGB. Took them on a tour of Shimbashi that usually works. The narrow alleys back of the station." Ludlow smiled at his hands. "Haven't seen them since, but I thought I ought to see you home safely. Least I could do after disrupting your evening."

"Yes. You certainly did. You're a son of a bitch. You know that? You didn't have to tell me. You could have just left it."

Ludlow sighed. "Okay. Maybe I should have. But it isn't healthy, what you've got pent up inside you. Give yourself a chance, for God's sake. Get rid of your past."

"It's true, isn't it?" Mori felt his pocket where he'd put the envelope. "I could tell you were speaking the truth. You're very honest for a *gaijin*, you know. Unusual."

"Afraid so, Ninja. And Colonel Yuki's involved. You really have no cause to protect him. Not now."

"He's a son of a bitch, too. I'm going to kill him as well. I think we can make a deal, American. That's what you wanted, isn't it?"

"I'm listening."

"If I get you into the National Police files, in return I want you to leave anything about Colonel Yuki out of your final report. I don't want some CIA hunter team doing my work. I want him myself."

"We don't know if he's really involved yet, Ninja. But okay. I won't say a thing. You'll get me into the National Police files?"

Mori nodded and held up a finger. "But you also give me the straight story on Kathy Johnson. Right? Whether she was an important spy for the U.S. government. That's my price." Mori got up. "You can take it or leave it."

Ludlow pulled out his pocket flask and opened it. "You're a hard man, Inspector. I really don't have any choice." He handed the flask across to Mori and said. "To the Japanese people. No hard feelings, I hope."

Mori took a deep swig. "To the American people," he replied. Then he went over to the fountain pool and was sick.

———

The National Police Agency was a dowdy old lady in despairing red brick like a dormitory in the Waseda Yard. Mori and Ludlow went downstairs to the Records Section in a creaking, ancient elevator.

The people in the Records Section were a special breed that didn't encourage intruders, foreigners in particular, no matter how meticulous their introduction. The section was a windowless subterranean cave of musty files and microfiche equipment in the second basement. This was the heart of the system, where the darkest secrets hid, guarded by a few former officers past retirement age, of unblemished record, breathtaking loyalty, and presumed financial need.

A duty officer at the narrow entrance had peered up from a pool of reading light to stare with surprise through bifocals at Mori and the *gaijin*. After removing his glasses and cleaning them carefully he listened to Mori's request. He was about to call Central Processing and send them both away when Mori suggested he check Special Categories List. Upon doing so he reluctantly stamped Mori's card with his signature chop, but insisted the foreigner remain in the waiting area. He noted how the two looked at each other; finally the *gaijin* nodded.

"And he mustn't smoke," the duty officer commanded after seeing a pack of Seven Stars magically appear along with a battered lighter in the huge *gaijin*'s hands.

Shelves rolled on into the murk, files piled on top of one

another tied with green tape and smelling of mold and damp cardboard. Mori searched the Current section for over an hour, for all they had on Colonel Yuki. His record was one of unparalleled success. Until two years ago. Then began an interesting adventure in Silicon Valley under the dubious title of Operation Avenge.

Three Dodge vans were acquired for the Fullerton, Sunnyvale, Palo Alto area. The vans housed a Danish device that could locate and reproduce on a TV monitor text appearing on targeted computer terminals. Yuki had been riding high as chief of the Defense Intelligence Agency. Besides the normal order-of-battle priorities, they collected the odd scrap of information about foreign high tech. Yuki had decided to turn a disorganized program into a full-scale assault. His early sorties into the U.S. computer industry had been promising and he'd quickly been awarded a substantial manpower increase.

Several Japanese high-tech firms had advised the agency on the types of data that were of highest value and on the location of U.S. firms believed to possess state-of-the-art know-how. The consultants also assisted in the screening of technical information picked up by the vans.

When a Securicom Congress in Cannes displayed the Danish device, computer users began to install aluminum screens or Faraday cages around their CADCAM systems. Without hesitation, Yuki abandoned the vans and moved into a direct purchase program. The final event, a year and a half ago, had centered on California again.

A purchase of design elements larger in value than anything yet attempted was organized. Three major Japanese electronics firms sent technical staff into San Francisco, although file detail was skimpy. Yuki had obtained the source and performed exhaustive checks on the man to confirm his authenticity. There the file suddenly ran dry.

The American consultant was identified only by the code name Carl. A terse announcement in an interoffice memorandum noted the detention by U.S. authorities of five Japanese high-tech executives and the American consultant. The charge was industrial espionage. The target was a leading microchip firm by the name of MicroDec. Three Japanese companies were implicated; one of them was Japan Electronics Corporation.

Yuki wrote the damage report and apparently had difficulty reconstructing what went wrong. The comments were brief and obviously intended to minimize the event. The prime minister's office directed a letter to the defense minister, reprimanding all involved. In his reply the minister of defense accepted blame, terminated all Avenge operations, demoted Yuki to a vastly scaled-down research section, and proposed that he himself resign. The resignation was refused.

———

"Thought you'd gone to the crapper and fallen asleep" was the only comment Ludlow made when Mori finally emerged.

"We can't talk here." Mori's head ached like a boil.

They went out into a brilliant autumn morning and walked to Hibiya Park, which was only a block away. The park, one of the better ones in Tokyo, boasted random walks and benches which they ignored, exotic plants with their names carefully misspelled in Latin, and a deserted amphitheater with rows of concrete slabs to sit on, where they finally landed. On all sides lush growth gave them privacy.

Mori sat on the edge of the stage and Ludlow stretched out in the front row with an ostentatious yawn of disinterest. All through Mori's briefing, Ludlow kept up the pose even though the Japanese left nothing out. The huge American stared around at the azalea, dogwood, and lilac as if he were considering the gardening profession. It was, however, how he always looked when engaged in intense concentration.

When Mori had finally wrung himself dry and had nothing more to tell, he stared at the American for several seconds. "Well," he said, and one could almost hear his own breathing had it not been for a siren that erupted suddenly over the steady hum of the city behind them.

Ludlow waited for the siren to fade. "I believe we have the one," he said quietly. An internal momentum was overtaking his voice. "Yuki is the killer. Motive is that wonderful Japanese capacity for revenge." His words began to bite hard and metallically into the steady hum of city. Overpowering the city. Destroying it. Twice during the ensuing discussion, Ludlow lit cigarettes to throw them away, half-smoked. Once Mori excused himself to make a telephone call and returned, his mouth set in a firm line to renew the exchange. The data confirmed that Colonel Yuki's career had been destroyed by the MicroDec scandal. More than adequate motive. In Japan, career was everything. Reputation. Honor. Work was the essence of life. The most important ingredient for the Japanese soul.

"But why kill Kathy Johnson?" Mori asked. "She was on the Japanese side."

Then Ludlow carefully explained the CIA operation to the inspector. How it had employed Kathy Johnson to set up Japanese companies that had been stealing microchip and computer high-tech secrets from Silicon Valley firms. Yuki, when he found out her role, killed her as part of his vendetta against those who had destroyed his career. Undoubtedly he had rigged the auto accident that killed Carl Lawson, although it would never be proven. "In fact," Ludlow concluded, "all we have right now is circumstantial evidence. Nothing we can wave in front of our superiors or a jury. Nothing that would hang him."

"Try this, then," Mori smiled. "The colonel visited Moscow earlier this year."

Ludlow stared at the Japanese. "To do what?"

"To visit with the KGB. Japan wants a new legalized security agency. Yuki was finding out how the KGB works. At least that was his initial objective."

"Good Lord." Ludlow threw up his hands. "It's just the sort of thing the KGB thrives on. They had the MicroDec nugget in their files. Knew of Kathy Johnson's involvement. Carl Lawson's. Valuable U.S. agents, who couldn't be eliminated under their new rules against executive action since Andropov. They fed the data to Yuki, knowing how the Japanese feel about revenge. No doubt they received an extravagant favor from Yuki in return. Then they just sat back. Brilliant."

"So what do we do?" Mori studied Ludlow for a moment.

"Nothing for now, Ninja. We can't go after Yuki yet. There's one more side to the equation. A Soviet operation that Yuki is involved in. He is the only one who can help us find out what they're up to. We just have to wait for the good colonel to make the next move."

CHAPTER 21

THE TEST

Before their nightly debrief, Pachinkov told another story. Tonight it was the one about Prokofiev when he was fifteen at Leningrad Conservatory. One day he had to show his assignments in orchestration to Rimsky-Korsakov before the entire class. The master found a number of errors in the work and became angry. Prokofiev bowed exultantly to the class. He had made the great man angry. Somehow he believed this increased his esteem. He never really learned how to orchestrate properly, as a matter of fact.

"Malik!" Sergei had grasped the point immediately this time.

"Yes." Pachinkov grinned at his friend's quick understanding. "I have received a cipher from Moscow. They have taken the Starfire operation out of our hands."

"Impossible!"

"Living a life is not so simple as crossing a field, my friend. We must face the facts. Malik tries to anger us. He will send a Center specialist in to collect Starfire."

"The bastard!"

Pachinkov winced at the explosive rage behind the voice. Sergei was his monster, a master of violence. Yet under it all he was basically a gentle creature. "Malik will use this man to achieve esteem. Enhanced power. Position."

"You mean the first directorate? He tries to take that position away from you?" Sergei's voice was a low shriek.

Pachinkov nodded his head. "I do not have the directorship as yet. He will do his best, it is now clear, to see that I do not get it!"

"But I have been counting on that, comrade. To live in Moscow again is our right after so many years in the field. We certainly deserve it. And perhaps a cottage in the Urals for weekends and vacations. I could cook! We could raise sables."

"Wait, Sergei. We get ahead of ourselves. Perhaps one day. But for now we must plan how to deal with the Shavki agent Malik sends us." The term was a disparaging one to describe small-time agents. "It changes how we deal with the American, Ludlow, you see. How is the surveillance going?"

"There is a small problem." Sergei opened up a pack of bitter Turkish cigarettes and offered Pachinkov one.

"Later. Well, out with it." From a dish he picked a sausage.

"Last night our best team lost him."

Pachinkov smiled. "Of course."

"It happened very suddenly. He drinks every night like a Russian. He was at a place called Isamu's in the Ginza. With that tiny Japanese sidekick. They look like something out of the Moscow Circus. A giant and a pygmy."

"How many times must I tell you the way they look has nothing to do with it. This is a dangerous American. And I believe we may be able to let him do our work for us. You must find him immediately."

"Our people didn't have a chance. He went over to Shimbashi after he left the Japanese. You know that maze of alleys behind the station?"

"It's not your fault, Sergei." Pachinkov shook his head. "But don't leave him out there alone too long. Who knows what he'll get up to."

After Sergei had gone he stood and paced his office, then stopped in front of the windows to stare across the city. If there was a caliber of talent here equivalent to Berlin or London, this would never have occurred. Even in Mexico City they could do better. Routine surveillance! When would he be allocated the resources he required for the importance of this hateful city? What did they think he was? Lenin himself?

Pachinkov forced his mind toward calmness. It was a test, he told himself, the final one, and he'd understood that from the very beginning. He'd been chief resident in London, Rome, and Washington. He had performed outstandingly with the best tools. In Tokyo they wanted to see how much of an improviser he was. And he'd shown them, hadn't he? Without the aid of T Directorate he'd set up the most productive high-tech espionage net in the history of the Asian apparatus. Some were even comparing him to Sorge! Computers and other high tech were flowing out of Japan to the USSR and Middle East like the River Danube at its April peak.

His mind slowly cleared. He turned on the stereo again and picked at the remaining food. Stravinsky. The strains were muted and intertwined, gradually building to something more, a crescendo of beauty in wood and metal. He listened to it all and felt the stillness return to his body. That patience was necessary for this work, he already knew.

CHAPTER 22

THE PARTY

It is said that the Japanese, as a people who must suffer conformity as few other races on earth, find peace in disharmony. If so, Tokyo architecture and layout is a confirming argument. Less a city than a kaleidoscope, Tokyo is a city planner's nightmare—an endless variety of patterns that mesmerize the mind.

"*Koko, koko.* Stop here." Mitsuko's sudden order caused the cabbie to swerve and nearly dissect a red Yamaha Princess motor scooter with a leggy girl in tight jeans aboard. Mori sat back quietly and let his wife direct the traffic. They were on Aoyama-dori near one of Tokyo's most fashionable shopping areas. Mitsuko led the way to a barely discernible lane less than three meters wide. It was busy with evening shoppers. A few stared at Mitsuko's elegant dress and Mori's black tie.

They turned again as the road narrowed further, coming to houses crammed inside stucco walls and occasional brick "mansions," as upper class apartments are called. The husband and wife were in Tokyo's inner city, a place of relative quiet and solitude. Mitsuko was in charge because it was the ICOT director's home, at the end of the block, that was their destination.

"You look nice tonight," Mitsuko said, smiling sideways at

Mori, and pushed the button on the gate to the director's home.

"Thank you," Mori said absentmindedly. He was still thinking of the *kanzashi* found in his mother's pillow; it had complicated matters tremendously at home. Without saying so, his mother obviously blamed Mitsuko. The tension between them had become palpable. Another "accident" like that and there would be an explosion. It was something Mori could not afford, with the issue of Yuki's guilt now confirmed by the American.

"Normally you don't dress up so nicely when we go out." Mitsuko gave him her best smile.

"I'm trying harder," Mori said.

A speaker in the gate asked for their names and automatically unlocked when Mitsuko gave hers. As they walked up the short path Mitsuko said suddenly, "Did you know Erika would be here tonight?"

Mori flushed as the paneled door swung open and Kazuo Suzuki, director of the ICOT advanced computer research program, beamed at them both.

Suzuki-san was taller than Mori by a good twenty centimeters. He had a deep, resonant voice, the voice of one who made many speeches. Mori had always felt that Suzuki was the ideal man for the ICOT job. A bachelor who hated the old copycat image of Japan and had set out to prove to the world that Japanese can innovate. A relatively young man, barely forty, who ignored tradition. Suzuki had quit a prestigious university research team to develop his own unique ideas; this sort of move was unheard-of in the staid electronics research community.

"The heavenly Mitsuko and her dedicated husband," Suzuki said, grinning charmingly as if he too liked a good joke. Mitsuko dove into the crowd like a swimmer who is familiar with the tides. Mori thought he heard her whisper, "Toilet," but he couldn't be sure. A hi-fi was rolling through a hit album by Anzen Jidai, the most popular rock group this year.

Tokyo parties, like other Japanese entertainment, conform to certain rules. One is that any insult is forgivable so long as the speaker appears drunk. This offers all kinds of opportunities to pass suggestions to superiors or keen rivals, to gossip, and to leak information. It helps explain why Japanese firms and institutions spend so much on entertainment.

———

The party was on in earnest, punctuated by bursts of laughter, female protests, and serious voices seeking to impress. The living room overflowed with a young crowd in the latest fashions of upper-class Japanese. The most striking feature of the pageant was its uniformity. The women were all in pastels and whites. Although there were some gorgeous creatures present, it was as if all the animals had been neatly camouflaged.

"I know just how you feel," Suzuki said, suddenly at Mori's side, calling a tuxedoed waiter who handed Mori another Suntory.

"Mitsuko is still a child. *Yoroshiku*," Mori said, observing male etiquette in which a wife is never praised. Mori then demolished half his second drink.

Suzuki called the waiter over to refill Mori's glass again and said, "All of our staff are young. Except for me of course. I am simply an outcast."

Mori detected the modesty of one who could afford it. In the past year Suzuki had been lionized by the media as the brightest star in the high-tech firmament. Another couple arrived. Suzuki whooped toward them and they embraced in a threesome.

On the buffet table were large black and red lacquer dishes piled high with sushi that was constantly being replenished. Mori took a *maguro* with his free hand and popped it into his mouth. The raw fish was succulent and cool, the burn of *wasabi* just enough to smart the eyes. Quite perfect. There were also shrimp and vegetable tempura, sticks of golden yakitori, and a dozen choices of salad. Mori filled his plate and moved through the crowd.

The talk around him was only of computers. It was as if he'd entered a world where a different language was spoken. "PROLOG work station attained a million LIPS . . . vast improvement on the von Neumann . . . Weizmann Institute's Ehud Shapiro said in his last visit . . ."

A tanned, athletic-looking young man was talking with Mitsuko. She'd taken off her jacket, revealing creamy shoulders
and the white curve of throat. Here among the elite of Tokyo's
scientific community she looked marvelous. Mitsuko saw him
and waved her wine glass.

He wigwagged his eyes at her to signal he wanted to talk.

She smiled distantly, an indicator that she was involved in
a business discussion. She was smoking a cigarette; she never
smoked at home. Mori felt somehow let down. He started
away. Her lips were forming complex words as if to disown
him: "The electromagnetic pulsar effect is negative . . ." He
wondered, not for the first time, if she was ashamed of him.

Mori nodded at people he'd met briefly in the first year of
Mitsuko's job, when he'd tagged along to several functions at
her insistence; there had usually been one a week then. He
saw their eyes unfocus, as if they were trying to recall where
they'd met. He went out into the garden.

Japanese gardens rarely boast grass, and this one was no
exception. However, it was charming and spacious, a place of
stepping-stone walks, pools, and viewing rocks. Guests had
spilled over into an area that was lit by strings of *chochin* paper
lanterns. Mori caught a glimpse of Erika deep in conversation
with a distinguished-looking gentleman.

Nearer to Mori was a girl he'd seen on TV. She was with an
older man wearing a ribbon on his lapel that indicated he'd
made the emperor's Honor's List. Suddenly, Erika was beside
Mori. She took his arm, snuggled against him. He could feel
the tautness of her breasts.

"I'm glad you could be here tonight. Mitsuko said she didn't
think you'd come. You don't like parties, do you?"

"Real parties I like," Mori said. It sounded somehow lame;
like something Yujiro would say in his detective series on
Channel 8. "Who's the old guy talking to the singer?" He
pointed a yakitori stick.

"That's Iwasaki-san, the head of IBM's Research Institute.
He invented the Iwasaki diode in the sixties. Maybe you've
heard of it?"

"No," Mori said. "Most of this is over my head."

"Don't feel too bad. We'd all be in the same boat at an MPD function."

Mori laughed. He appreciated her attempt to ease his feelings of inadequacy.

They walked together through the garden as far as a concrete wall marking the back of the property. From here you could see the expanse of house, and to one side a garage constructed Japanese-style; only columns supporting a roof to keep weather off the machinery.

"He's done quite a job, hasn't he?" Mori said.

"Who?"

"Suzuki-san."

"He's a maverick who's defying the Japanese system and getting away with it," Erika replied. "Most people didn't give him a chance to succeed in the beginning. Now some are very jealous; but most people admire him."

"Is my wife one of them?"

Erika looked momentarily confused, then followed his gaze. Mori was staring at the car parked under the roof in Suzuki's garage. It was a black Mercedes.

"Your house is not that far out of his way," Erika said.

"It's a damned good forty minutes out of his way."

"I told her you'd be angry." Erika tried not to look pleased. "Suzuki considers her the perfect Japanese woman."

"Why perfect? Because she went to Gakushuin undergraduate and rubbed elbows with royalty?" Mori was suddenly at a loss for peaceful words.

"Well, that's part of it, certainly," Erika admitted.

Mori icily suggested that ICOT's success didn't justify Suzuki making a play for his wife, did it? In a voice that lacked certainty, Erika said it was just a business relationship. Mori wondered why it was that in Japan success justified almost anything.

Mitsuko was fresh and upper-class, Erika was explaining. She used *keigo* naturally, not like the shopgirls at Mitsukoshi. *Keigo* was a form of polite, respectful Japanese that was considered the ideal of femininity. Further, Mitsuko was a member of the Tokiwakai, the Peer's School Club. Suzuki, on the other

191

hand, was a country bumpkin who'd made good. Mitsuko's willingness to work for him was flattering. She had left a prestige position at MITI to take the job, but that was very like Mitsuko, wasn't it? A very independent woman. She'd married Mori, after all.

The words stung, but Mori knew they were true. Mitsuko could have had whatever kind of life she wanted; luxury, the international set, maids and cars and European vacations. Yet she'd opted for a faded though famous name, a destroyed family fortune, an aristocratic and perhaps overbearing mother-in-law. In Suzuki she saw all those things she might have had; maybe realized her mistake.

Mori wasn't angry, he realized. Anger had nothing to do with it. The cuckolded husband in Japan felt shame. The reasons were difficult to define. He wished he hadn't raised the subject, so he turned the discussion around and asked Erika why she wasn't married.

Erika stretched like a cat and looked happy, as people do when they are asked about themselves. "I guess I'm a romantic." She tilted her face up to him with childlike innocence and smiled to show that she knew he could be trusted with a secret. "You'd have been just right for me," she said.

Mori felt the flush creep up his neck.

Erika didn't appear to notice. She looked thoughtful as she told him that when it came right down to the man she wanted to spend the rest of her life with, she preferred one who ordered her around and threw his clothes on the floor when he came home. "Someone like you, Mori-san." She brushed the hair out of her eyes and took his arm again. She lifted her drink and drained her glass. The liquid moistened her full lips. Mori felt her arm tighten against his, felt the pressure of her body, her warmth.

In a lighter voice, a happier voice that seemed suddenly released from a burden, she said, "Mitsuko told me how your family was very old-fashioned and strict about your upbringing. Mine was the same. I was taught to repress my feelings, to be of calm nerve, to fight with weapons—especially the *nagi-nata* sword. And also martial arts."

"What on earth for?"

"As I told you, my father was of the old way. He wanted me to be able to guard my personal sanctity."

"And did you?"

She giggled. "With ferocity. The Osakan men are very rough. But Osakan women are more violent than the men."

"Your father, what was his work?"

"Like you. In the police. Some special work he never would talk very much about. In Osaka, of course."

"Your house was of samurai ancestry, then?"

"Yes. Not a famous lineage like yours. But samurai all the same. I am of the old way and the new. Of the old way in spirit enough to accept being a second wife if the man loves me and I truly love him; I see nothing wrong in it. And of the new to fight for my rights, for my freedom to live and work as I wish, without being looked down on or treated as a sex object."

Mori understood what she'd meant that day at her apartment. Erika had the amazing candor of a child. He shook his head: "There are many branches to a river."

She escaped from his arm. "I do not take from someone what I cannot give." Her lower lip had gone to a delicious pout. Her eyes looked freshly washed and suddenly defiant.

Mori reflected whether truths realized by reason were superior to those attained by intuition. He knew what he wanted, but instead he said, "In Japan appearance is most important except to oneself. I will think about what you have said. We will meet again soon. Perhaps that would be better."

Erika brightened. As an intelligent Japanese woman, she ignored his words and read his *hara*, his emotions. "Good," she said as if everything were decided. "That makes me very happy." Suddenly she saw someone she knew. She gestured to Mori that she'd be right back. It was the last he saw of her that evening.

Just then, one of the tuxedoed waiters came up to him. "Are you Inspector Mori?"

Mori looked around, surprised. "Why yes."

"I've been asked to give you this note." He handed a small envelope to Mori, who opened it and read the message.

"Emergency. Car waiting for you in front."

Mori thought he would first find out what had happened, then come back to tell Suzuki or Mitsuko. He hurried out of the house and toward a green van that was parked in front of the gate. Mori didn't recognize the two men who were waiting for him. They had coats over their arms as if they anticipated a chill later in the evening. The coats were pointed at him. Underneath, he could just glimpse the vicious metal bores. One took the note from his hand and motioned toward the open door of the van.

The back of the van was outfitted with a rug and a U-shaped couch. Facing it was an armchair with some sort of console. The *gaijin* in the armchair looked around as Mori entered half-bent and was pushed from behind into the U-couch. Two men plopped down on either side of him as the van started moving. The one in the chair had silver-gray hair; that was all Mori could see of him in the dark. The only light came from the console, which had three dim banks of dials. The van was heavy with cigarette smoke that smelled bitter and foreign. The tip of the man's cigarette glowed suddenly as he dragged on it and exhaled.

He said something briefly in Russian and the van picked up speed. They had reached Aoyama-dori and were heading for the Shibuya district. The van had good springs and the couch was comfortable. It was a Toyota Camper, Mori decided, with some interesting modifications the maker probably would have been pleased to see. One of the lights on the console, a green one, started to wink. The man shifted his cigarette hand and picked up a microphone. He spoke softly into the mike as if he knew it intimately.

"*Poyekhali,*" the Russian said. "We have him and are proceeding." He switched off the mike. The cigarette glowed again and then the Russian spoke in passable Japanese.

"We apologize for the lateness of the hour and the disruption of your evening." He paused as if he expected Mori to demur. Then he continued.

"I have several questions I would like to ask you. Please answer them truthfully. Then we will drop you wherever you suggest. It should take no more than a few minutes. But I would like to emphasize that the questions are very important to us. So please answer them precisely. Are you ready?"

Mori nodded. But he was wondering how these people knew so much. How they had found him, for one. Exactly what to ask him, for another. Was there a mole inside his own organization? Yuki? He had agreed with Ludlow to keep quiet about Yuki. Ludlow had said, "Wait for Yuki to lead us to the Russians." Is this what has happened? he wondered.

"An official of our embassy sighted you in the company of an American three days ago," the smoker began. "Police HQ, I believe it was. The American has since disappeared."

They might be bluffing, Mori decided. Or they could be making an evaluation on how to proceed with the questioning—here, in the van, or under more secure circumstances. He decided his best chance for survival was to keep talking in the van. The truth, then.

"Yes. I've met the same American on several occasions."

"Thank you for being honest with us, Inspector. Now question number two, who is this man? What has he told you?"

Mori realized he had no choice.

"An American official with the U.S. embassy."

"Official, Inspector?"

"Yes. He's with their Public Affairs Department."

"So obviously he's interested in information. What kind of information have you been passing him, Inspector?"

"He is investigating the death of an American girl."

"Her name?"

"Kathy Johnson." Mori understood they were taping and that he was going in all the way. If he had been a real turncoat they would have enough incriminating evidence to run him for the rest of his life, no matter what their promises. It was all so frighteningly simple.

"And the name of the American officer?"

"Brown. Robert Brown."

"He is with the intelligence arm of the U.S. embassy; you did not know this?"

"No." His first lie, but not an important one.

The man shrugged. "That was the only name he gave you, Brown?"

"Yes."

The Russian was silent for several seconds. Mori wondered why they would be so interested in Robert Ludlow. They wouldn't be taking these risks tonight over something small.

"How do you make contact with Mr. Brown, Inspector? Let's suppose it is very important to reach him."

"I call a special number at the embassy."

"You do not know at what hotel he is staying?"

"No. All my contact is through the embassy."

"Excuse me a moment." The man turned and said something again to the driver, who turned toward Sendagaya, a quiet area of Tokyo which boasted parkland and stadiums.

"You can call that number any time of the day or night?"

"Yes," Mori said.

"And Mr. Brown's investigation of the girl's death. What is his conclusion so far? You can be totally frank with us."

"He believes that a third party is involved, interested in setting the KGB and CIA on a collision course in Japan."

"That's very interesting. Ah, here we are."

The van had pulled up outside a phone booth near the Olympic Stadium. The area was one of circular drives and trees, one of the few green areas of Tokyo. The escort to Mori's left got out, motioning Mori to stay where he was. He walked around outside the van for several minutes. This gave Mori the chance he wanted. He turned on the older Soviet:

"You are the ones who have been trying to disrupt my household? You've been watching my house?"

There was a barely audible sigh from the Russian. "We were watching your house. Yes. The watch has been discontinued. However, we did not disrupt your household. That we know nothing about."

"Then why was I put under surveillance. What reason?"

"The American. We thought we could track him through you. It turned out not to be, as you can see." The Russian smiled to himself in the dark. It was an irrefutable answer though totally untrue.

The Soviet who had been checking outside the van returned and rapped three times on the door. *"Poyezhaytye!* It is clear."

The older Soviet turned back to Mori: "We would like you to make a call to the U.S. embassy to leave a message for Mr. Brown. Request him to come urgently within one hour to this address." He handed Mori a slip of paper. It was a deserted area of Harumi, near the exposition buildings. Mori nodded and said, *"Hai."*

"You may get out now."

Mori let the man behind him open the door. He jumped to the ground and with the momentum caught the guard waiting there with a karate kick to the hip. The man went down. He felt a hand claw at him from behind, but he broke free and ran for the trees that lined the street. Once into the trees he raced desperately, keeping them between himself and his pursuers. He plunged into the miniature forest that surrounds the Municipal Museum. Something whispered by. Or was it his imagination? A branch whipped his face, making his left eye tear, and he nearly fell as he temporarily lost sight in that eye. Thicker undergrowth now. He plunged through it, then swerved left and began to zigzag. He could hear the van start up; the engine roar and the tires squeal as it accelerated. The sound came nearer, then started to fade. The engine slowed. He could hear voices. Sweat was cascading from his face down the front of his shirt. He kept running, driving his legs on, drawing deep shuddering breaths.

Then he heard another sound. Cars. He looked to his right and could see the entrance to the *shuto,* the expressway, a hundred yards off. There was a gatekeeper in a glass booth. He felt the stitch in his side as he lurched forward. The trees and branches thinned. A road appeared, the entrance to the expressway. Cars were lined up for the toll. Mori reached the toll gate and finally looked back. The Russians were nowhere in sight.

CHAPTER 23

SAFE HOUSE

The ride was conducted in silence except for the American next to the driver who spoke without turning around. Mori had phoned Ludlow's emergency number last night with the urgent message that the KGB was looking for him. Those in the car were under orders only to direct Mori this once. All future meetings with Ludlow, unless otherwise specified, would be conducted at this same place. The apartment was secure. Mori was to mention its location to no one—clear? Mori nodded and understood. Ludlow was taking no chances.

They dropped him on Ju-san-ken-do near the Yamate Line overpass with precise written directions and a fresh key taped to the paper. They told him not to take the key off the directions until he reached the address. When he did, the tape tore the paper and obliterated the instructions. These were the kind of people, Mori thought, who kept their money in post office savings accounts and never finished their drinks.

It was a gray cool morning; a north wind had blown mist in from the Pacific. Nearby were *rōnin juku* cram schools for unfortunates who'd not passed college entrance exams, a colossal sin in Japan. Student slums and light industry competed, but the factories were winning: producers of car deodorants, cosmetics for the young, box lunches, and bleached yarn. It was a place of transients who never looked one another squarely in the face, never asked questions, never knocked on neighbors' doors. It was, in short, a place conducive to privacy.

The apartment building was two floors in wood and spray concrete to match the clam gray color of local industry. Mori let himself in and lit the small Rinnai gas heater to dispel the dampness and the smell of mildew. It was a ten-mat tatami room with a low table, several dirty cushions, and little else. The tatami was shiny with wear and in several places had been incurably stained. There wasn't a speck of femininity in the apartment, no curtains or flowers or care. The only extravagance was a portable dual-tape stereo covered by a layer of dust.

At one end of the room was a sliding opaque glass door. When Mori opened it to let out the dampness it only allowed more in. The door opened to a dank alley with no hope of sunlight or even sky. The inspector shook his head and settled down to wait.

Ludlow was fifteen minutes late, his eyebrows jetting anger. He laboriously took off his shoes, carefully folded an ancient military raincoat, then crushed it to the tatami floor and nodded to Mori. He rubbed his hands together since the heater had not yet conquered the damp chill—nor would it, Mori decided.

"Cozy," Ludlow said. He rummaged in his flight bag, found several pieces of paper and a ballpoint pen, and dropped them on the table. Meanwhile Mori found tea and put on a pot of water to boil. When he returned to the low table he settled on a torn cushion opposite the hulking American who was by now sitting cross-legged on the floor. "Those bastards really have nerve." Ludlow stared angrily at the paper in front of him. Mori noted a new tension in his face: the alertness of the animal that is hunted. "I'll have the data on Kathy Johnson for you Monday, Ninja. American Club at three o'clock. An expert team from the U.S.A. is coming in to sort out her killing. Provide the final word, so to speak. They asked if you'd join the meeting."

Mori nodded. Then Ludlow had the inspector reenact, from

the beginning to end, the KGB kidnapping. When he was finished, Ludlow reacted negatively. What he was looking for, Ludlow explained finally, was a clue to the Russian side of the equation. If Ludlow's hunch was correct, they were the ones who had triggered the Johnson killing. They'd also fed Yuki names of CIA agents, knowing he would kill them. But before they could go after Yuki they had to find out who was the person at the KGB running the operation.

Ludlow rose, went to the radio, and found an interview show with Seiko Matsuda, the most popular female singer in Japan, as guest. Then he returned to the table and made a controlled crash landing on the *zabuton* cushion. Now he was ready to talk.

"My boss, Graves, has some operation underway with Yuki," Ludlow began. "Claims the result will be a 'reliably assessed defector.' That means a high-level defector from the Soviet side. Which also means lots of points for whoever reels him in. Graves would expect an assistant directorship. No less. However, Yuki wouldn't be wasting time on something not connected to his deal with the Soviets. So, somehow, what Mr. Graves and Colonel Yuki are up to is a clue to the Soviet side of the equation. Am I making any sense?"

"None whatsoever." Mori rose to remove boiling water from the Rinnai. He poured two cups of tea and set them on the table. On the radio the popular singer was explaining how she'd recently been asked to do a movie with Tetsu Tamba.

"It's a trade of some sort, Ninja. Trust me. The Japanese side—Yuki—got the names of his enemies, the ones who exploded his career. Kathy Johnson. Carl Lawson. And one more I haven't been able to figure out. All I have is the code name, Robin. Two of them are now known to be dead. The third may already be dead for all I know. But what did the Soviets get? That's what we have to find out. And I have a feeling the reason they're looking for me is part of the equation."

"You think Yuki did the actual killing, then? He was there in the intersection? With me, the foreigner, and the girl?"

"Right, Ninja. He was there, all right. The perfect crime. Send you out to watch the girl. One of the best in the business, correct? Then in front of everyone, he kills the girl. The whole thing was set up immaculately. From the timing so the lighting would be poor. To the crowd. To whatever disguise he wore. And, finally, the instrument he used to kill the girl with. A gun, but fired so no one near him would notice."

Mori rubbed his eyes wearily. "There are too many intangibles. Too many unknowns. For example, we are quite sure the foreigner on the intersection was a high-ranking Soviet. Why would Yuki—if he was working with the Soviets—kill the girl in a way that casts suspicion on a Soviet? The very people he is indebted to? It makes no sense to me."

"Right, Inspector. I'm frankly just as puzzled." Ludlow made a fist then opened his fingers one by one, Asian style, as he summarized the key questions. "One: Who at the KGB made the deal with Yuki? How did he benefit? Two: Why would Yuki set up a Soviet as the killer of Kathy Johnson? Three: What device did Yuki use to kill her?"

Ludlow had a moment of self-doubt. Everything he had was circumstantial. Could it be he had created this elaborate intrigue out of thin air? Ludlow had only three days to go. He would make his report to Harrington and Graves on Monday at the American Club. The expert team would take over. He'd be finished. Yet all he had were questions.

———

As it turned out the trip to Hakone with Hiroko was the high point of Ludlow's week, but not for the reasons he expected. The last typhoon of the season veered north. Weather in the mountains wobbled between cloudy and clear, which was considerably better than in Tokyo, where there were showers both days. The two climbed narrow trails over volcanic rock to emerge on treeless overhangs with breathtaking sweeps to the Pacific. They glimpsed Mount Fuji's majestic slopes from more angles than were found in the whole of Dogyu Okumura's works. They wandered through the brilliant greens of bamboo thicket and the purple haze of thistle-carpeted field. They watched the sky change.

At night they took luxuriously relaxing hot baths in the

marbled *ofuro* of the Fujiya Hotel. Afterward they walked naked except for *yukata* and sandals through musty-carpeted halls to their room. The room became their home, a haven after the active days, with its smell of good straw tatami and cedar *tansu* drawers. Outside the shōji-papered window a brook chuckled on its way east to the ocean. And for the first time in as long a time as Ludlow cared to remember, he relaxed.

He knew he could trust Hiroko. It was nothing tangible, simply years of instinct. And an unwavering directness about her eyes; an honest clarity of voice. He found himself talking freely without fear of walls or Official Secrets acts. She asked questions and he answered without considering motive. She fingered the scar on his knee and he told her of the Hindu Kush, how incredibly harsh it was. How the Afghans cleverly used the stark hills in ambushes. How the day it happened there'd been an omen, a rainbow in the sky. He feared them now, which she said was silly. Rainbows brought good luck. "For some," he'd said and looked away.

She touched a smooth round scar on his side and he explained the Vietnamese tragedy again. She listened with wide intelligent eyes and smiled sadly and wanted to know everything.

Finally, she picked up his lighter where he had left it and for the first time she saw the hesitation in his face. He told her it was just a lighter. Nothing more to it than that. But she asked again later when it was dark and they'd bathed and finished their first sake of the night. So he told her in a quiet angry voice about the lighter, why he'd kept it for luck since Colombo. Why in life the most dangerous times were just when everything seemed to be going right. Like now, he'd added.

Until Colombo he had played by the silly rules. Why not? He was on the fast track. His German was excellent. Assignment to Frankfurt, the glamour station of the vast CIA world network, the largest and most important station, was his for the taking. Frankfurt was where fast-track boys went first before solemnly heroic returns to Washington for the highest-stakes jobs. One could put up with a hellhole like Colombo with a Frankfurt assignment on the horizon.

In Colombo the operation objective had been relatively simple—authorization to penetrate the Aeroflot office near the Galeface Hotel. GRU sources were funding the northern Tamils. The Aeroflot manager was a GRU resident. Certifications in their safe would severely damage if not destroy Soviet prestige in Sri Lanka. All the more important because the Soviets were pressuring for port visitation rights; only Western warships had heretofore been permitted access to the strategic Indian Ocean harbor.

It was all spelled out to Ludlow in the ambassador's office one steamy hot Colombo afternoon. From the political side, quite a lot was at stake, although the mechanics of the operation were basically simple. Ludlow had been through a dozen similar safes, a Russian copy of an ancient Diebold. He set the operation up. The ambassador was assured nothing could go wrong.

The entry went like a piece of cake. So there he was in the Aeroflot office, at the safe. He had barely begun work on the old dinosaur when the shooting started. The Soviets took out two local Senegalese baby-sitters. A seal expert by the name of Goldman was smoking in the hall. Goldman was a friend, a good man with a penchant for wrist chains and dark-skinned women. He'd done a turn with Mossad and told marvelously funny stories about the Lebanese occupation. A Soviet 92 Parabellum at close range blew out his brains. Ludlow barely escaped by sorting a locked steel window shutter and storming by a surprised Soviet back-door sentinel, knocking him cold. Ludlow'd never carried a weapon. One of the Soviets came after him. A tall cocky blond with a Makarov.

Much later, when the Colombo disaster had been weighed by an expert sent in from Washington to assign guilt, they'd decided the blond Soviet had tipped it. He'd been a technical expert who got lucky checking security. Big promotion for him; one of the Senegalese forgot to lock a door. Since Ludlow had planned the op and was the only survivor, the Washington expert assigned him the burden of blame. His subsequent drinking bouts had been duly noted by superiors. That had been the turning point. Ludlow was reassigned to Peshawar and the dirty border war. Definitely not a step up; certainly not on the road to Frankfurt. He'd had nightmares for a time, which was normal. Gradually, his dreams of the blond Soviet faded.

"Forget him," Hiroko said and started to massage Ludlow's back.

Ludlow refilled their cups. "He who hath eaten salt drinketh water." He drained the tiny cup and felt the clear liquid deliciously burn the back of his throat.

She took the empty cup, put it gently aside, and kissed Ludlow very hard on the mouth. Then she pulled him on top of her and, for the first time, let him make love to her.

BLACK OPERATION

It was nearly midnight and from his apartment high atop Lenin Hills, Valeri Kovalenko, First Deputy of Directorate T, quietly smoked and watched the lights wink off in downtown Moscow. On the bed behind him Raya lay asleep, raven hair streaming over satin sheets. He turned to admire her again. In the pose of sleep her face held a childlike innocence.

His eyes strayed to the negligee carelessly thrown across the back of a chair and again he felt the warm tingle in his thighs. They had been lovers for over a year and she still astounded him in bed.

The blond KGB officer grinned to himself as he remembered her earlier tonight, firm buttocks planted against his thighs as she sat astride him screaming all the English obscenities he had taught her. She was a Georgian, with the deep sensitivities of that region. Laughingly he had finally consented to purchase the dress she had seen that afternoon at GUM.

She had lifted the negligee above her head, tossing her magnificent hair carelessly, her breasts milk-white, nipples somehow already erect like frozen droplets of good Caucasian wine.

"Khoroshy! Do you like?'' she asked enticingly, trying to imitate the girls with Vaseline lipstick who stood near the Kievsky Station entrance after eight p.m.

"Very," he'd whispered. "And must I pay?"

"Skolko?" She was laughing, a sound like a shiver. "For how long?"

"Sto lyet," he replied seriously. "One hundred years."

"Lenin, help me. You are bigger than Spassky Tower tonight."

———

The phone rang softly, urgently, jolting his thoughts. It was the special phone; the others had been turned off. Kovalenko, the second-in-command of the KGB Technical Directorate, lifted the receiver. He was the youngest ranking officer in the organization by at least five years, a virtuoso in his knowledge and proficiency in the strategic area of electronics, particularly computers that the USSR did not have. He looked quickly over at Raya; she had not been awakened.

Malik's voice was wry and conspiratorial. The leader of Directorate T said, "Fortune never seemed so blind as to those upon whom she has bestowed no favors."

It was a game they often played over drinks at the Caprice Club on Kalinin Prospekt. Identify the quote. However, Kovalenko knew that the late call from Comrade Malik meant more than games were at stake. T was part of the First Chief Directorate; its importance had been confirmed a month ago when the annual honors lists were published. The KGB Technical Directorate had won the lion's share.

"La Rochefoucauld," answered Kovalenko, wondering what was up.

"Ah-hah! You are wrong." Comrade Malik laughed just loud enough to suggest the hint of vodka.

"Then who?" Kovalenko was never wrong and he knew it. His English training was the best available in the KGB apparatus: he'd done the special school for illegals. He'd done Japanese and Chinese as well.

"Comrade Pachinkov is the author." There was a note of triumph in the chief's voice.

"The Region Seven director? The Tokyo resident?"

"Precisely. Do you not agree good fortune is essential to a successful intelligence career? His meteoric rise has apparently slowed. Ever since his team was involved in the unauthorized death of an American. I have just come from dinner with the director of the First Chief Directorate. He retires in December."

"What is it, then, comrade?"

"Your travel orders will be waiting for you tomorrow morning. It is essential that you reach Tokyo in time to attend a memorial service for an American girl. Please observe the operation sequence very closely. Three ranking officers and a psychologist, an expert on Japan, will brief you tomorrow. Unfortunately, I must be in Leningrad. Ten dossiers of Japanese were received by pouch today. One was selected. Do not reveal our choice to the Tokyo Referentura. They have another opinion and we don't want them to know the pieces we will play. Contact Comrade Pachinkov only after you have settled in and are ready."

"I understand." Kovalenko disliked the rivalry, the hide-and-seek each side played against the other. Yet he also knew it was necessary for the security of the participants. There were whispers of strange disappearances. Deaths. Rumors of a U.S. spy in their midst.

"The product is an AI prototype, the size of an electric typewriter. Avionics." Malik's voice was enthusiastic, building in pitch. "We want you to bring it out alone."

"A black operation?" Kovalenko tried to keep the surprise out of his voice. He'd struck a rich lode.

"We can't use normal channels; too much risk."

Kovalenko smiled because he knew the other reasons. Malik didn't want to share the spoils. The excuse was that Pachinkov kept his own operation to himself. The KGB had always insisted on a highly compartmentalized ship. Malik was using that policy to his own ends.

"Agreed," was all Kovalenko said.

"Nothing of the operation is to be revealed to anyone at the Soviet embassy in Tokyo, to protect your own safety. There is still a notable lack of discipline in that organization. Only meet with Pachinkov to let him know you're there. No details. He will be held responsible if there are any leaks."

"Of course," Kovalenko said. "Why isn't he handling it?"

Malik repressed a derisive snicker. "Pachinkov overreacted to a CIA operation. Originally, his team was to perform the surgery. As well, there's the annual hunt on inside Directorate T for a U.S. penetration. Such nonsense. However, absolute secrecy is essential for this project so I am handling it personally. Let's have a success, otherwise who knows what the Politburo will be told."

"I will not fail you."

"Your splendid achievements in Geneva, Colombo, Hong Kong, and now here were recalled to the director tonight. He wanted our best man on this assignment. He was quite impressed. I believe a dacha might be arranged. You would have to share for the first year; alternate weekends."

"That would be entirely satisfactory."

"Kuntsevo most probably. I hear the boar hunting is good in the fall. My best to Raya . . ." The chief of T was chuckling as he hung up the phone.

Kovalenko looked over to where the beautiful Soviet girl lay asleep. She was his supreme perquisite. Power had brought her to him. Success. With success came power, yielding the other bonuses as well: "special distributions" passes to Voyentorg, which provided the satin sheets, the stereo, and the imported appointments to his luxurious though small apartment; his chauffeured Volga. He might even love Raya, even though she no doubt reported everything to her superiors. Perhaps it was the nature of his perverse job; or the latent influence of an authoritarian father. Whatever it was, Kovalenko vastly preferred risk to certainty.

The blond Russian moved over to the window and stared out at the city. Moscow had been swallowed in darkness save for an occasional sweep of headlights and the lonely green pinpoints of gas streetlamps.

He understood it all, of course. Malik wanted the First Directorate chairmanship when it was vacated within weeks. It would be the next step up the rung for him. But it would represent the same step for several others, including Pachinkov. So a subtle documentation of blunders leading to the emergency insertion of Kovalenko's expertise into Region Seven would do it. Kovalenko's success would demonstrate superior tradecraft; show the leadership how operations are won. He, of course, would be pulled along in the backwash of Malik's promotion. The stakes were considerably higher than a dacha in Kuntsevo.

He began to organize the tools of his craft. The first fingers of dawn were reaching toward the spires of the Kremlin when he finally finished packing. He lay down beside the magnificent Soviet girl and almost instantly fell asleep.

CHAPTER 25

TYPHOON

Mori watched the morning news, about the typhoon that had hit Japan in the far north. The announcer's claim of its destructive force ran in counterpoint to the sounds of Mori's mother's koto. Her recital was scheduled for two p.m.

Waves were leaping over the breakwaters on Hokkaido and bamboo thickets near Sapporo were bent flat from gale-force winds. Gusts of up to eighty kilometers offshore, the stern-faced announcers warned. The networks, particularly the government channels, loved disaster. It allowed them to play father. There was repeated and detailed advice on what should be worn, which districts were safe, and what time the storm was expected to clear the northern districts. Tokyo could expect showers with occasional heavy downpours.

"I thought you weren't going to be late last night," Mitsuko said as she entered the tiny dining-living room.

"Something unexpected came up."

Instead of her normal house gown, Mitsuko wore a pretty blue and white print *yukata*, tied with a yellow sash. "You were drinking again, weren't you?"

"No, I wasn't drinking. Just a couple."

"You don't have to get angry."

The TV announced that ten people had died because of the storm. Enthusiastically the reporter predicted that the count would go much higher. Tokyo weather was still peaceful with only sporadic squalls. This typhoon would stay north, less a thundering brute here than a feline attacker, spitting and hissing and unpredictable.

"You look nice in your *yukata*. Something special today?" Mori had hoped for a peaceful day at home.

"No. Just that I invited Erika over for lunch."

"Did you have to do that?"

"Do I need a reason for everything? She's a friend. And I thought you two got along; that's what she says anyway."

"What did she say?"

"Oh, nothing. But you've seen her two times this week; that's more than I have. You've been silent since you abandoned me at Suzuki's party."

Mori nearly swore. "She's part of the case I'm working on. I was hoping to rest this Sunday. Something came up at the party, that's all."

"You can rest with Erika here, can't you? We never go out anymore. What came up? Was it something to do with your job?"

"I can't discuss it right now."

"Okay, if you won't bring it up then I will. Erika told me you saw Suzuki's Mercedes the night of the party. That's why you ran off and abandoned me, right?"

"No. I was called away from the party. An emergency."

"You're such a terrible liar, Mori-kun. If you like I'll tell him to stop picking me up in the morning."

"I understand perfectly; you needn't explain."

"Have you been drinking this morning? What's in that glass?"

"I wanted to relax."

"You always have an excuse, don't you?" She sighed and went into the tiny kitchen. She had really tried, she thought to herself. Done her best. But now she was certain. Their marriage was beyond all hope.

The doorbell rang.

Mitsuko served fish *nabemono* and *cha* for lunch. His mother decided to eat in her own room. Erika was very formal. She mentioned how well Mori looked, which was an outright lie, and then applauded Mitsuko's ingenuity as a homemaker in spite of the fact she was one of the busiest and most indispensable staff at ICOT. Mitsuko blushed at the size of the compliment and the particular emphasis given to the word *indispensable.*

"I understand she is highly valued by her boss." Mori tried a ridged potato chip which had been served with a dip for dessert.

Mitsuko smiled apologetically at Erika; her husband was being unreasonable. She got up to heat the coffee.

"It is a business relationship," Erika whispered, "pure and simple. Like I told you at the party."

Mitsuko returned from the kitchen with coffee on a tray. "What are you two whispering about?" She set the coffee down with a pitcher of cream and a bowl of cube sugar.

"Erika is just telling me I have nothing to fear," Mori intoned. "Your boss's interest in you is strictly business."

Mitsuko tossed her head. "Honest to God, can't we talk about something else?" She poured cream for Erika, then herself.

"There's a simple solution," Mori said brightly. "I will buy a Mercedes. Then Mitsuko can drive herself to work without suffering a decline in status. How do you get to work, Erika?"

"I take the subway."

"From tomorrow I will take the subway," Mitsuko said. "There, does that satisfy you?"

"It makes me feel like I have fallen short, to tell the truth. It makes me feel inferior that I did not think to provide a Mercedes."

"Our own house." Mitsuko took a sip of coffee, her nostrils flaring like a mare that had run too far too fast. "This is where you should start if you really cared about me. But you do not care! You spend everything you earn on people I don't know. You never tell me where you are, or when you will be home.

Lately you smell of alcohol every night so I can hardly sleep. Wednesday you didn't even bother to come home at all. I have had just about enough of your selfishness." Mitsuko finished her coffee, got up, and went into the kitchen.

Mori did not drink any of his coffee. He apologized to Erika for his wife's emotionalism and excused himself from the table to go upstairs. He settled in the study and listened to rain that had started to beat against the house. It came and went in waves, booming against the panes, then retreating in a whisper of receding sound. He poured himself a Suntory and drank it straight. What had gotten into Mitsuko? he wondered. Her job at ICOT had changed her, showed her there was more to life than taking care of a husband? He poured another Suntory and shook his head, then drained the glass and closed his eyes.

A half hour passed while Mori dozed. There was a sudden bustle of excitement from downstairs. He heard the high-pitched laughter of his mother, then a door slammed and it was quiet. He went downstairs. Erika was alone reading a magazine. The clock read 2:10.

"Your mother forgot the time and so did we." Erika looked directly into his eyes. "She was going to miss her recital, so Mitsuko went with her. They didn't want to bother you."

Mori went to the front door. The rain had increased again and the wind had picked up, driving the rain into his face.

"They're carrying the koto?"

"Mitsuko's helping her. They left in a rush."

"She should have called me," Mori said. He found his jacket and hat.

"They're probably at the Rojin Club by now. Mitsuko said it was just up the hill. Relax." She patted the cushion next to her. "Monday night is Tori-no-ichi Festival. Will you take me? Please?"

"My mother was wearing her new kimono?"

"She looked very nice. You know how she is when she makes up her mind. Mitsuko tried to get her to wait until the rain stopped. The TV says we're just getting a fringe. Your mother wouldn't hear of not going."

Mori sat down. "Monday night is okay," he said. He didn't know what else to say. She filled in the silence.

"I'm afraid I love you, Mori-san. I tried very hard not to let it happen. I'm sorry."

Before Mori could think, the phone rang. It was Mitsuko. She was upset. "She nearly fainted on the hill. I had to carry her here. Please come quickly. Bring the pills." The phone went dead.

Mori almost stumbled over his mother's koto abandoned to the rain near the top of the hill. He picked it up and reached the Ryojin Club nearly out of breath. His mother was fine. Several of the older ladies hovered around her. She waved when she saw Mori.

"My friend takes the same pills I do," she said proudly. "I'll just rest a few minutes. What time was it when you left the house?" Mitsuko was standing next to her mother-in-law, a strange, frightened expression on her face.

"Quarter past two," Mori answered quickly.

"That's what I thought too," his mother replied. "We had to run up this steep hill because I thought I was late. I didn't want to miss my own recital; I'd be the laughingstock. Look at the clock over there."

An old wall clock read 1:30.

"Someone deliberately put our clock ahead one hour to do this to me. And the *kanzashi* before."

Mitsuko's face had gone colorless. She was looking from her husband to her mother-in-law.

Mori shook his head as if to clear it: "Perhaps the clock needed repair; let's not be hasty." He felt the anger constrict his chest.

"There's nothing wrong with the clock," his mother cut in. "It was a gift from my mother and I have it checked every year. Someone did this on purpose. Someone who hates me."

Mori's mother was staring impassively at the door where Erika had just entered shaking rain from a pert red slicker. She hurried over.

"Are you okay, Oka-san?"

Mori's mother stood and stared at Mitsuko. "I'll live but

there are some people who apparently wish I'd just go away."

Mitsuko could no longer control her face. Tears streaming down her cheeks, she rushed into the ladies' room. Erika followed. Mori's mother shook her head:

"I don't want Mitsuko in my house again. Not anymore. That's final." She wiped a tear from the corner of her eye. "Now I can't give my recital either."

Mori started gathering her things. They called a cab but would have to wait two hours. He ended up carrying her *ombu*-style on his back after the rain slackened. When they reached home he made sure she was dry and put her to bed. By five o'clock, Mitsuko had not called and Mori decided it was just as well. For the first time since his marriage he slept alone. He didn't sleep well. He kept dreaming he was caught in a huge tsunami and it was carrying him farther and farther out to sea.

CHAPTER 26

SHINOBAZU POND

"What in the name of Lenin is going on here?" Chief KGB Resident Pachinkov stood suddenly, nearly toppling his chair. He slammed his hands against his waist and stalked the office. "We cannot even perform a simple operation anymore? What has happened to us, Sergei?"

The GRU chief sat humbly in front of Pachinkov's huge desk. "It was not so simple, comrade. This Japanese had special training, I am sure of it. His hands were like nothing you have ever seen. We were lucky he did not kill poor Popov."

"So Ludlow has disappeared and Mori didn't cooperate?"

"We will find him."

"I know you will, Sergei Ivanovich. I know you will. But we are out of time." Pachinkov came back to his desk and sat down heavily. He said, "Let me tell you what has happened." He then went through the whole miserable affair. The envelope had been left at the gate. The message itself didn't make any sense to the guards, fortunately. It was addressed to the chief resident. He'd needed only a quick look to understand what had happened. The message read: *Shinobazu Four ACGF Snow White.*

Sergei leaned forward with interest. "What did the note mean? Who put it there?"

Pachinkov grimaced. "I am to meet him Monday at Shinobazu Pond, the agent who has been sent in to run the Starfire collection. His name is Valeri Kovalenko. Directorate T. One of Malik's stars."

"It would be relatively easy for me to take him right away. An accident." Sergei's eyes squinted with shrewdness.

"If an accident occurs before he acquires the Starfire, we would be blamed. Besides, then we would never know for sure, would we?"

"If he is a lure?"

"Yes. If he has been sent in specifically to destroy us or if the Starfire is the true objective. It is quite a risky undertaking."

"You worry about the same thing."

"Of course!" Pachinkov exclaimed. "There has been no validation of the Starfire data. When in your memory has Center trusted a sole source? Never, comrade. So tell me why now suddenly we have a Shavki agent in our midst dangling like a worm on a hook? Tell me that, Sergei Ivanovich Vasilyev!"

"If you promise to erect a statue to my memory in Red Square, I will whisper it," Sergei answered.

"Oblivion is the natural lot of anyone not present. Pushkin wrote that, eh? You disagree with him, Sergei Ivanovich, eh? You don't think our good friends at T Directorate wish us oblivion? Now here is what I want you to do."

———

Shinobazu Pond is near Ueno Park and of good size. Walks divide it into three water courses, two shallow and marshy with reeds, providing ideal shoreline for the fall migrations despite the fact it is in a ward of downtown Tokyo. Today, these outer waters were filled by thousands of ducks. They basked in the unseasonably warm sun (days after typhoons are invariably clear and sunny), floating on the metallic surface, whistling and playing among the rushes or simply watching others of their rank approaching in wonderful formations that turned in line on the glide paths and swung cleanly into final approach.

On his way through the park, Pachinkov had identified mallards, pintails, and blue-winged teals. No doubt many had flown in from as far away as Siberia. That turned his mind to the work immediately ahead. Sergei should already be there.

An arched bridge in peeling red paint gave access to the tiny island. The Shinto shrine there was devoid of worship objects. At the altar was only a mirror. Pachinkov stood in front for a moment, then threw two coins into the wooden grate. For luck from their ten thousand gods. He recalled that the mirror symbolized the Japanese heart, the innate goodness of the race which stemmed from reflection rather than contemplation. He smiled. Another jewel to their uniqueness, admirers would argue, although history teaches that the Romans held similar views some three thousand years before.

Around the side of the altar he found stairs that led to a loft where Sergei would be—the one man in the embassy he could trust! They had gone over the details carefully after Sergei had obtained maps of the pond. The little shrine was at its very center, and from the third floor a sighting was possible on all sides. The electronics could be set up there. Whenever Kovalenko appeared, the sensitive equipment would be turned on. Whatever the Shavki from Center had to say would be used to hang him and Malik later if possible. The stakes were too great; nothing could be left to chance.

As Sergei also described it, the shrine had fallen into disuse. Across from the gate to Shinobazu Pond was Yushima Shrine, which was famous not only for its plum trees but also for the *shinjū* suicide of a famous geisha and her student lover. The Japanese were horrible snobs; anything that wasn't quite first-rate was ignored. The shrine was thus empty today.

He found the stairs steep and covered in dust. On the second floor was a musty room filled with soot covering idols of minor gods. From the third floor he heard a board creak. "Sergei, my old friend," he called softly. "Is that you?"

"Come quickly, comrade," replied the familiar voice. "I believe our friend is already in place."

Windows on all sides were without glass. The new portable directional microphones with amplifiers and antichaff devices had been set up on the south side. Sergei pointed out that window. For a moment Pachinkov saw nothing out of the ordinary. A sunny Monday afternoon; strollers were thinning along the pond's picturesque walks. Benches were emptying except for those occupied by less vigorous denizens of the downtown area who slept with newspapers over their heads. One of the figures stretched and removed his paper. He sat up, checked his watch, and Pachinkov had his blond.

"Did he see me?"

"No chance of it. I've been checking him since you entered the park." Pachinkov could hear the tension in his lieutenant's voice and checked the window again. The blond was glancing casually around. Looking for anyone irregular, no doubt. Very cautious fellow, this Valeri Kovalenko.

Pachinkov watched as Kovalenko walked leisurely to the edge of the pond and started feeding a growing crowd of ducks. The KGB chief checked his watch. It was almost time. He said to Sergei, "A cipher advised today that the head of the CIA's Directorate of Science and Technology will arrive in Tokyo. Named Harrington. It could have to do with the American girl's death or Starfire or both. We must be alert, and remember this is now between the CIA and Malik's agent out there. Not us. In any event, if we get the next few days right, we should be going back to Moscow very soon. Let us concentrate on that." He stood and saluted in the casual way of old friends. "Do it well, Sergei, and you shall have that cottage in the Urals and those sables." He started down the stairs.

"Do not forget the newspaper, comrade."

"Yes, Sergei." Pachinkov was still smiling to himself as he headed out of the shrine on his way to the rendezvous.

——

The agent from Moscow did not seem to notice Pachinkov as he made his first pass. The Tokyo resident appeared to be a relaxed tourist out for a walk with a newspaper under his arm; left arm and *Japan Times*. Right meant trouble. One turn of the pond if everything was satisfactory, then the recognition parole to be initiated. Kovalenko was to be hatless on the first turn, capped on the second to confirm all clear. Pachinkov felt like he was in the field again, not an entirely unpleasant sensation.

He was nearing the blond feeder again. The man was much too noticeable for his line of work; he looked like an actor from Mosfilm. Must have real talent, this Shavki. He tried to remember if he'd met Kovalenko before. Nothing came. The hat was in place now, a black baseball cap with braid, the kind the U.S. astronauts wore. Nice little piece of insubordination there. If this fellow kicked it in any way, Pachinkov would have his career.

"Where are you from?" The voice was low and firm. The words were English, perfectly spoken. Up close Pachinkov could see the youthful cockiness of the man's grin. He very nearly lost his temper.

"New York City," Pachinkov replied in a guttural accent.

"Chicago myself." Kovalenko seemed to be enjoying the chief resident's discomfort. English was not one of Pachinkov's better languages.

"A very windy city." Pachinkov struggled with the accent but finally the procedure was completed. He turned and walked away. Kovalenko fed the ducks the last of his bread and caught up, his long legs narrowing the distance easily.

"Thanks for coming." Kovalenko put his hands in the pockets of his raincoat and hunched slightly as if to deemphasize the slightly shorter stature of the chief resident. "There are several points I needed to discuss."

"Then go ahead," Pachinkov urged. "I have little time."

"Yes, of course. First I bring greetings from Colonel Malik of Directorate T. Your splendid work with Japanese electronics firms is a model and inspiration to us all."

Pachinkov ducked his head in acknowledgment. Malik would have him skewered and demoted if he could. An entirely untrustworthy peer. Muddying his waters too. It came to him then where he had met Kovalenko before. The face had not changed that much, really. Geneva, at least five years ago. There'd been a big push to obtain DEC PDP-11s plus a more powerful VAX range through a setup in the city. Kovalenko had been running it and with more than moderate success, he recalled. They would ship a kit into Geneva airport with legitimate end-user certs; then it would disappear. Great people, the Swiss.

"I hope you'll not be disrupting any of our in-place programs," Pachinkov said vaguely, but the threat was clearly there.

"I will handle it alone, which I believe should relieve your fears." Kovalenko spoke sincerely and watched the older man's face for reaction. He barely caught the flash of anger that momentarily captured Pachinkov's features.

Pachinkov folded his face into a patient smile. Except for the eyes. "Good," he said. "Then you will only need our assistance on the prototype exit procedure . . ."

"I will handle that alone also, Comrade Chief," Kovalenko said without looking at Pachinkov's face. "The prototype will be taken out using my own channel. Center believes there will be less risk."

Pachinkov was speechless; he wanted to shout obscenities at this confident Muscovite. To tear into him and shake that calm cockiness from his face. He turned instead and took a few steps away and his shoulders heaved as he took a deep breath. When he turned once again, he had regained control: "But there is a second channel for the special pieces. An absolutely secure routing."

"I have heard of your special route. Quite unique. My compliments. If it was in my power, I would change the orders. Things would be far simpler for myself. Unfortunately, there is great urgency in Directorate T for the product. The drawback of your special channel is the time it would take, I think you would be the first to admit."

"That I will admit."

"Furthermore a transmitter could malfunction. A crate left on a dock by mistake unattended, exposed to the weather."

"Certainly you are not considering taking it out by yourself. Without support?"

"That I am not allowed to mention to anyone, Comrade Pachinkov. You will understand of course. The orders are quite strict. It will be a northern route."

Pachinkov flushed. "But it could jeopardize my entire operation if you are caught. It has taken years to build what we have achieved. Center shows obscene disregard for our future."

"Then I suppose it is in both our interests that I get out unharmed, Colonel."

Pachinkov's mind screamed for retribution. Malik had done this to goad him, to force him to an error. Could it be that the operation was the key to whether he or Malik obtained the directorship of the prized First Directorate? Malik the bastard! His mind churned with alternatives. "Emergency contact then?" Certainly they would require at least that!

"No, comrade," Kovalenko said politely. "I have a carefully detailed instruction. Any special situations have been covered completely." Kovalenko knew this wasn't true, but also that he must keep this man out of it to minimize the danger to himself. He had heard stories of how vicious the infighting could get in the field on operations tens of thousands of kilometers from Moscow. Even to the point where it resulted in unexplained deaths.

"If there is nothing more, then I will leave you here," Pachinkov said, looking at his steel watch. The jauntiness had returned to his speech, as if nothing bad had passed between them. He waved as one would after chatting casually with a stranger, then headed for an exit that led to a street next to Ueno Station which advertised small but intimate porno films. When he was out of sight, Pachinkov again checked his watch and smiled. Sergei would be on him now. Let's see if that smart aleck son of a bitch from Directorate T could shake him.

———

Kovalenko spent the rest of the afternoon sitting at an outdoor coffee shop on Omotesando just down the road from the Tokyo Union Church, which he visited last. A nice lady in administration at the church checked the bookings and confirmed in a thin voice edged by sadness that the memorial service for the American girl would be held on Wednesday. Three thirty in the afternoon, right after a baptism. Things were a little crowded just now. Kovalenko took one of their cards with the address written in Japanese. "For flowers," he smiled and did a little bow when he left.

Such a nice boy, the motherly lady said to her assistant when he'd gone. Usually only the older people were so thoughtful.

CHAPTER 27

HARRINGTON'S FAVOR

Mori and Ludlow arrived at the American Club early so they could talk. There was a Sony on in the bar tuned to highlights of the Japan World Series, which had concluded last week. Cooper, Harrington, and Graves were to show in a half hour. Mori was in a quiet mood.

When the drinks came Mori lifted his glass in a toast: "My wife left me." Then he downed half the glass.

Ludlow said how sorry he was. "I hope it has nothing to do with the case."

"I never could get her pregnant," Mori smiled. "That was the problem."

In the awkward pause that followed, Ludlow handed the Japanese police officer an envelope with the promised data about Kathy Johnson. Then the big American went into unnecessary detail on how he was being taken off the case. A team of experts had arrived and would be in the meeting today.

Mori glanced briefly at the pages in the envelope. Ludlow had included a summary of Kathy Johnson's activities in the MicroDec case; a review of her Exodus Sixty activities in Japan; the need for a gun, false passport, and escape route to North America as a part of that work. There was nothing really incriminating or indicative of illegal espionage activity. "We all done then?" Mori asked.

Ludlow shook his head. "I want to find out what the Russians are up to."

"Very patriotic, but aren't you off the case? In Japan disobeying orders means tearing up your career."

Ludlow swirled the ice in his Bushmill's. "I'll figure out a way to stay involved."

"I don't see how," Mori said, but it was the answer he'd wanted to hear.

"This expert team doesn't know anything," Ludlow said. "Within a week they'll be itching to go home. I'll stay close to them. Become their liaison man. There are a hundred ways I can stay involved."

"You are sometimes very much like a Japanese."

"Devious."

"No. Pragmatic. It is a result of superior education. We have a saying: It takes only twenty years to grow a forest from saplings; but one hundred years to grow an educated person."

"Then trust me, Ninja. We're buddies. I'm not going to let you down."

There was a burst of noise from the TV. The Giants had won the first game. Mori scowled and emptied his glass. Ludlow ordered another Bushmill's for himself and Suntory and water for Mori.

Cooper showed up first in a freshly pressed suit and nervous grin, looking like a branch manager whose boss is in town. He nodded at Mori and turned to Ludlow as he sat down, "Harrington is going to ask you a favor. Thought I'd warn you."

"Have a drink," Ludlow said. "You've just ruined my afternoon but don't let that stop you from enjoying yourself."

Cooper ordered a vodka and tonic and stared around the bar. "Has to do with the FSX," he said. "Can't tell you more. Well I'll be damned, there's Joe Turner! Hey Joe!"

They exchanged waves and then Cooper told the story of Joe Turner, an expatriate entrepreneur who'd made a fortune in Japan then lost it. Mori split his attention between the game and the conversation.

Turner had heard about a water shortage in the Tokyo area each summer and set out to determine the cause. Surprisingly the source was Japanese female concern for losing face in the public toilets. Farting was bad manners, you see.

"Wait a minute," Mori held up a hand. "You mean to tell me it isn't bad manners in other countries?"

Cooper smiled. "No, but Japanese will go to absurd lengths to prevent people from seeing or hearing reality."

"Nonsense. It's just superior manners."

"Like people urinating in the streets in broad daylight?"

"That is just old people who don't know any better. The youngsters have manners."

"Let him tell the story, Ninja," Ludlow interjected. "I can't figure out how farting relates to a water shortage."

Women, Cooper went on, were flushing toilets every time they expected flatulence so no one would hear. All this flushing had driven up water bills and created the traditional summer water shortage. Turner set about to solve the problem and make himself a million. He invented a machine that made a flushing sound when you pushed a button and could be installed in all the booths. Solved the water shortage.

"Yankee ingenuity will win every time." Ludlow toasted the others.

"Sounds pretty farfetched," Mori kept his eyes on the TV.

"Actually it's true," Cooper said, "only he didn't make his million. The locals reverse-engineered his gadget, copied it, underpriced him, and drove him out of the market. Sound familiar?"

"Good old Japanese ingenuity," Mori said. "Don't tell me you believe everything that happens to America is Japan's fault?"

"No," Ludlow replied. "Forty percent. Maybe an even half."

Cooper took off his glasses, pinched his nose, and stared at Mori. "What you did to our microchip industry was unethical. You sent a wave of people into Silicon Valley and stole our know-how."

Mori stared back at the American in disbelief. "Most of what was given us was of your own free accord. Now Americans are crying because we worked harder with what we had."

Cooper pointed at the TV screen. "We invented baseball. You copied that too."

Ludlow held up his giant paws. "Gentlemen, gentlemen. I'm afraid we're not going to solve this one today. I make it points even and suggest an adjournment for tea." He held up his glass and winked at Mori. "It's the leadership anyhow that sets the course. To the Japanese people."

Mori picked up his Suntory and nodded reluctantly. "To the American people."

Cooper added, "To all losers everywhere." They finally drank to that.

Just when it looked like Harrington wasn't going to show, he appeared with Graves and two others, strangers to Ludlow. Harrington was rangy and Presbyterian, with thick hair cut athletically short. He was youthful enough to be envied but with a directness of eye and firmness of handshake that older men would respect. There were those who claimed Harrington was a trifle impersonal and others who insisted he was cold-blooded with subordinates—the kinds of complaints that always revolve around the highly motivated and the singularly successful.

The head of the most prestigious directorate in the CIA was young *and* rich. He'd made two Massachusetts fortunes in computer software by the age of thirty, when Route 128 and Foxboro was his home. Now it was Silver Springs and a Maryland Tudor townhouse. In the business of U.S. computer security he was creating his own legend. He had come to espionage late, Ludlow reflected; maybe that's why he excelled at it.

The two strangers were introduced around: "George" and "Mike." The expert team. Both were from the Science and Technology Directorate and attentive to their boss's moods. George was the leader of the two, Ludlow decided, by virtue of age and being introduced first.

To the table Cooper explained that Harrington was in Japan as a member of the Military Technology Commission; everyone knew what that was, didn't they? To his surprise no one did. The MTC, as Cooper called it, was legalized by the peace treaty after the war. That treaty prohibited Japan from military export except to the United States. The treaty remained in effect today; Japan could export strategic technology, armament, and military aerospace products only to the Pentagon. MTC cherry-picked and negotiated the price of Japanese military high tech during periodic buying trips. Its members, including Harrington, had been appointed by the president.

Harrington assured everyone, but mainly Mori, that it was a two-way street. The treaty was fair since in return Japan was allowed to stand under the U.S. military umbrella. Also it received contracts. For example, the U.S.A. had licensed Japan some years ago to produce the F-15 fighter.

"Mitsubishi is doing a fine job, too, sir," Cooper added in the pause. Ludlow nodded. He'd heard that Mitsubishi had bettered what U.S. plants had turned out with the same blueprints. Of course, the F-15 had been an obsolete fighter when it was licensed.

So they were partners, then, wasn't that so? Harrington had smiled for the Japanese and Mori took one ear off the baseball to mollify the grand dragon of the DS&T.

"It is so," said the inspector.

"Then," Harrington said, looking hurt and puzzled at the same time, "will somebody please tell me why our government hasn't been officially informed of the Starfire? The MTC supposedly is advised of all new technology in the pipeline. Is that true or isn't it?" Harrington turned to Cooper.

"True," Cooper said sadly.

"Maybe it doesn't exist yet," Mike said, and grinned vaguely at Mori. "Maybe it's just a code name and a piece of paper." Mike tapped a thick finger on the side of his drink. His cherubic features glowed with finality. His voice was totally committed.

"Inspector Mori," Harrington chuckled. "You can ignore anything Mike, here, says. He's our expert. That means he doesn't believe you or me or our governments. On top of that he likes to insult people. Don't take anything he says personally. He's my pit bulldog."

Mori tugged at his collar and stared at the TV screen, where a Seibu batter had just homered in game three. He wasn't sure whether the Americans were being insulting or sincere. "Perhaps you should discuss the Starfire with my government."

"We fully intend to." Harrington beamed at Mori as if he'd just made a very incisive suggestion.

George, the second expert, was measuring the TV screen. "That home run would have been an out in any U.S. ballpark except Fenway," he said with total confidence. He had a New England accent and a craggy face like a field full of stones.

Harrington turned to Ludlow. Mike and George, he explained, would take over the investigation into Kathy Johnson's death. Their minds were totally open. They were very impressed with what they'd heard about Ludlow's work on the case thus far and the efforts of the Japanese police. Graves cleared his throat and added that close cooperation between Operations and DS&T was essential. Harrington nodded and turned the floor over to Ludlow.

Ludlow kept his presentation short. If he knew anything about experts, it was that they didn't like to be told answers. Also, he didn't want Graves tipping Yuki. So he concentrated on the equation concept: that there was a Japanese side to the assassination, and a Soviet side. With Mori's help he had traced the source of the bullets to a gangster group in Yokohama. However, three puzzling questions remained:

"First," he said, "what device was used to kill Kathy Johnson? The seventy-six-degree angle on the head shot means someone other than a tall foreigner killed her."

George held up his hand slowly. "Careful on that one, Bob. Don't know I even buy your angle since it wasn't our lab data. As I recall the head shot was a Glaser frag-point."

"Right." Ludlow took a deep breath.

"So how did they get an angle on a bullet that fragged inside the victim? Not that it can't be done but we'd like to see a bit more before leaping to conclusions."

"There was a six-centimeter entry," Mori said, "before the fragmentation occurred. The way the bullet is designed the force of the burst is directed inward to maximize damage. I asked the same question of our forensic lab. Their detailed reply is in Japanese but I can assure you the calculation is quite accurate."

George nodded politely. "I'm not doubting their professionalism, Inspector, but we would like a copy of that report if you don't mind. Now what were the other two questions you had, Bob?"

Ludlow nodded. "Both have to do with a misdirection shooting theory. A misdirection is a format where, while the victim's attention is on an obvious threat, another person shoots her; in this case using a device that did not resemble a gun, carried in a manner that was nonthreatening."

"Jesus, Bob," Mike piped up. "What you been smoking? That's an awfully complicated series of assumptions there. Anything to back it up?"

Ludlow scratched the side of his nose. "Not if you don't buy the angle theory. Everything's based on that."

"Look, I've got an idea." Harrington understood the meeting was rapidly getting out of hand. On the surface, anyway, it was necessary to maintain the semblance of goodwill between Operations and DS&T. His boys were shredding the Operations theory based on its source, not its credibility. "Let's hold off attacking Operations' conclusions until we have a chance to review the reports again. Let him finish."

Ludlow wound up the presentation quickly. He reviewed the second question: If someone other than the foreigner had shot her, why was the foreigner set up, or was his presence accidental?"

George didn't bother to raise his hand this time. "Japanese Homicide got a description of the man, didn't they?"

"Over fifty eyewitnesses have given information," Mori said. "However there is little consistency in reports."

"Never is." George smiled. "Ever see an accident then ask someone else what they saw? Like two different events. We've had a run at the Homicide data already using computers. I think we know who the culprit is. As for him being set up by someone else, I personally don't think so. However, we'll consider every option."

Harrington nodded approvingly. "Perhaps we could get to

Bob's last point then?" He pulled out a handful of Schimmel-penninck cigars and passed them around. Ludlow stuck his in his pocket and continued:

"If a Japanese team was working with the Soviets, what kind of deal has been struck? Who at the KGB was behind it and what did he gain personally?"

George folded his arms and rocked back in his chair. "In for a penny, in for a pound," he smiled. "Everything is hypothe-sized around your misdirection theory, Bob?"

Ludlow's throat was dry. He knew they weren't buying it, but what did he expect? "That's as far as we have gone," he concluded and drained his glass.

Harrington cleared his throat and said what a fine job he thought Ludlow had done. He said he especially liked the idea of a Soviet plot with a Japanese tie-in. Then he turned to Inspector Mori. "How do you feel about that, Inspector?"

"As your expert says," Mori began, "everything is specu-lation. To answer your question, yes, I believe a Japanese could have been involved in the shooting. In that case, however, it was a Japanese working against the interests of Japan and for a foreign power. A traitor, then."

Harrington thanked the inspector for his insight and began a summary to draw the meeting to a close.

Graves had said little through all of this. He wasn't surprised by the attempts to discredit Ludlow's theories. No doubt they'd drawn up their own game plan. A DS&T coverup was in prog-ress. There was nothing he could do about it now. Harrington, especially, he didn't like. Too young, too sure of himself, too cagey. Too well prepared. Graves was reminded of another time in his career: Brussels.

A member of the KGB had contacted Operations, willing to supply data. Graves's job was to lead him about the city, totally sanitize him, then get him to a meeting with the deputy di-rector of Operations, who had flown in from Washington. The DDO also wanted Graves's opinion on whether the man was an authentic.

Graves had plenty of time while they chased around the city together. But Graves felt the KGBer was too meticulous, much

too smooth, terribly sincere. And he seemed to have anticipated all of Graves's questions. Graves called the DDO before
meeting time with a negative and the event was scrubbed. He
simply left the man on a streetcorner.

A month later came a second contact. It was the same man.
This time the director of Operations handled it personally. The
Soviet turned out to be authentic. Graves very nearly lost his
job. At the Soviet mole's insistence, the Operations director
interviewed him alone. His identity had since become the most
tightly guarded secret in the Operations Directorate. No one
besides the director knew exactly who the KGB agent was or
where he now worked inside the KGB. The word was he was
more valuable than even Penkovsky had been.

———

The meeting lasted through the final game of the Japan World
Series TV highlights. When Seibu won the game and the series
Mori was allowed to buy the final round.

In the American Club lobby as they were sorting cars, Harrington suggested Ludlow ride with him. He also offered to
drop Mori, but the Japanese declined since he had to go across
town for his date with Erika and the subway was faster. Mori
and Ludlow agreed to meet Tuesday at the safe house to compare notes. Mori shook everyone's hand before he left. Ludlow
smiled to himself, wondering what had become of that bitter
anti-American he'd met the first day.

The car was one of those air-conditioned Cadillacs, with a
flag on each fender, that the bigwigs get to use. Ludlow relaxed
against the fine upholstery and considered what might be on
Harrington's mind. Then he remembered what Cooper had
said: that the DS&T director needed a favor.

George was driving. His compatriot, Mike, had gone with
Cooper. Harrington told George to stop at the Okura first and
then take Ludlow where he wanted to go. Harrington seemed
in no hurry to talk to Ludlow. He sat back studying the scenery
for several minutes. They were passing directly in front of the
Soviet embassy. By the gate, a Japanese police van was pulled
up on permanent duty. The building looked deceptively quiet,

with lights blazing cheerfully from the twin towers where the living quarters were.

Harrington pointed to the embassy. "Like any service," he said, "they have some good people and some rotten apples." Then he told Ludlow there was hard evidence that Tokyo KGB had a large operation in progress. He sprawled with his head back, his lanky frame relaxed against the cushion like a boxer between rounds.

"Starfire," he said. "That's what the KGB's after." He lit up another cigar, took several puffs until it was glowing a nice cherry red. The Japanese had clammed up about the Starfire for months now; nothing but a little announcement when the project was started. Then zip. Before this they always came running with every new idea they had. Harrington shook his head. "Isn't that right, George?"

"Yup. Puppy dogs they used to be. Wag their tail, lap your hand. They've turned, y'know. Sadder than Solomon. And now they want their own fighter-bomber."

"Yes. I was coming to that next, George. Fighter support experimental they call it. For short, the FSX." He sighed and took a deep drag on his cigar. Then he launched into the background because, as he explained, it was all tied in to the Starfire problem.

The Japanese military wanted to design and build their own fighter-bomber to defend their islands into the twenty-first century. Although the program was highly secret, some American congressmen got wind of it and figured the Japanese were going to develop their own airframe industry and do to us in aerospace what they'd done in TV sets, videocassette recorders, and microchips. After considerable debate, Defense was pressured into offering Japan F-16 technology on a license basis. The most advanced fighter-bomber in the world, of course. Give them the entire kit, the congressmen argued, the works. Help the balance of payments.

Just as this was to be announced to the media, critics began to complain that the technology was too valuable to give away. The press conference was delayed until the end of this month. Now the Starfire NO-SPEC that Ludlow had sourced at Kathy

Johnson's apartment further complicated matters. Since the new data started to circulate the Department of Defense, everyone was rethinking the whole deal. A Starfire in an F-16 would make the plane untouchable. A growing crowd in Washington lobbied to scrap the FSX deal. Let the Japanese build their own plane. Meanwhile, U.S. leadership was trying to decide what position to take in the press conference scheduled for the end of the month. They were about out of time. Harrington looked at Ludlow. "Begin to add up?"

Ludlow nodded.

"Put the Starfire in the most advanced jet fighter-bomber in the world and what do you get, George?"

"More arrogance if you want my honest opinion. Do the work of three of ours."

"Ten of ours if that NO-SPEC holds," Harrington corrected. He looked out the window. "And always so damnably polite. That's the key to their success, isn't it, George?" Harrington took a puff on his cigar.

"Bet your sweet ass it is, sir." George's New England accent had become more pronounced.

They were close to Tokyo Tower, which had all the colored lights on and looked like a garish Christmas tree. Harrington said, "That's one reason we've decided to send you into the JEC research lab to collect the Starfire, Bob."

Ludlow took a deep breath. "Preempt the Soviets?"

"Yes. And have a good look to decide the implications of the sale of F-16 technology." Harrington folded his arms, still holding the cigar between his fingers. "The other reason is a bit more arcane."

The DS&T chief delicately tapped his cigar into an ashtray. Then he leaned back and spoke as if he were making small talk; only Ludlow knew it was not small talk.

"There's a few people, and they include Cooper and Mike but not me, who believe the Starfire's too good to be true. That it was set up as a lure by the Japanese to create a scandal. Entrap any country that sent in a team to collect it."

Harrington paused just a moment. For effect, Ludlow thought. This guy didn't need to collect his thoughts.

"Imagine the unfavorable publicity! The local media would have a field day. They're already accusing us of bullying tactics on economic issues. This could be the other reason the Japanese government hasn't come forward with any specifics."

Harrington turned to face Ludlow square on. "So, for God's sake, don't get caught. If you do we're going to have to deny you. You are only on contract after all."

Ludlow pulled out his lighter. He wondered what happened to an agent who refused an assignment. This one disturbed him. "Five days," he said finally.

"Make it four."

Ludlow deliberated and finally nodded.

Harrington snuffed out his cigar and turned to smile at the Operations agent. "You gave our people in Washington quite a scare, you know, blundering around with that data of yours."

"The Starfire test data?"

"Right. Nearly gave us all away, you did."

Ludlow stared at the DS&T director. "What do you mean?"

"Well, now you're a member of our smuggling ring, I can put you in the picture. Confidential, mind you."

"You mean the NO-SPEC test data I found at Kathy's apartment—she'd copped that?"

"This isn't a barbecue at Crane's Beach out here, Bob. You, if anyone, should appreciate that."

"Cooper lied to me?"

"Good Lord, man! Do you realize what's going on in Japan today? Of course he lied to you. Every night you'd been out with that Japanese Bruce Lee of yours. We weren't sure what you were up to. Thought you'd gone queer for a while, some of us. Coop's one of the best in the business. Going to have my job one day, mark my words. Did he lie to you! You've been in the relatively honest side of the trade, haven't you then, Bob? You only steal things? Some honor in that I suppose."

"So she'd been issued the radio, the camera, the rest of what I found at her apartment by Washington DS&T?"

"Well after all, Bob, we were putting in about two thousand word-groupings a month through the Misawa dish relay to that little radio set of hers. Everything going so well, too. Damn shame."

"She was taking out Japanese high tech?"

"Lord no. Nothing small, Bob." He smiled ingenuously and said they'd never had a resident in Japan, had they? Of course not. Ally and all that. Nor had they ever found a Japanese who was trustworthy, who would spy on his own countrymen, you see. Then Japan did it to us economically, didn't they? Took us on and ran right by us before we knew they were in the race. Economic superpower. Japan. Who would have believed it ten years ago? They were always bowing and scraping and telling you how much better you did things. And the young crowd in the Diet—the crowd that didn't lose the war—they're aggressive people, these youngsters. Like Mori, he supposed. Want to double the military budget for openers, which was fine we say. But there were a few at Langley who always kept a wary eye out, know what I mean? We're both superpowers now, allies, but fiercely competitive economically. And who knows? they say, these people who walk very softly in Washington's corridors. Who knows? So they came to him and told him, Roger, this is just outlandish and we apologize for it. But our job is to make sure in thirty maybe fifty years we haven't made any silly mistakes. We think it is time you get busy in Japan. Then they'd smile sadly, shake their heads, and walk away. Orders, Bob, that's how it's done.

"Looked all around for the right person. Couldn't be just anyone, with the stakes so high. And Kathy'd come off that magnificent MicroDec op beautifully. Still on a high. And credible as a cherry blossom in Japanese eyes. They hadn't suspected a thing, had they? Perfect, she was.

"Called her in for a chat. 'A few more years, Kathy, before you go back to being a woman again. What do you say to becoming our Japan resident?' What a girl that one was. Didn't even have to think about it. Knew it was dangerous."

Ludlow sat, arms folded, stifling his fury. Knowing it was right and wrong as these things always are. And that there was nothing he could do but become a part of it.

So they'd floated word of Kathy's desperate situation, Harrington continued. "No job. Out of money. Sooner than we thought the Japanese were there cruising around like sharks giving it a look. Easy it was, although we had to be careful. The more so for the political tension inside the CIA. The few Operations Directorate people who knew were furious, of course. They saw it as a huge defeat. Usurping their prerogatives. The beginning of the end for exclusivity in field teams and all the rest. Well, after all, it was inevitable. Everywhere you cared to look intelligence services were shifting emphasis to their technical directorates. Ability to produce or acquire know-how had become the key to national power. Economic and military prestige. Kathy knew the score, she'd have to keep her activity hidden from the Tokyo Operations Directorate. It was for her own safety as well as the political reasons.

"Once she reached Tokyo she started building the network right away. Making the contacts. Building the relationships inside the technical groups they needed. Zaibatsu and the rest. She was damn good, too. Learning Japanese. Lots of charm," Harrington winked. "Then this awful Starfire business came up." Harrington shook his head.

"Give it a whack, we said. Pinch enough for a call on what it was, first of all. She did. We saw Starfire had huge potential. More data was requested. To decide meaning for the FSX. Enough for us to decipher why they were trying to hide it. But don't lose your balance, we told her over that little radio of hers. The other work was by far more important. Within two years we expected to have an information network that penetrated every major Japanese company in the strategic high-tech field. Ludlow would come in to make the Starfire collection. She was meeting for the drop location on the final piece of data you found at her apartment when she was blown away. And very cruelly." Harrington turned to his driver. "Just when you think things are perfect, that's always when it happens, right, George?"

"Storms after the best weather, y'know. Never fails. But we have his name, yes, sir."

Harrington nodded and his eyes narrowed. "A real bad one, George. Top GRU man in Japan, although he hasn't surfaced since the killing. Isn't that what you've decided, George, after reviewing the descriptions Japanese police provided?"

"Sergei Vasilyev," pronounced George from the front seat. "We're going to get his ass. Wherever he hides."

"Eye for an eye, Bob. That's the rule. But the name I really want is behind some desk in Moscow. No matter who pulled the trigger. Whether the Russian did it, or some Japanese as you believe. Although frankly, Bob, I don't understand what weapon he could have used to satisfy that angle theory of yours. When you unravel this turkey there'll be a smiling Slavic face in Center at the last desk. Believe me. That's the man we really want, isn't it, George?"

"That's the man we want," George said softly.

Ludlow was watching both men. He said quietly, "You think Operations could have leaked data to the KGB to throw a wrench into your operation?"

Harrington agreed that Kathy's death had been a stunning blow to the DS&T and a huge victory for Operations. However, he was an optimist. "I look for the good in everyone," he said. "For now."

"Then you put that faked picture in her apartment to throw everyone off?"

"Deniability, Bob. With all that expensive equipment lying around her place we needed an out. No matter how madcap it was. Somebody trying to set up our poor baby, we'd holler. Just to buy a little hesitation. A little stutter step to get her out of the country. Any clown could see it was faked, of course." He turned to Ludlow. "Put you off, did it? Well I'm glad to hear at least we got something right."

"What's the future then? You going to try again?"

"I'm afraid, as far as the network goes, we lost our chance, right, George?"

"Gone," George said with finality. "Operations has won."

Ludlow was staring at Harrington. "So you're Robin?"

Harrington did not have time to answer. Their car suddenly swerved and stopped. George cursed and hit the horn. A pedestrian had crossed in the middle of the block, unheard of in Japan. (The police report would later state that the pedestrian had panicked and fallen, blocking the road when the big car loomed suddenly.)

A figure suddenly wrenched the door on Harrington's side of the car. It would not open. A gloved hand lifted an attaché case. Ludlow screamed a warning and shoved Harrington down on the floor. With the same motion his right hand came up with his Walther but a hail of bullets had already smashed against the bulletproof glass. Ludlow kicked his door open, dove, and rolled, coming up near the rear of the car. The assailant saw him. Aimed the attaché case. A spray of bullets ricocheted off the pavement. The Japanese ran for a car parked against the opposite curb. He was nimble but not young. A cold mask covered his lower face. Dark glasses. A brimmed hat putting his face in shadow. Ludlow cursed and aimed. Who was it? There was no telling in this lighting, under these conditions. Just like in Ginza then. The figure opened the door of a black Toyota, turned, and fired a last volley. Ludlow got off two rounds just as the door slammed. The tires spun, smoked. The car catapulted away. Scoring on occupants inside a moving vehicle was virtually impossible. Metal angles, even glass deflected rounds. But Ludlow still kept firing.

The car disappeared. Ludlow stood numb for a moment as the shock waves captured him. Then he turned back to the shambles of the embassy Cadillac.

Harrington was struggling to open his door, jammed shut by the force of the bullets, which had not been able to penetrate the bulletproof glass or the reinforced steel door. The lifeless figure of George was sprawled by the open front door.

Harrington was shaken but unhurt. He stared at George's body, the shock still in his eyes.

Ludlow came up to him. "You okay?"

Mutely, Harrington nodded.

"Still want me to go ahead with the Starfire?"

Harrington started as if coming out of a trance. "That was a Japanese, Bob! That bastard was a Japanese! And did you see what he used? Of course I want you to go ahead with the collection. Only now bring it out in three days."

CHAPTER 28

TORI-NO-ICHI
FESTIVAL

Mori waited for Erika at the great wooden gate of Otori Shrine in Asakusa. It was already dark when she called out his name.

She ran to him and grabbed his arm and swung around him like a child around a maypole. She was laughing, her head thrown back in the simplest form of joy. When she stopped she took his arm in both of hers and yanked it like a temple bell.

"I missed you," she said and pulled him toward the throngs entering the shrine.

She was wearing a sweater several sizes too large, which kept sliding off her shoulder. Her smile was rapturous; she was excited by the crowds, by the nice evening, by the festival itself, by being with him. "I love Tori-no-ichi," she said. "I didn't go last year. Give me a kiss."

Mori kissed her on the cheek.

"You call that a kiss?"

"I'm out of practice," Mori said.

"It's okay. I still love you." She glanced at him slyly then burst out laughing. "Stop looking *hazukashii*."

"I wasn't."

"Embarrassed," said Erika. "That's how you looked. Your eyes didn't know where to stop."

"There are police about, you know, after pickpockets."

"*Maroo* on your police." She squeezed his hand. "It's Mitsuko, isn't it? Well I don't know where she is. She went off somewhere with Suzuki-san the last I saw her."

Vendors sold candied apples, *okonomi-yaki* from steaming irons, sweet bean cakes, amulets for immediate wealth. Lights had been strung over their wood stalls, which lined the wide stone walk leading to the shrine buildings. The crowd bumped and giggled with the good-natured harmony of Japanese at ease. They oohed when they saw a huge square of *chochin* lanterns over the stage where samisen players were performing with drummers. The round lanterns with red *kanji* brush writing flickered into the black cedar boughs which protected the grounds from the night sky.

"It's beautiful, isn't it?" Erika's eyes shone and she pressed even tighter into his side.

Mori guided her along the paths until they reached steps leading up to the main shrine. Here the crowds thickened, waiting their turn. At the top of the steps was a stone basin. They washed their hands and rinsed their mouths with a wooden scoop. The water flowed from the mouth of a fierce dragon. As they approached the main shrine they saw a large building with clean lines in untreated wood. At its front was a long *saisenbako* offertory with a wooden grate above which hung a huge bell on a thick white rope. When they were close enough, Mori pulled on the bell rope and clapped his hands three times to attract the gods. Then he and Erika tossed coins into the wooden grate and prayed.

Shinto has no written texts or philosophy. For most Japanese, who lack interest in philosophical speculation, it has little more than ceremonial meaning. Yet it is an acknowledgment of the sacredness of natural phenomena. It fences off and sanctifies trees and rocks among other things. But the major attraction of Shinto is that, according to its teachings, Japanese, when they die, become gods themselves. Mori, like most modern Japanese, believed little of this. In his case, however, he saw in Shinto a justification of the life of refined poverty and rustic simplicity. This was what he had decided people should search for.

"About what did you pray?" Erika was looking up at him happily as they moved away from the shrine. The departing crowd flowed in a spray of bodies parting like a horizontal fountain to the sides of the main building. More stalls here were manned by priests selling serious fare: *kumade* ornamental rakes to gather fortune, masks of the seven gods of good luck, white arrows with rubber points, and bells to ward off evil spirits.

"I prayed for the spirit of the American girl," Mori said. "That she would be avenged although I have not been able to help her. What about you?"

"I prayed that Colonel Yuki will not be mad."

"What do you mean?"

"I have been working for him." She smiled anxiously up at him as a child does when it wants to be reassured. "He said it was for Japan. He said it was for your own good. Those were his words. I thought about it since the party. Yesterday I told him I was quitting. Also ICOT. He's very angry."

She held onto his hand tightly as they went into the area of great stalls where large *kumade* were displayed and sold. Before each stall were knots of people of whom one or two were the center of attention; these were the buyers who bargained skillfully for a *kumade* of their choice. Erika stopped before one of the stalls and offered him a bright smile: "I shouldn't have told you. You didn't know, did you?"

"That the antique hairpin *kanzashi* was the colonel's idea? No. I didn't have the slightest notion."

She reached up with her face and kissed him. "I'm sorry for everything, darling, really I am."

At the stall in front of them a buyer had agreed to a price. The *kumade* was lifted down from the huge display. A child's mask, lucky carp, small kegs of sake for wealth—all woven to a bamboo stake. Each year a larger one was purchased and fortune increased proportionately. The hawkers were scanning the crowd for another prospect.

Mori shook his head. "You fixed the clock, too, I suppose?"

Erika didn't reply. She raised her hand and a path opened to the *kumade* stall. She pointed to a beautiful one, a gold ship in a silver sake sea of lucky carp. "Five thousand yen," she said firmly.

Three men ran the booth, *yakuza* from one of the smaller families. One with a rough but good-natured face collapsed with helpless laughter. The second held his stomach as though he'd been cut in two. The third looked at Mori's watch for perspective but found none.

The first gangster's voice, when he found it, was strong with the experience of talking to small crowds: "Yes, well, I've heard virtue carries a lean purse. You work in Ginza do you?"

"Of course I work in Ginza, *danna*." Erika imitated the lilt of the Ginza hostess trade. The crowd laughed.

The gangster had put his fingers to his lips, hamming for the people. "Tell you what. Because you are so beautiful I'll take eight thousand, which is half its worth, but not a sen less." His two partners looked aghast.

Erika smiled at Mori then back to the gangster. "Five thousand five hundred." Then to Mori she said, "Are you angry?"

"No," Mori said. He hated himself for saying that but deep down he knew it was true.

The first gangster was nodding his head. "Of course he's angry. You're trying to rob me. Lucky I'm even-tempered. Tell you what. Six thousand five hundred but I'll hate myself for the rest of the night. Just look at that workmanship."

"*Kimatta!* I'll take it!" Erika shouted with forced glee. "But you have to do a *gambatte*. For my friend."

They handed her the beautiful *kumade* and the three gangsters clapped their hands in unison to the ritual, followed by the spontaneous applause of the crowd. Then she bowed and led Mori away. She handed him the *kumade*. "It's for luck," she said.

"You didn't have to do that."

"I know." She put her arm around his waist. Her fingers found their way under his shirt and played with his back muscles. They walked slowly to the street where the cabs were. Mori finally asked the question he had to ask, the one for which he had no answer:

"Why, Erika? Why did Colonel Yuki want to separate me from my wife?"

Erika waved her free hand. "He never tells me anything. Just 'Do this' and 'Do that.' He is not generous. I do not like him anymore."

Mori tried to keep his anger from gathering too quickly, from doing something headlong and rash. "What if I asked you to help?"

"Good! I knew you needed me."

They had reached the street. The crowds had thinned, flowing into an endless line of polished taxis. Mori knew he would never trust her again. "Can you find out why they wanted to separate Mitsuko from me?"

Erika adjusted her oversized sweater. "Of course I can if I try."

She climbed into the next taxi and turned to him with open arms to accept him into her warm embrace.

CHAPTER 29

THE UENO LIAISON

From a pay phone Ludlow called Mori. He wanted to tell his partner ("partner," Ludlow smiled to himself—who'd have thought that?) about the shooting. Also that Harrington was Robin and had escaped by the narrowest of margins. That the pieces of his theory were finally fitting into place. Mori, recognizing the urgency in the American's voice, agreed to meet him immediately. Also he did not ask questions when Ludlow said that the safe house was unsuitable. It was obvious Ludlow's American handlers would be taping every word. They finally agreed on Ueno Park.

———

The sign read BEWARE OF DANGEROUS ANIMALS in *kanji*, German, and English. Ludlow waited on the nearby gravel path and watched a knot of spectators in front of the panda cage. October mornings are busy at Ueno Zoo with school trips, late season tourists, lovers stealing time from office politics, retirees looking for something to do.

Except for the giant panda cage, Ueno had very little to differentiate it from other zoos in Asia. If anything, its uniqueness lay in the contrived precision with which it was run. All animals were fed on strict schedule, a fact which disturbed the newly arrived pandas for a time, accustomed as they were to Chinese irregularity.

Mori was late. Ludlow shrugged deeper into his old raincoat. The first chill of winter filled the early morning wind in that part of Tokyo. It fluttered the winter flowers that marked the narrow walks. It stirred the rows of conifers, in dormant watch over concrete benches that lined the asphalt paths like cenotaphs.

A footstep behind him. Ludlow turned. Mori's hand gestured Ludlow to follow. Mori headed silently up the path, away from the pandas, the knots of spectators. They rounded a curve in the footpath, which branched. The choice was jungle cats or monkeys. Mori chose the cougar cage and allowed Ludlow to pull abreast. "I don't have much time. What's up?"

"The Japanese side of the equation made a move after you left us."

"Against you and Harrington? Last night?"

"Yes. Remember the code name Robin? Kathy Johnson's control? Turns out to be Harrington. Last night someone tried to kill him."

"Where?"

"His car on the way to the Okura from the American Club."

"Who?"

"Hard to say except it was an Asian, Japanese I'd bet. He wore a cold mask, dark glasses, and a hat. Probably the same gear he wore for the Ginza killing."

"Yuki?"

"It had to be him."

"Harrington's all right?"

"Yes. But not George."

"Dead?"

"Yes."

"Sorry to hear that."

Ludlow pursed his lips. "I've a way to stay involved in the operation. Harrington asked me to join their team."

"Excellent. So Yuki escaped? What about the weapon he used?"

"One of those comic book devices our side would never use. Nor the Russians. An attaché case with the trigger in the handle. It was silenced of course and they used smokeless powder."

"The same as he used in Ginza then. It would give the right angles."

"Yes. Now we know what weapon was used to kill Kathy Johnson. One of the questions is answered. Still, we have a long way to go."

Mori stared at the cougar cage in front of them. The animal's yellow eyes glared back at him. "I saw Erika last night."

"Erika?"

"Yes. Maybe I haven't mentioned her yet. I didn't think she was important till last night. She works with my wife at ICOT."

"What about her?"

"She's been working for Yuki. He's trying to separate me from my wife. Does that make any sense to you?"

"Your wife works at ICOT? What kind of work does she do?" Ludlow was astonished at this revelation.

Mori started to walk and Ludlow followed. He stopped in front of the tiger cage. A big Bengal male was pacing back and forth. "She's assistant to the director."

"Does ICOT have a connection to the Japan Electronics Corporation lab? Is your wife or the director a part of the connection?"

Mori stared at the tiger. "I don't know."

"I'd ask around, Mori-san. I wouldn't waste any time."

Mori nodded. "Where would you ask first?"

"Right at the top. The head of the JEC research lab that has the Starfire. Have you checked with him before?"

"I haven't met him. I read the statements he made to investigators from Homicide."

"Meet him. Maybe he can lead you to others. Time is running out."

Mori looked at Ludlow. Ever since the phone call this morning he'd noted the urgency about the big American. As if Ludlow had a new timetable. So far he hadn't given Mori a clue. "You want to tell me what really happened between you and Harrington?" Mori said. "He asked you to do something, didn't he?"

"What makes you say that?"

Mori stared at the pacing tiger and thought a moment. "At the American Club, Cooper said Harrington was going to ask you a favor. Something about the FSX fighter-bomber. What was it?"

Ludlow hesitated momentarily. "It wasn't a favor exactly. It was news they had. The KGB is mounting an operation to steal the Starfire prototype."

"So what did he ask you to do about it?" Mori stared at the tiger. It was a beautiful animal. A shame it had to be locked up in a cage. It belonged in the wilderness. Free.

Ludlow wanted him to know, but it was impossible. Reluctantly he said, "I can't tell you the details."

Mori began to walk again. So the limits of their friendship had been reached. "It would be a national disaster if the Soviets stole Starfire," he said.

Ludlow kept his eyes on the ground. "Of course," he said. "I assume it is well guarded?"

Mori turned to face the American. "The most advanced electronic surveillance protects it. As well there are round-the-clock armed guards."

"Good. Then there is little chance . . ."

"There are other ways," Mori interrupted. "For example there is a memorial service for Kathy Johnson tomorrow. Key JEC executives will be there. Security will be difficult. A terrorist attack, the taking of hostages, would be child's play."

"To be traded for the prototype?" Ludlow mused.

"It is a possibility."

"Not the KGB's style. Too public." Ludlow scratched his cheek and flipped up the collar of his battered military raincoat against the chill wind. "They wouldn't do anything that could be traced to them. They'd use a proxy just like they did in the killing of Kathy Johnson. However, every precaution should be taken."

Mori nodded. "I think you should attend the memorial service just in case. I'll be in a police van parked outside; we're setting up video-camera surveillance of the congregation. Perhaps someone interesting will show up. Tomorrow at three thirty. Tokyo Union Church." Mori gave Ludlow the address.

As they were parting, Ludlow turned to Mori, a note of concern in his voice. "I don't want to worry you, Inspector, but I'd have a talk with your wife. She might be unwittingly a part of the Russians' game."

CHAPTER 30

NIGHTMARE

The social leap from the grease and the sweaty camaraderie of manufacturing to the air-conditioned gentility of the building service side had not been an easy one for Hiroshi Tsuna. He had not made the move from his beloved Nagoya plant willingly; he had had to be pushed. Since he was nearing the mandatory Japanese retirement age of fifty-five, however, there was really very little he could do.

Two years earlier, when the new Japan Electronics Tower had been completed in Shinjuku, Tsuna was appointed to run its plant: heating, electrical, air conditioning, maintenance, cleaning, and security. For a man of his computer engineering background and experience, the job itself presented little difficulty. The most agonizing part was the move to Tokyo. The frenetic pace of the city, the *tsumetai* coldness of Tokyoites behind their polite faces, the dedication to pleasure, left him and his wife feeling very much alone. After they'd found a small apartment in Hachioji, he'd thrown himself into his work.

The job itself had turned out better than he'd expected. Although his new staff was youthful and inexperienced, they were gradually whipped into shape and became a team that worked decently together. Eventually, Tsuna came to enjoy wandering on the daily rounds of his domain; the hushed carpeted elegance of the executive suites on the upper floors, the paraphernalia of the highly secret research team in the heavily guarded middle levels, the bustle of the lower floors where the plush and not so plush conference rooms were, and finally the unceasing rush and turmoil of the lobby. This magnificent building was like a city in itself, and this shining steel and glass tower became his real home.

He kept his city running well. The time to upgrade equipment, make repairs, he'd learned, was the winter, when systems weren't being used. JEC let out sizable contracts in security, maintenance, and cleaning, and there were going to be no lapses while he was running things.

When the call came from the German, who was only going to be in town for a week, Tsuna said he would be happy to see him. He was thinking of new security equipment. Not that he expected to buy anything from a foreigner; he'd stick to Japanese security equipment. However, German equipment had a very good reputation. They agreed to meet at four o'clock.

———

The meeting was held in the tiled first basement in the building superintendent offices. Tsuna started out by saying they'd never purchased from a foreign firm, since Japanese equipment normally satisfied their needs; however, he was pleased to listen to whatever the German had to say.

The salesman nodded amicably, then explained that there had been dramatic change in the range of equipment available during the past year. Mr. Tsuna perhaps already knew this. How old was the JEC security system, by the way? About two years, Tsuna guardedly said. The foreigner smiled and suggested JEC should consider several options. The German firm, whose name was Hilde GmbH with a Stuttgart address, was Europe's leader in the field. Tops in precision, he exclaimed a bit too heavily and pumped his lips like he was attacking a tuba.

For example, they had a new pressure differential system—

just the thing for closed areas and more advanced than anything on the market. Was JEC's a twelve-volt system? Yes, he thought so. Research-and-development security area, wasn't that right? Tsuna suggested he might take a look at the brochures. As the foreigner handed them over he reminded the building superintendent that German equipment could be fitted right into the present electronics; it wasn't like computers where you had to throw out one system to bring in another. Mercy.

After scanning the full deck of brochures, the Japanese engineer agreed that the German firm had several excellent ideas. However he really didn't need a pressure-sensitive system, since vaults weren't used. Most of their targets were in the open, equipment prototypes mainly. The salesman nodded wisely. The Tokyo Police crime-prevention officer had rated his system as excellent, Tsuna added proudly, and inquired whether the German would like a soft drink or coffee. If it wasn't too much trouble, coffee with cream would be perfect, the big foreigner had replied.

Fortunately Tsuna knew his security system thoroughly and didn't mind showing off: "We offer the intruder a wide choice of entrapment option," he grinned mischievously. "Sonic detectors are used in open areas to detect the slightest change in noise level." The engineer smiled radiantly. "A whirring air conditioner does not trigger the alarm of course. Only interruption of the constant sound pattern. Ours is the most advanced Japanese system available. A Sanya 587."

"How does the alarm trigger?" the salesman asked, still skeptical. "A bell alarm, lights, a remote?"

"A remote system," Tsuna smiled proudly. "In addition, we use ultrasonics. The pulses are spread over a wide area covering all targets. Any movement near the equipment triggers the attenuator."

The foreigner nodded, impressed. Picket-fence lasers he guessed that a mouse couldn't get through.

"But we don't stop there." Tsuna was shaking his head with disdain. "Heat sensors. Passive infrared. They pick up the heat from any humans. After the shunt lock is keyed, that is."

Slowly, the foreigner began to shake his head in admiration. His next question was given with a note of resignation, as if he knew there was nothing he could supply them: "You keep the only key then?"

"The security company has a duplicate," Tsuna confirmed.

The salesman shook his head in awe, checking at the same time the wall panel behind the engineer's desk where the banks of lights indicated operability of the total building security system. His eyes languished on the phone below the system, focusing on the center disc, which showed a number neatly typed by an IBM electric. It was a number he could read.

"Proximity detectors?" the foreigner suggested, his last gasp at making a sale.

Tsuna sniffed as if he'd been given an inferior bottle of sake. "No interest, I'm afraid. They only lock onto measured distance from targets and trigger with any change. I'd say we've covered that with our other equipment." Tsuna was smiling patiently now, looking at his Seiko watch.

The foreigner slapped his remaining brochures shut. The dial number was registered in his brain.

"Nobody's ever done you then?"

Tsuna chuckled suddenly. "Matter of fact someone tried. Three men posing as service engineers got past the night security. Triggered the MPD command center computer system they did. They were arrested photocopying some of our computer manuals, for the new JPP-33 as I recall. Totally bizarre. They could've walked into any of our sales offices and received manuals free. The thieves were traced to a run-of-the-mill industrial espionage firm and the client turned out to be some foreign exporter in Hakodate. Stupid of them. Finn-Pacific was their name. They came with presents and apologies, explaining it was all a huge mistake. Of course, we don't know what it was about. Went on to the prosecutor's office, but finally all charges were dropped. We got a little play in the papers. It was only three months ago. But it does prove how airtight we are."

"You've taken my measure, I'm afraid. Unless you're into

trip wires and geese." The salesman rose and held out his hand.

Tsuna laughed dutifully and showed him to the door, where the foreigner paused:

"That looks like a direct line to the Metropolitan Police Department headquarters, right?" He waved vaguely in the direction of the phone and panel. Tsuna turned to view the impressive array of switches and lights.

"Yes. Automatically dials the police emergency number." His reply was a trifle clipped. "It's all computerized of course. Ex-directory phone. I'm sorry, but I have another meeting."

"Certainly," the salesman responded with sincere appreciation. "You don't have any other plants with R&D that might be in the market for a security system, by the way?"

"No. The only other major R&D is in the Nagoya plant, but that's prototype testing mainly and upgrading present models. Sorry I can't be of more help."

———

Going up in the elevator, Ludlow was amused by how easily it had gone, and how vulnerable the building was. There'd been no trap on the phone that he could see. The line to the telephone was external cable, unprotected. Jesus, what an unsound fortress. The Japanese, obviously, had no idea. The doors in the basement were all concertinas with steel-framed sheeted walls, which meant that to get at the control box he could simply unbolt the doors where they attached to H-type girders and swing a door inward without touching the locking mechanism. And there were a number of ways to attack the security here. His mind reeled with the options. Also that little bit about Finn-Pacific gave him another lead to follow in the girl's death. He could add that to the Soviet name—Sergei—he now had for the foreigner involved in the shooting. And the weapon the Japanese used in the car attack, an attaché case. Two of his three questions were at least partially answered. Harrington had also mentioned that the KGB were after the Starfire. No doubt they'd sent in a team to test JEC defenses. Copying manuals indeed. Tsuna'd mentioned that Finn-Pacific was located in Hakodate. Was it coincidence that Graves during their meeting with Colonel Yuki had once referred to a proprietary in the north? A company acting as a front for the Soviets? Part of the Soviet espionage network? Perhaps it figured in the Soviet side of the equation.

Once he reached the lobby, Ludlow hurried into a men's room positioned behind the elevators. In a booth he removed a one-meter length of thin invisible plastic line from a side pocket. Back in the lobby, he moved past a statue of a nude girl near the public telephones and opened a rear exit door quickly and looked out. The door opened to a parking lot which was apparently full. Expertly, he fastened the plastic to the door's crash bar and pulled to make sure it was tight. Then he threw the free line outside the door and shut the door tight against the thin invisible plastic. Even if a guard on his rounds did spot it, which was unlikely, the plastic looked entirely harmless. It had all been done within seconds.

Guards politely bowed in the lobby as he ceremoniously returned the guest pass. He'd used a name card given him by an executive of the German security equipment firm in Hibiya. On the street, the nervousness hit him, as it always did when there was a big operation coming down and the odds favored him.

Ludlow sat massive and impatient in the Japanese cab. On the way back to his hotel, his eyes roamed the crowded streets bustling with well-dressed passersby, jammed with cars, weighted down with neon signs just coming on and cluttered by overhead vines of wires.

His cabby sighed at stoplights that ran crazily out of sync with every other street in the city. Congestion backed up on too-narrow roads. The city operated on occasion with the precision of a Japanese watch, but most of the time it ran quite otherwise.

His mind developed a schedule. He would make the JEC lab entry in two days. That gave him tomorrow to attend the memorial service for the dead girl. He reviewed the preparations he must make. It would be a busy two days. Time, indeed, was running out.

There are three kinds of subcities within the sprawl known as Greater Tokyo. The cultural subcities, such as Jimbo-cho and Ueno, are full of bookstores, schools, museums, parks, a zoo, and temples. The shop subcity Ningyo-cho is famous for its hand-worked dolls and Ginza for its fashion goods. Finally, there is the playground subcity, known for its bars, nude shows, cabarets, and erotic-merchandise shops. Such a place is Shinjuku, and it was to the Takadanobaba section that Ludlow directed the cab. The driver let him out near an ancient hotel.

Ludlow had dinner alone in a sushi shop near the station. A bottle of third-rate sake accompanied the raw fish. The shop had only a wooden counter where you sat looking at glass cases showing the variety of fish available. He ate a little more ginger than usual, since it prevented stomach problems and the shop was not one of the better places he'd been in. His earlier buoyant mood had given way to one of reflection. He still didn't like the fact that he was being ordered to steal from an ally, despite the evidence that Japan had apparently stolen from the United States. He didn't like the idea of being programmed by Cooper's lies to cheat someone he considered a friend now. No matter how you cut it, he had dishonored his own word. Maybe Harrington was right. Maybe he was too honest for this business after all.

He called Hiroko from a row of phone booths in the square. She was just on her way out; an embassy party. Would he like to come? "Rain check," Ludlow replied. He was not in a celebratory mood.

Back at the hotel he soaped and showered leisurely. The noise woke up the rats that lived on the other side of a vent in the wall. It was an old hotel but sturdy. He'd heard somewhere that rats chose buildings that were safe from fire. They appreciated value perhaps better than most humans. He had chosen this hotel for its sturdy door locks and the variety of exits in an emergency. In bed now, he checked that his gun was loaded and ready to fire. It was a precaution he had taken every night of his life since Colombo. The rats quieted. Finally he went to sleep.

———

He could smell the river through a row of trees, although he could not see it; the fetid stench of all Asian rivers. He was running. His legs were strong and without pain again. A bullet snapped by him, close enough for him to feel its anger. His legs drove harder but the pursuers were gaining. Through the trees he plowed, branches slapping at his face, and the black river was suddenly there.

He took it in a shallow dive then glided to the safety of its filthy bowels. The blackness surrounded him as he sank lower; the depth began to punish his chest. He estimated that he had reached the middle currents before he began his fight to surface, but the syrupy thickness of the water slowed his movement, sucking him ever deeper. Then he heard the noise. A clicking noise louder and louder magnified by the water. He could not breathe . . .

Ludlow forced open his eyes, feeling the sweat on his back and the drenched sheets under him. The dream was always the same; the face of the enemy he could never see. The sound of danger. His instincts told him not to move. Gradually, he could make out the dim familiar shapes. Nothing alien. Then what . . . the noise began again. A clicking noise; the door. The lock.

He slowly raised his head and checked the slit of light under the door for telltale shadow but there was none. Someone competent then. Someone who knew his way. He sat slowly upright; let them think he still slept. Quickly he put on clothes. Even quieter with the gun, his Walther, small and deadly.

Silently he went to the window and pulled the curtain aside. The hotel looked onto a square and beyond that a police box and the station itself. The middle of the square was filled with a flower bed and the statue of a Japanese girl wearing two doves and little else. A stone plaque commemorated World War II dead. The police box was brightly lit and alive with a late-night drunk. Otherwise the square was empty. Then he saw the three men who stood to one side in the shadows. One watched the police box, a second the hotel entrance, and the third spoke into something he held in his hand.

The sound at the door had stopped and Ludlow heard someone moving carefully away. The dead bolt was their problem, he guessed. But they could have stuffed the door with plastics and been well away when the explosion blew the room apart. So whoever it was out there wanted him alive.

The man with the radio gestured to a shopping bag in front of him. The hotel watcher picked it up and hurried toward the hotel entrance. Tools. They would have to cut through the dead bolt to open his door and were bringing up noiseless torch equipment. He considered his alternatives. The door might be momentarily unguarded. They thought he still slept. He felt the sweat running down his back although his hands were cold.

No sounds still from outside the door. Could he risk it? He went to his suitcase and pulled out two sets of documents. His hand hesitated, then yanked a small, heavy alarm clock strapped to the lining. It came free and he adjusted the alarm for eight minutes later. They should be coming through the door just about then. He put the alarm by the bed, returned to the door, and opened the drop bolt gently. No reaction from the hall. He pulled his gun and felt its deadly weight. Gamble, his instincts told him.

He opened the door quietly and slipped out, his back against one wall moving toward the stairwell away from the elevator. He heard the elevator working. Someone was coming up. He turned and raced down the carpeted hallway to the fire exit, which opened to his weight. He chose the roof.

Two days ago he had reconnoitered the roof, ostensibly to take pictures of the quaint square. The adjoining buildings were only several feet away, land prices in Tokyo being what they were. There was a ten foot drop to one; twenty feet to the other. He decided on the greater drop if he were pursued, since an outside fire escape on that building led down to an alley. Ludlow reached for the roof door.

As he opened the metal door a man turned around, surprised. He had been talking by handheld radio and leaning over the edge of the roof looking into the square. He shouted something into the radio in Japanese and tried to organize his hands; put the radio down, reach for a weapon. The man saw Ludlow's gun and froze.

Ludlow backed across the roof until he was near the edge. Then he aimed carefully and fired. The bullet hit the radio squarely, pitched it into the air momentarily where it disappeared off the edge of the roof. Ludlow turned and jumped.

For a small eternity there was nothing below him; then he felt a corner smash into his knee and his legs crumple under him like tissue. There was a sudden concussion, a distant muffled sound of glass shattering, and he knew the bomb in his room had gone. It was a low-grade nonlethal plastic, a warning to create fear and instill respect.

He willed himself up. From the square he could hear the phone in the police box ringing. He stood holding the knee. A bullet whined near him and splashed concrete into powder. He ran for the edge of this roof, searching desperately for the fire escape which had been so obvious in daylight. Metal railings. He plunged recklessly onto them, feeling them give under his weight and hold. Police whistles now. From where? He clambered down the metal rungs, feeling searing pain every time he bent his knees. He swung off the escape to another of more substance several floors down, conscious of the commotion above him now. Shouts. The stairs ended on another roof. He ran looking for a way out. His legs screamed for rest. Then he jumped again. A ten-foot fall this time. More pain, shooting now the length of his leg. A stairway was in front of him, leading where?

He plunged down the stairs until an alley opened below, and he made the final leap, trying not to cry out with pain as the pavement crashed into his legs. Someone moved from the shadows and his heart fell.

A couple emerged; the girl, her blouse undone, hastily covering yellow breasts and the darker oval of nipple. He was by them gulping air in huge draughts, telling himself the pain didn't matter. He lurched through a maze of narrow back streets, heading away from the hotel and off the main roads. Putting distance between himself and the enemy.

Finally he reached Meiji-dori, stopped a cab, and struggled in. The driver was a nighter and used to the unexpected. Without asking questions he slapped the meter down and headed for Shinjuku station.

Ludlow suddenly realized he had nowhere to go. He couldn't return to the embassy compound. Soviet watchers were outside waiting for him.

"Shinjuku. Bathhouse," Ludlow said in Japanese, although he couldn't remember its name. The cabbie understood.

Then Ludlow began to take stock. His hands were badly scraped, the left knee was throbbing, the pants on his right leg were wet, and an ugly black welt was rising where the Afghan wound had been retorn, and was filling with blood. He prayed that it was only a minor rupture.

With deep breaths he gathered his strength. How had they gotten on to him? And for how long? It must have been teams. He'd have seen it otherwise, wouldn't he? Briefly he wondered if it was age. The cabbie slowed.

The Ushida baths of Shinjuku were the largest in the city and catered to the late-night and early-morning revelers of Kabuki-cho and other less notorious districts. They offered steamy, scalding respite from the screaming hilarity of the crowded bars, the pounding rock of the discos, and the flirtatious eyes of the cabaret girls. The dragon slept reluctantly; not before three a.m. did the winking neon begin to dim and the clubs begin to empty. Those who had not negotiated love hotel partners for the remaining hours before the earliest suburban trains started running headed for the baths. Ludlow had ended up there many times on previous trips.

There was a special from three a.m.—a flat one thousand yen for the baths, towel, locker, and space on the tiles to sleep if you could find it. By five there would be little room left anywhere. Ludlow made it just before the final early-morning rush. He soaped on the tiny wooden stool, poured scalding water over his head, then slipped into the huge bath, separated from other bathers by the dense steam. The heat worked through his skin and soothed the tension from his muscles. He decided the final entry into the JEC lab had to be made tomorrow night. He'd lost his base. He must collect the Starfire and get out of the country as quickly as possible. That was his only alternative. His mind went back to his pursuers. Who were they? They were well organized and numerous. They didn't look like KGB hirelings. Police or Yuki's people, probably. If so they'd at least charge him for resisting arrest and perhaps for a whole lot more. The implications were too awesome to consider for the moment. He dragged himself out of the bath and found a space barely large enough to crawl into a fetal position. Before he knew it he was asleep.

CHAPTER 3 1

AFFAIR OF
THE HEART

At first, Mitsuko wanted to die. Her whole life had become a nightmare since the weekend. All Monday she could hardly get any work done. Mori had phoned several times but she'd refused all calls. Tuesday had started out better. She told herself it was just a fight with her husband about a stupid clock. She had done nothing wrong. The next time Mori phoned she would agree to talk it over. That made her feel better. Then Tomu called. He was a new man who worked in personnel. He'd come from somewhere inside the vast government bureaucracy; it was best not to offend such types. When he'd asked if he could talk with her privately, she told him to come right over.

Tomu was short and stocky with jet black hair combed straight back. Mitsuko indicated a chair in front of her desk and Tomu sat down, unbuttoned the jacket of his new Italian suit, and came right to the point.

He said he'd taken his car home for lunch a week ago last Monday. It had been raining, Mitsuko might recall. As he was leaving his parking place he spotted Miss Erika standing on the curb so he'd offered her a lift. Her apartment was in the complex next to his. A man was with her. Mitsuko felt the shock begin to register. Tomu-san cleared his throat gently. The man had identified himself as Mitsuko's husband. Miss

Erika had been called in earlier, and after careful questioning she had admitted a romantic attachment with Mitsuko's husband. Tomu stumbled on for several more sentences. A decision had been made today that it was best for Erika to leave. He cleared his throat again, said how sorry he was, apologized, and left.

Mitsuko picked up a pencil on her desk and broke it in two. She took a deep breath, trying to control her racing heart. She felt the tears welling in her eyes. No! She must keep control. She was an intelligent Japanese woman and this was something that every Japanese wife eventually faced, was it not? She would not cry! No hysterics! She bit her lip until the pain overcame her anger. An icy emptiness replaced her rage and fury. Her phone rang.

"Your husband is on the line," her secretary said.

"Put him on," she replied, amazed at how calm her voice sounded. She heard the line click.

"Listen, I've got to see you." Mori's voice sounded urgent and distressed. Good, Mitsuko thought.

"*What is* the problem?" She let her voice sound distant as if she were talking to a child.

"Everything is a big mistake. I've found out some things that . . ."

"So have I," Mitsuko cut in icily. "About you and Erika at her apartment." The brief silence on the other end of the line did not surprise her.

"That must be part of it," Mori finally murmured.

"Part of what?" Mitsuko's voice started to rise in anger. What was he mumbling about?

"A plan. A plan to separate you and me. Erika was part of it."

"You're just talking nonsense," Mitsuko said evenly. "You're talking rubbish. Call when you have a better story, will you?" She carefully hung up the phone and leaned back in her chair, proud of herself. She hadn't shouted and screamed at him. She'd held herself together. Yes. That felt so much better. And one thing was certain. The idea of a reconciliation with Mori any time soon was ridiculous. The confrontation had cleared her brain; given her new energy to deal directly with the problem.

There were many alternatives. One of her friends had taken on a younger lover when faced with the fact of her husband's unfaithfulness; another took up religion; a third flung herself into overseas trips. Divorce was the final but least acceptable option in Japan. Would she ask for a divorce? It ended careers for Japanese men, she knew. Divorce signaled weakness, an inability to handle the most basic of problems. Mori's career wasn't going anywhere anyway, however. No, there would have to be a better way of evening scores with her husband, of returning the hurt he had given her. She set her mind to work.

First, she called Suzuki-san to ask if she could use the company apartment indefinitely. Normally, the spacious rooms were used for ICOT receptions or placed at the disposal of visiting dignitaries. When Suzuki heard her request he did not ask any questions, which did not surprise Mitsuko. Personnel had no doubt informed him about Erika. Suzuki gently told her that she could use the place for as long as she wished and let it go at that.

Mitsuko hung up the phone, thinking about her first option. Suzuki-san. She knew he liked her very much. She would only have to snap her fingers and he would gratefully become her lover—or her husband. But did she really want either? She explored her own feelings. No. She respected Suzuki-san, but whether she could love him or not was a very difficult question. She certainly didn't know. Of course love could come gradually; it didn't have to be like lightning and thunder. She would keep Suzuki-san as an option, then. But she would look for others.

Most of the afternoon she kept to her private office, pretending to be busy with a budget presentation due next week. Erika was absent as Tomu-san had promised. In Japan no one was ever fired. Erika would quit very soon, however. She had lost face to her superiors in the worst way. Someone had started a rumor that she'd resigned.

It was nearly closing when Mitsuko happened to glance at

her diary and saw she had a five p.m. appointment penciled in. She'd nearly forgotten. Normally Erika would handle foreigners, particularly Americans, but this one had asked specifically for her. He'd been charming on the phone. He was from some electronics group in the U.S.A.; she'd forgotten the particulars. He didn't insist on meeting her, simply explained she was the best qualified to handle what he wanted to discuss. She finally consented. Now she was glad she had. It allowed her to delay going back to that empty apartment.

When the American was shown into her office precisely on the hour, she glanced at him appraisingly. He was wearing an impeccable dark blue suit and a conservative tie, which offset his shimmering flaxen hair. *Kinpatsu,* the word nearly fell from her lips. The "gold ones," Japanese called true blonds. His thick hair had the burnished effect of real gold. The receptionist gave Mitsuko a little wink and went out of the office with an extra swing to her hips. The girls would be bubbling about this one for a while, Mitsuko thought.

He presented his name card, which read MCC, Microelectronics and Computer Technology Corporation. She knew the name, of course. They competed with ICOT. His name was Mark Curtis, which had a nice strong sound to it. She read it out loud and looked at him to see if she'd pronounced it right.

The American smiled at her with even white teeth. "Very good," he said. "Do you speak English?"

"No, no," she demurred, trying not to sound flustered.

As it turned out, Mark Curtis spoke Japanese quite well, and he was straightforward in revealing his background. In America, he began apologetically, government and industry work poorly together. Nothing at all like in Japan. Several U.S. institutes had been formed, each with overlapping and often competing programs. There was a good deal of waste, he said, in talent as well as dollars. Maybe that was why the United States was behind Japan in new-generation computer-development programs.

Mitsuko read the name on the card again. Mark Curtis. He was not the usual kind of American she met. Normally they were old men, smelling of cigars, pretending to be polite but with their distaste for Japan's recent success written in their eyes. At least Mark Curtis had done his homework. He understood how Japanese should be approached. He understood the Japanese viewpoint. Implicitly he had thereby established that his firm could be an understanding partner. She also felt attracted to him personally. He had clean-cut good looks and he was tall: at least 185 centimeters. He had long, straight legs that he crossed casually as he spoke. She liked the way he carried himself too, lean and athletic. He had a slight tan; perhaps he sailed or enjoyed water sports. She stopped her mind from going further. This was silly. He was here for a business proposal. The past few days had made her giddy, vulnerable. She would have to watch herself.

The conversation moved to why Mark Curtis had requested the meeting. It was really quite interesting. MCC was a privately funded group: corporations, donations. It was pure computer research with no hidden meanings. DARPA, on the other hand, was the major large and competing U.S. research team. Everyone knew they were controlled and funded by the Pentagon. The purpose of their computer research was to further U.S. weaponry, pure and simple. Privately, MCC did not share this goal. Peaceful use of all types of computers was their sole objective. The American smiled at Mitsuko benignly. She agreed that that was laudable.

Then he came to the point. He proposed an affiliation with ICOT. Here, the American smilingly held up his hands as if to ward off an out-and-out refusal. Nothing formal, mind you, in the beginning, he said. God forbid, he understood Japanese preferred to have informal private contacts first. No feelings would be hurt if things didn't work out. All he was proposing was a concept, an exploration of the possibilities.

Now Mitsuko understood why he hadn't wanted to see anyone else. A matter such as this would only be handled by Suzuki-san. Astutely, the American understood that Mitsuko would be the best one to bring it to the director's attention.

It was nearly six. Mitsuko glanced at her watch and, to wind up their conversation, said that normally she didn't meet anyone who simply called on the phone. A letter was usual procedure in setting up a meeting. However, in this case she'd found the meeting most interesting. She hoped something would come of it, although she could make no promises. She stood and held out her hand.

Mark Curtis stood but did not take her hand. Instead he bowed like a Japanese and apologized for his rudeness. Normally he would have written, he said, but to be truthful another urgent matter had brought him to Tokyo quite unexpectedly.

Mitsuko looked at him, surprised and pleased. His manners were not at all like a foreigner's. He really was a gentleman. She immediately regretted being so abrupt in closing their meeting. "And what is this other matter that brings you here? I hope you'll not think my asking is rude."

"Not at all," the blond foreigner said softly, and averted his eyes. "I'm here to attend a memorial service for Kathy Johnson. She and her mother were friends of the family. Her mother died last year."

"You don't know how sorry we are about Kathy Johnson. How I am." She stumbled over the words in her embarrassment. Actually she hadn't known the American girl. However, Kathy Johnson's death had brought her husband together with Erika and thus affected Mitsuko's marriage. How ironic that this foreigner should be another link. Perhaps that was Mitsuko's fate.

"I have one final favor to ask, then I'll let you get back to your work." The foreigner glanced at his watch, noting the late time. "Could you suggest a place to eat around here somewhere? I'm tired of hotel food and want a little change. It doesn't have to be fancy."

"Of course," Mitsuko said and, after a moment's thought, suggested a famous Japanese noodle shop several blocks away. She explained how the noodles were made of a special wheat from a secret recipe. Suddenly she found herself craving one of the shop's tasty dishes. She had an inspiration. "Tell you what," she said, surprised by her own boldness. "I was thinking of eating there myself tonight. How about letting me treat you? An introduction to the real Japan."

"I'm afraid it's too much trouble, and I certainly couldn't let you pay, really . . ."

She smiled at him. He had reacted just as a Japanese would, turning down an invitation even though she could tell he would like to have dinner with her. "It's no trouble," Mitsuko said. "In fact it might do me good." She thought for a moment. "I have a few things to tidy up," she said. "Go downstairs and and I'll meet you there in a few minutes." She pushed the button for the receptionist and held out her hand without thinking. This time he took it and when he touched her she felt the strength and certainty of him. It was almost as if he'd known all along just what was going to happen.

As she was about to leave, Suzuki-san wandered in. He seemed to have very accurate radar for her departures. The usual adoring puppy-dog look was in his eyes.

"Dinner?" he asked brightly.

"Busy today," she replied, and watched him try not to look disappointed.

"Maybe tomorrow then," he murmured, and shuffled out of her office. For some reason she couldn't understand, she felt a little guilty.

Free from the office, she lost her gloom. Her problems were minor compared to this American's. Perhaps he and Kathy Johnson had been close. Perhaps even lovers. And yet he was putting on such a brave face. She must be more like this foreigner, she told herself, she must not let the changes in her life get her down.

The *udon* noodles were delicious. She'd decided to pay, and when she insisted and asked for the check, he good-naturedly let her. The dinner had gone too fast for her. Mark Curtis had talked of his travels and of places he'd been. He'd seen all the places she'd dreamed of going.

As they parted he suddenly said, "It's not fair!"

Startled at the tone of his voice, she wondered what had gone wrong after such a perfect time. "What is it?"

With a boyish smile, Mark Curtis said, "You have bought me dinner and now I will never have the chance to repay you. What do you say I take you out just tonight? The rest of the evening will be mine, though. On that I must insist. Then I shall never trouble you again. My conscience will be clear."

She laughed, somehow pleased this new friend was not truly upset. She realized then that the short time she had known this American had changed her entire day.

They went to Pub Cardinal for starters, then to the nearby discos. He was witty and knew all sorts of terrible jokes. She noticed he didn't drink much either and would just take a sip or two each place they visited. The night was costing him a fortune, but he didn't seem to notice. He must be quite rich.

For a nightcap they visited the appropriately named The Last Twenty Cents. They left their shoes at the door since it was a Japanese-style club, and danced in their stocking feet. Although it was late, the crowd was young and enthusiastic. She realized that she was enjoying herself. Although it was—unbelievable—past two o'clock, she was not the least bit tired. She felt free and alive again. He kissed her twice after they slow-danced and she didn't pull away. Her tiny watch read three a.m. when he finally took her home.

———

She thought about sleeping with him, sensed he wanted her. But she'd never been unfaithful during her marriage. If she took a lover, even for one night, her break with Mori would be irrevocable. Like most Japanese women, she clung to the pure, safe images of her past: the summer nights dancing in white kimono and red *hakama* to *kagura*, god-music, wailing flutes and drums, on the raised platform near her local shrine. She let Mark kiss her when she said good night at the door and held on to his hand as he started to walk away.

"Can I see you tomorrow?" he asked. "After the service for Kathy Johnson we can go to dinner. I'll give you a call about time."

"Certainly," she answered without thinking.

Then he walked away and she turned to face her empty

room. After she closed the door she stood there for a while wondering what had become of her.

———

The director of JEC R&D, Minobe-san, greeted Mori, who had arrived for his appointment a bit late. He was a well-groomed intellectual with a dignity that comes only from the highest levels of personal achievement. He started to talk before Mori could open his mouth.

"I'm terribly sorry, I do have a lunch in thirty minutes. Will that be enough?" A glance at his watch. It was good form to apologize when your guest was late.

"More than enough."

"Good. Well, I understand you've come about the American girl?"

Minobe proved to be quite a talker. Mori wondered if it was anxiety. The R&D director began by complaining that the circumstances of her death were a little bit vague, if Mori didn't mind his saying so. An accident was what the MPD advertised, yet all his requests for specifics had been brushed off. There was a church memorial service for her this afternoon and they were having trouble with the eulogy. Mostly because the cause of her death was uncertain. Minobe made an exasperated sound with his lips. Mori nodded encouragingly.

"I can tell you we are all terribly, terribly sorry; I just hope it had nothing to do with our role. No, I suppose it didn't."

"Your role, Minobe-san?" Mori shifted in his chair.

"Yes, certainly." Minobe then launched into one of those brilliantly vague project capsules that are usually reserved for friendly boards of directors at project-funding presentations. It all had to do with superconductors, as Mori had hoped. And Kathy Johnson had been involved. Instead of using metallic alloys as conductors, JEC had decided to go with metallic oxides, or, in other words, ceramics. Compounds of barium, lanthanum, copper, and oxygen. They had already reached 200° Kelvin with wire-thin ceramic rods using liquid nitrogen to supercool. It was very exciting.

"I understand the brilliance of your research," Mori interrupted, "but what is the connection to the American girl's death?"

"We were only trying to ensure that nothing went wrong." Minobe took off his glasses and wiped them carefully.

Mori measured the man and asked, "Wasn't her background checked before she was hired? Isn't that normal?"

Minobe stared abjectly at his hands. "Oh, my, yes. A very severe check was made and she came through it beautifully. In retrospect almost too perfectly."

"What do you mean?"

"The Defense Intelligence Agency came to us last spring. Nothing concrete, mind you, the colonel said. Just some doubt that it was best to clear up. I suppose you do this sort of thing frequently in your police work."

"All the time. What did the colonel suggest?" Mori tried to keep the excitement from his voice.

"A test of her loyalty."

Under gentle probing Minobe explained that the idea had been to let her see, periodically, test data that quite exaggerated what JEC's modest results had been. It would be a way to see how she reacted, the colonel had proposed. First, they claimed a breakthrough with a new vacuum chamber that allowed production of thin films for superconductors that tested consistently positive. Since such conductors were resistance-free and therefore did not release heat, miniaturization of a 5G computer would theoretically be possible. "Actually it is somewhat more complicated than that." Minobe pursed his lips and paused.

"In other words," Mori concluded, "you don't have a workable mini 5G computer in the JEC lab at the present time."

"Nothing that works," Minobe agreed. "You really have to solve the thin-film problem first, and then work out a new design architecture to hope for an operating mini 5G. It will take some time. The dummy prototype we made looks right, however. And the NO-SPEC report was very convincing."

"You were concerned that this prototype and the experiment on her loyalty were somehow related to her death, then?"

"We didn't hear anything, mind you. Not a word whether she had done anything untoward."

"How long had this test been in progress, Minobe-san?"

"Oh, from April I'd say. Less than six months. She was a very bright girl, you know. I was quite sure she'd see straight through the whole thing from the very beginning. Then how would I explain it to her?"

"How far along is your thin-film research, in fact?"

"Well, roughly speaking we're at the point where we can consistently produce SQUIDS."

"SQUIDS, Minobe-san?"

"A preliminary etching system for thin films. We can consistently produce electronic patterns in the thin films that make quantum interference devices called SQUIDS."

"Do you think she saw through the deception?"

"Well, I suppose we'll never know the answer to that now, will we, Inspector?"

Mori produced a pack of Seven Stars, but the director politely refused.

"Do you mind if I smoke?"

"Please. I hope nothing I've said has disturbed you. You were aware of this program, I assume."

"Of course." Mori lit a match by flicking his thumbnail against the match head. She hadn't been in the business long enough, Mori decided. A sixth sense came only with time. She'd found out about the dummied data but she'd played it wrong somehow. And it cost her her life.

"There was one more thing, although I don't think it's related." Minobe checked his watch. "A German salesman for security equipment had a meeting with our building superintendent yesterday. As a matter of course the superintendent phoned me after the meeting. I asked him to send the brochures up even though he hadn't seen anything special. One of the German devices caught my eye—a pressure-differential system—so I gave the firm a call right away. When I asked for the salesman, he said that he had never called on us. Nor did they have records of any contact with us. Odd, wouldn't you say?"

"Yes," Mori said. "What have you done about it?"

"Well, I called Colonel Yuki and put him in touch with our superintendent. I understand a description was given and the colonel said he would handle it. Apparently he knew who the man was."

"Good. Sounds like it's been taken care of. Anything else?"

"No. But it's been one thing after another lately." Minobe sighed and again peeked at his watch. Mori nodded sympathetically but said he didn't think a phony salesman was anything the R&D director should lose sleep over. Mori needed the answer to one more question before he could leave. Minobe's reply provided Mori his second shock of the meeting.

The R&D lab was absolutely secure from unwanted visitors. No one was allowed in by security guards besides JEC staff with special cards. Even they had to go through a security check before entering or leaving the lab. Of course the ICOT director and his personal assistant, a woman, also had access. They occasionally brought over one of their foreign VIPs to impress them, he supposed. ICOT had contributed immensely to development of the 5G, particularly in design architecture. JEC tried to comply with any favors they asked. Minobe apologized that he really had to run. Perhaps Mori could phone him if there was anything else he could do?

Down in the JEC lobby, Mori considered the two astonishing pieces of information he had uncovered. First, Starfire was a scam, a setup. Just as the American MicroDec operation had been. Was the Japanese government attempting to get even? And, second, his wife was one of only two people outside JEC with access to the highly secret lab.

He found a pay phone and finally reached Mitsuko. She was less sarcastic on the phone today for some reason. She seemed lighthearted. But only after he explained that it was a matter of utmost urgency did she finally agree to meet him that evening for a chat.

CHAPTER 3 2

CATCH ME IF
YOU CAN

The interior of the Tokyo Union
Church combines new Christianity with ancient Japanese or-
thodoxy; cream stuccoed walls, cantilevered stained beams,
and nailless joints reflecting Japanese shipbuilders of old. An
intricate harmony resulted. Crucifixion of Christians might
never have taken place.

When Mitsuko arrived, Mark Curtis was already in a seat
at the front reserved for close relatives. He turned as she came
in and nodded imperceptibly. An usher showed Mitsuko to a
seat more than halfway back, behind the large group of JEC
mourners who were impeccable in dark blue business suits for
the men and blue uniforms with white pointing for the women.

The organ was playing "Closer My Lord" in muted tones,
and the last arrivals were rustling in their seats. A middle-aged
and fatherly minister appeared and knelt in the sacristy facing
away from the congregation. Mitsuko stared around the church
fascinated by the formality of the Christian ceremony about
to begin. She was struck by the large number of foreigners who
were attending. Kathy Johnson must have had many friends.

———

In the front pew Valeri Kovalenko felt a twinge of anxiety.
Two police vans had been parked outside the church on Omo-

tesando Avenue. The street, a fashion center for the young, also had a carnival atmosphere today. It was worse than on his last visit. Hawkers lined the sidewalk and fortune-tellers plied their trade. He scowled. It made surveillance too easy. He should have expected that the police would be here, if only for security reasons; the congregation included several members of the elite. He'd recognized the head of the JEC R&D lab from Center photos he'd been shown. And the U.S. ambassador with bodyguards. One, however, startled him; the head of the CIA Science and Technology Directorate, Roger Harrington. Had Center known he was in Japan? Why then hadn't he been informed? He put that aside for now. With Harrington was a large phalanx of burly Americans. They were taking no chances. The Center agent must let neither the Americans nor the police complicate matters. So long as he stuck strictly to the plan, they shouldn't. He must assume Center had considered every angle—even the ones they did not tell him about. However, he was committed to the schedule: Have a good look at the JEC lab today and collect the Starfire tonight or tomorrow night. If he accomplished everything tonight, he'd have two days to make the Hokkaido coast, the fishing village of Nemuro where the boat would be waiting. It would be a Japanese boat manned by a local who was trustworthy. Code name Samurai. He'd be in touch. Mitsuko Mori, sitting in one of the back pews, now was the key. How she reacted over the next several hours would determine not only the fate of his operation but much, much more. He closed his eyes pretending to pray but in fact reviewing all the steps that must go right from this moment on.

———

Mori sat in the special police van listening to the crackle of radio traffic and trying to make up his mind. One of the foreigners in the crowd that had entered the church for the girl's service stood out in his mind. A heavy-shouldered older man. Gray hair at the temples. Mori squinted his eyes, forced his mind back to that awful moment on the Ginza intersection again and tried to compare images. Possibly. Very possibly. The radio crackled.

"Car two-three-oh, car two-three-oh."

In the driver's seat, his friend Watanabe took the call. "This is two-three-oh. Go ahead." The radio was a special high-frequency type that let out a thin background scream. Watanabe turned the speaker switch so Mori could hear.

"Two-three-oh we have an ID on that first request." Mori nodded his head at the good work that had gone into this simple statement. Special hidden TV cameras had been rigged to cover the congregation. The church had been most cooperative when told the reason—that a number of important foreign government officials would be present and that such security was required procedure. The remote camera operators picked out the row a suspect was sitting in for front and side angles. The pictures were relayed from the cameras to the vans over special lines rigged from the church to equipment in the vans. A transmitter in the van then relayed pictures to the huge third-floor command center at MPD headquarters, where requests were monitored and targets compared with available pictures on computer scanning equipment. It took only seconds to get validations. Nor was there any need for Mori to enter the church. He could watch three monitors set up in the police van.

"Go ahead," Watanabe said. "Identification please."

"Sergei Ivanovich Vasilyev. Passport USSR. Government assignment. Aeroflot office director. In Japan since since 1 August 1984. Japan residence valid through 1 August 1988. Nothing against. Any questions?"

Watanabe looked back at Mori who was sitting in the rear of the van, his eyes fastened on the monitors. Mori shook his head.

"Thank you. Over and out."

Mori continued to stare at the monitors as he spoke. "So he's Aeroflot, which means he's GRU. A hard-nose."

"Yeah," Watanabe agreed. "Aeroflot is usually cover for GRU."

"Right."

"And that's the one you saw in Ginza?"

"I'd almost swear to it. Except there's no scar."

"What scar?" Watanabe turned around to stare at the inspector.

"Back of his left ear. Like a knife slash. Or shrapnel in the war. Who knows? Red welt on the neck behind the ear. Saw it clear as daylight. And the videos show nothing in the closeups."

"So what do we do?"

"Stick with him like glue."

"What about your wife? Did you know she was going to be here?"

"Yeah, she told me on the phone. However we weren't told the U.S. ambassador would be here; lack of trust I suppose. Sergei Ivanovich is our main event nonetheless. He may be the missing piece to the puzzle. Besides I have a date with my wife at eight. She and I can talk then. And the U.S. ambassador can take care of himself; he's surrounded by U.S. security."

"Where's your American friend today?"

"Don't really know. He was supposed to meet me here. Something came up, I suppose."

———

Robert Ludlow squatted on the roof of the old ivy-covered apartment complex across the street from the Tokyo Union Church. The four-story building must be prewar, he guessed from its aged look and the fact that there were no elevators. He'd walked four floors to the roof unchallenged. The tenants were merchants selling clothing and other ware from converted apartments, as well as permanent residents used to people coming and going. Ludlow focused a pair of binoculars on the broad steps of the church across the street. The wide double doors were open. He'd had an eventful day thus far, using every trick he knew to keep from being detected. In spite of thick foliage impeding his view, he'd managed to identify the major players going into the service. Harrington and Graves. A crowd who had JEC lapel pins. An assortment of foreigners, many of whom looked to be American. Several who might have been

KGB. But the one that caught his attention was an early arrival. A lanky blond in a DAKS raincoat. He looked familiar. The trees made it difficult to get more than a glimpse, and Ludlow might be imagining things. Still, his subconscious was trying to tell him something.

There were quite a few loungers on the street attracted to the commotion around the church. Ludlow had noted the police vans and the remote TV lines going into the church. Mori was no doubt in one of the vans; however, contact now was out of the question. Those who had tried to take him last night were not KGB, of that he was sure. They were locals, which meant either police or Colonel Yuki's crowd. He had not yet been able to figure out why they had come for him. Both teams were represented at the church, and no doubt a liberal number of onlookers were watching for him or ensuring that nothing untoward happened to the VIPs inside. In any event, he was going to be very careful. He noted several hawkers had set up on the sidewalk. Sellers of cheap jewelry, watches, and a fortune-teller. He knew what he had to do. Wait until the blond came out. Then move in for a close look without setting off a stampede.

———

Sergei Ivanovich Vasilyev had known from the very start that this was not going to be a good day. It was in his bones. First, the man who was supposed to watch Kovalenko on the morning shift had called in sick. A severe case of vodka, Sergei suspected, although there was nothing to be done about it now. Neither did he have a replacement. This was a delicate assignment and he could not bring in the entire watch team, particularly the senior, more experienced men. Someone was sure to realize that they were in fact watching one of their own. Embarrassing questions might follow. Why would they put a visitor from Center under surveillance? The timing would be most unfortunate in terms of his own and Pachinkov's career. So the shorthanded team of relatively inexperienced watchers had been informed that the target was an American CIA specialist. That was all. And Sergei's decision to take over his sick agent's assignment this morning was having a bad effect on his digestive system.

He stared up at the lectern once again. It was a handsome piece in carved oak, but this was not what had caught Sergei's attention. Bouquets of flowers had been piled around the lectern, lilies and iris mainly, in whites, purples and golds. Somber flowers for a somber occasion, Sergei thought, and would have turned his attention elsewhere had a tiny flash of light from a bouquet directly in front of the lectern not caught his eye. Strange, he thought, and began to consider the possibilities. After several minutes he came to a distracting conclusion. He had seen police vans outside, with cables spilling from one across the sidewalk. There were visiting dignitaries, including the U.S. ambassador, here to mourn the girl's death. Surveillance cameras had no doubt been hidden in the church to monitor the congregation. One of the remote cameras had been ingeniously hidden in flowers piled around the lectern, where it could pick up head-on shots of mourners. A remote-controlled camera would swing on command, and light reflected from a moving lens would result in a flash such as Sergei had just seen. Not a miracle then. The notion that his face might be being monitored was a very disturbing one.

He had been very careful since the Ginza killing. This was his first venture out in public. What if he was recognized? He had covered the scar on his neck cosmetically. But his features could not be disguised. What if the CIA realized who he was? What would they do? Or the police? He had another agent waiting outside to pick up Kovalenko when he departed the church. The young Central Asian, Konstantin, would stay with him for the rest of the afternoon, keeping in constant touch with Sergei by radio. The immediate problem was how he could get out of this church and off-camera without attracting too much attention. Procedurally, he could not leave the church until Kovalenko did, until the Center target had been safely passed on to the next watcher. Sergei kept his head down out of view of the front camera and tried to figure the best way to make his escape when the time came.

Valeri Kovalenko waited until the service had begun to put the first stage of Center's plan into action. There was an opening prayer, then a hymn. At the end of the hymn he started to cough. He tried to stifle the cough at first but it was no use. He took out a handkerchief and held it to his mouth. That did no good. The coughing continued. The minister looked at him several times as he began the sermon, a brief account of the girl's life. An American next to Kovalenko looked over at him. "You better go outside for a minute." Kovalenko nodded and stood, shook his head as if to clear it, and remembered to bow in the aisle. Looking extremely embarrassed and perplexed, he made his way up the aisle, stifling coughs as he went. Mitsuko glanced at him with concern as he passed. He made a motion with his head. Outside. He was going to get some air.

On the sidewalk, outside the church, Kovalenko took a deep breath of air. The coughing disappeared. Leaves on the *keyaki* trees of Omote-sando Avenue rustled and turned their white backs to the breeze. He shrugged into his tan DAKS raincoat and appeared to pause, uncertain of direction. His eyes carefully scanned the street on both sides. If she had informed on him it would be here that he would know.

There was no sudden movement, no car careening to a halt in front of him with doors banging open. No crack of a sniper's rifle. She trusted him. The first test had been passed.

Robert Ludlow saw the blond come out the door of the church and without hesitation bolted for the roof trap that led downstairs. Taking the steps three and four at a bound, he raced to the first floor, then managed a casual stroll out onto the sidewalk. His eyes frantically searched the other side of the street. The police vans blocked his view. The blond was not in sight. Dodging cars, he dashed across the street. Gotcha! The blond had walked twenty meters down the hill from the church and was leaning against a wall as if waiting for someone.

Since he couldn't risk being noticed, Ludlow sat down at a fortune-teller's table. She'd set up on the sidewalk under a tree.

On the tiny round table were joss sticks, cards, and other paraphernalia of her trade. She was a young girl with a nice face. "What kind of fortune would you prefer?" The girl leaned doubtfully across the small table.

"Describe the options," Ludlow suggested.

The girl studied Ludlow's face, lapel, and hands; the mirrors of sincerity, affiliation, and wealth. "Two hours for fifteen thousand yen," she said. "You pay the hotel. One hour is ten thousand. Special service is five but I don't take off my clothes."

Ludlow shifted on the stool so he could look down the hill as if considering the options. The blond had not moved.

"I thought you only told fortunes."

She picked up a joss stick and tapped it against her cheek. "You looked like someone who would be interested in more. I throw in your fortune for free."

"That is still quite expensive." Ludlow watched as a Japanese lady, quite attractive, came out the door of the church and walked down to where the blond was. They started to speak. "Ten thousand for two hours and I use the room for the night," he said.

She made a face while her eyes clung to the offer, weighing certainty against probability. The blond and the Japanese lady stopped talking; she took his arm and they started to walk slowly down Omote-sando toward Meiji-dori crossing.

"Thirteen thousand five hundred." The girl tapped the joss sticks suggestively against her lips. It was then that Ludlow saw the two plainclothesmen. They had gotten out of an unmarked car and were studying the people on the sidewalk, slowly turning his way.

Ludlow kept his eyes on the pair. "Listen, I don't have time to negotiate now. I will come back later." He stood.

The girl watched him. "Ten thousand yen. This is the best you will find. Talk to any of the others. Go ahead. It is a very fair price." Through the open doors of the church Ludlow could hear the congregation and choir singing "Rock of Ages."

Ludlow took out two thousand yen, put it on the table, and checked the blond's progress. Still in sight. The two plainclothesmen were ambling his way. "If I do not return you can keep it."

She picked up the money. Suddenly her eyes flared wide. Ludlow felt a hand on his shoulder and a guttural voice said in English, "Down, Mr. Ludlow. Let's sit back down. I too would like to have my fortune read."

———

Sergei had watched the blond Kovalenko walk up the church aisle after faking a fit of coughing. What on Stalin's grave was he up to? As he watched Kovalenko out the door, however, he breathed a sigh of relief. Now he could get out of this mousetrap. He was sitting in the very last row so that when it came his turn to stand he could do so unobtrusively. He stood, half expecting all the CIA toughs there to come charging up the aisle for him. They didn't. He headed for the door and felt the cool breeze tug at his face as he walked down the church steps onto the wide sidewalk. Konstantin was lounging against one of the cars reading a Japanese newspaper. Sergei sighted the young Soviet Central Asian and got the recognition signal. Now the blond target was in Konstantin's hands. Lenin help him if he screwed up.

As Sergei started to stroll up the hill, away from the blond, he checked the sidewalk for possible trouble. A number of people were out today, strollers, loungers, hawkers. He noted the fortune-teller, who hadn't been there earlier. And she had a guest. Sergei looked again, hardly able to believe his eyes. It was that bastard American who had made him look like a jackass to Pachinkov. It was Ludlow!

He stopped in his tracks, deciding what to do. He knew he didn't have much time. The cameras inside the church could have identified him. He must escape. But this was too ripe an opportunity to pass up. Ludlow had stood and was looking down the hill. Sergei came up behind him and put his arm on the American's shoulder.

The American sat back down at Sergei's gentle suggestion. Sergei put a newspaper on top of the tiny table. Then he put his hand under the newspaper. In his hand was a gun. With his other hand he found Ludlow's weapon and spilled it to the sidewalk under the table. He gave it a vicious kick, sending it to the gutter. Then he smiled at Ludlow. "Much better now, isn't it?"

Ludlow looked down the hill. The blond and the Japanese lady were nowhere in sight. He stared at the Soviet. "Listen, Russkie, you people are responsible for that girl's death." He jerked his head at the open church doors. "You want to tell me about it?"

Sergei's grin broadened. "This is what I like about you Americans. I could put your brains through that van window and you sit there asking difficult questions. This is glasnost. Haven't you heard? We are going to work together. In fact I was going to propose something specific. Do you have a few minutes?"

Sergei took a small transmitter out of his lapel pocket and spoke hurriedly in Russian. A pickup on Omote-sando. In front of the church. Extreme urgent priority. Sergei put the radio away. Perhaps today wouldn't turn out so badly after all.

———

Mori sat in the van watching developments on the sidewalk. They'd monitored departure of the Russian target Sergei Ivanovich Vasilyev on the TV, then picked him up visually as he came down the steps. It wasn't until he went over to the fortune-teller that they noticed who the client was. Ludlow. That put a definite crimp in their plans. They'd hoped to follow Sergei unawares. The Russian might give something away. But whatever was going on between the Russian and Ludlow didn't look good. And now Mori could see two of Colonel Yuki's goons circling the two warily. Something was about to happen. He turned to his sidekick, Watanabe. "Out. Let's break up whatever is going on. I'll chat with Colonel Yuki's people first. You take the Russian, protective custody for questioning. Then I'll get Ludlow."

Watanabe looked over at Mori. They'd both seen Mori's wife

come out earlier, meet the tall good-looking foreigner, then saunter down the hill together. Mori had contained his anger. But now it was showing.

"Okay, Inspector. Let's just keep it cool, okay?"

Mori looked at his friend quizzically. "Sure," he said and opened the door.

Seeing Ludlow and the other foreigner engrossed in conversation, Mori approached the larger of Colonel Yuki's men. "What's going on?"

"We have orders to pick up the American sitting over there with the other foreigner." The big Japanese agent was chewing on a toothpick and gave Mori a please-don't-get-in-my-way grin.

"What on earth for?"

The grin froze slightly. The toothpick momentarily stopped bobbing around the mouth. "We don't know. He's done something illegal no doubt. We're just following orders."

"Lay a finger on him and I'll split you in two," Mori said good-naturedly.

The Defense Intelligence officer was a good ten centimeters taller than Mori. He smiled and gave Mori a push.

What happened next was hard for witnesses to agree on. Some said the small Japanese exploded a karate kick that caught the large one in the kidneys. Others said the hands came first, two pistonlike chops that sawed the large one's neck. He swayed for a moment, as another Japanese rushed in to pull the small one away, then fell to the pavement. He was out for over ten minutes. No one seemed to notice the minor action at a nearby fortune-teller's table, which suddenly overturned as a large foreigner with a mean expression rudely grabbed another foreigner who cursed in what sounded like Russian as he was hurled against a tree, lost his balance, and fell to the ground. Meanwhile the large foreigner took off for the Omote-sando subway entrance with the speed of a gazelle on dry, flat ground. Once there he disappeared into the bowels of the underground.

At this moment an unmarked car pulled up. The cursing Russian was seen to be helped in, then the car drove away.

Watanabe stood watching the Russian car head up Omote-sando. "I told you not to lose your temper."

"Arrogant bastard." Mori shook his head.

"What do we do about the Russian now?"

"Let him go." Mori took a deep breath. "Sergei will head for the Soviet embassy. Nothing we can do about it. I'll haul him in for questioning tomorrow. They were trying to take Ludlow. The Russian must have called for backup and it came just a bit too late."

A crowd was gathering.

"Back in the van, Inspector," Watanabe coaxed. "Think it's time we head home. Not much more going to happen today."

It wasn't until later that the police officer found out how wrong he was.

CHAPTER 33

DINNER AT MAXIM'S

In the church Mitsuko had seen her American leave hurriedly and she rushed out to him, a worried expression on her face. "Are you okay?"

The blond nodded and explained that an old allergy had returned; perhaps the flowers in the church had caused it. Mitsuko told him not to mind, the Christian ceremony was difficult for her to understand anyway.

"Look," he apologized, "I'm sorry I insisted you come only to—"

Mitsuko cut him off. "No," she said. "It's all right." Then she blushed. She was about to say she'd rather be together with him than sitting rows apart in a foreign church. It came to her that she'd been thinking about this man since they'd met. No good, she warned herself. A total stranger, a foreigner to boot, and she was about to hurl herself into his arms? She'd heard the arguments on the late-night TV shows that Japanese women were immature; that they lacked the emotional so-phistication of their more experienced American and European counterparts. Was this true? Was the fact that she'd had no other experience with men before she met Mori affecting her judgment now? She shrugged the thought away. She knew that Japanese women were changing, but that they were still very pure. Their innocence showed in their outdated emphasis on pleasing the opposite sex—the silly stress on cuteness and youth, their vulnerability to foreigners. In her case it was a matter of revenge, retribution for her husband's disloyalty. An affair with this foreigner would cleanse her; begin the repayment. As they started to walk away from the church, down the gently sloping tree-lined boulevard, Mitsuko took the arm of the person she thought to be an American.

When they'd nearly reached Meiji-dori intersection, where the street begins to climb toward Meiji Shrine, this "American" pointed to an open-air coffee shop. It was the one he'd reconnoitered several days earlier. "How about a cup of coffee," he suggested. "Better than sitting inside a stuffy church."

Mitsuko agreed, noting the tension in his voice. "I feel so sorry for you," she said helplessly. "The emotional strain." She wondered again about the relationship between the foreigner and the dead girl. He'd said he was a "friend of the family." Had they been lovers? She felt a pang of jealousy, then guilt. God, this was completely unlike her. Pull yourself together, she told herself. Enjoy it. You're going to seduce a very handsome foreigner but you're not going to let yourself become emotionally involved—just like a foreign woman. They quickened their pace and soon had reached the St. Tropez coffee shop.

As they waited to be seated, Valeri Kovalenko felt the adrenaline building. Her words had been uncannily correct. He was now under an emotional strain. But the weight he felt was for reasons other than the ones she thought. Every move he made from now on would be vital. He must concentrate, accept whatever happened, and deal with it quickly, mercilessly if necessary. He felt the comforting cold steel of the Makarov in the scarf pocket of the DAKS.

Unlike most customers, he asked for a table in the back. They were shown to one near the phones, just as he'd hoped. For a moment he envied the people around him, enjoying the pleasant afternoon. Carefree. It was always easier to be mentally honest in a foreign country, he'd found. A certain part of the brain was let out of the cage that had been built over years of conditioning, of living in a controlled society. Communism meant little to him, except as it affected his own career. Communism, Marxism, like every ideology of the intellectualist cultures of the world, had its inner soft core that was essentially ludicrous. For him the only matter of importance was to succeed with this operation. Center was counting on him. The most difficult part lay immediately ahead.

Both ordered coffees named after famous European playgrounds, Cannes and San Remo. The shop was a favorite pickup spot for foreigners, and a mixed couple did not attract attention. There were a number of other *gaijins* with locals at the tables, perhaps seeking brief but meaningful relationships. Several males sat alone, appraising the parade of chopped trousers, bagged skirts, and ribboned hairdos on the sidewalk outside. Harajuku was a fashion mecca for the young. One of those who sat alone was a smooth-featured Asian who did not appear to be Japanese.

Kovalenko tried to shut out the fact that Mitsuko was an elegant and exotic woman; that he had lied to her to bring her to this place at precisely this time. For a moment he wondered what it would be like to have a truly honest relationship with such a lovely creature. His mind quickly shrugged off this dangerous notion. The sun was waning. It made her skin even paler, her eyes deeper, more attractive wounds of black. Kovalenko shifted in his seat: "Before I leave Japan there is one more thing I must do in Kathy's memory. I want you to help me." He took her hand and held it in his.

"I'll do anything I can," Mitsuko said, and squeezed his hand in response.

"I want you to take me to where Kathy worked. I'd like you to show me her desk. Let me sit there, feel her presence for the final time. It will have more meaning than the church. In your religion I understand it is custom to visit the abode of departed spirits."

Center had calculated that the research-and-development laboratory at Japan Electronics Corporation would be nearly deserted. Everyone would be at the memorial service so long as the leader, Minobe, was there. With luck he might get Starfire out with ease.

Mitsuko stared at him in surprise. "I can't possibly do that."

Kovalenko tried not to let the panic show on his face. He preferred not to force her; there would be greater risk. He said, "It's too bad; I'd wanted to make my last day meaningful."

"Your last day?" Mitsuko tried not to let the disappointment show in her voice. Her plans were shattered.

"Yes. I have a flight out tomorrow. I'd hoped we could stop at JEC for a few moments, then head over to my hotel for cocktails. Tonight we're going to Maxim's."

Maxim's? She wasn't thinking of fine dining now. But that wasn't all that bothered her. Her friend's tone had changed, become too intense, almost threatening. Or was she imagining things?

"I would only stay a few minutes at her desk." Kovalenko's voice interrupted her thoughts. "Just enough to feel her spirit, her soul."

Mitsuko pondered what he'd said. She wanted to be reasonable. "Many Japanese relatives visit Pacific islands where loved ones were killed during the war to commune with departed spirits. What you want to do is the same. I respect you for that; you're like us."

"Then what do you say?"

"I want to help you," she said sincerely. "Each summer we have a festival to our departed spirits. In our homes are altars to loved ones and ancestors, so we are reminded of them daily. Most people pretend not to care, yet in their hearts they do. But the JEC research lab is a restricted area." Mitsuko sighed and took a deep breath.

"That's okay. I don't want trouble for you, Mitsuko. But I cannot go back to that church." Kovalenko once more considered the alternative. Force.

Mitsuko bit her lip. She could see how disappointed he was, even though he tried to hide it. Kathy and he must have been lovers. She shouldn't be envious and small. His lover had died tragically. She would help him if she could. She knew that, occasionally, foreign visitors were allowed into the lab. Minobe-san wouldn't know; he'd be at the church service for another hour.

"The guards might allow us a few minutes inside," she said, "if they know it is someone very close to her." Mitsuko studied his face for a moment. "Do you have ten yen?"

Kovalenko handed her the coin, knowing it was all a formality. Center had confirmed that she and the director of ICOT were the only two outsiders with the power to authorize JEC R&D guests.

She dialed hesitantly, looking back once at the handsome blond. She bent over the mouthpiece and he saw her body tense and her free hand fly to her hair as she started to speak. For a time she appeared to be answering questions. Then she hung up and came back with a broad smile. "I told them you were her fiancé," she said.

They took a taxi the short distance to Shinjuku and had no problem getting past the downstairs lobby guards. It was on the R&D floor of the Japan Electronics Tower that Kovalenko's troubles began. He spotted the security equipment as they alighted from the elevator: an infrared oven for hand-carried articles and a sensor body check. The only good news was that a monitor was turned off.

Two young guards manning the equipment waved at Mitsuko. She apparently was a favorite. Kovalenko took off his raincoat with the Makarov and folded it over the hand luggage. Inside the flight bag were clothes purchased by First Directorate in the United States. He set the bag and raincoat down: "I'll leave my luggage here where the guards can watch it," he grinned. "We'll just be a minute." He felt his senses become keenly alert. He must identify all security devices inside the lab within a very short time. And he had to appear casual, disinterested.

They went through the body check and Kovalenko made an awkward attempt to bow; the two young guards smiled at one another. One escorted them down the hall to the R&D door.

"Normally, you're supposed to give us a one-day advance notice." The young guard held the door open as they reached the laboratory.

"I know," Mitsuko replied. "It is greatly appreciated." She gave him a nice warm smile and led the way into the lab.

So that was it, Kovalenko thought, as he followed her past a series of cubicles where the technicians worked. He chuckled at the thought of the Center expert's face when he explained how far theories of Shinto psychology had gotten him. Security had been breached because one of the guards had a crush on Mitsuko.

They reached an immaculately clean open work area. Computers on rollable metal tables were in various stages of assembly. There was no one in the section. At the far end was a large desk with a clean top. Minobe's desk, Kovalenko guessed, as he saw Mitsuko glance furtively toward it.

However, the Starfire was nowhere in sight. Center had briefed him carefully on its probable dimensions and shape. Mitsuko was motioning him on into another lane of cubicles which ran by windows that faced out across the city. Only a handful of the work desks were occupied, the occupants too engrossed in their labors to look up. Kovalenko tensed. His mind raced through plans of how he might get the prototype past the two guards—if he found it. Nothing felt right.

Quickly he inventoried the security devices he'd seen. Formidable, as he'd expected. Electric sockets in the walls gave away laser beams. A camera mounted in the ceiling. In the floor he'd seen a pressure-sensor system. Troublesome but not impossible. But he'd have to attack it from the control box, wherever that was. Considerable time would be necessary.

Mitsuko had stopped and was looking nervously at her watch. "If Minobe finds out I've brought in a foreigner I haven't cleared with him he'll behead me."

"Who's Minobe?" Kovalenko asked innocently.

"It doesn't matter." She pointed. "This is her desk. Do you want to be alone?"

"If you don't mind." Silently he sat down at the desk. Mitsuko patted his shoulder and he listened to her footsteps fade in the direction they had come from. She'd go back and chat up her friend the guard, he hoped. But he musn't expect too much. He checked his watch. They'd already been inside three minutes. He forced himself to wait until he was sure she'd cleared the assembly area. Through the window he stared at the vastness of Tokyo that ran on into the horizon.

When he rose he was glad he'd worn the rubber-soled shoes. The floor was of spotless tile that picked up and echoed any sound. Noiselessly he returned to the assembly work area, stopping along the way to make sure he was not seen or heard.

Again he searched the benches. Most of the computers were large mainframes. Nothing remotely resembled what he had been told to look for. He searched for the camera mounted in the ceiling and scrutinized the design. This was something new; perhaps a digital encoded-dot system he'd only heard about that remotely triggered anything which changed picture sequence. Fortunately it wouldn't be turned on until tonight. His eyes studied the lens carefully. Chances were they'd have it focused on their prize even though the system wasn't activated until after working hours. He traced the camera's trajectory. Its focus was on a small metal box.

He raced over to the object, then stopped to listen and be sure there was no one near. When he hefted it he was surprised by its lack of weight. The metal cover was obviously a casing to protect the equipment inside. It fitted the Center specs, however. Quickly he worked the lock on the cover; it opened easily. Lifting the cover off, he stared for a moment in disbelief at the tiny computer. It was beautiful. His hand touched the metal surface, fingering the keys. Then, reluctantly, he fitted the cover again over the computer and returned the case to the exact position where he had found it. His mind was whirling. If he could believe what he had just seen, JEC had joined a sequential inference or logic machine with new data-base equipment. Marvelous! And what a a beautiful job of miniaturization they'd done. How was it possible? The chips, of course. The chips were the key!

"What are you doing here?" Mitsuko came on him suddenly, with a puzzled expression that was quickly turning to one of rage.

"I was just on my way out," Kovalenko stammered.

"No you weren't!" Mitsuko's voice whipped at him. "You were examining the equipment!"

Kovalenko smiled and walked toward her.

His next move was reflexive; he hit her precisely, a killing blow chopped to the delicate elegant neck, pulled ever so slightly at the last instant. He didn't know why.

Her eyes rolled back into her head as her body froze, then sagged to the floor.

Kovalenko ran by her to the door of the R&D lab. Voices were screaming in his mind. He summoned his will to walk calmly out into the hall. The two guards looked up at him and nodded. He went over to his luggage and picked up his raincoat woodenly. Deliberately, he unzipped the scarf pocket and grasped the handle of the Makarov.

"Mitsuko-san?" One of the guards was staring at him, then at the lab door.

Kovalenko shrugged. The guard who fancied her started toward the laboratory door.

"No!" Kovalenko drew the Soviet handgun clear of the raincoat.

"*Yarō!*" the young guard hissed at Kovalenko. The Russian had the weapon fully extended in front of his body, legs slightly bent to take the recoil.

Both guards drew at the same time. For a moment Kovalenko hesitated, amazed by their bravery. Then he squeezed the trigger. His bullet took the first youngster in the side of the head and blew his brains into a round rising sun against the immaculate wall. There was no sound from Kovalenko's silenced weapon, just the hard slap of the bullet splintering bone. Then an explosion as the second guard fired and Kovalenko felt a puff of wind from a near miss.

Kovalenko fired again. His round hit the second guard in the throat. A bright scarlet geyser erupted, a gun clattered and spun along the polished floor.

Without thinking now, Kovalenko raced to his overnight bag, threw the contents on the floor, and sprinted into the laboratory along the cubicles to the assembly area. Someone inside was calling for quiet. He forced the tiny computer into his bag and dashed back to the elevators. As he pounded on the down button, he tried not to look at the two guards crumpled in pools of blood in the hallway. One was moaning, the other lay still. Mitsuko's form in the work area had also been deathly still. For some strange reason he hoped he hadn't killed her.

The door opened and two people got off. He pushed past them, hit the ground-floor button, and heard screams as the doors closed. There would be panic now, and his main job was to keep cool until he was outside the building. He gulped air and felt his nerves begin to steady. Mother of Lenin, why had they given him a Makarov with armor-piercing bullets?

He went through the downstairs lobby with a nod to the guards on duty and outside felt the cold air engulf and revive him. The stir was beginning in the lobby as he flagged a cab. It was a bungled operation, but that didn't matter now. The end was everything. He sensed the release and exhilaration surge through him. He was out. He had won!

CHAPTER 34

LUCK OF A
THOUSAND CRANES

From the church, Mori and Watanabe had gone directly to the HQ command center to review tapes, process the data, and make out their reports. The Tokyo Metropolitan Police Communication Command Center was a huge, hushed room of intense activity. There were banks of several hundred CRT display units on gray desks manned by operators taking the more than two thousand emergencies called in daily, and organizing responses. So highly sophisticated was the system that on-scene time after receipt of a call was under four minutes. This was one of the reasons the Keishicho was reputed by professionals to be the finest police force in the world.

While Watanabe struggled with a report form, Mori conferred with the operator who had provided audiovisual link to the church scene. Soft overhead lighting, soundproofed walls, the atmosphere of intense concentration, and the hum of air-filtration equipment lent the command center the atmosphere of a library. The impression was deceptive. Mori glanced up at the huge screen at the middle of the room. One half of the screen was a map of Tokyo covering 864 square miles and over twelve million inhabitants. Red lights were silently flashing at locations where emergencies were in progress. There were ten in all; late afternoon was a slow time of the day. The other half of the screen was a huge video blowup map of the Kanda area, where the major current emergency was in progress. This half could also relay video pictures from monitors at banks or firms that had security-link alarm systems to the MPD.

The operator with Mori began to scroll through each of the camera tapes. Mori stopped him every time he wanted a still or to check someone in the crowd. Watanabe was tapping his pencil irritably against the desk, trying to get a wording right. A new light blinked on the map and the blowup went to live video, the inside of a research lab. Mori inspected the screen, then went back to his work. It looked like a laboratory on the big screen. Computers of some sort. Computers! His eyes returned to the screen. Somewhere in the center one of the operators was dealing with the crisis, calmly speaking into his headset while his hands punched at buttons to get things rolling. The main-screen camera went to a hall monitor: elevators, a security check, and two inert forms on the floor.

Mori hit the operator on the shoulder and motioned to the screen. "Which channel?" He plugged in a headset and let the operator set the computer-aided digitizer system where audio headsets and CRT displays could monitor any incoming action. The voice on the other end was excited:

"One of the guards is gone. The other looks very bad. The woman is showing weak life signs . . ."

"We have three paramedic units converging. First arrival," a pause, "two minutes. Clear an elevator so they can go right up, please. Which floor?" The voice was ice-cool.

"Thirty-third. The R&D laboratory."

"Thank you. Hang on, I'll get this to the para teams."

The line blanked out momentarily while the operator relayed information on voice links to the units screaming through Tokyo's streets.

"Where?" Mori shouted into the headphone, then realized he could only monitor from this desk. He had a sinking feeling in his stomach. He hoped he wasn't right. He tore off the headset, checked the emergency number on the big screen, and turned to the operator. "Plug me in to seven eighty-nine up top. Now."

Watanabe was staring at him and at the screen. "What the hell's happening?"

The operator hit a button and Mori put the phones back on. The "top" was a glassed-in booth running across the rear of the two-story command center. Inside, supervisors monitored every step of every emergency. Occasionally they made corrections and noted names. Mostly they just listened.

Mori identified himself and asked for location on emergency number 789. A disembodied voice asked him to wait.

"Shinjuku," the voice returned. "Japan Electronics Corporation."

"Who's down?"

"We have the guardmen's names, Kita and Saodome. The woman is unidentified; someone working in the lab we believe."

"What were they after?"

"A Fifth Generation minicomputer code-named Starfire. The prototype is missing."

"Perpetrators?"

"Not in custody. An unidentified blond. No nationality. That's all we have right now. We're trying to get these people out alive." The voice was clipped.

"Thank you, sir." Mori switched off and turned to Watanabe. "Shit."

Watanabe put his pencil down. "They hit where Kathy Johnson worked?" He was staring at the screen in disbelief.

"That's right," Mori replied. His voice sounded harsh and strained to his own ears. He was trying to sort out what had happened. The superintendent general and top brass had expected this. Had encouraged it. An attempt to steal Starfire. The only thing they hadn't expected was that it might cost lives. Or that it might succeed.

"Paramedics." Watanabe pointed to the screen. The hall monitors tracked the elevator doors opening as the first paramedic team rushed out. Four men. They went to one form, then to the next. One man ran off camera. The inside laboratory monitor flicked on. It zoomed in on an inert form. The paramedic reached the form, bent over it, then began hooking up a portable oxygen supply. The inert form was of a woman, somehow familiar. A woman with a long delicate neck, now bent at an awkward angle. Blood was coming from her mouth and nose. Mori felt a searing cold wind tear through his body.

Watanabe stood up, pointing to the screen. "It's Mitsuko! Mori-san, it's your wife!"

Mori's mind had become an echo chamber of sights and sounds. The headset had returned to the monitor channel and Mori could hear the professional voices describing the arrival of stretcher equipment. She was being carefully strapped in. The victim's life signs were weakening. They would have to hurry. Her pocketbook was checked for ID. The name was Mitsuko Mori. A disinterested voice read the address, Mori's address. Mori barely heard it. He saw Mitsuko's face as it had once been. Laughing and well. He saw her again at the church. Coming down the steps looking elegant and beautiful. She had walked over to the blond foreigner. Blond! Dammit, what had he been thinking about? He turned to the operator.

"Put the front church camera on again," he hissed. "I know I saw a blond in the first row."

Watanabe was looking at him sympathetically. "You okay, Inspector?"

Mori just shook his head. "The blond my wife was with at the church. . . . I don't have time to explain. Find out which hospital they're taking her to and get a car ready. Be downstairs in a minute. I have one more thing to do here." He turned back to the videotape as Watanabe scuttled off.

It took five minutes on fast forward before Mori found the frames he wanted. He requested stills and gave a distribution list. As he rose from the desk, a junior officer came running up and saluted smartly. "The superintendent general would like to see you urgently, sir."

————

The chief slammed his fist on the desk. To use defeat, that was the Japanese strength, *desho!* He looked up at Mori, who was standing at attention before his desk.

"*So desu*," said Mori. Of course.

298

That was why the terrible incident at the JEC lab must not cause anyone to falter. "And of all people, using your wife." He paused to consider a paper in front of him. "She's arrived at the Joshi Idai Hospital, gone straight to intensive care. Women's hospital, you know; they'll take good care of her." He looked at the report again. "On the way the paramedics' unit did its job. Her vital signs are starting to improve."

"What's the diagnosis?"

"I thought you knew. She's got a broken neck."

Mori again felt the cold anger in him, and stilled it. Time. It was not yet time. He made a formal half-bow. He knew he could not bring up the matter of Colonel Yuki and Erika yet. There was only her word against the colonel's. There was much more to do. "I apologize for the inconvenience my wife has caused." The words tasted bitter in his throat, but he continued. "It is entirely my fault."

The chief waved a blunt-fingered hand. "Don't punish yourself, Inspector. Could have happened to any of us. Understand from the colonel you've been having troubles at home." The chief made a clicking noise. "Such a beautiful woman too."

Woman, Mori thought. She had been used by the state and so was graduated in status from a "girl" to a "woman." She could die for that acknowledgment, or be paralyzed for life.

"I have spoken with Minobe-san," Mori said calmly. "He has told me how the Starfire prototype was dummied at Colonel Yuki's instruction."

The chief leaned back in his executive chair, clasped his hands behind his neck, deliberated, then nodded to himself. "Wasn't your piece of the operation, Inspector. You know the rules. They did a marvelous job over at JEC, I must admit. Too damn good, perhaps."

Mori knew he must hold his temper. Some Russian mastermind and Colonel Yuki were behind the tragedy. The chief had merely been used. He wished he knew their final goal. He wished . . .

"Let me bring you up to date." The chief snapped his chair forward and glared around at his desk until he found a folder. He opened it and motioned Mori to a chair. "Well then." The chief leaned on his elbows and began to lay out the facts. The blond killer was American. He read a passport number and name. A Japan entry date less than a week old. A company affiliation, which was being checked. Several minutes ago an anonymous tip was received that the killer would board a bullet train and head north. Self-Defense Forces troops were being deployed at stations as quickly as possible. Within two hours all stations to Morioka would be under tight security. Airport checks were also being set up, and road blocks around Tokyo and other escape routes. Ludlow was in hiding and could know the blond's escape route. Ludlow was wanted as an accessory to murder. Here the chief put the file down and looked up at Mori. The inspector's face was impassive. The chief nodded, satisfied, and started reading again.

Ludlow had passed himself off as a German security equipment-firm salesman to meet with the JEC building superintendent. Picked the super's brains about the R&D lab security system and god knows what else. The chief sighed and stared out the window a moment.

"When did all this happen?"

"Yesterday. The building super called Minobe about the meeting as a matter of routine. Minobe asked for the brochures, found something interesting the super missed, called the security firm. They knew nothing about any JEC meeting. Minobe became suspicious and called Colonel Yuki. From the detailed description, Yuki identified Ludlow. Yuki's team tried to pick Ludlow up last night at his hotel. Unfortunately he escaped."

Mori shook his head. Now at least he understood why Ludlow hadn't contacted him. Why Ludlow had run after the fight at the church. Both Soviet and Japanese teams were after him, apparently for very good reason. "I'm afraid I didn't help matters at the church. I should have been told what was going on."

"We realize that now, Inspector. However, technically you have interfered with apprehension of an accomplice to murder. Had he been picked up, the JEC entry might have been thwarted."

Mori silently bowed in shame. The words hurt, but he understood that they were true. He felt the cold anger flow again. Soon, very soon, he would let it off the leash.

The chief picked up the folder again. The MPD was holding off releasing anything except the fact of the break-in to the evening news, but there were already several leaks. The *Asahi* newspaper called to say they were planning to imply American involvement. Trust them to jump on the Americans first. MPD public relations has issued no comment. The chief spun the file to a far corner of his desk and rubbed his eyes. His voice sounded tired when he spoke again; this had not been one of the MPD's better days. After escaping from Yuki's team, Ludlow had spent the night at a public bath in Shinjuku. He had showed up at the church and Mori had helped him to escape again. The chief stared at Mori. "You figured out which side you're on yet? The colonel asked me to put that to you."

Mori smiled at the irony. There were many sides in this game now. "I know which side I'm on, Chief."

The chief nodded, then explained to Mori what he wanted the inspector to do. First, he must find Ludlow. The American could lead them to the others. Everyone who was involved must be caught, and that meant the plot leaders, no matter how high up. Here the chief added a footnote; Harrington of the CIA had been asked to remain in Tokyo until the matter was satisfactorily settled. As soon as all Americans were captured, there would be a huge press conference, televised internationally. The chief sucked air in a long hissing noise through square white teeth and fell silent, waiting for the inspector to respond.

"I will find Ludlow and the blond," Mori said quietly. "Japan will have its new security agency."

The senior police officer nodded calmly. In that case, Japan's gratitude would be generous. Mori would be a hero like his father and grandfather before him. The chief shifted his gaze to study Mori more carefully. "There is more than a security agency at stake, Inspector," he said. "Considerably more. May the luck of a thousand cranes ride with you."

CHAPTER 3 5

A PROMISE

The hospital had only recently begun to look prosperous. They'd put a new facade and shiny glass doors at the main entrance. The building was glass and old concrete, from a period of postwar afterthought. The staff taught at an affiliated medical college and published frequently, reinforcing an impression of quality.

Mori hurried through the front door. Colored lines were painted on the floor for queues to a wide counter. Crowds waited in remarkably straight lines for medicines, for clinical results, for room reservations, for operation schedules. He turned left down a hall with an arrow and the word LIFTS. Steel operating tables piled with soiled linen lined the walls. Children scampered after one another. Patients in light green unisex smocks spoke in hushed tones to visiting condolers. Others sat on chairs before open doctors' offices, pretending not to hear intimate testimonies inside. He went to the fourth floor. Why would they put her on the fourth? he wondered angrily, the fourth was unlucky. At a counter he asked directions. Two young nurses turned from sorting medical trays to look at him. Suddenly frightened by their stares, he asked, "How is she?" One nurse came over, her eyes sympathetic and curious. "Mitsuko Mori, yes?" She picked up a chart and studied it. The examination showed trauma to the neck, concussion, and a crack in the second vertebra. No severance of nerve or rupturing. Blood in her lungs was the main problem; she'd have died if the paramedics hadn't sorted that on the way in. She was doing very well now. The neck had been set and she was on an intravenous system to offset shock. "You're the husband?"

Mori nodded.

"Doctor will be looking in on her shortly. No other visitors allowed. We've had several calls from TV networks, and there are a dozen reporters buzzing around downstairs. No one except you knows her room. You can have ten minutes with her." She smiled at him as if he were a celebrity.

He stopped in a men's room to splash water on his face. On the sink were glass bottles and tubes. The ache behind his eyes had become acute. He looked at his face in the mirror and was appalled. He searched for her room, wrinkling his nose at the stench of antiseptic which hung in the air like poison gas over a battlefield. Room 402. He knocked, heard no reply, and went in. There was a white curtain around her bed separating her from the other patient. He pushed the curtain angrily aside. Was there no privacy anywhere in Japan? Her eyes were closed.

"Mitsuko, can you hear me?" There were tubes leading from her arms to bottles hung over the bed. Her neck was encased in a steel brace. She looked very white and frail, smaller than he had ever seen her. Her eyes fluttered open. She tried to move her head and could not. Fright captured her eyes as she remembered. She saw her husband and the fright was pushed aside. Mori smiled at her. He touched her arm lightly.

"I will find him," he said. "I will find him and I will kill him."

The fright returned to her eyes again. He shook his head and tried again. "Look," he said, wondering if the patient beyond the curtain was listening or asleep. He should have checked. "I love you very much. I'm sorry about everything. You and I were used. They tried to separate us to get at the Starfire."

"Americans." Her lips formed the words although no sound came.

"We know. We understand. Do not think about it anymore."

He touched her hand; the skin was cool. She could not move it. I will kill them all, he thought. Every one of them.

"Your mother?" Again her lips soundlessly formed the words.

Mori nodded understanding. "When you are better you will come home with me. My mother will be told about the clock and the *kanzashi*. It was all to split up our family. She could not come today but will visit you soon. I'm sorry I had no time to get flowers."

Mitsuko smiled for the first time. It was her broken-promise smile. It was a smile that said, you will never change, but I love you anyway. He grinned suddenly and squeezed her hand. "When you are well we will take a trip. To Hawaii or Europe, wherever you like."

Mitsuko's smile broadened and now there was a sound, the sound of a childlike laugh.

PART FOUR
NIGERU
(THE ESCAPE)

Love revealed to one's lover while alive is
not profound; to die with love kept to
oneself is superior to all other forms of love.
—Yamamoto Tsunetomo,
Hagakure

BULLET TRAIN

Ludlow made Shinjuku by 8:30
that night. He'd taken a bus from Osaki just to be safe. Plainclothesmen were crawling all over the station West entrance.
He ducked off the bus away from the brassy neon that surrounds the square; the great searing neon blues and whites of
the Keio department store, the fire red of a moving Minolta
sign, and the yellow and green of Sapporo beer. Everything
moved or danced or glittered. Lights crawled over pedestrians
below in tribal patterns and reflected from the glass and shiny
metal of new buildings.

He skirted a long taxi line. People waited patiently with
their shopping spoils. Lovers leaned together. Taxis pulled out,
leaving rooster tails of exhaust in the blazing neon forest. Ludlow hurried toward the JEC Tower.

Japanese shopkeepers were sweeping sidewalks in front of
stores and closing up. Throwing buckets of water to settle the
immaculate dust. He passed Yodobashi Camera, which advertised forty percent off in glaring window ads and shrieked with
a punk-rock disco sound.

From a distance the JEC Tower surprised him by its somber
elegance, somehow more substantial than in daylight. It
bulked up into the night sky, an ebony shaft, a branchless tree.
Around its roots, sparkling like magical flowers, were swirling

arctic-blue lights. As Ludlow approached he saw they were attached to the tops of police cars.

He cursed and circled the JEC building like a hunter stalking prey. Police were on guard at all the entrances, even in back. Detectives in civilian clothes were huddled inside the brightly lit lobby. He abandoned the area and walked until he found a pay phone.

"*Omachi kudasai,*" the voice of the 101 emergency desk officer was neutral, showing no surprise that a foreigner would be phoning for Inspector Mori after the close of office hours.

Then Mori was on the line.

"What happened?" Ludlow asked.

"Deep deep shit, Robert-san." Mori's voice was stone-cold. "You must be out of your mind. Where are you?"

"How bad is it? I'm in Tokyo."

"Two guards dead. My wife recovered long enough to make a statement that it was an American. They're not sure she'll pull through. You're a dead man, Robert-san."

"Wait a minute, will you! I haven't been near the building until a couple of minutes ago. Christ, there are police all over it." Ludlow's mind was racing ahead in a frenzy. "The computer, is it gone?"

"Sorry, Robert-san. That just won't work. The building manager, Mr. Tsuna, positively identified you posing as a German security-firm salesman. We know you ran the scope. They found your prints on a rear unused fire door and a length of clear plastic attached to the crash bar. There's no way your people can escape with the equipment. Why don't you give it up? I'll see what I can do."

"It wasn't Americans!" Ludlow shouted and slammed the phone against its hook.

———

Even though Ueno Station was packed with Wednesday travelers, Kovalenko played it safe. He bought a platform pass and went through the ticket barrier with a crowd. A ticket puncher would be less likely to remember him than a ticket-window clerk, who also could give them destination. Punchers looked at tickets, not faces.

Ueno had a large domed ceiling over the main hall, but there was only the barest hint of elegance in the gray stone. So unlike the glitter of revolutionary mosaic in Moscow's train stations, Kovalenko thought distastefully. Wood, that was the Japanese element, with all its frailties. Stone was for Russia.

Center had briefed him about the bullet train and he had been shown pictures. He followed signs down escalators that led to the sleek blue and cream coaches poised like a greyhound on a far track. Before boarding, he found a public phone and dialed his hotel for messages. There was one. A Mr. Samurai. He'd heard the news and would be at the agreed location in twenty-four hours.

Precisely on schedule, the bullet started up. Kovalenko unzipped the overnight bag and searched under the computer until he found the watertight padded envelope. He gently inserted the delicate machine, then put his precious cargo back into the luggage and hefted it to the overhead rack where he studied it for a moment to ensure that it looked nondescript like the other baggage. Satisfied, he leaned back in the reclining seat while his mind raced ahead.

It would take four hours and twenty minutes to get to Morioka. Then he must take a local train to Aomori City and cross the strait to Hokkaido, the northernmost of the Japanese islands. After that, he could rent a car for the final leg to Nemuro. The rest would be up to Samurai. He recognized the wisdom of Center experts, who had ruled out air travel. But the schedule was tight; it had to be. The longer he lingered in Japan, the greater the chance that the slow-moving Japanese police and Self-Defense Force might stumble onto him. Within two days he must be making rendezvous with a patrol boat of the Soviet Sakhalin fleet. The agent code-named Samurai would meet him at the fishing village with a boat. He wondered who this Samurai was, that Center trusted him so. A high-ranking government official was all they'd tell him. It was better not to know too much.

The train slowed and he glanced at the darkness outside. The outskirts of a small Tokyo suburb, Oyama, flashed past. The train was traveling at tremendous speed and required nearly eight minutes to come to a full stop in the station. At this pace, Kovalenko thought, he'd have no trouble making the last ferry across to Hokkaido tonight. Suddenly he was starved.

He went down the aisle quickly, with the lithe stride of an athlete, and swung off the train with the last of the departing passengers. Keeping his eye on his watch, he hurriedly reached a station kiosk and purchased two boxes of sandwiches and Japanese tea in a clay pot. The electronic warning was sounding as he took his change. Metal barriers on the platform that swung open when the train had stopped would soon lock shut. The barrier was swinging as he reached it; he leaped through and swung up onto the train. The heavy doors hissed shut behind him. It was all automated, Center had warned him. The Japanese were losing their humanity. He checked his watch as he made his way back up the aisle to his seat. Exactly two minutes. That checked against what Center had told him as well. He settled again in his seat, poured a cup of tea, and realized there was now a major decision he had to face.

The Japanese would be in full cry soon. No matter how clever he had been, he must not underestimate them. The guards in the lobby of the JEC Tower would surely have provided a description by now. They'd know he was blond, his approximate height, the color of his eyes. They would also know that the Starfire had been taken. Only two hours ago he had been inside the JEC Tower. It was now 6:15. Center had reckoned it would take them three hours to organize their hunt. If that was correct, he had another hour. He removed a schedule from his pocket and studied the train's stops and times. He would be at the next station, Utsunomiya, in forty-five minutes. That would be all right, but after that he must be prepared for anything.

He hungrily ate the sandwiches and tried to relax. He stared at his reflection in the window glass that shivered from speed as the bullet train screamed into the night. And then he sensed that something was wrong. Perhaps it was just that he was keyed up—nervous exhaustion from the day's events. He glanced at the computer in the overhead rack. It was still securely in place. What then?

A face, he remembered. A face had bothered him as he reboarded the train. Slowly he stood up and headed again toward the front of the car. As he went, he casually checked the seats, which were barely half full. Near the front of the car sat a foreigner. Kovalenko could only glimpse the stranger as he went by. He was not a young man. The hair was graying. A warning sounded in his brain.

Numbly he went through the frosted-glass door that separated washrooms from the passenger compartment. The door marked WESTERN TOILET was empty. Inside there was a small window to look out, a metal sink, a urinal, a stainless-steel toilet with metal railing on each side, and a diagram describing its use. He stared out the small window at the blackness rushing past. KGB, he was quite sure of it. The man's clothing, his hardened, weathered face and ice-blue eyes. Kovalenko would have a good look at that face on the way back to his seat. The question was, what was he doing here?

There were two possibilities. First was that a Center escort had surfaced. But in that case why not reveal himself to Kovalenko? In the Center briefing they were uncertain whether a shepherd would be employed. If so it would be someone sent by Center who would make himself known if he had an emergency. But the likelihood that this man was a shepherd diminished the more Kovalenko thought about it. That left the second, more dangerous option.

He flushed the toilet and opened the door. The corridor was empty. He went up to the door to the passenger section and cleared his mind. Everything depended on what he saw or heard in the next few seconds. He visualized the seat where the Russian sat. Casually he opened the door and strode up the aisle. In the seat where the KGB agent had been a few minutes before was another man, this one quite young, with smooth unwrinkled features and obviously Asian. Somehow the man looked familiar.

Back in his seat, Kovalenko checked the overhead rack again. His bag was there. He dared not touch it now, for fear of pointing out his precious cargo to other watchers in the car. His mind was careening through the options. What should he do?

The fact that they had more than one man on him explained why he had not been able to pick them out. Pachinkov had assigned a team of watchers to follow him. What a desperate fool! They were not there to protect him, of that he was quite sure. They were going to try and stop him!

For the first time since he had reached Japan, Kovalenko experienced a real prickle of fear. The train started to slow. Utsunomiya. A few minutes. The outcome of the operation might depend upon what he decided next. He had two considerations. First was that so long as he stayed on the train he was safe. Knowing KGB mentality, he understood they wouldn't try to take him in front of the other passengers, even though they now must understand that he was on to them. They would wait until all the conditions favored them. It would be meticulously organized. Probably at the last stop: Morioka. The more he thought about it, the more certain he became.

The second consideration was his own time pressure. He had to be out in the middle of the Sea of Okhotsk within forty-eight hours. If he left the bullet too far from the straits across to Hokkaido, he'd be stranded. He would miss the rendezvous. In that case, the pattern would revert to a pickup every other day, an hour earlier each time. This would give the locals or Pachinkov's Region Seven team ample time to take him. At all costs, he must make the rendezvous on schedule. Therefore he must leave the train as close to Morioka as he could risk.

He heard the clatter of a bridge and looked out to see the glimmer of a wide river. Seconds later they pulled into Utsunomiya Station.

Passengers moved up the aisles past him, getting off. He heard the hiss as the heavy outside doors opened. Carefully he scrutinized each face that passed. All were Japanese, with averted eyes and the sense of urgency typical of homeward-bound passengers. Kovalenko directed his attention to the platform outside his window. A minute had passed. The steel barrier railings were still open. The railing served one purpose: to keep passengers away from the edge of the platform and the frequent expresses that whipped through stations at over 150 kilometers an hour. The barriers had been installed after one person had been sucked into the side of a bullet by the vacuum created by the tremendous speed of the train. The victim had been dismembered and ground to pulp.

Kovalenko checked his watch again. Two minutes almost. The warning should be sounding. A team of ticket inspectors marched along the platform and disappeared to the rear of the train. Two minutes had passed with still no warning. Something tugged at Kovalenko's brain. Why would there be a change of conductors here? And why were they marching in formation? Conductors would normally walk in a loose, care-free group, wouldn't they? Even in Japan? Furthermore, the faces were young, suntanned, and tough. He glanced at his watch again. Three minutes had passed; too much time for the punctual Japanese. Something was seriously wrong.

He stood up suddenly and tore his luggage from the overhead rack. Brusquely he shoved aside several boarding passengers and ran toward the back of his coach. Outside, the all-clear whistles sounded. He reached the door between cars and hurtled into the passageway and down the steps toward the station platform just as the big outside door started to hiss closed. A safety activator stopped the travel of the door as he lunged through it and out onto the platform where he crashed into the steel railing barriers which had just slammed shut.

The force of impact nearly catapulted him back into the side of the train, but he caught his balance and, cursing, leapt over the metal railing. Pain flooded his thighs where they had struck the railing. The platform master was looking at him in surprise from his position near the front of the train. Hurriedly, Kovalenko followed other passengers toward exit signs and escalators at the far side of the platform. The all-clear was given, and the bullet sighed as it started to move out of the station, rapidly gaining speed.

Kovalenko went to the top of the escalator and looked down

toward the ticket barriers. Three Japanese in National Defense blues with combat field caps perched on their close-cropped heads and truncheons in their fists lounged in front of the wickets. He turned back toward the platform and walked slowly to the far end, looking at his watch as if waiting for the next train. How was it possible?

As he walked, he checked up and down the platform. Aside from several knots of well-wishers who had seen passengers off and were waving at the receding lights of the train, the platform was empty. Owing to the distance between them, Kovalenko could not see that one of the well-wishers was a stocky young man with Asian features that did not look quite Japanese.

———

He kept moving until he'd reached the bridge. No one had seen him time his jump off the end of the station platform just as a train from the opposite direction was entering the station enclosure. All attention had been on the sleek snout of the latest bullet arrival. Kovalenko had followed the wide rails, listening for any approaching bullet trains; at the speeds they traveled there would be little warning. Carefully he crossed the trestle, which had been constructed solely for the bullet trains. When he reached the far side he swung off the bridge onto the embankment and tumbled down onto the riverbank, clutching the computer to his stomach and protecting it as best he could.

For several minutes he sat on the bank contemplating his predicament. The police and Self-Defense Forces couldn't possibly have mobilized that quickly. Without question, the resident had leaked his route to Japanese authorities. Pachinkov had decided to let the Japanese dispose of him. The law would be efficient; it would keep Pachinkov's hands clean. There would be no proof of Soviet embassy complicity if Kovalenko was captured by the Japanese. Pachinkov would have won an easy victory. And Directorate T, Comrade Malik, and Kovalenko all would be the losers. He tried to calm his fury. There was still a way out. He only had to think it through.

CHAPTER 37

APPLE OF SODOM

It was ten minutes past midnight when Mori emerged from the subway. He passed the school and the Rojin Club and started down the steps toward his house. He'd barely caught the last train and his thoughts remained in turmoil from the hospital visit. Mitsuko had regained consciousness but was still critical. She had smiled when she saw him, but couldn't speak, and couldn't move.

A large dark figure merged with the shadows of the schoolyard, then disengaged as Mori passed. It followed the diminutive Japanese down the steps. Halfway, Mori stopped and turned.

"Who's there?" His eyes ached with fatigue as he vainly searched the darkness.

"I want to talk," Ludlow said in a low voice.

"*Kono yaro*, you son of a bitch." Mori started back up the stairs. He saw the big shadow now. It did not move.

"Let's go somewhere else." Ludlow's voice had not changed tone. "I need to talk."

Mori hesitated, put his hand on his service revolver, and said, "There's a park; two blocks." He turned and went back down the stairs. At the bottom of the steps he paused to confirm the *gaijin* was following, and went right instead of straight on to his home. Ludlow kept some distance behind.

It was a small park in a slight depression with a pond, two benches, and wisteria bushes which shielded it from the street. A gas lamp near the benches cast a bluish haze over the area, giving it an aura of unreality. On the globe of the lamp a lizard embraced its faint heat.

Mori sat on a bench farthest from the light; Ludlow took the closer one without apparently realizing or caring that he was nicely backlit. An easy target.

The American flipped out a cigarette and offered Mori one. Mori held up the palm of his hand in refusal and Ludlow lit his own, then blew smoke at the lizard. He understood it wasn't going to be easy.

"What time did they hit the laboratory today?"

Mori laughed harshly. "Four twenty-two exactly. He came out at four forty-six. I assume you know this already from other members of your team. I'm going to have to take you in."

"How's your wife?"

"She's better." Mori tried to focus unsuccessfully through the haze. If he had to shoot there was little chance he'd miss at this range.

"I'm not saying it wasn't one of ours." Ludlow took a puff on his cigarette and stared at his hands as if they were new and interesting objects. "I'm just telling you I had nothing to do with it, that's all."

"I'd like to believe that," Mori said. Funny, he thought, he meant it. "Unfortunately the facts interfere with your logic. As I told you over the phone we've already talked with Mr. Tsuna and he's identified you."

"That's what I wanted to tell you." Ludlow said. "I had scoped their security. Left that strip of plastic on their back door. It was a piece of cake. There was no need to do what they did!"

"Crap, Robert-san." Mori stirred impatiently. "JEC had a mountain of security electronics around the research-and-development area. Your people opted for a frontal attack because it was the only quick way."

Ludlow grinned unconvincingly at his hands. He had not

looked at Mori once yet. Then he spoke: "Three thousand years ago, Mori-san, the Romans used geese to warn their legions if the Gauls were coming. Intrusion systems are still basically the same. Just a bunch of electronic geese."

"You trying to tell me they're easy?"

"For one who knows." There was no conceit in Ludlow's voice.

"JEC had lasers, vibration detectors, pressure systems, cameras . . ."

"Doesn't mean a rat's ass, Mori-san. Believe me. They're all sensors, however you cut it. They're unimportant. Control systems and attenuators, Inspector. There's the red meat!" Ludlow finally looked at Mori, the confidence growing in his eyes. "Controls interpret what the sensors are seeing or feeling and decide whether or not you've got a hostile intrusion. Turn them off and what good are sensors, Mori-san? That's my point. Attenuators sound the alarm if controls decide they have a hostile. What if the bell doesn't ring? What good is that pile of crap in the R&D, tell me? Good Lord!" Ludlow shook his head disgustedly. "No one need have died or been hurt. It was a clumsy, stupid attack. Not the sort of thing an American team would mount."

Mori shook his head. "The evidence is that it was an American operation."

"Did you check the attenuator, Mori-san? You know what they're using at JEC for that pile of junk they call a security system?"

"An autodialer," Mori said wearily. "They plug into our new command center system. Everything's computers. The brain of our genius Aoyama has achieved this."

"Yes!" Ludlow shouted. "An autodialer. So, Jesus, I could have unplugged the system beyond the control box if I wanted, recircuited the line—put in a loop—or come up with the autodial number. Lord almighty, JEC uses a two-way."

"That number is a well-guarded secret." Mori's voice was strong with confidence. "Every number is unlisted."

Ludlow pulled out a cheap ballpoint pen and notebook. He wrote a number, tore off the sheet, and threw it at Mori's feet.

"Okay, Ninja, go dial that number. Then when you hear the answer click tell your friends to smash the JEC lab door down, collect anything they want, and walk out the front door. The remote alarm at police headquarters won't trigger until you hang up. The line's engaged, get it?"

Mori bent to pick up the piece of paper and stared at the number. He pulled out his own thumbed notebook and compared the numbers with the ones he had recorded. Slowly, he shook his head.

"There was no need to blow all those people away." Ludlow stared at his hands. "Mother of God, I'm sorry about your wife."

Mori crumpled the paper into a ball and threw it into the carp pond. The colonel had said this man was a highly trained expert. Now it was clear in what area his expertise lay.

"Downstairs security had a pretty good look at him." Mori watched the paper bob on the surface of the black water for a moment. "He was young, blond, tall, clean-cut. He looked like an American, Robert-san. My wife called security before she came in. She talked with the chief of the afternoon shift, Kobayashi-san. The story she gave was that Kathy Johnson's fiancé had come to take a last look around her desk."

"The police check that out?"

"We have a Minneapolis company affiliation; data has been requested." Mori looked at his watch. It would be nine a.m. in Minnesota.

"Don't hold your breath."

"Right," Mori said tiredly. "The company was no doubt just a cover. Still . . ."

"My good Lord, Mori, that's not enough!" Ludlow stopped in midsentence. A thought was screaming in his mind. "Did your artists do a mockup of the face yet? A composite?"

"Better than that," Mori said, and extracted several stills from the church videotape.

The American stared at the photos for a moment in silence. Suddenly, there was something incomprehensible in his face, a sense of violence that Mori had never seen there before, even after that day in the police forensic lab.

"I'd like to help you find this man," Ludlow said simply. But the extent of his hate was clearly etched in his words.

It reminded Mori of a dance he had seen as a child. It was a very distant memory, since only when his father was alive had the two daughters of the white-suit dancer, Kenjii, performed for him. There had been lacquered hats to represent royalty, and wooden daggers in shiny sheaths as symbols of position and power. As the dance progressed the hats, knives, and other trappings came off. In the end there were only the two beautiful girls in the white suits. Truth. So now his white-suit dancer was a foreigner. Not exquisite or supple as the daughters had been, but more enlightening by what he did not say. The shape was gaining substance. The special gleam that had come into Ludlow's eyes, which even the shadows could not hide, had been triggered by the description and then the pictures of the blond killer. Mori understood the extent of the change this shocking discovery had made in the normally taciturn, almost withdrawn American.

"You're still wanted, you know," Mori said. "The police have a hunter team assigned to capture you. Rumor is your own people have labeled you a renegade."

Ludlow smiled and shrugged. Then he told Mori who the blond was. A Soviet he had met before. In Colombo. A member of their T Directorate. He worked in Center now. That was all he knew about him. Not even his name. But the Soviet had killed a good friend of his. He had made Ludlow look bad. So maybe now he was beginning to better understand the Japanese concept of revenge.

"You've still got nowhere to start." Mori stood up and stamped his feet as if they'd gone to sleep.

"A company in Hakodate," Ludlow said. "A Soviet proprietary. It might be a dead end, but my wooden leg says it's worth a try. If they know the KGB resident as well as I think they do, our trip should prove fascinating."

"Where did you get the company?"

"Good. I knew you'd see it my way. There's an eight-fifteen from Haneda. I've had a busy week. A shootout in Mamianacho. An attempted heist of one of your computers. A visit to one of your public steam baths after being rudely awakened quite early one morning. I'll fill you in on the way."

Mori caught up and walked beside Ludlow. He didn't quite come up to the American's shoulder. Ludlow reached into a back pocket and pulled out a pocket flask.

"To the Japanese people," Ludlow said and handed it to the tiny Japanese.

Mori took a swig. "To the American people," Mori said and handed it back. "But you still have to prove to me it wasn't an American operation."

"Apple of Sodom," Ludlow replied. A grin rose to his cheeks and closed his eyes for the briefest of seconds. "That's what an Israeli friend killed in a Colombo accident would call it. Your concepts are full of circumstantial promise, Inspector. Short on reality. Evidence but no proof, as the Langley boys like to say. Dust under the skin." Ludlow's chuckle sounded like the wind.

C H A P T E R   3 8

THE NOVICE

Kovalenko took his bearings and headed east toward the Pacific Ocean. His shoulder throbbed gently; he'd probably bruised it in the fall at the bridge. He shifted the computer to the other side. There was no doubt now that he could make it, he felt sure of that. However, he was off the Center plan. He was on his own. He would follow the river until he figured out what to do.

The riverbank gradually flattened as he walked. He kept close to the river where he could follow a worn path. To his left was the blur of lights from Utsunomiya. The surrounding fields were dark. A dike rose beyond the fields, menacing, to a height of over fifty feet. Occasionally, the path he was on branched off and he could see that it led to the dike and steps going up.

He kept a steady pace. The river turned north; around the path, the grass became thicker and the underbrush more dense. He could hear the movement of small animals in the darkness; water rats, he guessed. Snakes. The smell of mud flats and polluted water offended his nostrils.

After twenty minutes the path was the only way along the riverbank. Thickets of undergrowth rose above his head and he could no longer see the ominous outline of the dike, although he knew it must still be there. Occasionally he stopped to listen to the sound of a motor. Beyond the dike and the river a road would follow the course. He must get farther away, however, before he went back into the open.

Each time the path branched off, he carefully checked the new trail; all he found were refuse dumps that yielded nothing. A first wave of doubt tugged at his brain. After what seemed like an hour, the path came abruptly to a larger crossing. Here the double ruts of a well-worn car track came to the river's edge and led back toward the dike. He could see tire tracks in the dim moonlight.

Downriver the brush had been cleared and a small makeshift dock constructed. Fishermen, he decided. For holidays. The ocean couldn't be that far. He reached the dock and then jumped back. Something was coiled on the old wood. He strained through the darkness to identify the shape. A length of rope had been hitched to a piling and the loose end trailed under the tiny dock. The unused portion had been neatly coiled. Kovalenko pulled the rope and out from under the dock came a small rowboat half-filled with water. He felt his heart lift.

Searching along the bank, he found a refuse dump and re-covered several usable cans. With these he quickly emptied the boat of water. Although he looked all around the dock area, he could find no oars. The owners apparently had kept those to ensure their leaky boat against theft. Back at the dump he came up with several planks that would work as makeshift oars. He hurried back to the dock, carefully loaded his baggage into the middle of the tiny vessel, and cast off.

The current was slow at the edges of the broad river, swifter in the middle. He decided to keep to the bank as best he could until he learned to manage the unstable craft. He saw black holes in the river, signaling rock. Carefully, he steered, using the current for power. The river was a good kilometer across here. There were small islands about, which had snagged debris with whirlpools he learned to avoid. Gradually, as he gained confidence, he moved toward the middle of the river. The current churned here. He guessed that he was making ten to fifteen kilometers an hour. He should reach the ocean within several hours if his luck held.

At one point he took out his map and spread it across his knee to make out where he was. He could see the line of river near Utsunomiya but couldn't discern distance. Soon, he hoped, and urged his craft into the heart of the strong current.

He found himself thinking of Raya. It seemed years since they had touched. The last night they'd gone to Tsentraenaya on Gorky Street to celebrate. He'd reserved a curtained booth where the grand dukes once played. It had been marvelous. The restaurant was where the elite of Soviet society gathered to solemnize, to honor, and to commemorate under the crystal chandeliers. The atmosphere of power was overwhelming. Raya and he had toasted to Kovalenko's success, to their new dacha. Now he understood why the operation had gone wrong. It was because he had been forced to kill the girl. Perhaps her soul pursued him. And they had underestimated Pachinkov when they insisted that Kovalenko meet with him. That was Malik's vanity. How much better off Kovalenko would be now if the locals had not been made aware of his presence until it was over.

Kovalenko's lack of concentration on the river caused his first real crisis. At a bend of the river the strong current shot him toward shore, where he glimpsed a black vacuum of rock. The small craft began to spin. Although he struggled desperately against the force of the river, he rode into a whirlpool of eddies. Barely scraping by several rocks, the boat threatening to overturn, he frantically battled the river with his clumsy plank paddle. Finally, he slowed and drifted toward shore, which was only several yards away now. He sat becalmed, trying to catch his breath, cursing his own lack of concentration.

Had he not been near the riverbank, he probably would not have seen it at all—a dock of more substantial construction than the first one. And swinging with the current at the end of a short rope was a large, sturdy, sleek-bowed riverboat with the bulk of an outboard engine in the stern. Eagerly he headed for the dock. He came alongside the larger boat and looked around carefully. The area was deserted. He tied his boat to the dock and gingerly lifted the computer to the safety of the pilings. Then he clambered up after it.

His new acquisition was built for rivers and speed. A check of the gas tank showed that it was at least half full. He pulled the starter cord three times before the engine caught. He was delicately lifting the overnight bag with the computer, trying not to use his sore shoulder, when the Japanese stepped out of the shadows, a fishing rod in his hands.

"*Tomare,*" the Japanese ordered, and pointed the pole at Kovalenko. The Russian saw that it was a rifle. Suddenly a strong light blinded Kovalenko's eyes. Reflexively he raised his hands to protect his face. Japanese civilians were not allowed to carry weapons. Their police were not issued rifles. This must be one of their security people. But how could they have reacted so quickly?

"American," Kovalenko said and took a step toward the stocky stranger to close the gap, cut down the disadvantage. Stick with the story, Center always advised for capture situations. Talk freely but give them nothing. Find out as much as you can. Kovalenko took another step.

"Stop," the man shouted and Kovalenko thought for a moment he might pull the trigger. Sounds came to him more clearly, as if his brain had been suddenly emptied. The gurgle of the river, the sound of a train far off. A horn. The beat of the outboard engine.

"Lost," Kovalenko pantomimed with his hands. "I'm an American tourist."

"The bag. Move it here!" The voice was harsh. Unyielding. This was no ordinary footsoldier.

Kovalenko slowly bent to pick up the overnight bag.

"No!" the voice ordered. "With your foot, move it there." The light lowered from Kovalenko's face and shone on the planking between them. In that instant Kovalenko glimpsed the reflection on his opponent's face. It was the young Asian from the train.

Kovalenko moved the bag with his toe toward the designated spot.

"Enough," the Asian ordered. He placed the flashlight on the ground pointing at the computer. Without taking the short-barreled rifle from its position aimed at Kovalenko's chest, he bent down, picked up the bag, and hefted it. Kovalenko waited. He saw that the gun was a Soviet Elba, a copy of the Israeli Uzi. It could be disassembled and the stock folded easily. Perfect for carrying in luggage. An automatic weapon.

For the first time the Asian smiled.

"A Japanese computer, isn't this?"

Kovalenko shrugged. "What is this all about? Who are you?"

"My name is Konstantin. I am assigned to the Soviet embassy in Tokyo. We are here to protect Japanese property from thieving American hands."

Kovalenko heard his own sharp intake of breath. It was incomprehensible.

"But I am a Russian citizen. Assigned to Directorate T of the Soviet KGB." Kovalenko spoke rapidly in Russian, trying to keep his voice calm.

"Admirable language facility," Konstantin said icily. "But that does not prove anything, does it?"

"My name is Kovalenko," the Soviet agent yelled. "I am Deputy Director of the Technical Directorate, you fool!"

"I see," Konstantin answered. "And a few moments ago you were an American tourist. Lost. Which is it to be then?"

Kovalenko understood finally. The chief resident of the Tokyo embassy and director of Region Seven, Comrade Pachinkov, had been more than clever. He could not let his own team know they were after one of their own countrymen, and a KGB operative at that. Too many questions, certain to cause eventual embarrassment, might be asked.

"I report to Andrey Malik, chief of T Directorate. My identification code is 3-252-759. I am on covert duty and am to rendezvous with a Soviet escort vessel near the Sakhalins tomorrow. You will be tried and shot if your actions are reported, Comrade Konstantin."

The young Soviet Asian shook his head with admiration.

"Yes. That's very good. Your briefing was excellent, no doubt. Now may I have some identification?" His voice was matter-of-fact. Methodical.

Kovalenko stared speechless at his young interrogator, skewered on the thoroughness of all Soviet agents who go abroad. They went completely clean. Even to the labels of clothing they wore. Their shoelaces. Nothing was Russian. He carried no papers to prove he was a member of the KGB, of course. To do so would be foolhardy.

"I can't give you anything right now," Kovalenko shouted. He realized that the inexperienced Russian in front of him was going to follow his orders whatever Kovalenko did or said. It was useless. The young KGBer was a novice.

"Empty everything from your pockets," Konstantin demanded. "Do it now."

Kovalenko did as he was told. He threw the wallet, the fake American passport, American credit cards, everything, on the ground in front of the Russian.

Konstantin stooped to pick them up. For the moment the barrel of his automatic weapon pointed off away from Kovalenko. In that instant, Kovalenko dove for him.

He had hoped at the very least to dislodge the weapon, but though they both fell sprawling onto the pier out of the light, Kovalenko felt the butt of the weapon smash against his chest. He swung desperately and his fist sank into soft underbelly. He heard the young Russian grunt. Kovalenko drove a second punch, better aimed, to the face. The gun clattered away. The Central Asian staggered to his feet, searching the darkness for his weapon and Kovalenko tackled him again, driving him to the hard planking and rolling on top of his smaller adversary.

He felt the sudden sharp pain in his arm and saw the knife. The blade was sticking through his muscle above the elbow. He slithered away, the knife still in him, taking a more total interest in his opponent now. He drew the knife clear and felt the sticky warm flow of blood stream down his arm, cascading off his fingertips. He sprang to his feet and almost in the same movement drove his heel into the young Soviet's jaw. In the next instant he landed a second vicious kick to the groin. He jumped back to view his handiwork, the adrenaline firing now. The pain in his arm was gone. Under his feet he felt a hard object and picked up the automatic weapon.

Kovalenko saw his adversary slump with despair. He retrieved the flashlight and shone it on Konstantin, who had collapsed dejectedly on the ground.

"Up," he ordered harshly.

The Soviet struggled to stand, taking deep sobbing breaths.

"Take off your jacket," Kovalenko ordered.

Konstantin slowly removed his jacket, his eyes reading the scene with disbelief. He dropped the jacket on the ground and kicked it toward Kovalenko with his foot.

Kovalenko patted the pockets until he'd found the keys. "Where is it?"

Konstantin jerked his head defiantly in the direction of the road.

"Stolen of course. You saw me jump from the station platform then?"

Konstantin's eyes glared with hate at Kovalenko. He did not answer.

"You watched me jump off the bridge. The rest was simple. You drove here and waited. Probably you planned to put a hole in the boat if I was out in the river. I never could have made it to shore. The computer was of no value to you. I was to be eliminated, weren't those Pachinkov's orders?"

A frigid stillness fell over the young Soviet. Kovalenko did not need an answer. He lifted the rifle and shot Konstantin in the head.

He had to search for five minutes before he found the car. It was a relatively new Toyota. He started the engine and listened to it for several minutes, watching the dash. The gas tank was full. That was strange, or very lucky, if it was a stolen car. It then dawned on him that he had a key. How could the car have been stolen if Konstantin possessed the keys? Unless he'd found one that somebody had left carelessly unlocked with the keys inside. Certainly too much to hope for, wasn't it? He opened the glove compartment and took out the registration. The car was a rental.

The papers were made out to . . . he squinted in the faint overhead light . . . Finn-Pacific Ltd., with an address in Hakodate. He searched his mind. Hakodate was a city in Hokkaido. There were special handling instructions. But these were in Japanese. The car must have been awaiting Konstantin's pickup in Utsunomiya. But how on earth could Pachinkov have known he would detrain in that city? He couldn't, of course. A car had been spotted at each station along the Shinkansen route. Extravagant, Kovalenko thought, but in terms of the prize worth every yen. Then Finn-Pacific must be a Region Seven front company operating in Japan's north. The company must have something to do with Pachinkov's conduit for moving his stolen computers and electronics out of Japan. Of course.

But how had Pachinkov known he would take the northern bullet? The answer rocked him with the force of a bomb detonating. He felt a rising tide of fright creep up from his stomach.

Pachinkov was close to the head of the KGB, was he not? A well-known fact. One of Pachinkov's connections could have somehow found out about the plan. There had been a number of people in on the briefing, after all. One could have talked without realizing what he was giving away. Malik wouldn't have let others in on his secret, that the operation was the key to a huge promotion. Damn Pachinkov. If the locals couldn't take him out along the way, no doubt Pachinkov was preparing a reception when he arrived at the fishing village of Nemuro. Mother of Lenin, what should he do?

Kovalenko sat staring through the window of the car as if in a trance. Then he shook himself. There would be no immediate answer. He must get started. He could think it through along the way. Carefully he put the car in drive and slowly crept along the dirt road that led for a short distance along the river and then turned toward the dike and started to climb.

The road became gravel where it crossed the dike. On the

other side it turned to asphalt, where it intersected a good road paralleling the river. Briefly, he consulted his map. The river was the Abukuma, by his guess. He was close to a small town named Date. Inland the map showed mountains that could slow him down and certainly be more difficult to drive. He chose the shore route, which would be more obvious to pursuers, but which would give him a better jump on Pachinkov's team. The hunters would soon be scouring the perimeters of Utsunomiya. The quicker he reached the ferry crossing to Hokkaido, the better. He checked the map a final time. Aomori, where the ferry embarked, was 400 kilometers north. With luck he'd make the first ferry tomorrow morning. He turned right, pressed the accelerator to the floor, and felt the Japanese car leap forward. He was exhausted, light-headed, but that didn't seem to matter now.

THE PERFECT
FLOWER

The entrance to the Hiraga Res-
taurant boasts a huge moss-covered stone reportedly insured
for twenty million yen. The minister of justice eased out of
his car and briefly admired the famous object. As a worshipper
of form over content, he took such things seriously. To escape
media attention and the lack of privacy at most Japanese offices, and to keep from reinforcing the notions of foreign jour-
nalists who insisted that Japanese banking, business, and
government were in close lockstep, the minister accomplished
all his important communication at night.

Delicate chords of a koto mixed with the hum of city. The
sky was clear, a good sign. It was still harvest moon period
and the excuse for this evening's gathering of the most powerful businessmen in Japan was a moon-viewing party. When
truly important issues were at hand in the fall, the most common venues for resolving them were the geisha restaurants of
Ginza, Tamagawa, and Akasaka, where upper verandas opened
their shōji to the southeast quadrant while hard-boiled dis-
cussions were held. There were other innocuous occasions that
provided excuses for such gatherings, since Japan boasts
twenty-five cultural holidays throughout the year, but in the
fall moon-viewing had clear preference. Few ever saw the
moon.

A manager rushed out to lead the minister of justice inside. The minister bowed to the rows of kimonoed geisha and *maiko* lined up to greet their most honored guest. He knew that all he had to do was snap his fingers and any of these pretty girls would share his bed tonight. But he looked forward to the glimpse of another whose beauty alone made her worth ten thousand of these.

The manager hovered near him, scolding the shoe boys to hurry, inquiring if the humble Sakura Room would do—as the establishment's premium moon-viewing location, it would—and sending an urgent message to the bar for heating of a Minokawa from Niigata, the minister's favorite sake. Word also flowed to the kitchen to begin preparation for the feast. Lastly, the manager informed him that the superintendent of police had already arrived, a fact the justice minister assumed from the numbers of heavyset visitors near the cars and in the halls of the restaurant.

The chief appeared from one of the many waiting rooms looking flushed and pleased. They went through the ritual of bows while management looked on with appropriate awe, then led the way to the upstairs room for the evening's program. Six security specialists were completing a thorough check as the two powerful figures carefully settled in the deep silk *zabuton* cushions like ancient shōgun. The ceiling of woven rush had been swept with electronic devices, as had the ornate *tokonoma* with its sacred calligraphy and its offering to the gods. The specialists were now worrying the incense burners, but finally approved and reluctantly backed from the room, bowing to the two men, now deeply engrossed in conversation at the long polished table.

The chief was bringing the minister up to date. A tip had indicated the blond was on a bullet train heading north, and spot checks of train personnel confirmed a blond was sighted on the 5:45 p.m. for Morioka. The chief glanced at his watch. Colonel Yuki was now flying to Sapporo to lead the hunt. According to his theory, the American would try to reach Chitose Airbase.

The first bottle of Minokawa arrived and, since it was not

considered impolite to begin before the others arrived, cups were filled and the first drinks of the evening taken. As host, the minister of justice was, by form, required to appear before his guests. The arms industry leaders would arrive in sequence of power, with the chairman of Tekkohashi last. His would be the deciding vote.

"Well, then, everything is splendid, is it?" The minister generously refilled their cups.

The chief nodded and explained other preparations. Roadblocks had been set up on all roads near Chitose Airbase. The Americans were being asked to cancel all Chitose flights.

———

The chairman of the Riko Group arrived first, as expected. The chairman bowed at the door, surrounded by a covey of giggling house girls who would serve them, then cut a path toward the low table where the two government officials were seated, using his right hand, as a sumo wrestler makes his way to the arena to meet his opponents in *tachiai.* The room was large, and smelled of delicate incense and the clean perfume of rice straw from the immaculate tatami, which boasted the purple and black border of Iwaname and Company, straw weavers to the emperor.

The Riko executive's brilliantined hair still had a good mix of black and gray in spite of the fact that he was well over sixty. He wore a blue pinstripe with a dark tie, and his strong voice was resonant with success as an old seashell catches the ocean. The minister of justice knew this man was a staunch supporter of the military and would be agreeable so long as no serious objections were raised by the others. In the later stages of their occasional evening gatherings, when considerable sake had been consumed, the Riko chairman was known to expound the unique and superior racial qualities of Japanese, which he would list at length as the basis for unrivaled national achievement since 1945.

The superintendent of police's interesting dossier on this gentleman also revealed his hobby to be breeding German shepherds. Apparently he was applying his genetic theories to the highest level of creatures that current law permitted. It was said that his experiments had given moderate success.

"Awful news, isn't it?" The chairman accepted a first cup of sake and raised it to his host. The evening editions had printed front-page accounts of the double murder, citing rumors of foreign involvement.

"The madman will not escape." The justice minister firmly downed his cup of sake. He had unbuttoned his jacket, exposing a generous girth of stomach. He brushed the crumbs of hors d'oeuvres from the folds of his shirt of Egyptian cotton, then looked up to the Riko chairman with all the contrived geniality he could muster: "You will recall, Chairman"—the hot sake had lubricated the minister's vocal chords and his voice had taken on a decisiveness earlier lacking—"that during the reign of the Cloistered Emperor Go Shirakawa, whenever the monks of Mount Hiei had an important issue, they would come down into the streets of Kyoto and demonstrate. There would never be widespread bloodshed. Only a few people would die. However, it focused the public's attention. The monks would get what they wanted and go back onto their mountain. Unfortunate as the JEC incident is, we expect to reap two huge dividends from this murder by a foreigner."

There was a fanfare of voices at the door, and a second guest was ushered in. The vice chairman of Matsu Company arrived with a subdued smile and apologies for the illness of his chairman. This by itself would not have deterred the chairman were it not for the doctor's orders on alcohol. "Comes to us all," he offered in a self-deprecating manner, as if not to implicate anyone outside the Matsu Group. The vice chairman practiced his art of humility magnificently. He was known as a man of great loyalty and organizational talent, and it was so marked in the comprehensive police dossier. He never spoke of his successes, which were immense; only of his failings. A true traditionalist. The police notations also included the little-known fact that his chairman had an unusual weakness for winning large golf bets, which the vice chairman had shown exceptional organizational talent in satisfying. That loyalty had no doubt speeded his meteoric rise within the group, which otherwise claimed dedication to seniority advancement systems.

The superintendent of police had always made it his business to understand the minor failings of the national industrial deities. This understanding perhaps made him somewhat more confident in his expectations of Matsu support; unfortunately, however, most of Japan's economic leadership was remarkably free of aberration.

The first wave of geisha had arrived and now bustled about them, being careful to touch thighs or lean closer than necessary whenever they poured sake—generally making their perfumed presence unintrusive but pervasive, soothing away the strains of tension by their laughter and good humor whenever conversation lagged for the briefest of seconds. They scolded the justice minister playfully for staying away so long—mainly for the benefit of his guests, since he had been there three nights before—and all the time watched the entrance for their next arrival.

Earlier than usual, the chairman of the Riko Group had launched into an exaltation of Japanese uniqueness. He was in the process of reviewing the nineteenth-century Shinto theologian Hirata Atsutane's claim that the Japanese islands were produced by ancestral gods and that the inferiority of the world's remaining populations stemmed from the fact that they were reared on earth produced only from sea and mud. At that moment the president of Sumigawa was announced.

There was another wave of bows and introductions, which seemed to carry the mood of importance and expectation in the room to a higher plane. With the arrival of their last guest expected shortly, the four industrialists in the room would represent the most powerful armaments firms in Asia, with dedicated work forces and tentacles reaching around the globe. Their combined corporate assets produced eighty percent of Japan's total arms. The minister of justice understood very well that the attitudes of his guests tonight would decide the future of Japan. And as with any Japanese group, one man would be allowed to dominate. The president of Sumigawa, who led the second largest of the firms next to Tekkohashi, would want assurances that nothing could go wrong. His was the most conservative voice of the three guests present. He was a gentle, silver-haired plutocrat, quite tall for a Japanese at 180 centimeters, with a tendency to introversion stemming from an isolated childhood. He'd demonstrated talent early in his research-and-development days, assimilating foreign product strengths and incorporating them into Sumigawa brands, which remained basically very Japanese. Later in his career, he'd been a key figure in Sumigawa's remarkable expansion of the seventies. Most recently he had embarked on an acquisition program that left some managers, who regarded that an exclusively American tool, shaking their heads. His extraordinary success was said to have come about because of an innate open-heartedness and candor—ingredients often lacking, it was said, in Japanese organizations, although not in the Japanese people themselves. Because of his conservatism, his vote would be difficult to secure; but he was considered basically in favor of the strategy.

Inside the Sakura Room, a koto player now arrived. She knew all the guests' favorites, although they tested her with requests such as "Utanomarino" and others which dated back three hundred years.

———

The chairman of Tekkohashi arrived just on the Hour of the Dog, a shade later than might have been polite had this not been an informal occasion. Moon-viewing parties never required fixed arrival schedules so long as sequencing was observed. This was the man most puzzling to the superintendent general of police. He had climbed to a position of power in Japan, effortlessly it seemed. There had been no trysts or bloodlettings along the way; he was afflicted with no enemies. Although of extremely practical nature, he showed great reverence for his ancestors and family name; he had even endowed a chair at a famous university for a ninth-generation ancestor who had been high chamberlain for ceremonies and fifth in line to Emperor Kanmu's throne. The chairman was known to have a great love of natural beauty and himself was an artist of some merit in *kanbun,* the Chinese writing system. He was also known for an immaculate sense of taste in clothing and personal cleanliness.

This evening the chairman of Tekkohashi was in a formal Japanese men's kimono. His scrubbed features looked like something out of the past as he was led to their table by one of the most attractive geisha.

The justice minister did not rise, as he did not want to appear the supplicant. He bowed from the sitting position, a feat made sufficiently ludicrous by his girth but accepted with dignity by the most powerful man in Japan.

"Domo-arigato, thank you for coming this evening," the justice minister said by way of introduction. "Our meeting tonight will establish the foundation for a new level of economic expansion unprecedented in our nation."

The chairman of Tekkohashi smiled agreeably, as if the minister had just told a very acceptable joke, and he turned to exchange jibes with his competitors and cohorts. They met more often in one capacity or another than their counterparts in any other capitalist country in the world. They, more than other economic experts, recognized that present international economic trends signaled trouble ahead. Thus, while the minister's words were overtly ignored, it was just such promise that had brought them together here tonight.

The justice minister quickly checked his watch and noted the ricksha from Shimbashi with its precious cargo would have started its journey minutes ago. She had cost a fortune but would be well worth it, of that he was quite sure—if she could keep all the men in the room apart.

Geisha fluttered about now like butterflies unable to alight, serving sake, offering courses of food, touching the important men, matching their careful banter with an escalation of mood that would climax when Hana made her entrance. The Perfect Flower.

Beyond the room, in the halls now crowded with security and waiting entourage, management orchestrated, monitoring the preference of the men for the women presented to them, always conscious of the fragility of the moment, leaving nothing to chance.

The ricksha man, whose name was Goto—Hana had claimed him personally, since he brought her luck, and would allow no others to transport her—was contacted via a small Sony two-way secreted beneath his *yukata,* and confirmed his location. He had crossed Itabashi intersection and was now moments away. Management ordered the last and highest-ranked of their geisha into the room, where they massaged the dignitaries with their musical voices, accounts of the latest scandals of the famous, and their kotolike laughter.

Already the minister of justice had laid the groundwork, delicately yet securely. Here in 1987, the Japanese economy was at the threshold of an unprecedented round of expansion in spite of gloomy forecasts based on growing protectionism around the world and the stronger yen. Even the United States government had recently cautioned the prime minister to be more security-conscious about Japanese high tech.

The fact was that increasingly sophisticated Japanese technology in defense-related areas was rapidly overtaking that of the U.S., who feared Japan's technology would fall into the hands of hostile powers. So wasn't that the nub? Japan had been unable to guarantee the security of its own burgeoning high tech. The minister smiled for all. No one in the room disagreed. More than other Japanese or the world at large, they understood the size of the problem.

The Japanese government, in so far as the minister could speak for it, had two goals, one dependent on the other. The first and primary goal was to somehow gain Diet approval for a decent security agency to protect Japanese high tech from foreigners. The second was to destroy the American monopoly on Japanese strategic high-tech military and aerospace hardware. Otherwise its huge potential would be denied them.

Both problems were complex, requiring a catalyst that on one hand would create public support and pressure for a new legalized security agency, and on the other would deny the legitimacy of the American control over Japan's military export. "Now we believe we have one," he said.

The minister of justice felt the rustle in the room, heard the deepening silence of anticipation in the listening audience. The geisha had retired to the hallway for the moment, relieved that their work was nearly done.

As everyone had read in their evening newspapers, the minister continued, there had been a terrible tragedy in Shinjuku this afternoon. The JEC lab had been broken into by foreigners, and two guards were killed. A Fifth Generation avionics computer prototype was stolen. What the public did not know as yet was that the break-in was an illegal act backed by the U.S. government.

The four powerful executives sat in stunned silence.

"Based on all the facts we have so far." The police chief smiled for the room.

The minister nodded. "Once the Japanese people realize that the illusion of American friendship and protection is unreal, public complacency will turn to fear of an ally and protector turned thief. The public will demand a decent security agency to protect them from outsiders. Possibly more."

The minister went on to describe the next steps. A unilateral declaration that the American export-monopoly agreement had been violated by their act of piracy. The U.S. would have nowhere to present its case. Off would come the gloves of the Japanese military-industrial complex. For the first time, Japan would be able to compete in one of the fastest-growing and largest export markets—arms trade, defense industry, high-tech strategic equipment sales. Aerospace.

The Matsu vice chairman nodded and said, "But Minister, the world is moving toward peace. The Russian presence is weakening in Europe. The Poles want independence, as do the Yugoslavs and Czechs. There is rumor that even the East Germans are not solidly behind Moscow anymore. They want reunion. What if the Soviet empire crumbles? Who would need arms?"

The minister of justice smiled broadly. "Suppose these fantasies were to happen: a new order in Europe, Soviet troops withdrawn, Germany united. What is one of the first things the new leaders would do?" He turned to the chief of police.

"Replace the vacuum left by departure of Soviet forces," the chief replied. "Buy weapons. Ensure newly won independence with the latest toys."

The justice minister spread his hands and beamed. "Of course. In fact it would greatly expand the market, not diminish it; particularly if our good friends, the Germans, get together."

There was healthy laughter all around.

The chairman of Riko raised his hand and was given the floor. He had already agreed to give the seconding speech. As everyone knew, he began, there were two categories of high tech—commercial and strategic. Commercial grade could be exported worldwide. No limitation. Strategic high tech was another matter, however. It had recently made headlines with the Toshiba case, where sales to the USSR of equipment for making submarine propellers had angered the United States. Normally, Japan's strategic high-tech capability was never mentioned in Washington, as if the U.S.A. didn't want anyone else to know it existed. Laughter here. Japan had always been faithful to their word on military export, hadn't they? However, the Toshiba case represented what everyone felt: It was time to break the U.S. shackles. The subsequent press treatment of the Toshiba top-tier executives (they had been forced to resign) as national heroes who had sacrificed themselves— "performed professional hara-kiri," as one journal put it— made clear once and for all how everyone felt. The justice minister's commitment couldn't have come at a better time, as far as the Riko Group was concerned.

The minister of justice then spoke in a low but intense voice: "I've had my planners draw up forecasts for a totally committed Japanese military-industrial complex. If we assume sales to Free World countries of our most advanced technologies, and slightly less advanced to COMECON and Third World, within five years we estimate exports alone in total to double Japan's present export numbers. Five years ago Japan was state-of-the-art in only one hundred strategic high-tech areas. Today the number has soared to over one thousand, and is climbing daily—in electronics, robotics, and ceramics."

The fact was, the minister explained, increasingly sophisticated Japanese technology was rapidly overtaking the United States in vital military areas. Yet Japan's own defense industry had maintained a closet mentality. Ashamed of the past. Afraid to be seen in public. It's time all that changed. The minister had come to his main point.

"I have asked you to join me here tonight to secure your consensus on two points critical to Japan's future. First, that you will agree to an expanded counterintelligence agency and help drive it through the Diet. It would mean that in order to protect our industry from Soviet and U.S. intelligence in particular, we would be placing government personnel in your plants to supervise all security for some period. This would not be a takeover by the government of any industry prerogatives." The justice minister stopped here to stare candidly at each of his four quarries. "Rather it would, as in the past, symbolize the growing partnership between industry and government. A new counterintelligence agency is now on the drawing boards to service the anticipated explosion of the Japanese defense industry in the near future. This is of course the second point of consensus I seek.

"Will your conglomerates support a defense industry that will dwarf present exports? The Japanese government was already of a mind with Adam Smith, that the market should be let open to the forces of free competition. For one thing this would allow prices to find their true economic level. Under such conditions sales could be unimaginable." The minister of justice then clapped his pudgy hands so that the service girls and geisha would be allowed to reenter the room. He wanted these men to be given time to consider the words he had spoken. There could be only one answer, of course.

In the oblique discussion that followed, in spite of the women's presence, there was at first subdued, then growing enthusiasm expressed as the plan's potential was confirmed around the table. One executive after another began to nod his head as he thought of his own group's resources and work-in-process planning. But the chairman of Tekkohashi, although he joined in the optimistic banter, did not commit his vote.

Obviously he was letting all the implications work in his mind.

At this moment, the door to the room slid open and Hana entered. So unexpected was her appearance, and so total was her beauty and freshness, that the men momentarily lost the thread of conversation—a pause which caused the other geisha in the room to smile knowingly.

Hanna-san did not look at any of the men but understood she was in command of all eyes. She had bowed beautifully as she came through the door, not slowing the pace of her mincing steps, the immaculate white tabi-stockinged feet swishing against tatami. She bowed again as she approached the main table, the scarlet-lined train of her white silk kimono trailing behind like the first consort to a reigning emperor. Ornaments in her upswept hair moved and caught the light as she stopped to kneel and bow in front of the guests with perfect grace and just the right amount of blush. The totality of her presence diminished all other females in the room as she greeted the justice minister first, since he was host, and then the others in turn. Although she had seen none of the guests before, a detailed brief on each one's personal likes and dislikes had been part of the evening's dossier. She repeated each guest's name and then her own, intertwining them deliciously.

Although the chairman of Tekkohashi was introduced last, she rated him highest with the promise of her eyes. She was aware that Japanese male pride could destroy the most expensive of evenings and wreck months of negotiation. The structure must be maintained so that each knew his place. Hana understood how to keep men apart in their competition for her so that they vied not with each other but within themselves for her attention.

She chose to sit by the minister of justice first, a move of consummate skill. It allowed the chairman of Tekkohashi to drink deeply of her. Hana, geisha of geishas. One of the miracles that happens less and less frequently in recent decades. A woman whose fame and beauty set her clearly apart. Her face had the arched brow, the delicate nose, the rouged lips that would have been equally at home in the days of the Kyoto court. A genius of Gion District upbringing and education that had spawned those of historical fame before her. Like her predecessors, Hana was trained in every nuance of pleasure. She knew without being told what was necessary and expected. And still a child. She and her sponsors had agreed that everything would be up to the Tekkohashi chairman.

A fresh round of sake was produced. Hana poured. Here she demonstrated her magnificence. She chose the Tekkohashi executive with her expressive almond eyes and he raised his empty sake cup almost too quickly, with relish and anticipation; an artist admiring a work of art. She imparted her own special touch to the way she held one long, elegant kimono sleeve with her free hand and poured with the other, revealing porcelain-white skin of wrist and forearm, for which she was justly famous. The act, by its utter simplicity, somehow conveyed the utmost eroticism to the enchanted chairman and other male guests.

She was to look for certain signals from the justice minister as to when she could leave to make her toilette and when she could not. She was experienced enough to understand that a matter of great consequence was being weighed tonight, although it might have surprised and amused her to learn that an important destiny of her country was being arbitrated.

The decision would be symbolically stated, and Hana was the symbol. To an extent more than the minister of justice cared to admit, a satisfactory conclusion to the evening was now in the hands of this fantastically beautiful woman-child whose very presence made his body ache for her.

———

After the last course had been served and the shōji windows opened to the moon, the justice minister signaled Hana to leave for the powder room. The other girls immediately followed her out. The guileless face of the minister beamed at his guests. He leaned forward over the highly polished surface of the cleared table, his face reflecting in the shine with the curious alertness of a bear searching for honey.

"I thought it was time we decided about combining forces." The minister cackled loudly in spite of the obviousness of the statement. Their forces had been combined since the Meiji era turned their samurai forefathers from soldiering to greed and trade. It was time for the members present to cast their votes.

The four industry leaders showed neither surprise nor overt interest. A quiet had descended again on this room. The time had come when the silences would count more than the words—as in Japanese architecture, where space gives form to the whole.

"I understand what you are attempting," the chairman of the Riko Group said carefully, "and I believe it is the proper course of action." The chairman leaned back from the table.

"Go over again how large you believe this new industry will be." The Matsu vice chairman liked numbers, since his background was financial. Someone coughed.

"The Japanese character for prediction is derived from the symbol for uncertainty," the justice minister smiled sincerely. "The fact is no one really knows. In the report I have provided you, a conservative estimate is given, I believe. My opinion is it will be larger by a multiple than the present entire electronics industry within five to seven years. The limit is a function of your ability to engineer, build, and sell."

At this the chairman of Tekkohashi seemed to blink imperceptibly; in the intense atmosphere of that room it was noted and recorded by all. He addressed his question to the superintendent general of police:

"You are quite sure this will not create another embarrassment as was incurred in California last year?"

The superintendent smiled. "The law here is ours, sir."

The Sumigawa president belched as he leaned forward to speak. "Your American, Mr. Superintendent, how soon do you expect his capture?"

"Within one day by our latest estimate."

The chairman of Tekkohashi folded his arms, closed his eyes, and spoke as if to himself. "We cannot know everything, yet we must exclude nothing." Then he nodded to himself, eyes still closed.

In panic, the minister pressed a button under the table for the women to return.

There was no time for further exchange as the women flowed back into the room like a scented river. Hana again made the men almost forget what it was they had come to discuss. No one appeared to notice the fine beads of perspiration that had collected on the minister's upper lip like summer sweat on a cake of iced tofu.

————

Goto the ricksha man received the news over his Sony two-way as the guests, entourage, and security personnel were streaming out onto the lava rock path in front of the restaurant to leave: Hana would enjoy the splendor of the gentleman from Tekkohashi's limousine for her onward transportation. He smiled for her. The evening had been successful, then. She had no doubt received a substantial contract and he himself would benefit at the time of her weekly payment with a special envelope she would slip to him when they were along the way. She had hinted at enough money for a day at Funabashi next week if it went well; there were several horses he was quite sure about. Truly he was a lucky Japanese.

BARTER TRADE

Hakodate is an oversize fishing village with a well-situated harbor on the northernmost island of Hokkaido. One point of the harbor is crowned by a colossus of rock, Mount Hakodate, which squares off with wrathful storms that swirl across the Tsugaru Strait.

Lines of rain struck at the city today like arrows of a vengeful god. From where he sat, Mori could see beyond buildings to a harbor overhung with mist. The hiss of a gas heater and the warmth of the waiting room made his eyes momentarily ache for sleep. Next to him, Ludlow studied a travel guide he had picked up at the airport.

They had arrived in midmorning by ANA Flight 603. As they landed, the runway lights were flashing like the warning signals in Mori's brain. It had been almost too easy slipping Ludlow through airport security. At the arrival lounge in Hakodate, he swore he saw Erika's face in the deplaning crowd. When he'd searched for her, the mirage had disappeared. His mind was playing tricks.

Outside, shades of gray merged with sea, land, and sky. Shortlegged men with soaked cotton gloves and shiny yellow slickers scurried on docks. Noncombatants roamed the safety of inner streets, hands in pockets, shoulders hunched against the storm. Occasionally a bright bamboo umbrella interrupted the drabness.

Mori sipped hot tea that the Finn-Pacific secretary had offered out of sympathy for their disheveled condition. He stared around the inauspicious premises. It was impossible to imagine that this unimpressive firm could be responsible for the damage Ludlow implied. Behind the reception desk were two small, empty clerical spaces, and a display case for products Finn-Pacific apparently exported: canned mandarins, crabmeat, sardines, and tuna. On a second shelf were small electrical motors, portable cassette radios, and several less-well-known brands of miniature TVs.

Ludlow had called it a "proprietary," which meant that in addition to its normal, legitimate business it shipped stolen goods on orders from the KGB.

"Mr. Lerikk will see you soon." The Japanese secretary came out of the manager's office to balance on one leg and smile encouragement at her tired guests. "A possible export contract," was all Ludlow had said when they arrived unannounced. They would discuss details face to face. The secretary had gone out of her way to be helpful. "For our barter business, is it?" she had inquired enthusiastically.

"Well now that's a possibility." Ludlow's reaction had come before Mori could blink.

"It's been growing rather nicely," the girl admitted. "Did you have a specific product in mind?"

"I wasn't sure about the market, you see," Ludlow smiled charmingly.

"Well it's the Russians, isn't it?" She'd nodded shyly, suddenly uncertain of their cause.

"Wonderful, the entire venture." Ludlow's voice had purchased all the shares.

Her face had lit with renewed inspiration. "Actually, the Soviet Friendship Association suggested the program. Being Finnish, we often act as intermediaries."

"You must be proud of your role"—Ludlow glanced at Mori—"in international cooperation."

"Boardings were the problem?" Mori stretched and pretended to yawn. The papers were occasionally full of the troubles in northern waters. The Japanese had always resented the way the Soviets took the Sakhalins at the end of World War Two. Mori said, "Since Soviets control the richest fishing grounds off Hokkaido, Japanese catches are limited. Soviet patrol boats make periodic boardings." Mori stared at Ludlow for a moment to underscore the point.

"The fishing co-ops, of course." Ludlow nearly slapped his thigh. "They must have jumped at the idea."

"Yes," the secretary said demurely. She was clearly pleased that they understood how important her company's role had been, that it had a small place in history. "This is seen as a huge step forward in international goodwill. In glasnost. Before, the penalties for exceeding catches were severe—impounding of boats, imprisonment of crews . . ." She'd shaken her head with revulsion. It was at this point that the manager had called her.

Lerikk's tiny office had striped curtains in the windows and dusty flowers in a vase. Ludlow delivered his card with his left hand and shook hands with his right in short stabbing blows, like a boxer warming up.

"American?" Lerikk's close-set eyes ricocheted from the name card to Ludlow's clothes, then to his face. The Finn was so stout that his arms were limited in frontal movement and protruded at a half-raised angle as he held the name card out to read it. He was ruddy-complexioned, with little hair. His breathing was noisy. He wore a chalkstripe double-breasted suit which simply made matters worse. Each trouser leg must have had a thirty-inch circumference.

"Right," Ludlow said with a deprecating shrug. The change in his demeanor was astounding. Ludlow's shoulders now sagged, his eyes had gone uncertain. His strong torso seemed to shrink. It was the mark of the truly great ones, Mori knew, this ability to change physically before your eyes. Mori wished he possessed that artistry.

"Electronics for your barter business." Ludlow's voice wavered as he cleared his throat. He waved a humble hand toward Mori. "My Japan representative. We haven't printed up cards yet, I'm afraid. Newly appointed." Ludlow shook his head as if that oversight was also entirely his own. On cue, Mori bowed.

Lerikk's face had grown a superior, skeptical smile. "Quite frankly, our barter crates do very little by way of electronics." The Finn folded his arms. "Mostly food you know. But please do sit down."

"Ah." The word leapt from Ludlow's lips as if he'd just understood a very good riddle. He sat down slowly.

Ignored, Mori found a hard-bottomed chair and tried not to breathe. He would let the charade go only so far.

"Food, is it?" Ludlow stared admiringly at the unimpressive desk behind which the Finn had settled.

"Well yes." Lerikk was drumming fingers of his left hand against his right forearm, a mild stress signal. "Food and sundries mostly." His English was thick with mispronounced consonants, the mark of one who has tried diligently to master but has fallen short. On top of his desk were several piles of letters which his eyes glanced toward to suggest he didn't really have much time.

Ludlow spoke hurriedly, still very much the supplicant. "My firm is looking for a conduit; high tech mostly."

Mori stared out the window in silent protest. Lerikk had swung toward him misunderstanding.

"But surely you have a local agent."

"No," Ludlow apologized. "Mori-san is merely a representative. Not a legal entity. That would require the nuisance of incorporation. Taxes. Not that I lack patriotism. Yes, sir. We are looking for an established firm. One that could act on our instructions. Export mainly. Items difficult to get out of the country. We're looking for a little ingenuity."

"Why not Tokyo then?" said Lerikk. There was a new ring of indecisiveness that comes with curiosity.

"Mr. Lerikk, if I may interrupt." For no good reason Mori came to Ludlow's aid. A hunch, perhaps illogical. The ring of uncertainty in the manager's voice had somehow decided him. "Please understand exports are easier here. This is the oldest

348

free port in Japan. The customs in Tokyo or Yokohama are time-consuming and inflexible." The way Mori said "inflexible" left little doubt. Ludlow was nodding his head admiringly.

Lerikk's stubby fingers found a pen. He lifted it expectantly. "Perhaps you have some reference?"

"The goods are not destined for U.S.A. buyers." Ludlow enunciated each word now as one punched rivets into yielding metal. He'd noted that the top letter on one of the piles displayed the seal of the Soviet embassy. "Middle East only. Iraq and Iran to be exact. The name I was told to supply you was Pachinkov. Oleg Pachinkov, Mr. Lerikk. Do anything for you, sir?"

Lerikk's face did not betray change. However, his jaw began to clench each time he took a breath.

"I don't believe I know that name." Lerikk picked at Ludlow's name card to erase the doubt. "Mr. Thomas."

Ludlow drew his chair closer to the front of Lerikk's desk and folded his massive hands on the scarred top.

"Then perhaps you should read your mail again." Ludlow indicated the letter from the Soviet embassy. It had been easy to read the signature upside down.

Lerikk's eyes bounced from the American's hands to the letterhead to Ludlow's impassive face. A tiny bubble of sweat appeared at what many years ago would have been his hairline.

"They might not have told you yet, of course." Ludlow's voice had taken on a sudden frosty edge.

"Who would that be, Mr. Thomas?"

"The Soviets, of course." Ludlow's huge hand suddenly shot out with surprising speed and gripped the Finn's wrist. "Look, I really don't have much time."

Lerikk did not struggle. His pupils dilated as fright invaded his eyes. Mori started to protest.

"Lock the goddamned door, Mori-san!" Ludlow rose half out of his chair, still holding his prey. Mori went to the door, unsure what to do.

"You want to call him to confirm, buddy?" Ludlow had still not released his grip. The Finn was momentarily unable to comprehend the sudden change in the American. Ludlow lifted the phone. "Call him." He shook the receiver under Lerikk's double chin.

Lerikk wobbled his head unsteadily. "He's traveling."

Ludlow replaced the phone. His face suddenly relaxed. He turned to Mori and motioned him away from the door. Then he released his hold on Lerikk's wrist. White marks there slowly disappeared. The American sat down again in his chair. A pleasant smile had returned to his features.

"Well, perhaps we can do some business after all, Mr. Lerikk. Traveling, is he? And where might that be to?"

Lerikk looked first at one of the faces confronting him, then to the other. With feigned despair he held up his hands. "They've rented a car."

"Here in Hokkaido?" Mori's voice was incredulous. Ludlow was smiling like a cat.

Lerikk nodded assuredly. "He's to stop at the Daisetzan Hotel tonight. Vacationing, I believe. After that they didn't say. I'll phone him this evening if you don't mind." He opened a drawer and, to steady his nerves, began methodically to put the letters on his desk into the drawer.

"Fine, Mr. Lerikk. That would be perfect." Ludlow stood and grinned with suspicious warmth. "We'll phone you to-morrow, then?"

Lerikk nodded agreeably but didn't bother to see them out.

The sky was darkening when they reached the street, and the rain had increased in intensity. They hailed a cab and Mori directed the driver downtown. The Nippon Rent-a-Car office was located next to the central fish market. The car itself smelled of mackerel, and they had to drive with all the windows open for the first hour. They left the storm behind as they neared the mountains of Central Hokkaido.

Evening comes early in northern Japan. The hot-spring hotel was on the outskirts of Daisetzan National Park, perched on a rise of grassy slope and Hokkaido pine. It offered the casual woody elegance that comes when Japanese architects succeed in blending the structural with the environmental; something they are rather good at, Ludlow conceded. As backdrop against a clear night sky, dark mountains dominated the silence. Their snowy crests were faintly luminescent from the half moon.

Somewhere along the way, Mori had asked Ludlow how he thought the barter system worked.

"Figure it out, Ninja." Ludlow's voice was up a notch. "The KGB people in Region Seven under Pachinkov have a very competent channel for getting high tech out. Tied into this barter scheme, don't you agree?"

"You mean it has Japan's tacit agreement?"

"To a point," Ludlow said. "I mean, when have the Japanese ever lived up to their international commitments?" That was not a criticism, Ludlow assured the inspector, simply a matter of historical record. One had only to look at the recent import treaties, or the Toshiba case. The Soviets knew that Japanese fishing co-ops were violating limited-catch pacts. Severe penalties hadn't worked. So the Soviets chose a common ground with Japan—the willingness to ignore a temporary illegality if it achieved a selfish goal. Finn-Pacific was granted a monopoly on crate supply. When a boat was boarded, so many crates were bartered for so many pounds over the catch limit. The Japanese co-ops paid for filling the crates with food the Soviets on the Sakhalins could use.

Mori turned the heater up a notch. "So, unknown to the co-ops, the KGB controls Finn-Pacific and is slipping stolen high tech in with the food and sundries?"

"Right. But since most items the KGB wants can be purchased off the shelf, they don't need to be stolen or shipped out in barter crates. They can be sent through the normal export shipping channel using direct contact on arrival to local freight companies so dummy return addresses won't be notified. Cash payments on all bills in transit. Fake customs declarations, since no one in Japan bothers to examine content anyway. Slick as goose shit on linoleum. Crates are just for special items."

They had parked with a sight line to the hotel entrance. Mori shook his head. "I still don't really understand it. Our trip could be a waste. I'll check the hotel for our two guests."

Ludlow appeared to consider the idea carefully. "You have

a weapon, Ninja? Or do you people rely entirely on clever martial-arts footwork?"

"You are all children," Mori shook his head. "You laugh too much. You get angry too easily. You tell too many jokes. You are never serious when you should be." Mori's hand reached for the door handle. Ludlow's arm blocked him.

"Better make sure it's loaded, smartass, lest they blow you apart in the middle of one of your fancy ninja moves."

Mori sighed and unholstered the Colt. He flicked the handle open and reset the cartridges. Then he replaced the weapon and patted the bulge under his jacket.

"You're worse than any of them," he hissed and opened the door.

Ludlow smiled, finally, after the Japanese had gone. Even Inspector Mori had his moments.

———

The night duty clerk was a cooperative girl with a high, pure voice and large, clever eyes. Before she could dive for a registration form, Mori had his wallet on the counter flicked open to the police badge. It glittered officially in the subdued lighting.

"An elderly foreigner who checked in earlier today?" Mori's eyes were scanning the off-season lobby. The assumption was that foreigners this time of the year were few and far between.

"He did not check in," the girl replied obediently. "A party arrived before him this evening." She opened a register, anticipating Mori's next question. "They're sharing an adjoining suite. Three-five-zero-five and -six. The name for both rooms is Balboa."

Mori remained berthed at the desk.

"What nationality, please?"

"Spanish." The girl's thin voice floated against the urgency of his questions like bamboo flute counterpoints to a *tsuzumi* drum.

Mori wondered if he had the right party. "How was the reservation made?"

She pirouetted and pulled a card from a box to study it briefly. "A company named Finn-Pacific. Their telephone is a Hakodate number."

"Did you see the party that arrived first? How many men or women?"

"A large man." Her head nodded in beat to the words. "Middle-aged but not old." A touch of caution in her eyes before she plunged on. "He insisted on carrying his own luggage. Strong he was. Like a water buffalo."

"Not a blond, then?" Disappointment seared Mori's voice.

"No." The girl understood she'd somehow failed the interview. Mori gestured to the rear of the lobby.

"The back door leads where?"

"A garden and tennis court," said the girl. "There is also an outdoor communal hot spring." Her eyes dipped modestly.

Mori nodded. "In their rooms, are they?"

The girl bowed. "Will there be trouble?"

Mori's answer was a long stare. Then he turned and left.

At an outside dispenser he bought two cans of Mountain Dew and handed one to Ludlow. He settled again in the front seat.

"That bad, is it?" Ludlow was studying Mori's face. He popped the easy-open can with one huge finger.

"Two of them." Mori drank half his Mountain Dew. The dry Hokkaido air had made him thirsty, after the humidity of the Kanto. "And neither was the blond."

"Sure," Ludlow said, finished his drink, and crumpled the can in his fist. "That confirms they're not working together. That means the blond is here to discredit our friend Pachinkov."

"And you think Yuki's working for the blond's team?"

"Everything points to it. Someone at Center is jealous of Pachinkov's success. Or there's a fight on for a big job. Has to be one of the two."

"So that's why the blond didn't bring the stolen prototype to Finn-Pacific to ship out through a barter crate?"

"Looks that way. He's going to take it out alone. I don't

353

think Pachinkov likes the idea. Neither he nor his friend. So we follow them and hopefully they lead us to their blond comrade. What do you say?"

"What if they're really on vacation?"

"What if frogs had shorter legs? They'd bump their asses when they jumped, right?"

CHAPTER 41

FLIGHT

The Japanese car was much better than anything Kovalenko had driven in Russia. His own Chaika was a clumsy cow compared with this sleek machine. It amazed him how smoothly the engine purred, with none of the squeaks or rattles common to even the best Soviet equipment after the first year. His dashboard was ablaze with interesting lights and buttons that offered to tell him how many miles he could drive on gas in the tank, the outside air temperature, the temperature in the car—anything he wanted to know. Why didn't they have such cars in Russia? Was it too much to expect? This machine was for the average Japanese citizen. He'd passed many like it on the road.

As he drove, he spent part of the time inventing stories he would use if he were stopped. Center advice was to keep to the simplest one: that he was a tourist.

If the police stopped him he would claim the car was rented through friends in Finn-Pacific. Should the police check, the company would no doubt stall until they found out who the driver really was. And of course, no check could be made with the company until morning.

Kovalenko had an international driver's license, acquired in Hong Kong, a fresh American passport with a tourist visa stamped by Narita immigration, plus various credit cards and a Social Security number. Center had made sure his documentation was complete; their thoroughness had almost been his downfall, he thought grimly.

If he were stopped now for any reason it would cost him valuable time. So he took every precaution. He observed all the speed limits meticulously. He skirted towns if there was a choice of roads, since travel through congested small-town streets created too many opportunities for a sighting or unforeseen accident. Japanese in rural areas took a reckless delight in moving furiously, whether with cars, motorcycles, or bicycles.

After dark, however, the traffic thinned. The later it became, the more Kovalenko eased his rule. Time was increasingly critical. By tomorrow morning he must be on Samurai's boat and underway toward his rendezvous in the Sea of Okhotsk.

He reached the northern coast of Hokkaido. Seaward lights flickered from boats out for flying fish attracted to bulbs trolled just below the surface. Small fishing villages blurred past. Thatched roofs in vague outline huddled together protectively. On one side was the blackness of the menacing sea; on the other, the thrust of harsh volcanic hills. They battled the elements year round here, he imagined. The ocean attacked incessantly, foaming against black volcanic beach. But the closeness of the Okhotsk Sea had lifted Kovalenko's spirits. He was glad he was not tied to this forsaken place. He could escape.

Jagged lava rock polished by the pounding sea rose in his headlights like prehistoric sea monsters hurled ashore and frozen in time. He slowed for a curve. The ocean's vast expanse spread out ahead momentarily. He imagined himself safely on the Soviet patrol boat, heading for the homeland with prismatic spray flying off the bow. Quickly he reined his mind in. Never to anticipate, that was his rule. He must concentrate on the problem at hand. He was close now. It was time to face his future.

Nemuro would be the last chance for Region Seven to stop him and the 5G computer from escaping. It followed that Pachinkov would come for him. His career, after all, was at stake.

He would be alone, probably, or with only one of his most trusted lieutenants. But surprise was with Kovalenko. Once he reached Nemuro and contacted Samurai he could choose the time. He should have no trouble in escaping. There were many ways. But escape to what?

A sense of unease had been curling behind the logic of his plans like a snake about to strike. Malik, his chief, never trusted subordinates with the complete truth, no matter how close they were. Again and again he had thought back to that meeting with Pachinkov at Shinobazu. Why had it been necessary?

Suddenly, it became frighteningly clear. Kovalenko shuddered. Fear seized him—a fear such as he had never known before. He pulled over to the shoulder and stumbled from the car, his heart hammering, bile rising in his throat. What his mind sought to shape could not be true, yet he knew with his deepest primal instinct that it was. He staggered to the edge of the sea as the salt wind tore at his clothing. He stared into the dark emptiness toward Russia. *Pyeshka* . . . the word echoed relentlessly through his mind: the pawn.

Malik had insisted he make contact with Pachinkov, hadn't he? To lure him! Malik had known Pachinkov would follow. That there would be an attempt on his life. He, Kovalenko, was the tethered goat! *Pyeshka.* He was the one who was supposed to die!

Kovalenko stormed back to the car and slammed the door. He shifted to first and pressed the accelerator to the floor. Tires spun in loose sand, then dug into hard asphalt underneath and squealed as the car roared to life. He rode the animal with fierce intensity until his arms ached from holding too tightly to the wheel.

When the rage finally ebbed, he slowed the car to a more considered pace. A plan slowly formed; his mind was crystal clear. He must get out. He must defeat Pachinkov. He would return to Moscow. And destroy Malik. That was how the game must be played. He could be the next chief of Directorate T.

He concentrated on the road and thought of what he must accomplish in the hours ahead. His mind now was focused, his memory deep. He had the address where he was to meet the one who went by the code name Samurai. He looked at his watch and calculated another thirty minutes to Nemuro. He would not drive through the streets of the town even though it was after midnight. Too much risk. He would park and approach the rendezvous on foot. The house should not be difficult to find.

THE BIMBO

Mori was driving, following the twin taillights of the KGB car. At 11:20 the two KGB officers had left their hotel and started north. At the wheel in the first hour, the American had twice nearly fallen asleep. Now they were heading toward the sea with Ludlow snoring in the back.

As he drove, Mori thought about Ludlow. He decided the American and he were alike in ways the American could not imagine. They were locomotives on parallel tracks, rushing toward their mutual destruction.

Mori paused in his thoughts to check his distance to the KGB car ahead, keeping it barely in sight. Then he scanned the rearview mirror again; a pair of headlights followed.

What he admired most about the American was his total fearlessness. Mori could not be like Ludlow. Mori was afraid, and not only of shame. He had numbed his consciousness so that he could face death, walk right up to it without faltering, but then what? He'd been in difficult situations before; yet always he had had the advantage. He couldn't imagine being in a foreign country and facing the kind of odds that Ludlow faced tonight. His own country had turned against him. He was hunted by all sides. Mori could escape. Ludlow had no chance. Mori's admiration was born of guilt and fear. The guilt struck him because he did not face the same risks as his friend. The fear was that, when the time came, he would not be able to save the American. That, as with his father, the nightmare of helplessly watching someone he cared for die would be repeated.

A warning tugged at his consciousness. He checked ahead and to the sides. Nothing. He opened the window and felt the wind wash his face, yet it gave no clue. Finally, he realized that it was the rearview mirror. The lights from the car behind had been with him for at least the past half hour. That by itself might mean nothing: it was late, and the road had little traffic and few turnoffs. Still, he could not take chances. It could be a KGB chase car protecting the occupants in the vehicle ahead. He kept his left hand on the wheel, unsnapped the holster with his right, and pulled the Colt, thumbed the safety off, then placed it on the seat beside him. Carefully, he considered his options. Before he could decide, the headlights in his rearview mirror began to grow in size. The decision was made for him.

He lifted the Colt and steadied it on the open window. He could see the headlights in his mirror suddenly swing to the passing lane, hear the roar of the motor in his ears as the car overtook him. He braced himself, and, as the car came abreast, looked across at its occupant. At first his eyes refused to register. The form behind the wheel was a woman's. The familiar profile echoed in his brain. Erika! Then the car was by him, rushing into the darkness.

For the next several minutes he could only hear the noise of the wind in his ears. Impossible! He must be seeing ghosts. He watched the taillights receding into the distance ahead of him. It was closing on the Soviet car. No. The Soviet car was slowing. There were lights ahead—a gas station and rest stop. Her car went by without slowing. Mori followed. The KGB car had pulled in beside one of the gas pumps. Mori no longer cared about them. He pressed his foot on the gas until he was keeping to her speed. A mile down the road the car suddenly turned off. When he reached the intersection, he followed and nearly passed the woman. She had turned the car around so it was facing back the way she'd come. He slowed, made a

U-turn, and pulled in behind her. In the backseat, Ludlow stirred but did not wake.

Mori walked quickly to the car, yanked open the door, and pointed his gun. "Okay, out of there where I can see you."

The figure did not move for a moment. The face was hidden in shadow. Then she moved, a tight skirt hiked up as she slid across the seat. A full sweater that slipped off one shoulder and revealed a shoulder strap. Finally the light caught her angelic face.

"Erika! What is this?"

She grinned. "Give me a kiss."

He ignored her provocation. "Tell me what you're doing here." He wanted to shake her, shake the truth out of this beautiful chameleon.

"You ask very stupid questions sometimes, you know. At the shrine Monday night you asked me to help you, no? How can I help you if I do not know where you are? I have been following you."

"How did you know where we were?"

"I do not like your voice or your gun. I am not a criminal. I do not answer such a voice." She folded her arms and turned away.

Mori put away the gun and shook his head. "Okay, why don't you tell me just what the hell you're up to."

Mori heard a car door slam. As Ludlow came up to them he angrily pointed a finger. "Who the hell is this?"

"Her name is Erika," Mori said. "She's a friend of mine. She's been following us."

Ludlow swung his head about as a bull does getting ready to charge. "Mori!" he roared. "You out of your *pima* imbecilic mind? What the hell is this all about?"

Mori shrugged. "It's a little bit complicated, but I can explain."

"Like hell you can. I want this bimbo out of here. Now!"

Erika was staring at Ludlow. "Listen, hairy barbarian," she said in clear English. "I'm not bimbo. And don't yell!"

Mori looked at her in astonishment. "Where did you learn that?"

Erika's mouth was a firm line and her cheeks had gone a healthy red color. "Never mind," she said.

Ludlow was glaring at her. "Who sent you? Who are you?"

Mori said loudly, "She's the one I told you about at Ueno Zoo. She's helping me. She used to work for Colonel Yuki."

Ludlow shook his head. "She's been working for the colonel, now she's working for you? What's tomorrow going to bring, Inspector? You lost your goddamned mind?"

Mori saw the lights of the KGB car flickering through the trees that lined the main road. The hum of the motor grew, then faded as it sped past their intersection. He turned to Ludlow. "What do you want to do?"

"Hell, we can't leave her here, that's for damn sure. For now she comes with us."

Erika started to protest. Mori took her arm. "Do like he says, Erika, we'll come back for your car later. You have some explaining to do. Now get your things!"

"*Chutto matte!* You don't have to yell." She pulled away from him, then grabbed a small travel bag and portable cassette player–radio from her car.

Mori made her sit in the front seat. He put his car in gear, hit the accelerator, and hurled the car onto the road after the Soviets. Within several minutes they'd picked up the KGB taillights again.

"You know." Ludlow leaned forward; a pleasant grin had swept all anger from his face. "I hate to sound stupid, but how did this young lady know where to find us?"

"I don't know," Mori sighed. "She was trying to learn what Colonel Yuki was up to. Why don't you tell us what happened, Erika?"

She went through it all in a soft, precise voice. How she'd done what Mori asked and begun to question Colonel Yuki to find out what he was up to. How Colonel Yuki was very co-operative, suddenly concerned with her welfare, insisting, finally, that she needed a guard. They took her to some awful building in Kanda that smelled like a warehouse with only a cot and toilet. They said it was just for a few days, but gradually she understood she was a prisoner. She'd waited her chance and escaped. After that she'd kept in hiding and, as soon as she could, gone straight to Mori's house. There she had stayed half the night waiting for him, until she finally gave up. She was walking back toward the station when she saw Mori come down the stairs, then stop and look back. She hadn't known what to do. When she saw the huge American coming down the stairs behind him, she'd run and hidden again. She'd followed them since. Caught the same plane, and rented a car after they rented theirs.

"How come you passed me then, why now?" Mori jerked a thumb toward his car. "The American is still with me."

"I just wanted you to know I was here. I didn't think you'd stop." Erika gripped the small travel bag and red radio on her lap. She looked straight ahead. "You don't believe me," she exclaimed suddenly, "but it's all true. Swear to the gods."

Ludlow leaned forward, so that his huge shaggy head was almost between the front-seat occupants. His eyes smiled at her as if she were a daughter. Tension lines around his clamped mouth softened. For a moment he was almost handsome. He clucked his tongue as if scolding a kitten. "Mother have mercy, child, we're not doubting you." His eyes picked up their cold, frightening passivity only when he took a good long look at the radio Erika held tightly in her lap. "So why don't you start from the beginning for Uncle Robert here? Let's have the entire program."

"Right," Mori echoed. "Tell us everything you found out from Yuki."

She began with Mori's wife. Yuki had ordered the *kanzashi* and clock incidents so that Mitsuko would leave Mori. It was somehow important that she be estranged when someone they referred to only as "the *Kinpatsu*"—"the blond"—arrived. Mitsuko was to become friends with the blond and help him to do something. Then the blond was to run north and a Soviet they called only Oleg would follow him. Mori looked at Ludlow and nodded: Pachinkov, of course. The blond would be in some danger, Erika continued, but Yuki would do his best to help him escape. At the right time, Yuki would call in an American he referred to as "the *bochi*."

"Cemetery," Mori advised.

"Graves," Ludlow smiled.

When pressed for more, she said Oleg would be arrested, but that she wasn't sure why and it didn't all make a great deal of sense. She would have found out more, but Colonel Yuki had gradually become suspicious of her questions. She turned to stare out the front window at the car they were following.

"You did a terrific job," Ludlow said after a moment's pause. "An absolutely terrific job." He leaned back and clapped his hands rhythmically like a Spanish guitarist for a particularly fine flamenco. Then, as if a thought had just occurred to him, he stopped clapping and leaned forward again. "You know, Erika, why don't you relax? You look uncomfortable with all that debris cluttering up your beautiful lap. Why don't we put it in back?"

"It's okay," she said. "I don't need anyone to help me."

"Maybe we were a little hard on you," Ludlow murmured mournfully, as if he were reciting a kaddish. "If so, we're sorry. Right, Mori?"

"Yes. We're sorry." Mori was puzzling out the change in the American. "Everybody relax. Put your things in back, Erika. Like he says."

"No," she said, but finally she passed her tiny suitcase to the American who settled it on the seat carefully beside him.

Then Ludlow said: "Didn't I also see a smart little portable radio? Want to put that in back, too, Erika love? No trouble at all?"

She held onto the portable and did not reply. With one great paw, Ludlow suddenly reached over the seat and scooped the radio out of her grip with such force that it appeared she'd handed it to him.

"Give that back!"

"I'm sorry, love, but I guess I am a barbarian, just like you said. I see something I like, I take it. This really is a fine piece of equipment, by the way. Where did you get it? One of those nifty little shops in Akihabara?" Ludlow started to work the dials of the radio.

Erika turned to Mori. "Make him give it back."

"In just a moment," Ludlow said. He looked up at her, smiling sincerely, then continued to examine the dials.

"Stop! You're going to break it."

Ludlow was examining the sides and top with greater interest. The mechanism was only easy to spot if you were looking for it: the tiny mesh on the side to speak into, the extra switch in back, the key button on the side. Ludlow turned the radio on; it picked up some Enka music.

"Very nice tone." He nodded approvingly at Erika. "Must have cost a ton."

"Give it back," she said.

Ludlow flicked the special switch and listened for a moment to the static, which suddenly cleared. A voice declared it was Car 55 and needed a repeat on the disturbance location. After a pause, another voice cut in giving a specific address. A building in Tokyo.

Mori said, "That's the Tokyo Command Center police net! It has a special crystal."

"Yes," Ludlow agreed. "I suppose it has." His eyes had lost their earlier merriment. He leaned forward in his seat so that his voice was close to Erika's ear. "You want to give Uncle Robert your call sign, child, or am I going to have to wring that pretty neck of yours?"

Mori swiveled around to shoot a look at Ludlow. "Her radio is set up to transmit, too?"

"She has a direct line," Ludlow said. "To the Tokyo Police Command Center. Want to place a call?"

"You mean she's been assigned to follow us?"

Ludlow's eyes had become distant, like those of a doctor about to tell a patient he is fatally ill. "Looks that way, Inspector." He turned back to Erika. "So how do you identify yourself when you want to report in, dear? What is it you say? I don't think you understand what kind of trouble you're in yet, do you now?"

She turned to Mori. "I was going to tell you about this but the American wasn't to know."

Mori nodded, his eyes still on the road. "Who told you the American wasn't supposed to know?"

"She's very good, I'll give her that." Ludlow was staring at the radio in his hands. "Went right to her fall-back story without blinking an eye. Takes lots of training, that does."

Erika had put her hand on Mori's arm. "I went to Watanabe-san. Your friend. He said I was not to trust the American."

"Who's Watanabe?" Ludlow demanded.

"The one we met for lunch. The one who gave you the background on Kathy Johnson's role in the MicroDec case. The one who lost his mother and sister in Hiroshima."

"How did she know how to contact him?"

"I gave her a special number and his name in case she couldn't reach me."

"Then she could be telling the truth?"

"I am," Erika said hotly.

"I think she is," Mori concluded. "Watanabe knew the chief wouldn't buy her story about the colonel being a traitor or holding her in a warehouse. So he did the only thing he could—made it look like one of his own operations. It's like him; he couldn't use anyone in the MPD, because getting authorizations would take time and tip off the chief or Yuki. So he asked her to follow us. He wanted to make sure I was okay. If there was trouble he'd come running because he's a friend."

Ludlow nodded. "Fine. But I think we better check it out. I understand he's not a big fan of the U.S.A.; that could explain his orders to Erika. He probably still thinks I ran the Starfire break-in."

Mori scratched his head, then turned to Erika. "When are you supposed to report in next?"

"I was supposed to contact him fifteen minutes ago."

Ludlow handed her back the radio. "Why don't you show us how it works? Ask if they can get Mr. Watanabe on the line. His friend, Inspector Mori, would like to have a chat." He looked at Mori. "That okay with you, Inspector?"

"Yes." Mori was trying to sort out his mixed feelings about this woman. How dangerous was she? What was the truth about her? If he lived through this, maybe he would find out.

In the ensuing five minutes, Erika showed them how the radio sending unit set up. They had to stop the car and take a special aerial out of her little suitcase, which they stood by the side of the road. It was actually quite simple. The button, when keyed, notified a console in the Tokyo Command Center, which dialed the special sending frequency assigned her. Watanabe came on after several minutes' delay. His voice was worried until Mori explained things. Relieved, Watanabe confirmed Erika's story: After Erika had told him about Yuki's connection to the blond, he had known it would be too sensitive for the higher-ups, so he had set the whole thing up on his own. To protect Mori in case the crazy American tried to kill him or worse, he laughed embarrassedly. Before Mori rang off, he promised to call in periodically.

Nobody said very much afterward. Ludlow silently helped fold up the antenna and put it into her little case. When they got back into the car, Ludlow offered to drive, then insisted Erika sit next to him in front. After they had found the KGB taillights again, Ludlow explained to her how it was better to err on the side of caution than of trust. This was the closest he ever came to an apology. Erika understood, and knew how she should handle it. First, she flattered Ludlow with just the right amount of distance, admitting that anyone else would never have found her out. Uncle Robert was a true professional. She had much to learn from him. However, she said, there was still quite a bit of confusion at Tokyo Police headquarters about Uncle Robert's role in the JEC break-in. How was she to answer their accusations that Uncle Robert organized the break-in and was party therefore to the murder of the guards? Or that the blond was an American, as everyone in Tokyo still believed?

"By which way the blond is running," Mori said. "If the blond was an American, he would have tried for the nearest American base. They are all far behind us now."

"Yes," Erika agreed. "We are nearing the ocean."

"It will be a boat," Ludlow said firmly. "Escape by sea to a vessel outside the territorial limit." He looked at Erika and smiled. "The people in the car ahead of us are KGB; they know where the blond will leave from. They are taking us to him." He looked over at Erika and winked. "But I'm not asking for your trust, child. That's a word we have to leave out in our game. If I'm wrong and the blond is not there and heading out to sea, then I will surrender peacefully for whatever awful spectacle your little heart desires. You can take me back to Tokyo." Ludlow patted her knee.

Erika smiled brilliantly at him. "But I trust you completely, Uncle Robert." Then she politely removed his hand from her knee.

The American shook his head, marveling at how she'd put him on the defensive and kept him there. "A natural," he said to himself and shook his head again. "A perfect little gem."

He drove steadily onward, reaching the ocean as an overcast sky lightened for a reluctant dawn.

———

They left Erika with the car. After they had reached the ocean and followed the KGB car east, it had finally slowed on the outskirts of Nemuro. Ludlow had been driving carefully, giving the KGB car plenty of distance. The Soviets had turned off on a road that climbed behind the village. They'd known exactly where to go—a lookout that gave a perfect view of the boats and dock and streets of the hamlet. Ludlow stopped the car a safe distance away and pulled into a deserted logging road. Before they got out, Mori said, "This is where you'll wait. You can see the road to the lookout from here. Stay near but out of the way in case we need the car, okay?" Erika nodded and watched them begin the climb into the woods beyond the road.

———

The American selected a spot that was steeply above the two Soviets and in trees. He leaned against a massive cedar and wiped his face. He pointed his handkerchief at the Soviets, who were busily making preparations at a lookout by the side of the road below. Pachinkov was using a pair of glasses to scan the dock and beach below them. The other man busied himself inside the car. Small fishing boats were pulled up all along the beach, and at the dock was a large, sleek trawler. On the dock was the office of the fishery cooperative that controlled all the boats in the town.

The final streaks of dawn lighted a low overcast horizon. In the village, smoke coiled from chimneys as cooking fires were set. No one moved outside. Ludlow turned to Mori:

"What do you think?" He indicated the Soviet who sat in the KGB car assembling what appeared to be a high-powered rifle with telescopic sight. The man certainly looked familiar. Even at this distance, Ludlow was almost sure it was the one who'd tried to take him in front of the church.

"Sergei Vasilyev, he works at Aeroflot," Mori said. "He also resembles the one I saw in the intersection that day Kathy Johnson was killed. Have to see his neck to be sure."

"His neck?"

"The *gaijin* in the intersection had a scar behind his left ear."

"Then let's go down for a better look and maybe a chat," Ludlow said. "You ready?"

Mori stood up. "Ready," he said.

———

Pachinkov's eyes felt hollow and his head ached from lack of sleep. He wanted to pour cold water from the ocean over his face, but knew that was impossible. Kovalenko was down there somewhere. They must wait for him to make the first move. They must watch.

A figure emerged from the village streets, crossed to the beach and was walking slowly down the row of boats pulled up there. In his hand he carried an overnight bag. Pachinkov put the glasses on him. Sergei got out of the car and came over. "Who is it?"

"A Japanese fisherman," Pachinkov said. "Or maybe not." He handed the glasses to Sergei. "See what he carries in his hand? Is that the overnight bag Kovalenko was carrying on the train?"

Sergei studied the figure for only a moment. "The very same." Sergei put the glasses down and picked up his rifle. "How do you want this done?"

"Several bullets through the bag first; I want the Starfire destroyed."

Sergei lifted the rifle and stared through the telescopic sight.

"Do not kill the gentleman unless you have to. Disable him."

Sergei steadied the rifle and began to squeeze.

The crack of sound was startling. Sergei's rifle disintegrated. The sight shattered, sending needlelike bits of glass into the Russian's cheek. Sergei turned, roaring like a buffalo, to face his unseen assailant, the useless weapon still in his hands. A line of blood was marching down his face.

Pachinkov's hand reached for his coat pocket. A second shot rang out and a bullet hummed by the Soviet resident's ear. His hand froze.

Lazily, the big American stood and walked toward them. Neither Soviet moved. There was a possibility of taking him, but both had seen movement in the bush behind the American across the road. Pachinkov signaled Sergei not to try.

Ludlow walked up to Sergei, took the weapon from the Russian and hurled it over the edge of the lookout. He studied the gash on Sergei's cheek with momentary disinterest. "Nice to see you again," the American said. He then searched Pachinkov and found a steel Beretta with pearl grip that was brand new. Next he took Pachinkov's binoculars and checked the beach.

The figure there had turned at the sound of shots and was staring up toward the lookout. Then, he hurriedly began to check the boats again. He found the boat he wanted and clambered on board.

"Do you know who that man on the beach is?" Ludlow asked, turning to face both men.

They shook their heads.

"His name is Colonel Yuki. I have a feeling he was expecting you to be here."

Pachinkov wondered what this American was talking about. It was then that the one who had done the firing stood and started to walk toward them. He was not large even by Japanese standards, but Pachinkov could see by the casual sureness of his steps and the steadiness of his eyes that this was no common Japanese. He carried the handgun pointed between the two Russians. Pachinkov cursed under his breath. The American had been unarmed.

Mori had stopped fifteen feet from the two Soviets and was staring at Sergei. "This was the man in Ginza. The welt on his neck is the same."

Sergei turned to look more carefully at Mori. "I have never been to the Ginza, sir."

Ludlow nodded. "Why are you here?"

"We are waiting for another." Pachinkov folded his arms. "It is a matter between only Russians; we suggest you leave him to us."

"I would love to, really I would, but unfortunately . . ." Ludlow put the glasses on Yuki, who was stowing the overnight bag in the wheelhouse. "How did you know your man would be leaving from this village?" Ludlow turned to look at the chief resident.

Pachinkov shrugged. "He stole one of our cars, which, unknown to him, had a high-frequency transmitter attached."

Ludlow clucked his tongue. His eyes went again to the beach, where Yuki was now frantically untying moorings that held the boat fast. "So—the same system used to move stolen high tech out of the country, then?" He turned to consider the Russians.

Pachinkov chuckled at Sergei, who shook his head with barely concealed satisfaction. They were some team, like old comedians making up their lines as they went. Ludlow could have watched it all day—but the starting of a far-off marine engine distracted his attention.

"The man on the boat down there just put a small bag on board." Ludlow made an approximate size with his hands. "That what your friend stole?"

Sergei shrugged. "Perhaps." He started to hum a Ukrainian folk song.

"It is what was stolen," Pachinkov agreed. "The man we want must be nearby. We can settle this ourselves."

Ludlow looked at Mori. "According to these gentlemen, Colonel Yuki just put the stolen computer prototype on board that sloop. Make any sense?"

Mori shook his head. "No idea, unless he's going for a ride too."

Sergei pointed suddenly. Yuki dove into the water behind the boat. Slowly the boat slid into the water under his exertion. Finally its keel floated free. Ludlow checked the name. *Minikami.* It was a powered fishing sloop with a single winch in the back to haul up the nets, which were now stowed on deck. Simple to operate. The engine revved and the boat steadied as the propeller took hold. It backed slowly away from the beach.

"They try to fool us," Pachinkov said. "They try to make it appear a fisherman goes out in his boat alone."

Ludlow was scanning the waves. Mori was now also straining his eyes toward the ocean for some clue. At first Ludlow thought it was a sea bird riding the waves, slender and disappearing periodically behind the roll of tide. He studied the object for almost a minute. Then he handed the glasses to Mori. "At ten o'clock." Ludlow said. "Between the boat and the breakwater. Tell me what you see."

Mori squinted into the glasses. "A snorkle. It's a damned snorkle."

Pachinkov's voice was suddenly sharp and authoritative. "Now, my friend."

Sergei dove for Ludlow, knocked the Beretta free, and drove a knee to Ludlow's kidneys. The vehemence of the surprise attack stunned Ludlow. He staggered momentarily off balance. Sergei scooped up the gun and covered Mori, all within fractions of a second. Pachinkov ordered Mori to place his weapon and the glasses on the ground in front of him and take three paces back. Ludlow was to keep his hands well away from his body. Mori bent to comply.

The report was faint, the echo against the hills fainter still. Sergei was thrown against the lookout wall, held it for a moment, then released his grasp. He rolled onto his stomach, twitched, and was still. A growing stain marked the northwest quadrant of his back. The bullet had gone clean through.

Ludlow grabbed Pachinkov and rushed the Soviet under cover behind the Russians' car. Mori hadn't budged. He turned to stare up the mountain, then walked over to Sergei's lifeless form and studied the scar behind his left ear.

"So now," Mori said, "he'll not be able to prove his innocence."

There were no more shots from the mountain. Ludlow gradually straightened. "We're beginning to understand, Ninja."

Mori walked to the edge of the lookout and stared at the boat moving slowly out to sea. A black form grabbed a trailing line and hauled itself up over the side. The figure swept the wet-suit hood off his head. Although he could not see at that great distance, Mori knew the hair would be blond.

"What do you want to bet," Ludlow said, "that the bullet they used matched the caliber of your gun?"

"They can claim anything," Mori replied. "It went clean through."

Three cars pulled suddenly into the lookout parking area. The doors swung open. Graves climbed leisurely from the back seat of the last car, a black American Chevrolet with blue embassy plates. No chrome. From the other cars six husky Americans in civilian clothes emerged with guns drawn aimed at Mori, Ludlow, and the KGB officer. The station chief waved to Mori. "Nice to see you. The famous Inspector Mori, isn't it? Would you kindly holster your weapon, sir? My people are a distrustful lot." Graves glanced at Ludlow as though they might have met before. Then he turned to appraise the dead Soviet on the ground and the other silently glaring at him. He spoke to the Soviet:

"Your comrade on the fishing boat will be allowed to escape. You will be executed for treasonous acts if you return to the Soviet Union. The American government offers you asylum."

Mori was blinking with disbelief. "You can't do that."

Ludlow shook his head with disgust.

"You are all fools," Pachinkov shouted suddenly. "Valuable Japanese high tech will fall into Soviet hands. You are letting a murderer get away. And your guns have killed an innocent man."

"A price for everything," Graves said pleasantly.

Pachinkov glowered at the station chief, then turned on Mori. "The man on that fishing boat, Kovalenko, spent one night with your wife, Inspector. We have tapes to prove it."

There was a silence. The others were staring at Mori. The police inspector nodded and smiled. "You make bad jokes," he said to the Russian and felt the tension go out of the air. Even if it was true, he thought, it wasn't her fault. It was his fault and the fault of the state.

"I am not interested in asylum." Pachinkov spit the words at Graves.

"Let's see how that plays after you've had some time to think it over, old buddy." Graves was smiling with the warm feeling of success.

Pachinkov's face suddenly contorted. "You have worked this out with Malik, haven't you? To destroy my career and advance his? Is he your spy, then? Is this why you wish him to head the First Directorate? By the soul of Lenin I shall not let this monstrosity succeed."

Graves made a motion with his hand. Two of the Americans took the Soviet, one on each side, and moved him to the car where they tried to conceal the fact they were handcuffing him.

Graves then came over to Ludlow. "As fast as you can, get to Misawa Airbase. At the gate give my name. They'll fly you out of the country. Don't waste any time."

"Damned sweet of you, Graves."

"Look," Graves snarled. "Temporarily I'm in a good mood so let's not change that, okay?"

"What about Yuki? Didn't you know he's working with that Soviet in the boat?"

Graves looked around to ensure Pachinkov was already in the car out of earshot. "Yuki is a true patriot, Bob. He volunteered to take the blond out in the boat. For this whole thing to sell, Pachinkov has to believe that comrade Kovalenko escapes safely, right? However, in truth, Colonel Yuki has an executive order with prejudice when he's over the territorial limit. Dump the body."

"How's he supposed to do that?"

"He put an Uzi aboard last night. Also a Stinger for the Soviet patrol boat if necessary."

Ludlow shook his head. "A Stinger is surface-to-air. It won't work on the ocean unless he's point-blank."

"You know something?" Graves wheezed. "You worry too much. This is Yuki's last hurrah. He retires when the operation is over."

"Yuki's working with the Soviets, Graves. He killed Kathy Johnson, attacked Harrington. It was a trade. In return he helps the blond escape."

"Jesus, Ludlow, give me a break, will you?" Graves had a resigned smile on his face. He slapped Ludlow on the back. "Look, get your ass over to Misawa Airbase. I've arranged everything. Plans takes care of its own. I have to be going." He gave Mori a victory salute, did a little jog over to his car to prove he was in shape, and allowed the driver to open the door for him.

The door to the Chevrolet slammed and the American car backed onto the road. The last Ludlow saw of him, Graves was turning around with a solicitous grin to say something in his atrocious Russian to their captive.

CHAPTER 43

CAPTAIN'S CHOICE

Using the Soviet's car, Mori and Ludlow reached the fishery co-op parking lot. Erika was not in sight. On the beach, knots of local men had gathered talking. No fishing boats had been launched, although it was well after seven o'clock. The co-op building was at the land end of the pier, which had concrete pilings and thick poured concrete escarpment. At the far end was a corrugated shed where catches were weighed and cleaned. Stacked against one wall were crates with the Finn-Pacific logo in red on the sides. Alongside the pier a sleek fishing trawler gently nudged rubber tires that had been suspended from the pier by ropes.

When Mori and the *gaijin* entered the office, several eyes turned to them, but in general they were ignored by the dozen-odd fishermen who sat at desks or lounged smoking and chatting in low voices. They wore rubber boots, flared worker's pants stained with salt spray and fish blood, and light sweaters or jackets against the early chill. The office smelled of the sea and the men's faces held the arrogance and respect of those who had conquered it many times. They were all walnut-tanned, but the face of the old man who was on the phone was most striking.

It was a face chiseled to the bone, with no excess fat, the skin drawn tightly over raised cheekbone and prominent white eyebrows. It was tanned from years on the ocean to a magnificent gold offset by a shock of thick white hair. His eyes glittered with the pride and stubbornness, the enterprise and boldness that embodied the Hokkaido fisherman. He was clearly the leader, deferred to by others in the office.

"No boats till we get the all-clear," the leader of the fishery cooperative said. "The *chikisho* bastards will break us all finally, won't they?" He hung up the phone and looked at Mori and Ludlow.

"Who the hell are you?"

"We need some help. There was an emergency on the mountain this morning. Perhaps you heard the shooting."

"So you say? I didn't hear a damn thing. Araki, you hear anything up on the mountain earlier?" A younger man broke off obediently from a conversation and shook his head. The leader turned back to Mori. "We didn't hear anything."

Mori took out his wallet, opened it almost reluctantly, and placed it on the cooperative leader's desk. "I'll need the fastest boat you have." He said this softly, but there was a quality to his voice that made people in the room stop talking. Through the thin walls you could hear the lap of waves against the pilings and the screech of gulls.

The leader was staring at the badge in Mori's wallet. "By the feet of Buddha, a police officer. And from Tokyo at that." He picked up Mori's wallet and turned it over in his hands as if looking for flaws. "*Yaroo*, it's all connected, I suppose. Last night that wild pig of an infantry colonel commandeered Araki's house as if he owned it and borrowed his boat." The leader turned once again to Araki.

"He paid money," Araki said by way of apology, "and his family is distantly related."

The leader nodded his head, "The officer rank. You can tell them any time. Users. Be lucky you get the boat back, and I hear he put a rifle aboard last night. Thought nobody would see."

"He paid a lot of money cash, Captain."

"See what a patriotic cooperative we have?" The captain put his bare feet up on the desk. "And now our boats cannot go out because of our patriotism." He stared momentarily at the young fisherman.

Araki flushed. "He said he's meeting a Soviet patrol boat and it could be dangerous. He had an official paper."

"There you are," the captain scowled. "What nonsense!"

Ludlow spoke softly in Japanese. "Yes, normally you can take care of a Soviet patrol boat with several of those crates out there, correct?"

The captain took an *oshibori* from his desk, unfolded the damp towel, and lowered his head into it. He stayed that way for several seconds. When he removed the towel, his face had regained a measure of patience. "And who in the name of the Seven Pleasures is this foreigner?"

"He works for the American government," Mori said.

"Finn-Pacific," Ludlow offered quietly. "You know this firm, of course?"

The captain nodded. "They are known all along the coast."

"They were hiding stolen high tech in the crates," Ludlow said. "They were using you, the Russians were."

The captain shook his head sadly and put his feet down on the floor. "And am I to understand that you do not wish to use us?" He leaned forward on his desk and folded his hands in front of him as if about to deliver a lecture. Everyone in the room began talking again in the quiet way of Japanese waiting for an argument to begin.

First, he explained that there was a lottery, since demand exceeded supply. And there was nothing illegal about it, since they had no intention of exporting the crates. The Soviets would board their craft and simply take them. All the fishing cooperatives on the Hokkaido coast considered it a desirable policy. In conclusion, he did not believe what the foreigner had to say. This nonsense about stolen high tech was as crazy as bean-throwing. The cooperative leader stared at Ludlow, who now threatened a very desirable understanding with the Russians.

"Transponders," Ludlow said abruptly. "Your crates with high tech have special high-frequency transmitters the Soviet radio ships can track easily. They simply board boats with high-tech crates."

The leader shook his head. "This I do not believe."

The door burst open, and this time all faces turned. Erika walked in, looking around at the men. She saw Mori and Ludlow and looked at them sternly. "What are you two doing here?" She came over to stand by Mori and smiled at the leader of the cooperative. Then she took out a name card and handed it to the captain with a bow.

For the first time the leader smiled. "Araki, get me my name cards."

He gave her one and then had Araki set a chair. The chair was placed alongside his desk as the captain had seen her legs. Mori strode to the window. The *Minikami* was a dot on the horizon now. He could feel the sweat under his arms.

Erika tut-tutted as the captain explained that the two intruders had ordered him to give them a boat. She apologized for them and gave a sigh; she had heard the argument all the way out on the pier. Had a boat with a blond in it set out this morning by any chance? she asked.

The captain grimaced. Well now, they couldn't be sure, but a pig of a colonel had taken one of their boats and forbidden any others to put to sea. He had acquired a passenger out past the breakwater who might have been blond, but the captain couldn't be sure. "Araki, you've got the best eyes of the crowd. Was that scuba diver your friend, the colonel, put aboard a blond or not? This lovely lady would like to know." He picked up Erika's card.

Araki looked pleased to be back in the captain's good graces. "When he took off the scuba hood, his hair shone like gold. I have never seen anything like it."

Others in the room nodded.

"Look," Mori interjected, "we're wasting our time here."

"You don't work for them do you?" the captain asked Erika incredulously. He was staring with distaste at the Japanese police inspector and the foreigner.

"Of course not," Erika replied sweetly. "Look at my card. I

work for the colonel, and these men are assigned to me." Then she turned and lectured Mori on giving rather than taking and how he shouldn't let his police training go to his head. "He's only used to dealing with criminals," she whispered to the cooperative leader with a smile of regret. Of course he had another side, she added. Was the captain by any chance a patriot who had experienced the war? Yes, she'd thought so. Her eyes rested on his features for an unnaturally long moment. And in a fighting unit too? How wonderful.

"Neither the Americans nor the French could handle Indochina, but we did: and easily if I may say so. Araki, go get me my bayonet."

They really had to be going, Erika insisted, since the village next to them had kindly offered the use of a boat and there was no time to waste. But perhaps she could come back later. She certainly would like to hear about his war experiences.

"Gadarukanaru also. I was there with the Kawaguchi Brigade. How long would the boat be needed for?"

Erika turned to Mori, who said they had to catch the *Minikami*. There had been a terrible mistake and the *gaijin* here must deliver a personal message from his government to the blond *gaijin* on the boat. It was in the interest of international peace.

"What is this nonsense he is telling me about our barter crates?" The captain pulled at his ear.

"Simply that," Mori agreed. "I don't know where he gets his information. If there were any problems I'm sure they will be corrected soon if not already. I wouldn't worry about it frankly."

"Now about your boat," Erika said sadly, "the next town of Kaga said they have faster boats than those here so I'm sorry we can't accept your very kind offer."

The captain stood up. "A lie, but not unexpected. They are thieves always poaching in our fishing areas. You will waste valuable time driving there even if what they said was true. I have the fastest ship on the coast moored alongside. I will ask you to pay for fuel."

Erika hesitated, then graciously accepted the captain's offer. She explained that any bills should be sent to the address on the card, if the captain didn't mind. Payments were usually prompt and he could confirm what she'd said by phone. The captain allowed that he knew someone he could trust. He picked up her name card and read the name "Defense Intelligence Agency" out loud in a satisfied voice.

Erika turned to the American and whispered in English. "I am sorry I did not believe you. This boat is my *on*, my repayment." Ludlow shook his head proudly like a school principal at a student who'd just graduated.

Meanwhile Araki had found the captain's bayonet and reverently handed it to his leader, who placed it carefully on the desk. He then pointed to the weapon and grandly explained he'd been in Indochina, Malaysia, and Gadarukanaru. He'd fought under the famous General Mori.

Erika was studying her fingernails and pointed one at Mori. "That was his father."

"The Tiger's son? I don't believe it. He was a tall man."

Erika giggled in spite of herself and said that war rations had stunted Mori's growth. Also that living up to a famous father had made him rude. "He wants his own Toranomon," she said. "His own Gate of the Tigers. He wants to do better than his father."

Mori had returned from the window to stand beside her. "Yes. It is all quite true. And here I am working for a woman in an unimportant operation on the coast of Hokkaido. Now if you don't mind, I think we should get under way."

The captain called out five names and headed for the door. The thunder of marine diesels soon brought the big sleek trawler to life.

Erika took Mori aside before he boarded the boat. "Please be careful, both of you. When you come back, I will make a party. We will get drunk and laugh and remember what we have done. May my ancestors forgive me."

"They already have. You did the right thing."

"Give me a kiss."

She kissed him very hard and very long on the lips, until he could taste the salt from her cheeks. She pulled away from him. "You will come back, won't you?"

"Of course," Mori replied.

She turned suddenly and ran as fast as she could toward her car. Even after she reached it, she didn't look back. Not even once.

CHAPTER 44

SAMURAI

Several days of rain had thickened the ocean green and made waves hard under the skin of hull. Spray flew like steam off the bow. The captain steered and watched the radar. Mori and Ludlow stood silently behind.

"The last time I met an American close up was in Gadarukanaru. You ever been there?" The captain fixed Ludlow with his stubborn eyes.

"I don't believe I know the city," Ludlow replied in his politest Japanese.

Mori poked him. "It isn't a city. In English you call it Guadalcanal."

"Yes, in 1943," the captain continued as if they were old friends now. "On Koror where we staged, they told us Americans did not like to fight at night, that they were effeminate. And at night the only thing they could do was dance." The captain laughed heartily and slapped his radarman on the back. Ludlow coughed and folded his hands behind him like a Marine at parade rest.

"When we were night-landed at Taivu Point"—the captain considered his radar again more closely—"no Americans opposed us. The surf gleamed like Ginza neon with shining water creatures, noctilucae. They stuck to everyone's leggings and made them glow. We laughed and there was no American fire. Everyone thought it was going to be like Malaysia."

Mori barely listened. His head throbbed. His eyes were fixed on a dot slowly gaining size on the horizon. Although clouds towered overhead, the sun had come out, producing a metallic glare. A rainbow flickered in dark cloudbanks to the east and was gone. The air was heavy with humidity. Inside the cabin, windows fogged with spray. Wipers were turned on.

Their objective had been Henderson Airfield, the captain was saying. Two thousand Japanese troops advanced at night, through darkness so thick that each man had to hold onto the belt of the man in front. Officers put white crosses on their backs for identification. Since nine was a lucky number, the charge was scheduled for then. A ridge blocked access to the airfield, so that was where they attacked. The officers shouted *"Totsugeki!"* and off they went. "That was where I met my first American." The captain twisted so he could see Ludlow's face, and winked. Then he glanced at the radar again. "Storm coming," he said to his radarman, and looked at the ship's barometer before resuming his tale.

In the interlude, Mori said to no one in particular, "Isn't it curious that the colonel would put a ban on any boats leaving Nemuro until his return?"

"An American jumped up in front of me." The captain took his hands off the steering and made a thrusting motion. "I speared him with my bayonet before he could fire. I remember his face . . . he was quite young. Yet he shouted orders into his radio as he died; it brought down a maelstrom of mortar shells that killed most of my company. In the end I alone escaped."

"There were good soldiers on both sides in that one." Ludlow's smile was devastating, but held evidence of one who also knew a lost war.

"I mean," Mori said thoughtfully to the horizon, "if I had to take a trip out alone with an enemy, I'd prefer to have friendly boats around me." He'd spoken in English so the captain wouldn't understand.

"Patriotism." The captain pounded the steering as if it were

384

yesterday. "It was where I learned that Americans had *seishin* also, that the war was not going to be as easy as our officers thought." He shook his head and stared back into his memories.

"Maybe he isn't intending to come back," Ludlow said absentmindedly. He was remembering the triple-canopied jungle and the uncanny accuracy of the Vietnamese enemy's rounds.

"Exactly what I was thinking," said Mori.

———

The speed with which they were overtaking the *Minikami* lulled those in the sleek wheelhouse to an assortment of melancholies, each stirred by illusions of certainty.

For Mori, the certainty of his discovery would not leave him. Colonel Yuki was in the process of defecting to the Soviet Union. He should have seen it long ago. Yuki had played the police chief, the minister of justice, and the rest for fools. The way it had turned out, they'd be left with nothing. In time they'd figure it out. Yuki wasn't stupid. He had realized he had no alternative.

Yuki had no doubt advised his Soviet contact about the dummied computer. Therefore, the purpose of the operation was obviously not to get the computer out but to destroy the man the Americans now held, Oleg Pachinkov. In that they had succeeded. The fact that the blond had not discarded the computer meant he did not know everything. He also had been used.

For Ludlow the certainty was somewhat different. Since he'd boarded the boat, interrupted only by a temporary rush of memory of Vietnam, his mind had been busy trying to sort the total operation. His melancholy correlated to the certainty that he would never know for sure. That was always the way it was toward the end of an operation. He had figured out the two sides of the trade, that much was true. Yuki had helped to set up Pachinkov in return for the MicroDec data the KGB had provided. Yuki had killed two of his three tormentors, Kathy Johnson and Carl Lawson, and had attempted to kill the third. The equation, if not fully satisfied, was completed. And Pachinkov had mentioned another called Malik, accused him of being a U.S. spy, which was to be expected. Malik was the one pulling the strings then, Pachinkov's enemy inside the KGB. He was the one who had set it all up, the one Harrington wanted. But who was he and where was he? At the end of an operation there were always more rooms within rooms. Mirrors reflecting mirrors. Truth was what you guessed at.

Mori interrupted Ludlow's thoughts. "What about Graves?" he asked in English. "How did he know where the blond would leave from? And that Pachinkov would be there?"

Ludlow grinned. "Yuki told him. You see, a week ago Graves bragged to me that he had an operation on with Yuki that would net a Soviet defector. Yuki knew where the boat would leave from, knew Pachinkov would be following the blond. Neat little trap. But don't give Yuki all the credit; the colonel was controlled every step of the way by someone in Moscow." Ludlow pulled out a pack of Seven Stars and offered them around. Then he produced his battered lighter and lit Mori, the captain, and the radarman.

"Make me a promise," Mori said, eyeing Ludlow's lighter.

"Certainly," Ludlow smiled.

"Next time you're in Bangkok, get me a lighter like that."

"I'll do better, Ninja," Ludlow said. "Here. You can have this one." He handed Mori the lighter.

"It is a lighter of character; I will repay you one day."

"You already have. You've taught me some things about Japan and the Japanese people I should have already known. You're not too bad a race after all."

They both looked up as the trawler adjusted course. The captain called them over to the radar screen. "Your friends know we will overtake them before they can get to their rendezvous. They are not acting friendly. Apparently, they've decided to head for the Kuriles."

"Land?" Ludlow looked with disbelief at the captain.

"Controlled by the Soviets and normally visible from the coast of Hokkaido." The captain waved his hand consolingly. "If it weren't for the weather we could see it easily. We are already too close to what the Soviets designate as a strategic zone. Anything entering can be fired upon."

"You have the choice, Ludlow-san," said Mori. "I will have the captain take you back and see that you are transported safely to Misawa Airbase. From there you can return to the United States without problem."

"And what about you?"

"I will borrow the trawler's lifeboat." Mori shrugged. "It has an outboard motor. I have come this far. It would be a shame to turn back now."

"You're sure he's not returning to Japan, then, aren't you?"

"The decision is mine alone," Mori said softly. "It is a personal matter. Between the colonel, the Soviet, and myself."

"Alone? In this sea, with a storm coming?"

"Where there is disadvantage there is also advantage."

"Enough of your damned epigrams." Ludlow angrily pulled out the KGB resident's weapon.

When the captain turned around to see what they had decided, he was staring into the barrel of a pearl-handled Beretta.

"You will put us in close to shore," Ludlow ordered calmly. "Then you are free to return to Nemuro. In this weather there will be few Soviet aircraft up."

"Don't make promises you can't keep." The captain scowled at them both, then adjusted course. The trawler swerved to lock once again onto the *Minakami*'s wake. Mori could almost make out the fishing sloop's deckhouse now.

"I'll not be able to wait for you," the captain muttered, "but I will wish you luck . . . whatever it is you are up to."

Mori could feel the perspiration on his hands. He hadn't been able to change clothes for three days. A bad omen. Condensation was rising off the water and the darkening low clouds created a veil of mist impossible to penetrate two kilometers ahead. The Kuriles must be close by.

Suddenly the veil began to lift like a theater curtain. First, a shoreline in distant brown, with a mix of greens further inland. Rocks and trees took form. Mori reached into his pocket and touched the grip of his Colt.

The *Minakami*'s deckhouse was clearly visible now, as was the stubby mast for winching up the nets. Colonel Yuki was distinguishable by his uniform. He must have changed into it along the way. There was no doubt about it. He was frantically working the steering, pausing every now and then to glare over his shoulder at the approaching vessel. The blond Soviet had taken up a firing position, cradling the Uzi at the stern. The captain kept their boat just out of range. The colonel had given Mori the answer he wanted. Obviously he was not a hostage. Two men were working to a single purpose. Escape.

Sooner and faster than Mori expected, land approached. Ludlow pulled a plastic bag from a corner of the cabin and ejected the bullets from his gun into it.

"Give me yours too," he ordered Mori. "Looks like you were right about your friend. He's defecting."

The captain suddenly shouted a warning. The Soviet had gone into the wheelhouse and come out with a barrel-shaped instrument. He set it on his shoulder and aimed the device at their boat. "Missile launcher," Ludlow said. He'd hoped Graves's information had been wrong.

"What do you suggest?" Mori looked at the American.

"Pray to as many of your gods as you can squeeze in." Ludlow was measuring the distance from their boat to the *Minakami*. To the captain he said, "Do exactly as I say and at the instant I say it. Back off. Give them more distance."

They watched fascinated as the blond Soviet leisurely lined up the launcher and slowly squeezed the trigger. With a puff of smoke, the missile was launched. "Hard left," Ludlow shouted almost in the captain's ear. The boat heeled over, water nearly rushing over the rails as the sleek ship obeyed. "Full speed," Ludlow shouted again, and they felt the vibration of the turbines as new power shook the boat and made it bolt over the waves. The missile whooshed past with an eerie scream. "Come about, face them again," Ludlow shouted. The Soviet was putting another missile in the launcher. Twice more he launched; each time they evaded. Perspiration stood on Ludlow's forehead. The captain pointed again. "Boat's heading for that beach; they've given up."

Their ship was slowing as it neared land. This side of the island was open coastline. Uninhabited. The *Minakami* was racing toward a small stretch of beach. They watched as the sloop rammed straight onto the black sand. Two figures jumped off and struggled up the beach and into undergrowth. Out of sight.

At one hundred yards, the captain turned to Mori. "I can't take you in any closer. We'll ground." His eyes were nervously searching the threatening skies. "There's something else I probably ought to tell you." The captain fished a folded piece of paper from his shirt pocket. "Radio operator sent this up a while back. Says the *Minakami* made contact with Soviet command headquarters in the Kuriles. They spoke for some time but we couldn't understand what they were saying. Everything in Russian you know."

The trawler was beginning a wide circle. As it reached the closest point to the beach, the two men jumped. Mori quickly found himself in shallows. He heard the trawler engines suddenly go to full throttle as the craft swung back out to sea.

———

By the time Mori made it to the beach, Ludlow was searching the cabin of the *Minakami*. He came out with a triumphant grin. In one hand he held what looked to be a launch device, in the other a small sleek aerodynamic missile. "Missile launcher," he announced, and loaded it before he jumped down onto the sand. "It's a Stinger," he added with pride of intimate knowledge. "Surface-to-air, which is why it wasn't very effective against our boat. Heat-seeker doesn't work head-on unless you're nearly point-blank on the surface." He handed Mori the bullets to his gun and showed him how one man could operate a Stinger easily, by arming the weapon, sighting through the eyepiece, and pulling the trigger. "Simple." Ludlow smiled, hefted the weapon easily over his shoulder, and started up the beach.

"I'll take the point," Ludlow said as they walked. "Just pretend I'm your military umbrella like it reads in the peace treaty." He winked at Mori. "If we get out of this I'll get you and your family to America. You'll be free. Last chance."

"I couldn't do that," Mori answered quickly. "If I get out of this, I'll be free right here."

There was no path. Silkweed and thornbush. Pines with roots that tangled the ground as if groping for freedom. Silvery birch with leaves like green coin. Mori felt his mind clearing, his fear evaporating like the seawater drying on his skin. Two halves of the circle were nearly complete. One more point would make it full. Life was simple, really. It didn't bother him anymore that he was on Soviet soil. No matter what happened, in Tokyo life would go on as usual. They had used him as they had used his father; as they used anyone to further the honor of Japan. Why should he be surprised? They had gone to war not for personal greed but for national honor. Both the military one in '41 and the economic one thereafter. The nation benefitted first, then its people. Japan was truly a nationalistic state.

Ahead, Ludlow thrust aside the brush purposefully. Watching everything. Mori wondered if he should reveal his new insight? But what did Ludlow care? He already knew that all agents were expendable. That he was part of some larger unknown equation. Ludlow would give them more than value. No doubt they were counting on that in Washington. Ludlow, who refused to run.

The giant American stopped to take his bearings and check the opponent's path through the brush. Mori crouched behind. Ludlow wouldn't give up. That was the way with some good men. Pursuit of a goal. It was a kind of greed, but not quite the same thing. Washington had counted on that too, hadn't they? No different from the leadership in Tokyo. Or Moscow for that matter.

They started off again and worked silently through the woods. They came to a clearing and, rather than crossing, Ludlow skirted its edges, ducking from tree to tree. They were nearly to the other side when the staccato of gunfire erupted.

Insects filled the air, humming their anger. Mori stumbled but regained his feet. He held the slippery bark of a birch tree for support. Pain crawled like a worm across his hip. When he pushed off from the tree to follow, a red stain marred the purity of silver bark. Ludlow was out of sight.

"Inspector Mori?" Strange someone should know his name here. It was not Ludlow's voice. One he'd never heard. Close. Very close and behind him. Mori turned. The blond was standing behind a large pine no more than five yards away. A Makarov was held loosely in his hand. "Drop your weapon, please."

Mori let his Colt fall to the ground. It was all wrong, Mori thought. There was no malice in the handsome Soviet's face. Why should there be? Mori decided. The KGB officer raised his gun and aimed it at Mori's forehead.

Strange thoughts filled Mori's brain. He felt no anger somehow. Only regret. Samurai performed their ablutions every day. Perfumed their topknots, filled their nails with pumice and buffed them with *hagane.* He regretted that he was not, as his father had been, well prepared to die. Unwashed. Bloody. Mocked by the enemy. He gathered himself to fling his body in a last desperate attempt.

The Soviet's finger tightened on the trigger. As Mori tensed, the Soviet's left eye suddenly erupted like a boil bursting in a fine mist of pink and bone fragment. The echo of Ludlow's gun hung in the silence. Kovalenko fell to one knee, fired wildly, then plunged to the ground as if trying to capture it. Mori froze, rooted to the spot.

Farther off there was a sudden burst as tracers poured into bushes not twenty yards away. He thought he heard Ludlow cough. Mori retrieved his weapon and fired in the direction of the tracers. The handgun offered only a dull click. He pried the Makarov from the Soviet's lifeless hand and cautiously made for the bushes. The Makarov was poorly balanced and too heavy.

Ludlow was lying on his back, staring at the sky through a hole in the trees. His automatic lay on the ground near him. It had started to rain and his face seemed to be accepting the gift of water with a sardonic grin. The ground was darker under the American's left side. Mori looked closer. A small neat puncture had gone through his shirt where the bullet had entered, above the ribs.

For a moment he stared silently at his American friend's face. Then he picked up the weapons: the Beretta with the one spent round that had cost Ludlow his life; the Stinger, which Mori slung over his shoulder. He felt the coldness of his anger seeping into every fiber. He looked at Ludlow a last time. "To the American people," he said tersely. Then he moved off into the forest.

———

The flight bag was on a slight rise, with the grass around it flattened like a deer had slept there. It seemed to have taken Mori hours to get this far, although his watch had recorded only ten minutes. Yuki had apparently fired from a prone position to steady his aim. Mori studied the surroundings, holding his breath. He could sense a closeness in the silence. No birds. The earth was still.

A slight sound not far away. A small animal perhaps, only they would have long ago fled the carnage. Yuki was of the old school. A man of action. There was an ancient saying, "Make up your mind within the space of seven breaths." Yuki would believe in such trash. Mori grasped the flight bag and noted the gleam of computer inside. He waited, lying on his good side.

The irony of his life was not deliberate, he thought; simply the discrepancy between expectation and results. He could be forgiven that, he hoped. He had only sought truth and honor— and had found them quite by accident. No doubt it had been ordained by fate. Erika was truth; not of the mind but of the spirit. Ludlow was honor. For a moment, Mori had the irresistible longing to begin his life over again. To thereby justify Ludlow's sacrifice. But the moment passed. If death was necessary to fulfill his own world, then it must be chosen. The only true tragedy would be to fail to complete the circle. The fierce eyes of his ancestors were watching him.

The form was khaki-colored, moving cautiously toward the

clearing and the flight bag. It stopped and sheltered behind a tree checking the terrain.

"Colonel Yuki," Mori called in a jovial tone. "I have come to take you back to Tokyo."

The colonel flattened against the tree. "Ah"—Yuki recovered his voice quickly—"so you have. So you have. And I see you have found the computer. Well done." There was an ominous click in the stillness as the colonel released the safety on his weapon.

"The American is dead," said Mori. "So you have nothing to fear."

"Then it is best to put your weapon down." Yuki spoke gently as if talking to an animal he was afraid of. "A platoon of Soviet soldiers will arrive any minute. I can offer you your life."

"I have already chosen death, Colonel."

Mori could hear the colonel's sharp intake of breath. Sense his shock. When he spoke, his voice was hoarse. "Do not be foolish. Attack me, and you will never escape. Give up now and I will see you are eventually released."

"You killed the American girl in Ginza and nearly Harrington, too. You killed Ludlow. You caused the death of the two guards with that dummied computer on the ground over there. And nearly my wife's death, too. You've made a pact with the Soviets. They gave you details on how you were set up by the CIA, and you helped to destroy Pachinkov's career."

"Yes, Inspector. Yes. I see it is already too late for you. You will not escape this island."

Mori felt the strength of his anger surge into a terrible battle cry that had been his ancestors'. It came not from his lips but from his soul. He rose with it and charged his enemy, firing with both guns as he went.

———

Later he remembered nothing of what happened, not the screams, nor the tangle of bodies. Nor his hands chopping again and again at the inert form. It all had transpired in a dream, as the Nihilists promised. He found himself sitting cross-legged beside the colonel's crumpled body. His own chest was heaving, yet he remembered no exertion. He could feel rain on his face. Smell the scent of pine and damp earth.

Deep racking sobs came from somewhere. He realized they were his own. They subsided. A purity of soul radiated from his heart to his very being. A strange new light shone throughout his body. He had found what his father and grandfather always knew. What he had sought. The pristine beauty of total freedom.

The sound of the helicopter was quite close. Mori looked up and could see the wash of propeller bending the trees when the machine came over low. As it flashed overhead, Mori saw it was a dark green color. On its side was a single red star outlined in white. Mori reached across and gathered in the Uzi that had fallen from the dead colonel's fingertips. Then he went back for the missile launcher and the overnight bag with its evidence of the entire deception.

———

Captain Yuri Bulganin had been finishing bitter Russian coffee in the mess when the alert came. He could still taste the dregs at the back of his throat. They'd wasted valuable time waiting for the platoon to double over from the barracks. Operations had picked up a faint signal on a Japanese fishing wavelength. There'd been no way to confirm, although the sender spoke Russian. There was no sophisticated hookup here to get through to Moscow quickly. The sender claimed he was a Soviet and aborting a rendezvous with the Vladivostok, a heavily laden communications ship disguised as a trawler. They'd put through a call immediately, but it took more precious minutes to raise the ship and coax confirmation from its reluctant captain. No details on open wavelength. It sounded like one of the idiotic schemes the KGB would get up.

Bulganin concentrated on the landscape and dropped the helicopter even lower. It was a new Hind, like some deadly praying mantis, with missiles in pods bulging from its sides. In Afghanistan the equipment had performed remarkably well.

Bulganin knew the machine intimately. He had spent ten months out of the last eighteen flying from Dagram Airbase, an hour from Kabul. The landings had always been hot, with those devilish new Stinger missiles the Americans were providing the guerrillas. This was a walk in Gorky Park by comparison. The co-pilot straightened from the heat-sensing devices and held up four fingers.

Bulganin spoke into the interphone. "The radio report said there would be only two. Are you sure?"

"Four," the co-pilot confirmed. "Three inert and one moving. En route our computer also recorded two vessels within strategic zone radar range. One on the beach up ahead. The other with full steam up and heading out. I'm also getting heat from the beach."

Bulganin studied the tops of trees that were rushing by underneath him. "Check with command but I'm not going after any ships until I get this land action sorted. We'll put down on the beach ahead. Keep your eyes open for any movement on that beached boat. It's recording heat but probably from engines."

The captain switched on his intercom and advised the twenty men in back. All but one sat quietly in full battle gear; paratroops, elite seasoned veterans of Afghanistan. A unit whose blue-and-white ribbon on their red shoulder flashing signified the Kamerov Medal, first order, for valor under fire—a prize few units that had come through Afghanistan intact could boast.

The final member of the party in back, the one not in paratroop uniform, had arrived by jet just as Bulganin was lifting off. That had been the final exasperating delay. From its wing markings Bulganin knew the arriving jet had been a MIG assigned to the wing squadron at Sakhalin Airbase.

The control duty officer had called from the tower and requested that Bulganin hold until the visitor was aboard—a Colonel Malik, who was on an inspection tour from Moscow. Bulganin suggested what the officer could do to himself, and held the helicopter on the ground.

When the visitor was driven up and strolled over to Bulganin's helicopter, he was wearing the winter-duty uniform of the KGB. Immaculate. Not a hair out of place. Middle-aged around the eyes, but with the trim body of one who dieted or exercised a great deal. There was a confidence about the man too that Bulganin didn't like, as if he had done them all a favor by making them wait. No apologies or excuses. He simply marched up to the open side door, stared momentarily at the machine-gun mount, then hopped briskly in and took a seat.

The co-pilot had poked Bulganin in the arm as they were finally lifting off. "Looks like we have Peter the Great back there." Bulganin had managed a grin.

Now as they were going to final hover, with the clutch in and the machine grinding to stay airborne, the co-pilot poked Bulganin's arm again. "Peter wants a word."

"Mother of Lenin. Plug him in." Bulganin's hands continued to maneuver the Hind for landing as he listened.

"You're doing a fine job, comrades." The KGB colonel's voice confirmed only highest marks. For what, Bulganin was not yet quite sure. "One of my men has brought a very valuable piece of equipment out of Japan. He's down there. A few hostiles might be with him. I'm quite used to these situations; I'd like to use your outside speakers."

Bulganin immediately sensed that everything he had just been told was untrue. As captain of the ship, he could technically refuse any onboard requests. However, there was an underlying sense of urgency in the KGB officer's tone which raised images of the severest reprimands should the demand be ignored and later prove decisive.

The speaker voice boomed out over the noise of the rotor blades. First in Japanese. "You will not be harmed if you come out with your arms raised over your heads. Do not show a weapon. Do not make any threatening moves once we have you in sight. Our soldiers will give you ten minutes to get to the beach and surrender. After that they will be instructed to hunt you down and use whatever force necessary." Then in Russian. "Comrade Kovalenko. If you have a weapon, in sixty seconds, fire it three times."

Colonel Malik handed the mike back to the co-pilot. Bulganin reluctantly admired the plan. Their job was made easier, certainly. It separated the birdseed from the bullshit. Orders were not to take any hostiles alive. Unless they were American.

The chopper settled, dipped its nose, then slewed around and hit the beach. The sand was lifted by the blades into a black cloud that hovered over the craft, blocking sight and filling the open door with choking dust.

The Hind had two coaxial rotors above the engine pods, and Bulganin looked up as he cut the engines and disengaged the clutch. The rotors slowed and there was only the huge swishing noise as their arc became more visible through the volcanic dust. Sixty seconds passed. Colonel Malik from his jump seat said "Son of a bitch" in a voice that didn't sound particularly disappointed. The co-pilot unbuckled and went outside to stretch. That was the last thing Bulganin remembered distinctly. The rest became part of a nightmare.

The report later stated that the figure burst without warning from the edge of the tree line some twenty-five yards away. Bulganin heard the shout from soldiers deploying from the helicopter. They were still bunched and unready. Incredibly, the figure was tiny. Not Russian or Caucasian. Japanese. It came screaming at the helicopter and the gaggle of surprised soldiers. In its hand was a stick that was winking off and on like a Roman candle. Bulganin heard the thud of bullets impacting the Hind's metal frame, and the scream from the KGB officer in back. One round disabled the rotor.

Bulganin reached for his sidearm and opened the port canopy. Eight of the troops had gone down in the first burst of fire. Soldiers were sprawling on the ground or running for cover. Confused orders were being shouted. Discipline had broken down. The Roman candle rushed closer and had developed an automatic bark. Bulganin steadied his weapon on the frame of window and brought the tiny figure into his sights. Soldiers had regrouped and were returning fire now, huddled near the helicopter for cover. The figure staggered and fell, then got up and came on again. It gathered speed and ferocity and leapt toward the lieutenant of the platoon, who was attempting to free his weapon. Bulganin almost felt an irrational sympathy as he squeezed the trigger. The opponent's nerve was a thing of exquisite and nightmarish beauty.

"*Nyet.*" The voice in Bulganin's ear made him freeze. His gun did not discharge. He watched helplessly as the lieutenant fell under the karate kick of the Japanese. He swung around. Blood was pouring from a crease in Colonel Malik's forehead. His immaculate uniform was spotted with blood. But what drew Bulganin's attention was the pistol in the colonel's hand. It was aimed at Bulganin's head.

"Let them handle it if they can." The colonel's voice was low and deadly.

Bulganin's mind was spinning. This was not possible. A member of the KGB? The words tore from his lips. "You are a traitor."

The colonel's eyes greeted these words with an exultant flicker. "Every human being is born with the capacity for honor and decency. Unfortunately, our state does not yet allow us to preserve either one."

Bulganin was measuring him; the colonel was only superficially wounded, though his reflexes could be dulled. If the surprise was complete . . .

Bulganin lashed out suddenly. He caught the KGB colonel with only a glancing blow, however. He heard the explosion begin and saw the spout of fire start from the colonel's weapon. Then he felt himself falling into a bottomless black eternity.

———

Mori retreated instinctively. The fire from the Soviets was growing in intensity and confidence. But above all, he had seen the gun come up in the window of the helicopter. Knew there was nothing he could do. Expected death. Even welcomed it. Yet the weapon had not fired. Instead, another shot had sounded and the pilot had slumped in the cockpit.

He reached the depression where he had dropped the Stinger and fell into it. Bullets churned the sand around him. These Russians were still in a state of shock. Mori grinned to himself. They had lost half their number within seconds, and their confidence was shaken. He must not let it return. He set up the Stinger on his shoulder, brought the helicopter into the cross hairs. He had not cared one way or the other, he thought. That was why he had not died. However, the mystery of the helicopter was an act of his ancestors. The enemy cared too much. And their ancestors were of little quality and did not protect them. Even now they were sheltering around the helicopter for protection. Only faintly did he feel the pain, remote and far away.

He stroked the trigger, cold and beautiful, like a sword under his finger. Steady. A form leapt from the open helicopter door and raced zigzag toward the water. Dressed not in combat fatigues but in a formal Soviet uniform. Instinctively Mori understood that this was the one his ancestors had used to save him from death. The figure reached the water and dived below the surface. Mori pulled the trigger.

———

The fishing sloop rocked with the waves that raced ahead of him toward home. His eyes still ached from the brilliance of the explosion that had mushroomed into the sky; white-hot molten lava sibilating into waves of orange, spurts of crimson, concluding in a huge black cloud that rose with the authority of death.

He had risen in the sand slowly, awed by the sight. He had gathered up the computer from where he'd left it in the undergrowth, and headed for the boat. Once away from shore he set the engine to full throttle. The pain began to surge as he watched tasseled whitecaps march past as in a parade. The wind was with him, he thought. And the spirits of his ancestors. In the wheelhouse was a tiny altar to the god of the sea. He thanked him, asked for a kind ocean to bring him home, then lashed the wheel in a setting toward the distant peaks that were Hokkaido. Finally he searched his pockets and found the battered lighter Ludlow had given him. That was the last thing he remembered.

Later, he recalled only vaguely the bump of a boat touching, shouts as ropes were secured and figures leapt aboard. The blurred forms that gently lifted him smelt of the sea and of fish, and it was then that he realized he was safe. Somewhere in the cloud of vagueness that surrounded him, Erika's concerned face swam. He tried to smile, because he understood without seeing her that she was crying. "It is all over," he said with great effort, which sent a meteor shower of pain through him and made him drowsy again. Then he fell into a warm and pleasant darkness.

EPILOGUE

A police band played "Kimino-
sato," several war marches, and "When the Saints Go Marching In" since it was the crown prince's favorite. There were
banks of carnations in circular patterns set on tripods at NHK
Hall entrance as well as on both sides of the huge stage. To
arriving dignitaries they had looked every bit like sugary targets in a heavenly shooting gallery. And as one observer
adroitly pointed out, "Inspector Mori had hit the bull's-eye in
all of them."

Experts generally agreed that an astute delay in denial of
American complicity, plus the huge media buildup to Inspector
Mori's award presentation, had generated the necessary public
outrage to win unanimous approval in the Diet for the new
security agency.

The prime minister put in an appearance, as did the ministers of defense and justice. They made speeches praising
Mori's love of country, love of family, and, finally but not least,
his fighting samurai spirit. There was frequent reference to his
famous lineage. And of course to the new security agency.

On the streets outside, traffic had come to a standstill.
Tradesmen manned stalls selling memorabilia, pictures, national flags with Mori's name, a brief biography put together

by an enterprising publisher to cash in on all the publicity.

The legend had begun even before Mori's remarkable recovery. "Six bullets in him," the *Yomiuri Shimbun* intoned. Miraculously, none injured vital organs. His most serious complication was loss of blood. Truly he had been touched by the gods.

Faced with calamitous proof that the Americans were not involved in the Starfire theft, the minister of justice had known he could not destroy the American monopoly on Japanese military exports. He'd finally turned to the chief of police with the words, "Half a kingdom is better than none at all." They had settled for the new security agency.

Although throughout his debrief Mori had described the key role of Robert Ludlow in breaking the Starfire case, the American's name was kept out of the media. And the assertion that he had given his life to save Mori's was turned aside. "That is something only a Japanese would do; die to save the life of another Japanese. You must be mistaken."

Aoyama was introduced as Mori's closest friend, and placed in charge of all releases to the public. He had done his usual superb job. TV coverage became so intense that Fuji newscasts were providing updates on Mori's condition in every one of their shows. The number of background teams roving Nemuro became so large that the local fishery cooperative had to limit interviews—since they were interfering with the annual mackerel run. NHK and Asahi ran hour-long personal profiles on Mori, underscoring the austere simplicity of his life, his humble rented abode, and several understatements from his mother in the best Japanese tradition. Her son had only been doing his duty, pursuing enemies and traitors. All the media added nightly embellishments to his heroic actions. By the day of his award ceremony, Mori's popularity had reached such proportions that he required a special police escort, even though he could walk now quite well by himself. He was deluged with requests for interviews, and he refused them all. The insanity of the media had extended to suggestions that he be nominated for the Diet.

In retrospect, it was later agreed that the success of the MPD media achievement had been bolstered by an unexpected and urgent note from the Soviet embassy requesting a meeting with the minister of defense. Delivered less than four days after the event, and before Mori's debrief had been completed, the note protested the fact that two armed Japanese nationals had been landed on Kurile Island. They had surprise-attacked a peace-loving Soviet paratroop platoon, the note claimed, causing deaths and serious injuries and destroying one helicopter. One of the Japanese—a full colonel—had been killed outright. Both had been landed by the Japanese government to infiltrate the island and provoke an incident, the Soviets concluded. Obviously the purpose was to inflame Japanese sentiment for return of the Soviet-held islands. The Soviet government lodged a most serious protest over the incident, with the curt footnote that it might present the entire matter to the United Nations if a satisfactory answer was not received. Thus in one stroke what the foreign press was dismissing as an unsubstantiated and local propaganda fabrication became an international event.

The Japanese counterattacked with the poise of those who know they hold all the cards. Starfire was their high tech, after all, they chided. A Soviet had attempted to steal it and a Japanese hero had prevented that from happening. Furthermore, a high-ranking KGB officer involved in the theft had defected to the U.S.A. and was unreeling a huge story of KGB technical espionage in Japan. The Soviets had no way of knowing that this last was untrue. Finally, a front company for transporting stolen high tech out of Japan had been uncovered in Hakodate. With this the Soviets realized their mistake. The Russian attack in the press subsided rather abruptly in one of those "Everything is a lie" blankets used by all nations to snuff out their most dangerous truths.

Three days before Mori's award presentation, the final piece nearly escaped them. On a back page of *Pravda* a terse announcement noted the wounding of the KGB's Technical Directorate chief and the death of his subordinate in a training accident off the Sakhalins. It was Mori who placed that in proper perspective. A short time later, the Soviet Collegium confirmed the wounded Soviet hero, Colonel Malik, as the new head of the KGB First Directorate. He was elevated to the rank of general.

———

Mitsuko was released from the hospital for several hours to attend her husband's award ceremony. She had regained much of her strength, although the neck brace would remain in place for several months more. In the prime-time newscast that evening she was seen in black silk kimono with the famous Mori crest in white, looking pale and beautiful.

Mori's speech, following the elegance of the crown prince's presentation, was suitably brief and simple. He first thanked his government for the medal, saying that it was not really deserved. The person to whom the award should have been presented was not able to attend tonight. For he had given his life to save Mori's, and by so doing confirmed that he and his country were friends, not antagonists. Mori cleared his throat and spoke firmly into the microphones: "The bravery of this man for Japan, a country he did not serve, will never be adequately recognized. He was a true samurai: a person of noble spirit, of honor, of trust. I would like to pass the medal I have received to the government Mr. Robert Ludlow represented." Mori stepped down and presented the medal to the United States ambassador, who had graciously agreed to attend the ceremony.

———

It was two weeks later that Erika threw the party in her tiny apartment, the party she had promised for Mori and Ludlow. Mitsuko was still in hospital and could not attend. But Watanabe came, as did Isamu, and several friends from the force, and the captain from Hokkaido, who flew down with his radarman; plus several other friends who came to drink. The captain brought a present and handed the package to Mori with the words, "You were holding on to this when we found you. Figured it might be important."

It was Ludlow's lighter.

Mori rubbed the back of his head, trying not to show how pleased he was. "I'll keep it till I see him again," he said.

Watanabe, who had lost his family in Hiroshima, offered the first toast to Robert Ludlow's dauntless spirit. Others followed. Then came Mori's turn. He paused, looking silently at his countrymen. Then he raised his glass.

He said simply, "Robert-san taught me there was more to life than revenge. I hope there are no remaining members of our leadership who need to learn this lesson."

———

The party lasted until after three a.m. When it was over, Mori took Erika for a drive. They went to Atami, which, at that time of the morning, and with the heavy car and skilled driver he'd been assigned, took only one hour. Instead of stopping in the lovely oceanside city, Mori ordered the driver on until he'd reached a parking area with stone steps leading to a hillside shrine. Here they stopped and Mori, with Erika, began the five-hundred-step climb. "It is in memory of officers and soldiers killed in the Pacific war. My father is here." It was now getting light.

In front of the alter, Mori clapped his hands to attract the gods. Then he prayed. Erika bowed her head and asked the gods to give Mori-san whatever he should want. He had suffered greatly both in mind and body. He had fulfilled his pledge of revenge to his father. Please let him be free, she prayed finally, although she knew it was impossible. She waited by his side until he was done.

They turned together and before them was the vast expanse of the Pacific. A red sun was rising.

"You will be busy from now on," Erika said. "I understand you will be given a position in the new security agency. It may be difficult for us to meet." She wondered why it was that meetings were always so easy for her, and partings so complex. Mori was a national symbol now. A hero. She could not chance the tarnishing of his reputation. She had no place in his life.

"You would have been right for me," Mori said and stared at the shimmering ocean.

She smiled because she had told him that once. It seemed so long ago. "Give me a kiss."

She felt his lips touch hers and concentrated very hard on how it felt because she wanted to remember it for as long as she could. She held on to him for a moment after their lips parted, then she let him go. She took his hand and they started down the stone steps together.

They could see the first fishing boats of the day setting out from shore. The god of the sea reached out to touch the Great Sky Father. The rising sun grew ever larger, ever stronger in the vast expanse of sky that towered above them.